THE VIENNA ASSIGNMENT

Olen Steinhauer's two previous novels, *The Bridge of Sighs* and *The Confession*, have garnered thus far an Edgar nomination, an Anthony nomination, a Macavity nomination, a Historical Dagger nomination, and critical acclaim.

Having worked as a dishwasher, librarian, assembly-line worker and English teacher, he was inspired to write his Eastern European series while on a Fullbright Fellowship in Romania. Olen was raised in Texas and now lives in Budapest, Hungary.

Visit www.AuthorTracker.co.uk for exclusive information on Olen Steinhauer

www.olensteinhauer.com

OLEN STEINHAUER

THE VIENNA ASSIGNMENT

HARPER

Harper
An imprint of HarperCollins*Publishers*
77–85 Fulham Palace Road,
London W6 8JB

www.harpercollins.co.uk

This paperback edition
1

First published in Great Britain by
HarperCollins*Publishers* 2005

First published in the USA by St Martin's Minotaur
under the title *36 Yalta Boulevard*

Copyright © Olen Steinhauer 2005

Olen Steinhauer asserts the moral right to
be identified as the author of this work

A catalogue record for this book is
available from the British Library

ISBN-13 978 0 00 721088 6
ISBN-10 0 00 721088 4

Set in Meridien by Palimpsest Book Prduction Ltd,
Polmont, Stirlingshire

Printed and bound in Great Britain by
Clays Ltd, St Ives plc

For
SP

ACKNOWLEDGEMENTS

Thanks to Robin Hunt for listening to, and reading, various incarnations of this story, and to Matt Williams for his continued vigorous support. Erik D'Amato, ever a good sport, generously drove us to Bóbrka, and for this I'm very grateful. Erika Papp righted my usage of the Hungarian language, while Anna von Pezold corrected my poor German; I'd never have got it right without them.

Thanks also to Krista Steinhauer for the use of her wonderful photographs. The last two images, on pages 273 and 365, were used in Dejan Atanackovic's 'Golem Project', which toured museums in Belgrade, Sarajevo and Florence beginning in 2003.

And for her great generosity in sharing her parents' stories, I thank Jelena Franković, without whom this book could not have been written.

This is the share due the priests from the people who sacrifice a bull or a sheep: the shoulder, the jowls and the inner parts.

— DEUTERONOMY 18:3

Prelude

15 August 1966, Monday

It was the smell that would stay with him when he remembered this moment: grass – yes, and flowers. Strong, musty. Then a glut of syllables. Rough tones. Eyes still closed, he tried to manage the sounds into words, then sentences.

'Stehen Sie auf!'

Guttural, crisp. Behind the voice, birds twittered.

And in his head something thumped, but the pain was manageable; he could hold it in his hand and squeeze it into submission.

'Sie sind Nicht tot, oder? Nein.'

Pressure – fingers gripped his shoulder, then shook. First hesitantly, then with confidence.

'Kommen Sie.'

He waited, because . . . he didn't know why. He only knew he should wait, a few seconds, before opening his eyes and proving that he was, in fact, awake.

Now.

A bright sun and, as he suspected, grass. His cheek was

buried in freshly trimmed blades, arms spread out. Hovering above, a heavyset man in a strange uniform smiled and scratched his moustache.

'*Da sind Sie ja. Stehen Sie jetzt auf.*'

German, Austrian accent. *There you are. Get up now.*

The policeman helped him up, straightened his jacket, and brushed him off with quick, economical slaps.

'*Bitte schön, mein Herr. Ist alles in Ordnung?*'

He nodded. '*Alles in Ordnung.*'

He could speak it, but the language wasn't his.

They were standing in a grassy semicircle bordered by geometric bushes that caged flowers. Roses or carnations – he couldn't quite focus yet. Beyond the policeman were trees, a young couple walking hand in hand, students lying in the grass reading, and a white-bearded old man leaning against a tree, staring at them.

'Drunk?'

He shook his head. '*Nein.*'

'Name?'

He opened his mouth. The policeman waited, blinking.

'Documents? You have documents, *ja*?'

He patted his pockets and glanced behind himself: a small Greek temple with a statue on a plinth – a young, naked man looking to the side. In his breast pocket he found a typed card with a name.

The policeman squinted at it. 'Bertrand Richter?'

'*Ja.*'

'This is a library card. Anything else?'

He shrugged. 'Sorry. At home.'

'What are you doing here, Bertrand?'

He had no idea. 'I was out late last night. I guess I fell asleep.'

The policeman smiled again. 'You have an interesting accent, Bertrand.'

'I travel a lot.'

'Doing what?'

'I buy and sell Persian rugs.'

'I see.'

The policeman considered him a moment, glanced into the sun, and returned the card. 'Be a little more responsible in the future, Bertrand.'

'Of course. I apologize.'

The policeman smoothed his moustache with thick fingers. 'Don't apologize to me. It's Vienna that doesn't want drunks littering its parks. Need help getting home?'

'No. No, thank you.'

He did not sell Persian rugs, and his name was not Bertrand. Although he could not remember what his name was, he was sure that this was not it. He walked south through the park – *der Volksgarten*, he remembered, Garden of the People – towards the spires of the Hofburg Imperial Palace rising above the treetops. The vast square in front of its arc was speckled with tourists and businessmen drifting past the statue of a man on a rising horse – this, too, he knew: the monument to Archduke Charles.

He knew Vienna, its geography and its histories – that much was apparent. But this was not his home – walking its streets gave him a vague sense of agoraphobia, and the German he spoke was strange, from somewhere else.

Just past the archduke he turned left, entering a tunnel that burrowed through the palace, where statues of long-dead royalty looked down from crevices, making him think of old wars on horseback.

And for a reason he could not place, those statues filled him with disgust.

He emerged on another square and sat in the shadow of

5

a white church beneath a high clock tower, then touched the throbbing sore spot on the back of his head. Underneath, the hair was stiff from dry blood. In his jacket pocket he found a slip of white paper, folded in half, with barely legible handwriting: *Dijana Franković*, followed by a telephone number.

He stared for a while, but could not remember her.

There was a telephone booth on the other side of the square, and he briefly considered it. But he felt that he should not call the number, and he was clearheaded enough to follow his muted instincts.

Between the church and the gloomy Raiffeisenbank, he followed Kohlmarkt down to Graben, a pedestrian shopping street choked with outdoor café tables where all of Vienna, it seemed, stared at him. He entered a café at random and found a bathroom with three sinks. Beside him, a businessman in a clean suit checked his straight, white teeth in a rusting mirror, then left.

He splashed water on himself and stared at his wet face. Round but thin, with three moles on his left cheek. He tried to guess his own age – somewhere in his forties, perhaps. He felt much older.

He removed his jacket, then rolled up his sleeves. That was when he noticed the blood smeared down his right forearm; it wasn't his blood. He washed it off.

It seemed that at this point he should panic, but he took in each new piece of information as if it were part of a checklist on a clipboard. *Don't know my name*. Check. *Woman's phone number*. Check. *Don't know age*. Check. *Someone else's blood on me*. Check.

He went through his trousers, and in a back pocket found another slip of paper – small, one inch square, a dry-cleaning ticket:

A phone booth directory told him that the Hotel Kaiserin Elisabeth was not far away – down Graben, then a right at the high, corroded Gothic of St Stephen's Cathedral. He paused at the Huber Tricot clothing store, but by now the path was coming back to him. Left, just a few doors down, past cigarette- and gold-sellers' shopfronts. Weihburg-Gasse 3. The Kaiserin Elisabeth was plain-faced and white, the glass awning held together by an iron frame. A thin bellboy in green stood before the wooden doors, hands clasped behind his back. *'Grüß Gott,'* said the bellboy.

He nodded a reply, then went inside.

The narrow entry was lined in marble – to the left, an alcove with lift and stairs; to the right, a reception desk, where a woman read a book. She smiled at him as he passed.

His instincts kept him shuffling ahead, beyond the desk. Which was strange. A reasonable course of action would be to approach the receptionist and ask the simple questions: *Do you recognize me?* and *What is my name?* But, as with the phone number still in his pocket, he could not bring himself to do what was reasonable.

Through double doors he found an empty sitting room, where a regal patterned carpet stretched beneath a domed glass ceiling. In a portrait above the cold fireplace, Queen Elisabeth looked as if nothing could amuse her. He settled on one of the padded chairs arranged around polished coffee tables and flipped absently through a copy of the day's *Kurier.*

He could wait here for hours – but for what? Perhaps nothing. He read that a German writer named Pohl had just died; the Americans had begun broadcasting on Radio Free Asia; and in the back, a concerned reader had written in to protest US President Lyndon Johnson's escalation of war in Vietnam.

But none of these could compare to his mystery. He folded the newspaper as the double doors opened, and the bellboy walked up to him. His loose blond hair hung low over his bright blue eyes, and his smile seemed completely insincere. 'Can I help you, sir?'

'I just wanted to get my key.'

The boy winked. 'Let me take care of that for you.'

'I appreciate it.'

He followed the bellboy back into the lobby and watched him approach the desk. *'Drei-zwei-eins.'*

The woman set her book aside and reached back to the wall of slots. She handed over a key on a weighted ring and an envelope.

The bellboy gave him both items, saying of the envelope, 'This was left for you last night.'

'By whom?'

The bellboy looked back at the desk clerk. She said, 'I wasn't here last night.'

The bellboy shrugged. 'Would you like me to accompany you, sir?'

'No, thank you.'

'Grüß Gott,' said the bellboy.

He took the lift up three floors without opening the envelope. His patience was a surprise. The natural impulse was to rip it open, but instead he slipped it into his jacket pocket and walked down the hallway to the door marked 321.

The room was large and clean but lived-in. He crossed the carpeted floor to an empty suitcase in the corner and found that the wardrobe was filled with clothes. Inside the envelope was a wallet – old, the leather well worn – with money, schillings and koronas (these pink and pale-blue bills began a trickle of associations), and a faded photograph of mountains he knew were the Carpathians.

There was no other identification in the wallet, but details were beginning to come to him. This room was familiar, and this —

He crouched beside the wardrobe and reached beneath. His fingers found it quickly, and he was soon peeling off the tape that attached a maroon passport to the underside of the wardrobe. He opened the passport and found a photograph of himself with his three moles. Above a name.

SEV, BRANO OLEKSY

Even now, with the evidence in front of him, his name was strange, three words that could not quite fit in his mouth. He was forty-nine years old. His country – he was an Easterner, and that felt right. But not comfortable. He stepped over and locked his door.

A passport, a wallet, and a phone number, which he took out of his pocket and read again. Dijana Franković. He lifted the phone.

It rang seven times before he hung up, and with each muted buzz another fragment came to him:

A party in a large, smoky apartment, full of people.

Him with a drink in his hand, asking a short, wrinkled man, *Have you seen Bertrand?* The man shakes his head and walks away.

A crowd of young people cross-legged on the living-room floor around a long-haired man strumming an acoustic guitar. Everyone singing in unison: *Love, love me do. You know I love you . . .*

A drunk woman with striking brown eyes edged in green,

and black hair pulled behind her ear. *Bertrand?* she says. *I tell him go to hell. Da. He is boring.*

Awkward dancing – him with the brown-eyed one, who whispers into his ear. *Brano Sev, I am in the—*

Again with her, but the air is fresh, her arm linked with his as they make their way down the sidewalk. *'Zbrka,'* she tells him, *is Serbian word what mean . . . confusion. Da. What is confusion of too many thing.*

Then blackness, but her voice: *You want I should read your future?*

He cradled the receiver and closed his eyes, trying without success to dredge up more.

In the shower he examined himself. There was no more blood but a remarkable number of scars. A long white thread etched down his right thigh, and there were two punctures above his left breast. Drying himself in front of the mirror, he found more marks on his back and a knot of white tissue on his shoulder. He wondered how he could have earned these.

Then the telephone rang.

'Herr Sev?' said a woman's voice.

'Yes.'

'This is the front desk. A gentleman is coming up to speak with you.'

'Who?'

'I don't know. But I felt you should know . . . he told me you had left town, and he was here to collect your things.'

Brano Sev was suddenly aware of his nudity. 'My things?'

'Yes, sir. I told him you were in your room, and he seemed very surprised.'

'Thank you.'

He dressed quickly, slipping his wallet and passport into his pockets. He was buttoning his shirt when the rap on the door came.

'Yes?'

A hesitant, deep voice, but not German. It was his own Slavic tongue. 'It's me, Brano. Let me in.'

'Who?'

A pause. 'You're not going to pull that code-word crap with me, are you? It's me, Lochert. Now open up.'

Brano unlocked the door and stepped back. 'Come in.'

He was faced with a tall blond man with a thin, half-hearted moustache above pursed lips. 'Well?' said Lochert. 'You want to hit me or something?'

'Should I?'

That seemed to relieve the visitor, and he closed the door. 'Look, Brano, I don't know what happened last night. I guess we were attacked. But at least Gavrilo's dead.'

'Who's Gavrilo?'

'What are you getting at, Brano?'

'Just tell me who Gavrilo is.'

Lochert blinked a few times. 'GAVRILO is the code name for Bertrand Richter.'

Brano reached into his pocket and handed over the library card. Lochert examined it.

'Yeah? And?'

'Why is Bertrand Richter dead?'

Lochert rubbed the edge of the card with a thumb. 'What's going on, Brano?'

'I don't remember.'

'What do you mean you don't remember?'

'Just what I said. I don't remember a thing. I woke up in the Volksgarten this morning and I don't know how I got there. I'm not even sure who I am.'

Lochert cleared his throat and pursed his lips again. He sat on the bed. 'Amnesia?'

'Yes. Amnesia.'

'You don't remember me?'

11

'I'm sorry.'

'Amazing.' Lochert stood again. 'Incredible!' He walked to the door, then back, tapping Bertrand Richter's library card against his thigh. 'Okay, right. Don't worry about anything, Brano. Where's your phone?' Before he could answer, Lochert had found it and was dialling. He covered the mouthpiece with a hand and said to Brano, 'Pack.'

Brano stared at him.

'*Pack*. You're flying out of here.' Lochert uncovered the mouthpiece. 'Yeah, it's me. I've found him. No, but you won't believe the condition.' He waved a hand at Brano and said to him, 'Come *on*.'

Brano emptied out the wardrobe as Lochert spoke.

'Exactly . . . Two o'clock, TisAir. Right. The main terminal.' Then he hung up. 'The ticket's being reserved. All you have to do is pay for it.'

Brano stopped packing. 'Where am I going?'

'You're going home, Brano. Where you belong.'

They took care of the bill together, the flaxen receptionist watching carefully. 'A receipt, please,' said Lochert, and she made one out under his name, Josef Lochert. The bellboy opened the front door and nodded courteously when Brano handed him a tip.

When they got into a white Mercedes parked further down Weihburg-Gasse, Brano noticed the plates. 'Diplomatic car?'

Lochert started the engine. 'Useful. I can speed if I want.'

Brano watched the city slide by as they made their way along the Ringstrasse past enormous Habsburg monoliths. They didn't speak for a while, until Brano asked, 'Did I kill him?'

'Bertrand?'

'Yes.'

Lochert stared at the road a moment, then shrugged. 'Yeah, of course you did.'

'Why?'

'Because, Brano, he was a traitor. Don't become moral on me, now. That man got what was coming to him.'

'But how was he a traitor?'

'He was selling us out to the Austrians. We used the code GAVRILO because we didn't know who he was. Is that clear enough?'

'Who's we?'

Lochert tapped the wheel and looked over at him. 'You really don't remember a thing, do you?'

He shook his head.

'Both of us work for the Ministry for State Security, on Yalta Boulevard.'

'The Ministry for . . .' Tourists jogged across the road in front of them. 'I'm a spy?'

Josef Lochert laughed a loud, punchy laugh. 'Listen to you! Major Brano Oleksy Sev asking me if he's a spy!'

'What about Dijana Franković?'

He licked his lips. 'She's nobody, okay? A whore. And trouble. Forget about her. And stop with the questions. You'll get all your answers soon enough.'

Lochert dropped him off at the Flughafen Wien departures door and handed his bag over from the back seat. Brano placed it on the kerb. 'You said it's reserved?'

'Yeah,' said Lochert from inside the car. 'Hand over your passport at the TisAir desk. It's the two o'clock flight.'

'Okay.'

'Have a good trip, Brano,' he said. 'Now close the door.'

Brano watched the Mercedes drive away.

The airport was cool, with a vast marble floor leading to a row of airline desks. He waited behind a businessman arguing with the young woman standing under the TISA AERO-TRANSPORT sign, until the man, frustrated, walked off. The woman smiled at Brano.

'May I help you?'

'I have a reservation.' He handed over his passport. 'The two o'clock flight.'

The woman examined a list on the desk. 'I'm afraid there's no reservation for you, Herr Sev.'

'But my friend made the call.'

She read over the list again. 'No, there's not one here, but it doesn't matter. There's a free seat.'

He paid for the ticket, handed over his bag, and asked for the bathroom. 'Just past the lounge,' she said, pointing.

He lit a cigarette as he passed tired-looking travellers sitting with their bags, some reading newspapers, others books. Beside the bathrooms was a line of pay phones, and he considered trying Dijana Franković's number again. Much later, he would wonder if calling again would have changed anything that followed. But there's never any way to know these things.

He washed sweat from his forehead and stared at himself again in the mirror. He was becoming used to this round, flat-cheekboned face and could even spot his ethnicity – Polish features. From the northern part of his country, perhaps. But that was all the mirror told him.

At the urinal, he felt dizzy again, the spot on the back of his head aching. A large man in a suit took the urinal next to him, then looked over.

'You all right?'

'I'm fine. Just a little dizziness.'

This Austrian, Brano noticed, didn't unzip his fly. 'You're Brano Sev, right?'

'I – ' He zipped himself up. 'Do I know you?'

'No, Brano,' said the Austrian. He reached into his jacket

14

pocket but didn't take his hand back out. 'Why don't you come with me?'

The dizziness was intensifying. 'Where?'

'We'll have a little talk.'

'I have a plane to catch.'

As the Austrian stepped closer, his hand withdrew, holding a small pistol. 'Forget about the plane, Brano.'

Brano's head cleared. He leaned forwards, as if to be sick.

'Hey, are you—' said the Austrian, crouching, but didn't finish because Brano swung his head back up into the man's nose, at the same time thrusting a fist into the man's stomach. The Austrian stumbled back, a hand on his bloody nose, the other trying to keep hold of the pistol. Brano kneed him in the groin and twisted the gun hand until he had the pistol. He stepped back.

The Austrian stared at him, covering his nose and his groin.

'How many more?' said Brano.

'Jesus, Brano. I wasn't trying to kill you.'

'How many more?'

The Austrian leaned against the sinks, then looked in the mirror. His eyes dripped and his nose bled. 'Just one. He's watching the front exit.'

'How long before he comes inside?'

'Ten, fifteen minutes. Look at this goddamned nose!'

'And you. You know who I am?'

'I wouldn't be any good if I didn't know who you were. The new Kristina Urban, the Vienna *rezident*.'

'Who do you work for?'

The Austrian was becoming impatient. 'Who do you *think* I work for?'

'Just answer the question.'

'The *Abwehramt*, obviously. What's with all these questions?'

Everything Brano had done in this bathroom had been

automatic, as if he were being controlled from somewhere else. Now he tried to think. The *Abwehramt* was Austrian foreign intelligence. He was the Vienna *rezident*, who controlled his country's intelligence operations in Vienna. And he had killed a man named Bertrand Richter.

'Why do you want me?'

'Because we were told to get you.'

'Why were you told to get me?'

The Austrian finally let go of his groin and uncovered his nose. It was beginning to swell. 'You've been in this business long enough to know that we just do what we're told, and we seldom know why.'

'Come here,' Brano said as he walked to one of the stalls. He opened the door. 'Come on. Inside.'

He stepped back as the Austrian entered the stall and turned around.

'Face the wall.'

'Christ, Brano. There's no need to shoot me.'

Brano swung the pistol into the back of the Austrian's neck and watched him crumple onto the toilet.

At the gate, he wondered when the man in the stall would wake up, rush out to his colleague or call airport security, and come to take him away. But over the next twenty minutes no one came, and as he paced he thought about the name the Austrian had told him – Kristina Urban. The name, for some reason, made him think of flight. He tried to work through the details – a dead man, a woman's phone number, a hotel, a man named Josef Lochert. Brano was a spy, the Vienna *rezident*, and the *Abwehramt* were after him.

He thanked the stewardess who stamped his ticket, then boarded the crowded plane.

His seat was next to a young Austrian – twenty, maybe

16

– who lit a cigarette as soon as he sat down and refused to buckle his belt. 'They make me feel trapped,' he said in a whisper.

Brano nodded, but at that moment he remembered why the name Kristina Urban evoked flight. Last month, the *Abwehramt* had tossed her from a high window of the Hotel Inter-Continental.

'Feeling trapped makes me anxious,' the young Austrian told him.

'Me, too.'

'You should try hashish. Settle you down.'

Brano was no longer listening. The dizziness came back, and he leaned forwards, settling his head against the next seat.

'You all right?' said his companion.

The stabilizing pressure of takeoff eased his sickness, and when the wheels left the ground he remembered more.

It had begun at home, in the Capital, in the office of a very old friend, Laszlo Cerny, a man with a thick, unkempt moustache, a colonel in the Ministry for State Security. GAVRILO was the subject of a file open in front of him, and now, on the plane, he remembered its contents. On 6 May, in Vienna's Stadtpark, a routine money exchange had been stopped by Viennese intelligence before the exchangers could even meet. Then, on 18 June, an apartment used to radio messages across the Iron Curtain had been raided. Three people had been caught – among them Kristina Urban, the Vienna *rezident*. Two weeks later, she was thrown out of the hotel window.

Brano closed his eyes as they gained altitude.

He arrived in Vienna just last month to replace Kristina Urban and to uncover the leak that the Ministry had code-named GAVRILO. Before setting up in the cultural attaché office of the embassy on Ebendorferstraße, he had specialists go over the building again. Seven electronic bugs were found, so Brano, to the dismay of the head of embassy security, Major Nikolai Romek, decided to work out of the Hotel Kaiserin Elisabeth rather than risk more security leaks. From there, he visited three suspect operatives and fed each one false information. Theodore Kraus believed that two men would meet and exchange codebooks inside the Ruprechtskirche on 14 July; Ingrid Petritsch believed that Erich Glasser, an employee of Austrian intelligence, would deliver classified files to a Czech agent in the Hotel Terminus on 28 July. And Bertrand Richter was told that a shipment of automatic rifles would be smuggled from Austria into Hungary near Szombathely on the evening of 8 August in a West German lorry.

Bertrand Richter.

He could see the man now. Short, with dark features, a foolish smile; a drunk. But a wonderful drunk. Worth all the schillings poured into his account, because in social situations information flowed around him effortlessly. So for two years the Ministry on Yalta Boulevard had used this excitable dandy, and in exchange gave him the means to remain in that social circle he most loved.

But on the night of 8 August, that arrangement ended when Josef Lochert – yes, Lochert was his assistant from the embassy – waited at the Hungarian border with binoculars and watched the Austrian police stop and search each lorry with West German plates. Lochert reported to him with a smile: *We've found GAVRILO.*

Which was why Bertrand Richter was dead.

'This is my first trip east.'

Brano looked at the young Austrian. 'What?'

'My first time,' he said. 'You study the Revolution from books, you read your Marx and your Lenin, but there's nothing like seeing a people's republic firsthand. That's what the leader of my discussion group says.'

'Don't get your hopes up,' said Brano, because now he could remember his home as well.

He unbuckled his belt and, holding the backs of seats to maintain his balance, began walking to the bathroom at the front of the plane. He watched passengers flipping through magazines and newspapers to see if any turned to look at him. Though none did, he didn't trust that that meant he was alone. The more he remembered, the more he was sure that someone on this plane would want to stop him from wreaking any more destruction on the world.

He had reported the identity of GAVRILO with a coded tele-gramme sent from the embassy and received the coded reply later that same day, from the office of his old friend Colonel Cerny.

The bathroom door was locked, so he waited at the head of the plane, watching faces. It had been his responsibility, he remembered, to make the arrangements for GAVRILO's death.

Bertrand Richter was holding a party, ostensibly for the Assumption of the Virgin Mary, on 14 August, yesterday – in fact, Bertrand hardly needed an excuse to host a party, but as an atheist he enjoyed the irony. Perhaps to extend this irony, he had invited Brano. From a pay phone, Brano called at nine-thirty and told Bertrand he could not make the party because of an emergency. As suspected, Bertrand wanted to know the details. *Come down here and I'll show you,* Brano told him. *It'll just take twenty minutes. Tell your guests you're getting more food, but don't bring anyone.*

Where?

The Volksgarten. Temple of Theseus.

Is this about the fourteenth of May?

Brano didn't know what he was talking about. *What about the fourteenth of May?*

Josef Lochert, standing beside him, waved a hand for Brano to hurry up.

Nothing, said Bertrand. *I'll be right over.*

The bathroom door opened and an old woman came out, smiled at him, and made her way back down the aisle. Brano locked the door behind himself and used toilet paper to wipe his face dry. He had worked for the Ministry twenty-two years; he was unmarried. Discovering his life as if for the first time, it seemed the life of a lonely man. But a man of no small importance – a major in the Ministry for State Security, located on Yalta Boulevard, number 36. Colonel Cerny, he also remembered, was his immediate superior, and he'd known him over two decades. He'd even helped this man, seven years ago, to deal with the suicide of his wife, Irina – a hotheaded Ukrainian whose photo remained on Cerny's desk to this day.

As someone tried the door, he sat on the toilet, holding on to the sink and breathing heavily.

Last night, at the Temple of Theseus in the Volksgarten, he and Josef Lochert had waited forty minutes, and when Brano returned to the pay phone and called again, there was no answer. So Brano went to Bertrand Richter's house in order to draw him out personally.

The smoky apartment was full of revellers in various states of drunkenness who never noticed the phone was off the hook. Someone had pulled out an acoustic guitar. He couldn't find Bertrand – no one seemed to know where he was, nor did they care – and then he asked the tall, pretty woman whose dark eyes had followed him around the house. Bertrand's girlfriend, he remembered. A Yugoslav tarot-card reader.

Dijana Franković said, *Bertrand? I tell him go to hell.* Da. *He is boring.* The whole room was singing 'Love Me Do' by the Beatles. She was very drunk, and she pulled him aside. *Brano Sev, I am in the love with you.*

It was too late, he decided, to follow through on the operation. Bertrand Richter could be killed another day. So when she asked, he walked her back to her apartment, listening to her lecture on the Serbian word 'zbrka' – *The essence*, she said, *is when is much too many thing, so nothing can you touch*. Despite his apprehension – a woman who would say 'love' to a near-stranger was plainly unbalanced – he submitted. He went upstairs with her, and after two hours returned to his hotel. An unsigned telephone message waited at the front desk: *Come now*.

He returned to the Volksgarten, thinking not of Bertrand Richter but of the contours of Dijana Franković's body.

Jesus, Brano, where the hell have you been?

While he was at the party, Josef Lochert had decided to wait by the front door. And when Bertrand returned to his home, drunk, moaning about the woman who had spurned him, Lochert suggested they go for a ride to clear their heads. He drove Richter to the Volksgarten and walked him to the Temple of Theseus. They climbed the steps and, once inside the temple, he beat Richter with a truncheon until he was dead.

Lochert had dragged the body behind the bushes that ringed the temple. It was after two in the morning, and he was unamused by Brano's disappearance. *Wait until Yalta hears about this, you just wait.*

Brano ignored that. *You've removed all identification?*

Of course. The wallet's in my pocket.

But Brano looked for himself and found a library card inside Richter's trousers. *What about this?*

Keep it as a souvenir. Just help me with him.

The last thing Brano remembered was rolling up his sleeves and dragging Bertrand deeper into the bushes. The man's head was a mess of blood and skull shards by this point – blood smeared across Brano's forearm – and he

21

remembered not wanting to look too closely. At midthought, his memory stopped.

Then he woke, with a dead man's library card and no memory, to the coarse sounds of an Austrian policeman.

'You're not getting sick, are you?' asked the young Austrian.

Brano sat down heavily. 'Flying's not easy.'

'Don't worry. Tisa Aero-Transport has a one hundred percent safety record. I checked on it.'

'The company's only been in existence five years,' said Brano. 'Let's hope they have a perfect record.'

The Austrian grunted, and Brano closed his eyes, working back over the morning – waking, the policeman, wandering to the hotel, and getting his keys. The envelope with his wallet. Why didn't he have his wallet on him when he woke?

It had been dropped off sometime last night, the clerk had said. But by whom?

The seat-belt indicator lit above his head, and he fastened his. The young Austrian smirked. 'They can't make me do it. Let them just try.'

'If there's turbulence, you could get tossed over the seats.'

'It's not my fault if they can't fly straight.'

Brano looked at him. 'Why are you travelling?'

'I told you. My discussion leader thinks it's a good thing. And since I just got voted treasurer, the others felt I should bring back the first report from the socialist lands.'

'I see.'

'Who knows? If I like it, maybe I'll stay.'

'That wouldn't be fair to your comrades.'

'Yeah,' he said. 'I guess you're right.'

Brano rubbed his sore head.

At the moment his memory stopped, he had been in an empty park with a dead body and a living man. Besides his heart, the foliage bending under the weight of Bertrand Richter, and Josef Lochert's heavy smoker's breaths behind him, there had been no sound. He was struck from behind.

Josef Lochert had knocked him out last night. Then he had taken Brano's wallet and returned it to the hotel.

Not to kill him, but to leave him there for the Austrian police to pick up, beside the body of Bertrand Richter.

He didn't know why, though that would come later, but he was sure of this story. Now he worried about where he was at this moment. On a plane, headed home.

You're going home, Brano. Where you belong.

'I'm telling you,' said the Austrian, 'You don't look right to me at all. You need some water or something?' He waved to a stewardess, but they were already descending.

As the plane taxied to the gate, Brano watched the other passengers unbuckle their belts and reach beneath their seats for their hand luggage. A child across the aisle muttered to her mother, then turned to smile at Brano. She was missing two front teeth. Brano tried to smile back. The young Austrian said, 'It's good to be among the workers again, eh?'

Brano walked to the front of the plane as the stewardess stood up without a smile. 'Please wait until we've opened the door.'

He nodded but remained where he was. She gave him a short look and went to the hatch to peer out the window. A man in orange work clothes was rolling metal stairs up to the plane, while behind him four men stood in leather coats, casting long shadows as the sun set. The one in the front, fatter and older than the others, raised his red face to the light. It was not Colonel Cerny but a man further up the chain of command, the Comrade Lieutenant General. An old-guard soldier who had distinguished himself fighting the Nazis, he was now an inveterate alcoholic running the counterintelligence division.

The stewardess grunted as she unscrewed the lock, then pushed the hatch open. Brano stepped out onto the stairs. The Lieutenant General spoke to the other three men, who jogged up to wait for him at the bottom.

As he descended, he realized he knew these men as well, but peripherally. Young, hard men adept at following orders. Once he reached them, two grabbed his arms and led him across the tarmac.

'Comrade Lieutenant General,' said Brano.

The older man tugged on his collar. 'Don't *com*rade me, Brano. You're in the shit now.'

He tried to control his voice. 'I don't understand. GAVRILO has been taken care of.'

'De*spite* you. Don't start with your stories, okay? Lochert's already sent in his report, and you . . .' The Lieutenant General shook his pink head. 'I don't even want to talk to you.' He turned and walked towards the airport.

Brano looked back at the passengers trickling out of the plane, staring in his direction. The young Austrian shielded his eyes, trying to make sense of the sick passenger who was being led away by three large men.

PART ONE

The Shoulder

8 February 1967, Wednesday

He left the Capital that morning, and at ten stopped in Uzhorod to fill his petrol, then continued up into the mountains, alert to each curve hidden behind clusters of snow-sprinkled pines. A small suitcase and briefcase shivered on the passenger seat.

His name was Brano Olcksy Sev. He had reached his fiftieth year the previous month with fewer scars than he deserved, and owned the same white Trabant P50 he had bought ten years before. He had replaced so many internal parts that likely nothing inside it had come with the original car. Even the steering wheel had been replaced in 1961 (31 October, the same day Stalin's sarcophagus was removed from its Red Square mausoleum), after he had taken a particularly sharp turn while trailing a suspect and found it sitting in his lap.

In Vranov he took lunch at the empty restaurant he knew from his last visit three years before, because this stop never changed. The waitress, a large woman with a cleft lip, frowned a lot at him. Then she leaned against the edge of the table, a faint odour of sweat misting off her cheeks, and asked if he was sure he didn't want a drink with that. 'We've got the best brandy in the region.'

Brano shook his head and watched her return, frowning, to the kitchen, then opened his briefcase and took out the case file with cold fingers.

Until last August, Brano had been a major in the Ministry for State Security, located on Yalta Boulevard, number 36. But for the last five months he had been a comrade-worker at the eternally noisy Pidkora People's Factory, the third man down the assembly line, fitting electrical wires into gauges so that the machines of socialist agriculture would never fail. Then, yesterday, he felt a tap on his shoulder. His alcoholic foreman stood behind him.

Someone to see you, Sev! In my office!

Brano followed him through the jungle of machinery to the glassed-in box in the centre of the factory floor. Behind the cluttered desk, holding a newspaper and smiling, sat the Comrade Colonel, Laszlo Cerny, wiping his unkempt moustache.

The foreman closed the door as he left, muffling the sound of machines.

Brano.

Comrade Colonel.

Sit down, said the colonel, tapping the newspaper on the desk. Then he held up the paper, which was Austrian. *Kurier.* He said, *You ever meet this guy?*

Who?

Filip Lutz.

Brano said he hadn't, then began to understand. This was the way meetings at Yalta Boulevard had always begun, with pleasantries and diversions. The Comrade Colonel even read out portions of that expatriate's slanders about the 'acts of barbarity' committed by the Ministry for State Security. *The lies he tells. Those Austrians will believe anything. Say, Brano,*

I don't suppose you'd be interested in leaving this factory, would you?

The waitress delivered his coffee with an arched brow. 'You're up here for work?'

Brano closed the file. 'How do you know I'm not from here?'

'Your accent. And your car.' She nodded at the mud-greyed window. 'Those plates are from the Capital.'

'That's very good.'

'So?'

'Yes?'

'Are you here on business?'

'You're very curious.'

'My husband says it'll get me into trouble one day.'

'Visiting family,' he said. 'In Bóbrka.'

'Bóbrka?' She crossed her arms over her chest and raised the mottled side of her lip. 'From the Capital to Bóbrka. That'll be a shock.'

'It certainly will be.'

He opened the file again as she walked away, and he looked at the top photograph, of a handsome man's face – wide, with faint features.

This was the reason for interrupting his day's work – Jan Soroka. Five and a half months ago, in August, this petroleum specialist had made it out of the East, to Vienna. Colonel Cerny shrugged. *Through Hungary, we suspect. Their border is full of holes.* Assumedly for asylum, Soroka twice visited the American embassy, then remained in Vienna for the following three months. In November, he reentered the American embassy and did not emerge again.

Well, we lost track of him at least. It happens. Just an oil rigger. Sometimes people slip through your fingers. But listen to this.

Ten days ago, Soroka had reappeared, magically, in Bóbrka – his hometown, and Brano's.

Brano had left Bóbrka in 1941, so Jan Soroka was un-familiar, as was his wife, Lia, whose puffy lips in her Galicia Textile Works identification photo made her look as if she'd just been hit. There were no photographs of their seven-year-old son, Petre.

And he hasn't been arrested? Brano asked.

Colonel Cerny shook his head. *He won't be, not yet, because that's what he must be expecting. His wife and son have joined him there. It's the 'why' we're after. And who would be best equipped to go in and work on him?*

Does this mean that I—

Cerny held up a finger. *Temporary and unofficial reinstatement, Brano. These might come in handy.* He reached in his pocket and handed over Brano's old internal passport, marked with the crest of the Ministry: a hawk with folded wings, its head turned aside. *The Lieutenant General wasn't in favour of it, but I used my influence. And if you distinguish yourself, then there's a chance—*

'That your wife?' the waitress asked.

Brano closed the file. 'Wife?'

'She's pretty.'

'Thank you.'

Among the papers he found a brief typed summary of the file's contents. Soroka had been born in 1934 in Sanok, to Wladislaw and Sofi Soroka, farmers. His childhood was not mentioned, nor his parents' 1947 transfer to the Bóbrka Petroleum Works, though it was noted that in 1950, at sixteen, Jan was part of a Red Pioneer trip to the Capital to shake hands with General Secretary Mihai and see the sights. When he was twenty-three, Jan applied for and received permission to move to the Capital, where he advised the Central Gas Industry Committee as part of the industrial reform pro-gramme Mihai had implemented the year before, in 1956, some months before his death. Before he disappeared, Soroka attended a conference in the spa town of Gyula on 'the future of power in the socialist neighbourhood', attended by scientists from all over the Empire, specialists in gas, petroleum, and nuclear energy. But a week after it ended, his wife, Lia, filed a missing person's report – Jan had never returned home. Militia Lieutenant Emil Brod investigated it – but without success. A line towards the end of the summary said, 'EXTERNAL ACTIVITIES: See attached.'

The Vienna report's five pages speculated on Soroka's date of entry into Austria – 21 August, six days after Brano had left – and listed various places he had visited. The list was not exceptional. There were the regular sights – the Stephansdom, the MAK, the Schönbrunn Palace – and bars where one might run into one's own countrymen, the most well known being the Carp, on Sterngasse. Then, on 25 August, a Thursday, he first entered the American embassy. During that five-hour visit, his hotel room was searched, but nothing of interest was found. Soroka returned to the embassy the next day, for only an hour. He then went to the Carp and got drunk.

On the following Monday, he appeared for the first time at the Raiffeisenbank and, as far as the agents could discern from their vantage on the other side of the lobby, opened an account. This was never properly verified.

The report became sporadic after that, skimming over the following three months with summaries. Soroka began eating in specific restaurants and going to a limited number of bars – the Carp most often – and made brief friendships before dropping out of touch. It was the life of a dissatisfied exile. A couple of these acquaintances were agents who tried to get the story out of him, but short of a full interrogation there was no way to learn more. He was not considered important enough to abduct – which, the report speculated, was probably a mistake, because on 18 November he returned to the American embassy and did not emerge again.

Brano said, *Who's the Vienna* rezident *now?*

Cerny pressed his lips together. *Josef Lochert.*

He— But Brano didn't finish the sentence. After his expulsion from the Ministry and five months standing beside an automated belt, this was, finally, something. *So where does Soroka say he's been all this time?*

The Comrade Colonel grunted his delight. *You'll like this. He says he's been with a mistress in Szuha – a small village near the Ukrainian border. Guess her name.*

I don't know.

Dijana Franković.

Brano flinched.

Yes, said Cerny. *I don't know what the Americans are up to. They know we're aware Soroka was in Vienna, but they're willing to send him in with a terrible cover. We want to know what's going on.*

We?

Myself, and the Comrade Lieutenant General.

I see.

Don't misjudge him, said Cerny. *What he did to you was what he thought he had to do.*

He wanted me in prison.

Colonel Cerny shook the newspaper at him. *Well, when Josef Lochert reported that you'd attacked him and tried to sabotage the operation . . . what did you expect him to think?*

Thank you again, by the way, said Brano. *For keeping me out of prison.*

You know I'd do much more for you. He stood up and looked through the glass at the factory that reached beyond his line of sight. *Maybe this isn't much better.* He stuck out a hand, and Brano took it. *So? Have I put something bright into an otherwise dull day?*

You've put something bright into an otherwise dull life.

Cerny tossed him the *Kurier. Enjoy the read. That stuff is no good for my bladder.*

Brano accepted the gift of a small roll from his waitress and drove through the mountains to the other side, passing Turka and then moving further north beyond the Carpathian hills. Giraltovce and Svidník glided past, and after dark he reached Dukla. There was a new billboard outside town, briefly lit by his headlights: General Secretary Tomiak Pankov, bald head shining above a blue suit, stood smiling, arms out, while around him a ring of twenty children danced. Beneath: THE SOCIALIST WORLD IS THE WORLD OF PEACE.

With children dancing in his head, Brano drove north into the forest.

He could not see the drilling machinery in the dark, but he knew it was there, among the pines. As he emerged into the sparse, rolling terrain that led to the village, he had an overwhelming urge to turn back. A couple of houses appeared on the left – new, unfamiliar homes – but the graveyard on the right brought on the subtle push of nostalgia he'd been waiting for. He took a left at the crossroad and drove into the centre of Bóbrka.

It seemed that everything was already known to him in this town of less than four hundred; everything was tactile. The lit windows with their rough lace curtains, the tyre-mangled road, the sharp grass springing up in his headlights, the fogged windows of the village's one bar and the old man shivering outside in the cold with a beer in his hand, watching Brano's Trabant roll past. Otherwise, the village was deserted. The bus stop was dark, though the yellow church with its statue of the Virgin Mary was lit by a floodlight. He followed the right-hand bend in the road, passing the small state shop his mother ran, continuing without looking at the prim homes leading up to hers.

Brano was genuinely surprised to see the house as it had always been, small and remote from the road. After the dynamism of the Capital, he was in a place that lived as if nothing had changed in the last fifty years.

He parked in the gravel, took out his suitcase and briefcase, and paused at the gate. He took breaths of cold air until the red tint in his cheeks began to fade.

The kitchen light glowed from around the side of the house, so he walked through shrubs to the kitchen door. Whitewashed by the thin lace curtain, she was still heavy, her thick elbows on the table, staring at the playing cards laid out before her. She jumped at his knock.

As Iwona Sev approached the door she squinted, and he leaned close to the glass to help her out. Then her head slid back, eyes filling with light before the smile came. She pulled the door open and shouted, 'Brani!'

He kissed her, then came into the kitchen, which had also never heard of progress. Wood-burning stove, gas lamp, a pail of fat in the corner. She held his face by the chin and turned it in the light. 'You're thin, thin. Are you all right? Is everything okay?'

He noticed that on her forehead, between her eyes, was a smear of soot. He kissed her cheeks again. 'I'm just taking a vacation. It's all right to stay here?'

'How can you even ask? It's not every day I have my son here. Or every year, for that matter.' She tried to take his suitcase, but he wouldn't let her. 'Get those to your room and I'll make something to eat. You must be hungry.'

He tilted his head from side to side.

'Of course you are. I'll heat some soup.'

'You've got a spot,' he said, touching his own forehead. She opened her mouth, blushing. 'Oh yes, yes.' She wiped the spot with a thumb and looked at her dirty print. 'If I had an electric stove, I'd be a lot cleaner.'

It could not really be called 'his' room any more. All personal effects – the toy oxcart with the broken wheel, the rotary board game, and even the set of French metal skiers with little metal skis and sleds – had been removed long ago, and his younger sister, Klara, had taken her possessions to her own home on the outskirts of Bóbrka. A group of framed photographs hung on the wall in a loose pastiche of half-forgotten faces. Uncles and distant cousins who were killed in the war, and their wives, who had remarried or stuck out the following years in solitude. A group shot of his mother's family from the 'teens, faces serious, as befitted the weight of such a sitting. Brano was also there, at two, and at six years old, with curls that made him look uncomfortably like a girl; Klara as a nine-year-old had the same intense features she had carried into adulthood. In the centre, a larger portrait of his father – his Tati – stood sentry over the others. It had been taken during the war, a young man's face with too many worry lines sprouting from his eyes. His mouth was open, revealing the chipped front tooth Brano always imagined when he tried to remember the face of Andrezej Fedor Sev.

He sat on the edge of the bed, gazing at that tooth. The man was probably dead now, one tiny fraction of the endless stream of refugees who made their way west after the war. But this man had been ordered to leave, by his son, on a frigid October night.

Brano wiped his palms dry on his knees.

It was not his room any more. It had become a home for guests. A guest room, and he was a guest. He put the suitcase into the wardrobe.

* * *

Her forehead was clean and the cards cleared away. She was heating pork stew in an iron pot and toasting bread. He asked her about the shop. 'Well, you know. Eugen is a good boy, but I don't need him. I could do all the work myself. It's a small place. But the State wants two employees, and who am I to argue?'

'You could bring it up at a council meeting.'

'Do you think that would help?'

'The State can't know things unless it's told.'

She hummed beneath her breath and stirred the fragrant soup. She added a spoonful of fat from the pail and let it cook a little more before ladling it into a bowl and collecting the toast. She poured him a glass of brandy and seemed pleased just to watch him eat.

He told her a few necessary details about the Pidkora factory and spent more time describing new construction in the Capital and everything that was changing. 'The metro was a fantastic success.'

'That's a good thing,' she said.

'When you travel you see the entire cross-section of the city – Gypsies and workers and university professors riding side by side.'

'And Politburo men?'

'Mother.'

'I'm only asking.'

He finished eating and sipped the warm brandy. She poured herself one and refilled his.

'And what about your personal life, Brani? Do you have friends? Any women you'd like your mother to meet?'

He hesitated. 'No, no women.'

'You're not so young any more.'

'I'm aware of that.'

'And when you reach a certain age you'll kick yourself for not having a wife.'

36

'It's possible.'

'Maybe we can find you a nice girl around here.'

'No. Mother, don't try that.'

'If you're not going to be sensible, then I'll have to be sensible for you.'

'Mother.'

She finished her glass. 'What, son-of-mine?'

'I'm quite happy with my life.'

'Nonsense. No one is happy with their life. Your Tati used to say that all the time, and he knew what he was talking about.'

He stared at his drink until she let the subject go. She went on to other matters, and by eleven had told him all about the happenings in Bóbrka. Alina Winieckim and Gerik Gargas had died in the last six months, the first of encephalitis, the other in a gory drilling accident. Alina's husband, Lubomir, got a permit to move to the Capital – 'Did you hear from him? I gave him your phone number.' Brano hadn't. 'Always unsociable, Lubomir. Always . . .' She twisted an index finger against her temple to signify insanity, then told him that the entire Ulanowicz clan had moved to Uzhorod.

Brano rubbed his eyes.

But there was good news as well, she told him. Wincet and Kalena Szybalski had got married after only a three-week courtship (though Kalena's soon-swelling belly made the reason clear enough). Also married were Piotr and Jolanta, and Augustyn and Olesia. 'There's love in the air,' she said. 'Maybe you'll smell it, too.' Krystyna Knippelberg was seven months pregnant with her sixth. 'You should see how ecstatic she is. But who wants six children? All she really wants is one of those Motherhood Medals, it's obvious.'

'Is that so bad?'

'It's bad when you can't feed the five children you've got. Krystyna will have to send one off to the orphanage, mark my words.'

The most spectacular news, however, of Jan Soroka's mysterious appearance did not cross her lips.

'And what about my sister?'

She yawned into the back of her hand, then took the bottle to refill his glass, stopping when she saw it hadn't been touched. 'Klara is doing well. Oh, very well. She and Lucjan are as happy as you can imagine. No children, though I talk to her.' She drank her brandy and put her chin in her hand. 'Maybe Lucjan is seedless. You can't blame a man for that, but I *would* like some grandchildren before I'm dead. Klara's not my only child, though.'

'Maybe.'

'You see?' she said as she got up. 'It's not just in the Capital that interesting things happen.'

She kissed him good night and left the brandy out, but he didn't drink any more. He sipped tap water and read Colonel Cerny's copy of *Kurier*. In a long column called 'An Eye into the Other Side', Filip Lutz told of his own interrogation in 1961, a year before he escaped through Prague to the West. He said that the brutal treatment he received at the hands of the Ministry for State Security was the sure sign of a paranoiac society in the advanced stages of collapse. He gave the regime three years at most.

When the words began to blur, he went to the bedroom, undressed and folded his clothes, then climbed into the cold bed.

Brano was not the kind of man who liked to recall his youth, preferring to forget that time of *zbrka* – Dijana Franković's word for 'the confusion of too many thing'. Before and during the war, he had stumbled through the stages leading to adulthood with his loud friend, Marek. The road to adulthood had been so clumsy and hesitant that even at the end of that life he was still unsure what to call himself. But after sending away his father, the *zbrka* dissipated. He was Brano Oleksy Sev, first a private, and then a sergeant, a captain, a lieutenant, a major. Then a factory worker. Now, he was neither an officer nor a worker but something undefined, lying in this cold room in the north of the country, where he always found the childhood *zbrka* waiting patiently for him.

As he warmed, he closed his eyes to focus on the provincial silence. It seemed clean to him, without malice, but then the noise did come, in little bursts, then a long high note: drunk men's howls wavering on the cold breeze, from far off. At least that was something familiar from the Capital.

9 February 1967, Thursday

His back was stiff from the too-soft bed, so he stood beside it and stretched his arms and twisted, then rolled his shoulders, the smell of breakfast rousing him. After a quick wash he ate bread and jam and two boiled potatoes. The eastern sun lit the dust in the kitchen while Mother talked about the people she expected to come to her store today, because villagers were as predictable as the clock on the wall.

They walked to the centre along the riveted gravel road, nodding at those who nodded, and he stood aside while his mother spoke hesitantly to old women before finally introducing him to Zuzanny Wichowska and Elwira Lisiewicz and Halina Grzybowska. He removed his hat for each woman, and though they gave him timid smiles, they did not offer their hands.

On each woman's forehead was a fading black stain. Yesterday, he realized, had been Ash Wednesday.

His mother's shop was a narrow, nameless place two doors down from the butcher's. She unlocked the door and opened the curtains to let in light. Shelves packed with canned foods and liquor bottles grew to the ceiling, and under the glass counter lay sausages and cheese. She showed him the back room filled with boxes her young assistant had yet to unpack, then made coffee on an electric coil. While they drank, a tall sixty-year-old man in a faded smock appeared with pallets of bread, the ash on his forehead sweated almost completely away. Mother asked how his wife, Ewa, was, then introduced him to Brano as Zygmunt. Brano shook his hand while she signed the invoice.

'You're enjoying Bóbrka?'

'Just arrived last night.'

'Different,' said Zygmunt.

'Bóbrka?'

'Different from the Capital.' He glanced at Brano's polished shoes. 'A big man in the Capital is just another man in Bóbrka.'

'The reverse is true as well.'

'It may be,' he said, taking the invoice from Iwona Sev. 'And that might be why I'm still in Bóbrka.' He touched the brim of his hat before he left.

Brano said he would go for a walk.

'To register with the Militia?'

'Of course.'

'You're as predictable as a villager, Brani.'

Without his mother as an intermediary, there was nothing to connect Brano to the ashen villagers who gave him cursory glances; there were no words to be said. He walked along the main road that branched out from the church, past yards with chickens and self-satisfied dogs, to where a single white Škoda was parked outside the Militia station, a small but austere concrete box with a tin

40

roof and its Militia sign propped in the window. The interior was dim and simple: a grey, scratched desk, a chair on each side, and an empty bulletin board. A portrait of General Secretary Pankov in a crisp fedora hung over the desk. Brano waited until a voice cursed from the back room.

'Hello?'

The voice silenced.

'Hello?'

The far door opened and a wrinkled uniform appeared: a young man with a black, greasy fringe swept over an ashless forehead. His sunken eyes were dark, his lips wide and without expression. 'Yes? Need something?'

'I'm here to register.'

'Register?' He moved to his desk and sat down.

'I'm from the Capital. I'm staying here now.'

The man motioned to the opposite chair and removed a stack of papers from a drawer. He went through them, pulling one out, then shaking his head and returning it to the stack and trying another until he found the form he needed. He turned it around for Brano. 'Here you go.'

Brano took a pen from a holder on the desk. 'This is for foreigners. I need form AE-342.'

The militiaman flushed. 'Yes, yes. How about that?' He returned to the stack. 'Here, of course. AE-342.'

While Brano filled it out the militiaman eyed him, the only sound the pen tip scratching paper. Brano passed it over and watched him read. The hawk on his blue Militia shoulder patch was dirty. Then Brano handed over his internal passport, and the militiaman's lip twitched at the sight of the Ministry hawk on the red cover.

'Uh, it says here you work at the Pidkora factory.'

'That's true.'

'But your passport—'

41

'Former employer. I haven't had a chance to change my documents.'

The militiaman cleared his throat. 'Well, Comrade Sev, it's good to have visitors in Bóbrka. I'm Captain Tadeusz Rasko.' He stuck out his hand and Brano took it, rising imperceptibly. 'How long will you be with us?'

'A week, I think. But my foreman is very flexible.'

'Very good,' he said. 'So you're here for a holiday?'

'I've worked hard this year.'

'I imagine.'

'What do you imagine?'

The captain's mouth chewed air for a moment. 'Just that you've worked hard, Comrade Sev.'

Brano nodded at his passport on the desk. 'Can you stamp that, then?'

'Of course.' It took another minute of desperate searching to come up with the proper stamp, then more to find the inkpad. But Captain Rasko did finally place the small purple entry stamp on a clean page.

Brano walked further out of town and then up the dirt road leading into the hills that surrounded Bóbrka. He passed old women he barely recognized from previous visits on his way to the windswept fields spotted by patches of snow. He tugged his hat lower and slipped his hands into his pockets against the cold. There were a few houses up here, one freshly painted, but he stopped at the low two-bedroom that needed a paint job more than any other.

The front door was open before he'd reached the steps, and tall, thin Klara looked down on him, smiling. The spot on her forehead was very black, fresh.

'Mother said you'd be by.'

'That was a good guess on her part.'

He kissed her cheeks and held her briefly before she drew

him inside, where the warmth encouraged him to strip off his coat and hat. There were more food smells here, pork and cabbage, and when she noticed him sniffing she asked if he was hungry. He was not. 'But you're so thin, Brano.'

'I'm fat enough.'

Klara began chain-smoking in the living room, while the fingers of her free hand pinched the fabric of her long brown skirt. He asked about her life, and she told an abbreviated story of the three years since they'd last talked, her dark eyebrows bobbing. While living with Lucjan's parents, they had built this little house (which, during his last visit, before he left for West Berlin, had been nothing more than a concrete foundation) and moved in two years ago. 'You've seen the outside, right? We got the paint from the factory in Sanok. Never use that stuff. It's just like chalk, washes away.'

'I'll remember.'

Lucjan was still working at the petroleum cooperative in a number of capacities, though these days his work was mostly administrative. 'He's immensely talented. He could do the work with his eyes shut.'

'He always seemed talented,' Brano lied.

'Lucjan's been making his own vodka in the basement. You'll like it. It's *fruity*.' She wrinkled her nose when she said that.

Then she asked, and he told her the same vague things about his life that he had told his mother.

'A factory, huh?'

'It's not as bad as it sounds.'

'But why?' she asked.

'What?'

'You told us you'd left the Ministry, but you never said why. Did you finally get disillusioned?'

He looked at her a moment, wondering if he could work

43

his way through that lie as well. No, not with Klara. 'I was fired.'

'Fired?' She straightened.

'Yes. I was working in Vienna, and a colleague double-crossed me. He sent in a report claiming that I had tried to sabotage his work. Can I have a cigarette?'

She handed one over and lit another for herself. 'Well? Did you?'

'Of course not. I'd never sabotage the Ministry.'

Klara seemed amused, as if this were something she could not quite believe. 'You were accused of sabotage and were then given a job in a factory.'

'If I didn't have allies, I'd be in a work camp now. Not everyone in the Ministry believes this man.'

'Who is this man?'

He stared at the glowing tip of his cigarette. 'Someone who wanted to get ahead and didn't care who he ruined on the way up.'

'And . . .'

'And?'

'And did he get ahead?'

Brano nodded as he crushed his unfinished cigarette in the ashtray. 'It's an imperfect world.'

'And now you've come here.'

'A little holiday.'

'But here,' she said. 'Why *here*?'

He wasn't sure what she was getting at. 'It's home.'

'You realize that everyone in town knows about you.'

'What about me?'

'What you do for a living.'

'What I did for a living.'

'It doesn't matter to them. No one here trusts you.'

'I don't see why they shouldn't trust me. My job was only about uncovering the truth.'

She flicked ash off her cigarette. 'Come on, Brano. They don't want to end up another Tibor Kraus.'

'Who?'

'You know. That man from Dukla, the butcher.'

'I don't know him.'

Klara sighed. 'It was in *The Spark*. He'd been using one of those machines for making meat pies. What are they called?'

'I don't know.'

'Well, he adjusted the gears so it made them with an ounce less dough. Then he sold the extra dough on the side. Made some money.'

'He was caught?'

She nodded.

'Good.'

'He was executed, Brano. Because of meat pies.' She waited, but he didn't say a thing. 'This is what I mean about the villagers here. You scare them. You know you do. Hell, what you did to Father is almost a legend.'

'I helped him.'

'You're the only one who believes that, but it doesn't matter. You know what they think, and that's why you never visit. It's not relaxing to be in a place you're not welcome.'

'So I'm not welcome here?'

'In this house, yes. But in Bóbrka . . .' She waved the smouldering cigarette in a circular motion and let go of her skirt. 'Who knows?' She stood up. 'We'll see you tonight?'

When he walked back into the village, the eyes that fell upon him had a different effect than they'd had an hour before. He had known he was not welcome, but Klara saying it aloud had made the idea flesh. A mutt behind a fence barked maniacally at him, and in the eyes of passers-by he saw not only a lack of welcome but actual hostility. The old women were musing over how to fit him into their wood-burning ovens, and the men were wondering where on his body a shotgun blast would best end his untrustworthy existence.

The bar in the centre was only large enough for three small tables and a short counter. One table was taken up by two old men playing cards on either side of a half-full bottle of rye vodka, and behind the bar a young man with a mono-brow beneath his ashy mark bent over a case of Żywiec, counting bottles. Brano waited until he stood up. The recognition flickered and then steadied in the barman's eyes. 'A beer?'

'Sure,' said Brano.

He removed a warm Żywiec from the box, uncapped it, and slid it over, then returned to his counting.

'And a paper?'

The man looked up. 'What?'

'Do you have a copy of *The Spark*?'

The barman took a coffee-stained copy of the day's paper from behind the counter. 'Anything else?'

The two older men took a break in their game to watch Brano sit on a stool by the lace curtains, sip his beer, and begin to read.

On the front page, General Secretary Tomiak Pankov looked back at him from behind a podium in a slender suit, his bald head ringed by a thin patch of grey, talking of peace. When Pankov took power a decade ago, his first preoccupied year had been spent purging the Politburo and security apparatus of anyone too loyal to his dead predecessor, Mihai. Brano had survived that purge by sticking close to Colonel Cerny, whose ability at side-stepping the hammer was almost famous. Once his power was secured, Pankov became what he'd always been, a Party bureaucrat who made speeches on industrial levels and agricultural output; he focused on the numbers. But after a heart attack in early 1965, his focus changed, and he reinvented himself as an enlightened man of peace. *The Spark* reported that twenty-six nations had been present at the most recent international summit, called 'The Doves of Peace' – Pankov was not known for his original titles.

Brano glanced up from the paper and peered out of the window; Pavel Jast had arrived.

Comrade Colonel Cerny had given him the name of his contact, shown him a photograph, and added, *An idiot, a gambler, and a drunk, but useful.* That seemed about right. He could read those characteristics in the swagger Pavel Jast shared with all small-town informants, as if the entire People's Army were marching behind them and would back up any stupid thing they did. So Brano returned to the paper as the fat man burst in, muttered something indecipherable to the two old men, then clapped a hand on the counter and demanded a vodka. He held the muddy glass to his lips as he rotated, leaning back to survey the tiny space. In the translucent window-reflection, Brano saw Pavel Jast's eyes settle on him. Jast produced a cigarette and winked at the two old men before approaching.

'Hey, you. *Com*rade. Got a light?' He winked a second time in the old men's direction.

From his pocket Brano took a book of matches marked HOTEL METROPOL and handed it to Jast without looking away from the window.

The first match faltered, but the second hissed and sparked until the cigarette was lit. Jast exhaled smoke and the stink of earlier vodkas, and Brano's eyes watered as he accepted the matches back. But this was a different book of matches, white and blank. Jast said, 'From the Capital, eh? Aren't you Iwona's boy?'

Brano drank some more beer, then laid a few koronas on the counter. He turned to Jast for the first time and saw the red web of punished veins beneath his flaccid cheeks and nose. 'I am,' he said.

Another wink at the old men, who seemed unsure they liked the performance. The barman ignored everyone. Jast grunted, the shot glass pressing into his chin. 'Well, you're not in the Capital any more, comrade.'

'I didn't notice,' said Brano, and only after he left did it occur to anyone in the bar that this had been a joke.

On the way back to his mother's house, he clutched the matchbook in his pocket, turning it over and opening and shutting it while he watched faces along the road. Zygmunt, the old man who delivered his mother's bread, seemed to be avoiding his gaze, but Captain Rasko acknowledged him as he stood in the mud with a young woman whose puffy lips made her look like the victim of abuse. He hadn't expected to come across Lia Soroka out in the open, but he managed the surprise by nodding back at Rasko and at Jan Soroka's unsmiling wife.

He didn't take out the matchbook until he had passed his mother's front door. He flipped it open and read the sweat-smeared pencil scrawl inside the cover:

<u>MIDNIGHT</u>
EMILIA 4

*

Klara brought a large dish of pork cabbage rolls, and Lucjan ducked his head as he followed her in with his vodka, sealed in a used litre-sized soda bottle. Lucjan was nearly two heads taller than Brano, ruddy in the face, his wide shoulders stretching the back of his shirt, but his handshake had almost no strength at all. Mother took the vodka from him and disappeared with Klara into the kitchen.

Lucjan tried to smile. 'Klara says you're on holiday.'

'That's true.'

'You don't know how long?'

'A week, probably. Just long enough to get some rest.'

'Must be nice, having that kind of relationship with your manager. He doesn't care?'

'He's a good friend.'

'Known him a long time?'

'Are you always so curious?'

Lucjan let out a nervous laugh, then settled on the sofa and began to roll a cigarette, his big fingers fumbling with the thin paper. Brano watched. 'She told me you're doing well at the cooperative.'

'Klara's an optimist.'

'But you're doing administrative work. That's a good sign.'

He licked the paper and sealed the cigarette. 'What about you? You're not used to working a factory job, are you?'

'Not so different. There are orders, and I follow them. I do all right.'

'That's the answer I'd give, too.' He offered the damp cigarette, but Brano shook his head.

Klara had known Lucjan Witaszewski all her life, and perhaps this explained the unimpressive choice she'd made at the age of seventeen. Brano had been working in the Capital for four years when the wedding invitation arrived in his mail. But that was 1948, and in the Capital there had been no end to the work. In almost every alley hid another criminal, the detritus all wars produce, and on top of that, there had been a new man in the Militia office named Emil Brod who had to be followed and examined and, finally, accepted.

49

So he had posted his response the next day: he could not come, but he wished them every happiness in their new, shared life, and had every hope that unity like theirs would be the backbone of their new, great society.

Klara had never replied.

Now, nearly two decades later, she placed two glasses of vodka on the coffee table and ran her fingers through her husband's hair. 'What's the subject?'

'Work,' said Lucjan.

'Just as long as it's not politics. Now drink.'

Both men did as they were told, and Brano admitted that Lucjan's apricot vodka was rather good. Lucjan shrugged his thanks.

They went to the kitchen table while Mother dished everything out. 'No ceremonies here,' she said. 'Just eat.' Brano followed the order, but Klara bowed her head – a quick prayer – before lifting her fork.

Conversation lingered on work as Lucjan revealed an unexpected excitement, describing the new drilling rig that had been delivered. 'The Austrians know what they're doing, I can tell you that. They sent over the Trauzl – a cable rotary rig on wheels. A real beauty!'

Brano noted that the factories in Uzhorod were pumping out record numbers of tractors and industrial machines. Klara wasn't impressed. 'These production records don't do anything for Bóbrka. You can see it yourself. Now that it's winter, we're hibernating, like always. Go out after dark, and Bóbrka's a ghost town. I suppose the Capital never gets like that.'

'It doesn't,' said Brano.

'Makes you wonder what goes on behind the windows,' Klara said. 'They're still living their lives.'

'They're eating their mothers' meals,' said Mother.

'And having more sex.'

50

'*Lucjan,*' said Klara.

Lucjan shook his head. 'What they're doing is playing cards. That's what.'

Mother frowned.

'There's a lot of gambling?' asked Brano.

Lucjan's face shrivelled. Klara looked up.

Brano opened his hands and gave a smile so small that it could be seen by no one. 'I'm not going to arrest anyone for it. That's not what I do.'

Lucjan shrugged. 'Everyone does it, right?'

'I do it myself,' he lied.

'But not like here, I hope,' said Mother.

'Like here?'

Lucjan looked at his plate. 'It's like in a lot of villages. These peasants run out of money, and the bets get a little strange. You know. *I'll bet my horse on this hand.* That sort of thing.'

'Not so strange,' said Brano. 'The same as betting your watch.'

'But what about your child?' Klara asked.

Occasionally, Brano had heard of this sort of thing during his years in the Militia office in the Capital, though it happened more often in the countryside: men betting the life of a daughter, a wife, a mother. It was a repulsive element of the old world that socialism had not yet wiped clean. But he pretended it was news. 'Child?'

Klara went back to her plate, her face as red as the Comrade Lieutenant General's, but not from drink.

'Some guy,' said Lucjan. 'An idiot. He was drunk, and he bet his little girl's life on a hand of cards. Can you believe it?'

'So what happened?'

Lucjan smiled. 'He won! Thank God.'

The silence that followed felt long, and they each looked

51

at him: first Lucjan, before facing his plate again, then Mother, who gave a fragile smile. Finally, Klara's stoic gaze held him for a long time before returning to her food. It was a look Brano could not quite decipher, but it gave him a sudden, overwhelming feeling that he was far from home and among strangers.

After dinner they returned to the living room and worked slowly on the vodka, Mother filling the silences with gossip Brano had already heard the night before. His sister and her husband had probably heard it all as well, for they only grunted into their glasses as she chronicled the love affairs of the town.

Then, with enough liquor warming him, Brano said, 'A while ago, I took a trip to Vienna.'

'Vienna?' said Mother. 'I didn't know you went there.'

'I did, for a little while. Work. A friend of mine was having a party. There was some food, but it was gone quickly, and everyone began drinking heavily. I ran into the woman he was dating – she read tarot cards for a living.'

Lucjan snorted. 'Tarot cards?'

'She was very nice to me. She had been drinking quite a bit. Someone was playing an acoustic guitar and leading the room in song.'

'You *sang*?' said Klara.

'No.' Brano set his glass on the table. 'After a while, this woman asked me to dance.'

'Did you dance?' asked Mother, looking around. 'Have you ever seen Brani dance?'

'Never,' said Klara.

'I did dance, but not at first,' said Brano. 'She continued to stand very close, watching me. So I asked her where my friend was. She said she had told him to go to hell. She'd told him he was a bore and she never wanted to speak to him again.'

Lucjan leaned forwards. 'She *told* him that?'

'Well, if he was boring—' began Klara.

'There's a difference between the truth and civility.'

Klara shrugged at Mother, who smiled back.

'It was none of my business,' said Brano. 'But I tried to defend him to her. She would have none of it. Finally, she grabbed my arms and pulled me close to her and said, *Brano Sev, I love you.*'

'She *didn't*,' said Mother.

Klara grinned. 'This is fantastic!'

Brano shook his head. 'I told her she was mistaken. We'd only met once before, and she didn't know who I was at all. She couldn't be in love with me. It was impossible.'

'Nuts, that one,' said Lucjan.

'We danced a little, and by then it was very late. Most everyone had left. I wanted to get out of there, but she was clutching on to me. So I told her I'd walk her home. She was drunk, and it seemed like the gentlemanly thing to do.'

Lucjan clucked his tongue. 'I bet it did, you rat.'

Brano looked at him. 'On the walk to her apartment she told me she had a vision of her future, living on a lake with an older man standing behind her, protecting her. It was fate, she said, and she said that man was me.'

'Was you,' echoed Mother. Klara winked at her.

'I got her to her front door, where she snatched my hat from my head and told me I'd have to come up and let her read my future if I wanted my hat.'

'Your *future!*' Klara burst out laughing. 'This is priceless!'

Brano didn't smile. He looked from one face to the other.

'So?' said Lucjan. 'Did you learn your future?'

He shook his head and lied again. 'I took my hat from her and went home.'

'Sure you did,' said Lucjan.

'I assumed that by the next morning she'd be so embarrassed by what she'd done that nothing else would happen. But I was wrong. She was still convinced she was in love.'

'And you saw her again?' asked Klara.

'Never. I left the next day. But she got my address and started writing me letters.'

'With your future?' asked Mother; then, realizing she'd made a joke, she started to laugh.

'It was a very strange experience.'

'You still get them?' asked Lucjan. 'The letters.'

'Sometimes, yes.'

Mother touched the bun of her hair. 'Here I was trying to set you up with some nice girls, and you're involved in an international romance!'

'There's always a surprise with Brano,' said Klara. 'He sits there, mute as a stone, then comes out with the strangest stories.'

'But I wonder sometimes,' he said, lifting his glass again, 'do you think I was wrong to say that?'

'Say what?' asked Lucjan.

He focused on Klara. 'To say she couldn't be in love with me. Do you think I could have been wrong?'

'There's all kinds,' said Klara.

Mother nodded. 'You just can't know, can you?'

Lucjan licked his lips. 'How come that kind of thing never happens to me?'

Klara elbowed him in the ribs.

The others had left and Mother was asleep by the time Brano put on his coat at the front door, pulled his hat over his forehead, then went down the front path, through the gate, and into darkness.

Bóbrka on a moonless night was a land of unpredictable pits and obstructions. He stumbled in a few potholes and ran into carts left on the side of the road. Despite all the koronas poured into the oil complex in the forest, no one had thought to equip the village roads with street lamps. The centre was barely visible by the muted light from some windows and by the spotlight illuminating the church. He stopped, looked around, and began walking east, towards the woods.

He'd never quite understood that night with Dijana, nor the letters she'd sent after he left. He'd even received one just before leaving the Capital for Bóbrka. *Brani, why this silence? What we have it is good.* He remembered standing at her door, and her saying in her stilted Serbo-Croat version of his language, *I want for to read your future.* Though she spoke German well, she chose out of adoration to speak his language to him, which she butchered mercilessly. *Brano Sev, I am in the love with you.*

He emerged into an open field littered with blackened pump-jacks tipping their heads like chickens, then continued up a gravel road to the Emilia 4 pump, a high wooden tower built four decades before on the Canadian model and lit up like the church, though now it was used as a meeting room for officials in from the Capital. As a child, Brano had often climbed up inside it, alongside Marek, and across the roof of the low administrative building that stretched along the tree line. As he approached he heard what he'd heard the previous night: drunken howls from far off.

The door to Emilia 4 was unlocked, and when he closed it behind himself, the cold darkness was an unwavering black. He heard the laboured breathing of unhealthy lungs close by. Brano lit a match and stared into the grinning, red-veined face of Pavel Jast. Jast's hands were stuffed in his pockets, and he reeked of vodka. 'Evening, Comrade Sev.' He stuck out a thick hand.

'What's the name of your friend?'

'You know who I am, I know who you are. What's the point?'

'Your friend's name, Comrade Jast.'

The big man dropped his hand. 'The glorious Archduke Ferdinand, Comrade Sev.'

'Thank you.' The match was burning his fingers, so he blew it out and slipped it in a pocket. 'Let's go outside.'

They walked shoulder to shoulder behind the administrative building, where the trees threatened to swallow them. Jast took out a cigarette, but Brano asked him not to light it. 'Of course, of course,' muttered Jast.

'So what do you have for me?'

Jast sucked on the unlit cigarette. 'Soroka's been staying in his parents' house – that's the two-storey one just past the church.'

'Cream coloured?'

'Yes, yes. His wife and boy go out to take care of errands – shopping, that sort of thing – but Jan I almost never see. A couple times I visited the house – clandestinely, you realize, just looking through the windows – but all I ever saw was the Sorokas eating and listening to the radio.'

'Radio?'

'Nothing like that. Just a receiving set. If he's sending, I wouldn't know.'

'What do the villagers say?'

'Villagers.' He sniffed. 'They'll say anything if it's entertaining enough. Wienczyslaw thinks he's working for us, preparing to turn Bóbrka into a New Town – tear down all the homes and build tower blocks. Armand has the paranoia to think he's working for the Poles, to redraw the border and take the region back. Only the old folks believe his cover story.'

'The one about the woman, Dijana Franković.'

'Exactly.'

'And you?'

'I try not to think too much. He's working for the West – I've been told enough by Yalta to know that. But what does the West care about a dump like Bóbrka? Our oil deposits aren't big enough to be important to anybody. All I can think is that he's going to try to take his family back with him.'

'That was my assumption,' said Brano. 'How do you suggest I make contact?'

Jast took the spit-damp cigarette from his lips and then replaced it. They had stopped and were facing one another. 'He does go to church.'

'Every Sunday?'

'On the two Sundays he's been here it's been regular. It's the one thing I'd depend on.'

They began walking back in silence, until Jast brightened and took something from his pocket.

'Here – look at this!' He handed over a ballpoint pen, and in the light bleeding around the buildings Brano saw on it the image of a shapely blonde in a red evening gown.

'Yes,' he said.

'Turn it over.'

Brano did so, and watched the evening gown slide down her body, revealing breasts, hips, and the dark spot between her legs.

'Pretty good, huh?'

'Very nice,' he said as he returned it.

'Got it from a friend who visited West Germany. The things they make there!'

As they rounded the corner of the administrative

building, Brano noticed two men approaching the wooden tower.

'Damn,' whispered Jast. 'The night watch is usually longer at the bar.' He turned back and waved for Brano to follow.

They entered the woods, where Jast soon found a barely discernible trail, cursing when he ran into low branches, his heavy feet snapping everything they touched. As they progressed, Brano explained the method of their future meetings. The cue would be an empty matchbook left under the bus-stop bench. 'We'll meet in the graveyard at eleven that same evening. Does this suit you?'

'Pretty morbid, yes, but it suits me fine. Damn!' He flailed his arms against unseen branches, then fell. Brano crouched, reaching out a hand. He heard Jast's voice. 'What the hell?' And then, 'Jesus Christ, what—' Then nothing.

Brano lit another match, which shook as his eyes focused. Pavel Jast also saw what he had tripped over, and leapt up, muttering, *'Oh fuck oh fuck.'*

On the ground was a shirtless man, short and heavy, mouth gagged tight over a beard, his stomach and chest and arms covered by numerous tiny cuts. They had bled, tinting the white body pink. Brano touched the sticky, dead wrist, then the still-warm chest, and glanced at the well-tailored black trousers and scuffed shoes. He dropped the match and lit another, while Jast jumped from foot to foot, babbling words Brano could no longer make out.

Before they split up at the edge of the woods, Jast told him how to get to Captain Rasko's home. Brano returned to the dark village, which was no longer haunted by howls from the forest, continued past the church, and near the Militia station opened the wooden gate to a low one-bedroom. He knocked on the loose front door, then did it again. Something fell behind a window; a light came on. The lace curtain was pulled back slightly. Finally, Captain Rasko stood in the doorway, hands shoved in the pockets of a grey robe, his black hair sleep-pressed into an angle. 'Comrade Sev,' he said, not bothering to hide his disappointment.

'Sorry to wake you, Comrade Captain. I'm afraid there's been a murder. In the woods near the cooperative.'

'You've got to be kidding.'

'I'm not.'

Rasko stepped back, and Brano entered. There were piles of clothes in the living room and a pungent smell from the kitchen. 'Last murder we had was two years ago,' said Rasko.

'You'd better come look at it.'

'And that murder was before my time. I've only been Militia chief a year. I don't even have a staff.'

Brano waited.

'I suppose I should get dressed.'

'I suppose you should.'

Despite the darkness, Brano was able to take him directly to the body. Rasko ran his torch beam up and down it. 'Jakob.'

'You know him?'

'Of course. Jakob Bieniek. I know him as well as anyone else knows him.' He crouched, made a face, and touched the gag, turning the head aside. 'After his wife, Janica, died – I guess that was five years ago – he became . . . well, strange.'

'How?'

Rasko used the torch to investigate the ground around the body. 'He was a hermit, Comrade Sev. He dropped out of touch with everyone, which is a feat in Bóbrka.'

'His job?'

'Delivered milk from the distribution point in Krosno. But even when he was driving, he wore these tailored suits.

See those trousers? And his shoes – always polished. He looked foolish.' Rasko shook his head. 'What happened to him?'

'Looks like a razor blade, or a few of them, used many times.' Brano followed the torch beam with Rasko, walking around the body.

'A match.' Rasko crouched to pick it up.

'It's mine.'

'Oh.' He paused. 'So what were you doing out here?'

'Just walking. I couldn't sleep.'

'So you came out *here*?'

'Aren't many trees in the Capital.'

Rasko stood still a moment, thinking. 'No one really liked Jakob, but I can't imagine anybody who'd feel this way about him.'

'Somebody did.'

Then they were quiet, staring at the now-cold body. Rasko took a length of wide red ribbon from his pocket and tied it to a tree. 'Let's go.'

At the militiaman's house, Brano drank a glass of tap water while Rasko called the village doctor, who would get the body in the morning. Rasko told the doctor to watch for the red ribbon. Then he poured a tall vodka for himself and sat across from Brano. 'Want to come with me tomorrow?'

'Where?'

'To Jakob's house. See if we can turn up something.'

'If I won't be in the way.'

'I'm alone here, Comrade Sev. Your presence can only help.'

10 February 1967, Friday

He slept lightly and woke at seven in a sweat. Though he could not remember it, he knew he had again dreamed of that week just after his return from Vienna, spent in the basement of Yalta Boulevard 36.

The Lieutenant General had accompanied him in the white Mercedes from the airport into town. Brano, with his memory now intact, knew better than to speak, and when the other three men guided him to the large double doors of Yalta 36, the Lieutenant General only said, *You better cook up some goddamned brilliant answers for us.*

But he didn't come with Brano as the men walked him past a stunned Regina Haliniak at the front desk, along the corridor of unmarked doors to the stairwell that brought them down to the basement. He'd led enough men to these damp, windowless cells to know the route, and even said hello to Stanko, the stout man with round glasses who kept the guardroom organized. Stanko, nodding, could come up with no reply.

A Ministry doctor visited him that night, listened to his heart, and asked him questions. For the memory loss, he could offer no authoritative explanation but suggested stroke. *You're not young, Brano.*

The interrogation began the next day, when he was dragged to another room with a table and two chairs. What would always strike him as the great irony of those sessions was that each morning on the table sat a glass of water and the headache powders Brano's doctor had prescribed, and only after he'd taken them did the Lieutenant General's assistants feel free to begin what the Americans liked to call his 'softening up'. Not until blood flowed did the Lieutenant General arrive.

You set up office in a hotel.

Yes, said Brano. *The embassy wasn't secure.*

Maybe you were afraid Major Romek would listen in on your schemes?

I thought nothing of the sort.

61

Kaspar.

One of the guards struck him across the back of the head.

Don't be impertinent, Brano.

Working back from the Lieutenant General's questions, Brano could piece together Lochert's inventive report. He claimed not only that Brano had attacked him in the Volksgarten the night of the Richter murder but also that over the previous month he had been trying to sabotage the investigation into the identity of GAVRILO. Brano had undermined security at the embassy, consciously casting doubt on the abilities of their head of security, Nikolai Romek, by planting electronic bugs. Why? Because Brano needed an excuse to run his operations outside the embassy, where he could not be watched, at the Hotel Kaiserin Elisabeth. From there he could meet with whomever he wanted.

Lochert, his report claimed, was confused about the *why* of Brano's treachery. Only after the incident in the Volksgarten was he able to piece together the details. Brano arrived late because of a liaison with a certain Dijana Franković, Yugoslav national, who, besides being the girl-friend of Bertrand Richter, was known to have entertained KGB agents in her apartment on Döblinger Hauptstraße. Brano, Lochert finally realized, was working for the Russians – who, for their own reasons, wanted to hinder Yalta Boulevard's investigation into the source of their Vienna leak.

This was all, of course, a lie, and two weeks later, after he'd been released from his Yalta cell and given his new labour assignment at the tractor factory, he and Colonel Cerny took a walk together in Victory Park. *But why?* Brano asked him. *Why did he do this?*

Cerny had thought it through over the last weeks.

Lochert's lived in Vienna almost a decade; he knows the city and its networks better than anyone. We sent him to Vienna because he grew up in one of those Saxon villages in the Carpathians; we felt he understood the Germanic mindset. And then Kristina Urban was killed.

He expected promotion.

But he's a simpleton, said Cerny, *because the Ministry never planned to promote a hired gun – a half-educated Saxon thug – to the level of* rezident. *Then you arrived, with only minor Austrian experience, and Lochert's pride . . . well, he couldn't take it, could he?*

If the Lieutenant General believes his story, why aren't I in prison?

Why aren't you dead, you mean. Cerny gripped his arm and whispered, *Because you've got me, Brano. I've still got a few tricks up my sleeve.*

He wiped the sweat off himself with a hand towel, and as he finished dressing, Mother stumbled to his bedroom door. She rubbed her bloodshot eyes. 'Where were you last night? Did you get any sleep?'

'Some. I've got to run.'

'Where?'

'To meet Captain Rasko.'

She leaned against the wall, stifling a yawn. 'Why on earth are you seeing him this early?'

'There was a murder last night.'

'There was . . . *what*?'

'I'll tell you about it later.' He kissed her forehead.

Captain Rasko had not yet dressed. He asked Brano to make some coffee, then sprinted back to the bedroom. Brano picked through piles of dishes for the coffeepot and cleaned it thoroughly. There was a bag of ground beans in the cabinet.

Rasko straightened his tie as he drank. 'This is better than my coffee.'

'I cleaned the pot.'

'Oh, is *that* the trick?'

Brano set down his cup and used a rag to wipe the counter clean. 'You told me you hadn't dealt with murder before. What kinds of crimes do you usually deal with?'

'Petty stuff. Fistfights and drunkenness. Thievery. Gambling – the boys here like Cucumber best – but I only become aware of gambling when it leads to fistfights or thievery. These guys are serious about their card games.'

'I've heard.'

'Had your breakfast yet?'

'I don't usually eat breakfast.'

'Good. Because we're going to see the body first.'

As they parked behind the doctor's house, two small blond boys in pale blue pyjamas ran out of the back door, whistling clouds of breath into the cold air as they reached Rasko's side. They called him 'uncle' and held his legs as he tried to approach the back door, where the doctor, an old man in a white smock, stood smoking. Rasko rubbed the boys' heads. 'Juliusz, meet Major Brano Sev.'

Juliusz came down a step. 'Sev? Iwona's . . .?'

Brano nodded.

'From the Capital, right?'

'Yes.'

The doctor held out a damp hand but didn't smile. 'Pleased to meet you.'

While the boys fought in their room, the men settled in the kitchen with coffee and cigarettes. Juliusz had picked up Jakob Bieniek's body just before dawn and made a preliminary examination. 'A savage. That's who did it. I counted a hundred and thirty-four slices, but my eyes got tired towards the end. There are more.'

'Was it done there?' asked Brano.

'Eh?'

'Was he killed in the woods, or was his body brought there afterwards?'

'The woods,' said the doctor. 'Yes, in the woods. He got leaves in his hair – what little he has – while he was struggling. And when he was attacked he still had his shirt on. There were fibres in some cuts.'

Rasko looked at his hands. Brano took a final sip of coffee and stood up. 'Shall we see the body?'

Juliusz had laid Bieniek on a table in a sunny room with large windows and white cabinets that held his equipment. One white napkin covered his face, another his genitalia. Between them, his stomach rose like a low mountain, etched, like his arms, with white marks, each between a couple of inches and half a foot long. The longer slices had split and puckered the flesh. All the blood had been washed away.

The doctor removed the face napkin and stepped back.

'How about that,' said Rasko. 'He kind of looks like Comrade Sev, doesn't he?'

The doctor bent over Bieniek's white face, which was blemished where the gag had stretched over his lips and cheeks, then glanced back at Brano. 'You know, you're right.'

They were both right. Like Brano's, Bieniek's face was wide and round, with flat cheekbones, and he even had a mole on his left cheek, where Brano's three moles lay. But unlike Brano, Bieniek was fat, his scalp was almost bald, and he had a thin beard that was more than a few days' forgetfulness.

'Here,' said Juliusz. He opened a cabinet and took out a brown paper bag that he handed to Rasko. 'These are the handkerchiefs used to keep him quiet. One in his mouth, the other around it.'

Rasko took the bag but did not open it.

'And these are his documents?' Brano pointed at a maroon passport on the table.

'Yes.'

Brano glanced at the passport photo – a clean-shaven version of the man on the table, smiling, with colour in his cheeks – and slid it into his pocket. 'Are we sure he died from the cuts?'

'I'd bet on it,' said Juliusz. 'Once the carotid artery was hit, the fight was over.'

'Razor blade?'

'I'd bet on that, too.'

'Any thoughts on the assailant?'

The doctor blinked a few times. 'Don't know how many there were – it could have been a single energetic killer. But whoever it was, he didn't know a thing about anatomy. Cutting that artery was dumb luck.'

'Fingerprints?'

The doctor inhaled. 'Comrade Major, this isn't the Capital.'

Brano looked at Rasko. 'Do you have any questions?'

Captain Rasko was staring at Jakob Bieniek's swollen ankles.

'Comrade Captain?'

His tongue danced inside his cheek. 'No, no more questions.'

Jakob Bieniek's house was on the edge of the centre, another two-bedroom surrounded by ridged, frozen mud. Like Klara and Lucjan's house, this one had been painted a Sanok white that the weather had quickly turned grey. There was no walkway, just a path of old boot prints leading to the locked front door. Rasko nodded at the window over the door handle. 'Shall I?'

'Be my guest,' said Brano.

He shoved an elbow into the glass, knocked aside some loose pieces, then unlocked the door from the inside.

The place smelled sour, as if something were rotting in the back room, but it was only the smell of a shut-in who allowed his unwashed body to fester in a small, airtight space.

'What a shithole,' said Rasko.

Unlike Dijana Franković, Brano Sev did not believe in fate, but as he walked through Jakob Bieniek's cluttered, musty living quarters, he thought that if fate had dealt him a different hand, this could easily have been him. The instinctual urge for solitude he shared with this dead milkman was a curse in a small town; it was punished by internal exile. Bieniek's exile may have been chosen at first, after his wife's death, but soon a whispered pact among the townsfolk had assured that he could not escape his sphere of silence. Brano had experienced that silence in the Capital, but unlike Bieniek, Brano had had Yalta Boulevard. Yalta had encouraged his hermetic nature; the Ministry rewarded the virtues of solitude and secrecy.

The furniture in the living room was threadbare, the kitchen worse than even Rasko's. But the stink was centred in the bedroom, where greasy plates and filthy underwear were spread about. At the end of the bed, a small, cluttered desk looked out the front window, and beside the desk sat two cardboard boxes stuffed with papers.

While Rasko opened the window, Brano squatted and leafed through the boxes. At first he couldn't decipher the quick scribbles. He brought a few pages to the desk for better light.

'What's that?' asked Rasko.

Brano read aloud: '*16 October 1966: Maria eats liver with potatoes on Mondays. She's done it three weeks running, so that is a rule of thumb. She does it for strength, maybe, because on Monday afternoons Wiktor comes to visit and she has to clean the house afterwards, before Krysztof returns.'* He looked up. 'Who are Maria and Krysztof?'

'The Rzepkas. Married. Live a couple streets away. Are all the pages like this?'

They were. The subjects changed, but the project did not. Jakob Bieniek had been keeping track of his neighbours with an unsettling eye for detail. He noted Lubomir Winieckim's suspiciously brief grieving period after his wife Alina's death, and before he'd been seen kissing the very pregnant Krystyna Knippelberg.

'I never realized he was actually crazy,' said Rasko.

Brano pulled out page after page of questionable activities – the Szybalskis, the Gargases, the Lisiewiczes. There was a method here, each sheet focused solely on one person, each comment preceded by a date. But the pages weren't filed alphabetically; they were erratic, the excitement of a hermit's secret knowledge leaving no time for order.

The disturbing sense of a missed fate swelled again. Not only did he share the reclusive nature of this dead man, the same face, too, but they shared the same profession. They were watchers and, each in his own way, judges.

'Some of this may be of use to you,' he said.

'Dirty laundry, that's all it is.'

'I mean for the case. Jakob could have been blackmailing someone.'

'Of course!'

Brano placed a stack on the desk. 'Why don't you go into town and ask around for information? The townspeople won't talk to me.'

'I suppose you're right.'

'And I'll let you know if I find anything useful.'

Once Rasko was gone, Brano settled on the floor, legs crossed. He started through the pages, sometimes pausing on a familiar name, reading a line here and there, but continuing until, a little after noon, he found what he was looking for.

SOROKA, JAN

28 January 1967: A surprise. Jan Soroka walks in the main square as if he's been here all his life. We all know (see K. Knippelberg – 11 September 1966) he left his wife in the Capital, and now, 5 months later, he walks through Bóbrka, smiling like a fool at everyone. When I passed him I remained silent to hide my surprise. I don't know if he noticed . . .

30 January 1967: Overheard at the bar: The gambler Pavel Jast said Soroka's been with a mistress these past months. A Dijana Franković, from Szuha. I never thought Soroka was that kind of man, but if nothing else my studies have shown me you don't know who anyone is, ever . . .

3 February 1967: Another surprise. Jan's wife and boy have arrived, everyone in his parents' house. What is this? I'm beginning to doubt the story of the mistress. Jan and Lia are not, as you'd expect, fighting. Through their window they look in love. I'd find their reunion touching if the suspicion of something larger wasn't getting to me. Jan drove his father's car to the train station today. A green Volga GAZ-21 was parked outside as well. I don't know whose it was, but the plates were from Uzhorod . . .

6 February 1967: When Jan isn't hiding inside his parents' house, he walks the western road out of town and smokes in the fields. From my car I saw him talking to a cow. Insane? It's possible. Perhaps I will speak with him. Perhaps I will not.

Brano got the Trabant from his mother's house and drove through Bóbrka, easily, as if he had nowhere to go. Just before the church he noticed the low gate and cream-coloured two-storey house, the tiled roof that needed repairs, the empty yard.

He turned around at the bus stop on the other side of the church and drove westward out of town, into the fields. Split-rail fences, half blown over by old storms, lined the northern side of the road, and occasional clusters of blank-faced cows appeared, a few stopping their meals to look at him. Then he spotted a figure coming over a low hill to the south, beyond the cows, where the earth rose into the base of a mountain. The figure was approaching the road, but Brano did not slow down. He continued over a second hill and, once out of sight, turned the car around and waited. He looked at his wristwatch, counting the minutes, then drove back slowly.

The man that walked alongside the road glanced back at him. Faint features, thinner than in his photo. Brano stopped beside him and rolled down his window. 'Would you like a ride back into town?'

Jan Soroka's surprise was evident in the quick growth of the eyes, the tension in the lips. Jan looked at the empty path ahead of him, considering it.

'A long walk back,' said Brano. 'Come on.'

Jan's shoulders relaxed, as if he'd got rid of some weight. The bump in his long neck jumped when he spoke. 'Thanks.' He had a high voice.

They drove for a minute without speaking. Jan seemed content to gaze out the window as if admiring the landscape.

'I'm Brano Sev, Iwona's son. Aren't you Jan Soroka?'

Jan continued looking out the window. 'I think we each know who the other is, Major Sev.'

Brano felt momentarily as he had when his steering wheel had fallen into his lap in 1961. He feared he might swerve off the road.

'Why is that, Jan? Why would we know each other?'

Jan Soroka finally turned from the window, his eyes still damp from the cold winds. 'Bóbrka is small. There's a whole communications network for each new visitor.'

'They don't have a lot more to talk about.'

'Exactly what I mean.'

The village was coming into view. 'Where have you been, Jan?'

'Just wandering. I do that a lot. To think.'

'I don't mean now. I mean these last five months.'

Red fingers grew into his pale cheeks. 'Haven't you heard? I got involved with a crazy girl in another small town. I suppose I wanted a little excitement. But I love my wife, Comrade Major. I love my boy.'

'Dijana Franković,' said Brano.

Jan Soroka watched a collapsed barn pass.

'Funny, I used to know a Dijana Franković.'

'Not so funny. It's a common enough name in the Serb villages.'

'But I didn't know her here,' said Brano. 'I knew her in Vienna.' He looked over in time to see Soroka turning his head fully away. 'And besides, Szuha isn't a Serb village.'

'I was misinformed.'

'You were. I'm not a major any more, either.'

'No?'

'I work in a factory, assembling tractors.'

71

'Oh?' Jan didn't look like he believed that.

'Have you heard about Jakob Bieniek?'

'Bieniek?'

'Turned up dead last night.'

'Dead?'

'In the woods. I'm helping Captain Rasko investigate it. If you hear of anything important . . .'

'Of course,' he said, turning back to the window. 'Of course I will.'

Brano took him to his house without asking for directions. He said nothing more because there were stages to go through in this kind of situation. What he had told Pavel Jast was true – he believed Soroka's plan was to take his family west. This could happen at any moment, but if Jan were planning to leave tonight, he couldn't have maintained his calm. He would have sweated and shook like so many men Brano had quizzed in the past.

The only risk was that, if he pressed, Soroka would panic and flee come nightfall, leaving Brano with nothing to give Cerny – nothing to assure his return to Yalta.

He lunched with his mother and her assistant, Eugen, a thin boy of about seventeen who tapped his foot continuously. They had bread and cheese and salami from the store's stock. Then he returned to Bieniek's. He came across a single entry for Lia Soroka:

4 February 1967: She and the boy cross the street and buy food for the house. She's much too elegant for this town, or for that fool who ran off with a peasant slut. What is this loyalty she feels? What ties her to a man like that? I could never do such a thing to her. Even after all these years, I've never been unfaithful to Janica.

There were two pages on Brano's mother, and a sense of decorum made him lay the sheets to the side, unread, on the floor. But after learning more on people he did not know or care about, the decorum left him and he found himself reading of visits SEV, IWONA made, weekly, to Juliusz, the doctor. Bieniek speculated on the 'carnal interests' of the doctor, whose wife spent much of her time in Krosno.

Brano's palms were sweating as he put down the pages, and he felt the beginnings of a headache.

It was already dark, the cold was seeping into the house, and he had so little to go on. But there was one thing that, in his growing impatience, he felt he could look into right now. One person might know the name of Soroka's contact, who drove a green Volga GAZ-21 with Uzhorod plates.

Pavel Jast's house was on the edge of the woods, separated from the next house by a field marked by ruts and pits that, in the darkness, Brano had to be careful to avoid. The house was small, with two very bright windows. The murmur of muted voices rolled towards him.

He approached from the back, along the tree line. The windows were fogged over by the breaths of many men, creating a diffused glow. He squatted beneath a window and rose slowly until he could just make out the forms. Men around a table. A voice said, 'Cucumber – you're dead!'

Laughter followed, and a few moans. Pavel Jast said, 'That's fifty-two koronas . . . *and* that lousy mule!'

Brano used the tip of his finger to rub a corner of the window clean. Five men sat at a table with faceup cards. Jast; Mother's assistant, the hyperactive Eugen; Zygmunt; Juliusz; and a fat man he didn't recognize. Jast collected the cards spread over the table and began to shuffle them like a satisfied pro. Eugen was smiling, drunk, and Juliusz was serene. Zygmunt looked sick; perhaps he was the one who had just lost fifty-two koronas and a mule. Yes – Jast set down the cards and leaned over to kiss Zygmunt's cheek. Zygmunt pushed him away.

The fat man he didn't recognize sucked on a cigarette and put it out in his vodka, then laughed. Behind Jast's large right ear was the German ballpoint pen with its naked woman.

He crept back across the field, tripping once, and made his way back home. Mother was asleep, so he drank headache powder with water, then took a glass of Lucjan's vodka to bed. He rolled his face into the pillow, closing his eyes, but not even his brother-in-law's concoction could help him sleep.

11 February 1967, Saturday
Mother was already awake. She crouched beside his bed, touching him lightly on the wrist. 'Brani?' He opened his eyes to her large features close up and felt momentarily like a child.

'Yes, Mama?'

'Brani, there's someone here to see you.'

'Who?'

'That captain,' she whispered.

'It's okay. He just needs my help.'

She pressed her dry lips together and stood up as Captain Rasko appeared in the bedroom doorway, hat in his hands.

The blanket fell from Brano's thin, pale chest when he reached to the foot of the bed for the shirt he'd folded the night before. 'Good morning, Comrade Captain. Can you give me a minute?'

Rasko nodded and left. Mother still looked concerned. 'What is it?'

She glanced back at the doorway. 'He asked if you were planning to leave. I said you weren't. You aren't, are you?'

'No.' He finished dressing and put a hand on her shoulder. 'Why don't you let me talk with him alone.'

She went to her bedroom.

Rasko, in a chair, was still holding his hat as Brano sat on the sofa. His hair looked dirty. 'What is it, Captain?'

'This is difficult, Comrade Sev.'

'Then do it quickly. That'll make it easier.'

'You see,' he began, shifting his feet, 'I went through the evidence Juliusz gave us. In that bag. The handkerchiefs found on Jakob Bieniek.'

'The ones used to silence him.'

'Right.' He passed his hat to the coffee table. 'Well, there was something inside the handkerchief. The one that was inside his mouth.'

'What was it?'

He clutched his hands between his knees. 'A matchbook.'

'Excellent. That's more than we had before.'

'It was from the Hotel Metropol. From the Capital.'

Brano leaned back. He struggled a couple of seconds with what to say next, remembering Juliusz's hesitation when they met. Then he knew there was nothing to say. He could point out that other villagers made trips to the Capital, but they both knew none of them could afford a night in the Metropol, nor a drink from its bar. And even if they could afford it, the coincidence of his arrival from the Capital and the matches in a dead man's mouth could not be ignored by any responsible investigator. So Brano asked the captain what he would like to do.

Rasko cleared his throat. 'I'd like to search the house for evidence.'

Brano stared into Rasko's dark eyes until the captain blinked. 'Be my guest,' he said.

While Rasko went through his room and the others, followed nervously by Mother, who cried out for him not to be clumsy, Brano waited on the sofa, turning over the one thing he was sure of. Pavel Jast had used his matchbook to frame him for the murder of Jakob Bieniek. Either he had returned after they discovered the body, or he had been involved in the actual murder and had stuffed Brano's matches between Bieniek's struggling teeth, encased in a wad of handkerchief. But why?

'Any luck?' he asked when Rasko came back, flushed, wiping sweat from his forehead. Mother stood behind him with crossed arms, silent now, utterly disgusted.

'Can you give me the keys to your car?'

Brano stood up. 'It's unlocked.'

Rasko first checked the boot but found only a spare tyre and a jack. He searched the back seat, which Brano had cleaned meticulously before leaving the Capital, then under the driver's seat. He reached beneath the passenger's seat and made a face. It wasn't elation, nor was it defeat. It was somewhere in between, and the expression remained with him as he drew out a crumpled white shirt with large splotches of reddish brown. Brano suppressed an involuntary shout as Rasko flattened the shirt on the seat, eyeing the bloodstained slices, each between a couple of inches and half a foot long.

Brano looked up at the house, where his mother had opened the curtains, her fat fingers tapping her chin.

Rasko exhaled. 'Well, I suppose you know what's next.'

'Of course I do.'

Brano walked behind his Trabant to the passenger door of the white Škoda. Rasko said, 'You want to tell your mother where you're going?'

She was still in the window, her hand now covering her mouth. 'I think she already knows.'

On the drive to the station house, his palms together between his thighs, Brano was not overly troubled. Surprised, yes, but many times in the past he had been faced with inexplicable turns of fortune. It had been an inexplicable night in Vienna as he was arranging the final hours of Bertrand Richter. The last thing he'd expected was interference from Bertrand's girlfriend, the tarot-card reader. And then, when he'd woken the next morning in the Volksgarten, a blow to the head briefly relieving him of the burden of memory — who could have predicted that? As he had then, he now calmed himself by measuring the length of his facts. Pavel Jast, the one man in town who was to assist Brano, had arranged a murder conviction for him. *Check.* Which could only mean that Pavel Jast had his own agenda in this larger investigation of Jan Soroka.

Which meant, most likely, that Pavel Jast was assisting Jan Soroka by making sure Brano would not hinder his and his family's escape.

But was Jast really so shortsighted? Once the truth came to light, Jast would find himself in a work camp, or in the eastern mines. Jast was too much of a survivor for that. He was the sort of operative that hangs on for many years, always a step away from being caught or being made redundant. His kind, the small-town informer, was as resilient as the cockroach.

Jast wouldn't wait to be caught. He would leave with Jan Soroka's family while Brano was in jail, perhaps in the back seat of that GAZ-21 with Uzhorod plates, heading westward.

'I'll need to make a call,' said Brano.

Rasko parked in front of the station. 'I already called Yalta. I wanted to clear this with them.'

'You knew you'd take me in?'

'I wanted to know what I could and couldn't do. The man I talked to told me to do what I felt necessary, and someone would call later.'

'What was the man's name?'

'I didn't ask.'

This, he understood – the Ministry would want to pretend they didn't know he was here.

The cell was no more than a large closet with a lock on the outside, a small, high window, and a mop in the corner, the room Rasko had been stumbling around in when Brano first met him. A low bench below the window was the only furniture.

'You want coffee?'

'If you're making some.'

Rasko stepped out. Brano watched the door close, heard the lock slide into place, then wiped his hands dry on his knees. He climbed on the bench to look out the window but could see only patches of blue sky. So he settled on the bench again and, as he often did when in need of assurance, remembered her.

He remembered their long walk back to her apartment that night, her drunken complaints about the *zbrka* of the modern world. He remembered that she had a long body, pale but dark around the eyes, and he remembered leaving her apartment after their sex, the kiss she had placed on his cheek, leaving damp marks he could not bring himself to wipe off. *Brani,* she'd whispered, *this not the end from all for us,* then drew back, smiling.

Weeks after the Lieutenant General's interrogation, he had begun receiving her idiosyncratic love letters with the apprehension of a man fearing the unknown, and sometimes on the way home from the factory he wondered if he'd find her at his apartment, waiting with a smile.

I not knoing what you will to say when this getting to you. Maybe you are thinking I am little crazi, I dont kno. We have only 1 night – not 1 night but 2 hour!

But no, dragi. I not kno what you was thinking, but that night it was for me very good. I am not so sentimental person, no. I more practic that what people think.

She wrote, *That night when we was together Bertrand he die. Police dont kno who kill him, but was no accident. He die in Volksgarten. It make me start to thinking. You kno death, it do this. I start to thinking why I am in Vienna? I not like Vienna. I love in the world only 1 thing only. You, Brano Sev. Are you understand me? In the world this one thing.*

She told him that she was a Vojvodina Serb from Novi Sad, born in 1939. Her father, a professor of economics, was in prison from 1954 to 1957, though she couldn't explain why. *Was only what Tito say, if he think you enemy, you is in prison.* Dijana studied economics as well, and in 1959 married Dusan Franković, a medical student who also played in a jazz quartet called 'Sol', or Salt. Two years later, her father died from injuries sustained in prison, and the following October her mother killed herself.

I then 22. I sudden tired for econometrics. I stop talk with friends and I read on Carl Gustav Jung and on other things, like occult. That when I learn tarot first. Dusan, he not understanding why am I so quiet and not interesting, and we fight. So in 1963 I go. I start to thinking Yugoslavia is a country from losers, so I go. My husband he very sad, of course, but now is ok. He marry again.

She told him everything, and he was surprised by the things he told her. He said that he would try to get back to Vienna, and if that didn't work, he would get her a visa to visit him. He even believed the promises himself.

Rasko brought two cups of coffee and sat with him a moment. They sipped in silence, pursing lips over the hot liquid and looking at the smoke-darkened walls. Brano said, 'The other day, I noticed you talking with Lia Soroka.'

Rasko nodded into his coffee's steam.

'Do you mind telling me about her?'

He tilted his head from side to side. 'What's there to tell?'

'Why she's come back here.'

'Because her husband is here.'

'And you believe that?'

'I take things as I see them, Comrade Sev. I'm a simple man.'

'Have you talked with Jan Soroka?'

'Of course. He registered when he arrived.'

'What did he tell you?'

'The same thing he's told everyone. He was with a woman.'

'And you believe that as well?'

'I see no reason not to believe it.' Rasko stood up, holding his cup near his chest. 'Is there anything else you need? I have some paperwork to attend to.'

'Just tell me when the call from Yalta comes through.'

For months he'd tried through regular channels to get papers to visit Dijana in Vienna, and it wasn't until his second refusal that he approached Cerny for help, in November, during one of their regular weekend drinking sessions in the old man's First District flat. Cerny had spent most of the afternoon complaining about the diet his doctor had put him on to regulate his diabetic condition. *The man says I can't eat rugalach – what kind of claptrap is that?* Brano admitted he didn't know, then broached the subject that had been on his mind all week. Colonel Cerny shook his head. *I've been waiting for this. I thought you'd ask earlier.*

I'm asking now, Comrade Colonel. All I need is travel papers.

Let me put you out of your misery. The answer is a strong no. That you could even ask after what happened in Vienna . . . this woman has already got you drummed out of the Ministry, and don't fool yourself. She's only a path to more failures. I'm not going to have one of my oldest friends compromised by a spy.

She's not a spy.

A Yugoslav living in Vienna? What makes you think she isn't? We have reports she's been entertaining KGB agents in her apartment. The girl likes sex – I'm not a prude, but what's she up to? She's certainly not reading their fortunes. He shook his head. *The Lieutenant General thinks you worked, through her, for the Russians. How would it look if you went back to her?*

But she's not a spy.

Cerny doubted that. *We've read her letters to you. They're something to look at. She needs a good lesson in grammar instead of making intrigues against my oldest friend. My God, man, she's half your age!*

Brano had argued more, testing the limits of Cerny's patience, but the man had an answer for everything. There were photographs of Dijana Franković with Russian agents in her apartment – Cerny had been to Vienna and seen them himself. She was clever, Cerny told him, clever enough to outsmart the very clever Brano Sev. *Maybe, Brano, you're just getting old.*

So Brano had put her letters into a box behind his wardrobe at home, keeping them as a reminder that, in this life, luck does not come without requiring something of you, sometimes requiring something you cannot give.

Rasko tapped the frame of the open door. 'It's the call.'

Cerny's voice was laboured. 'Do you realize you took me from my wife's grave?'

'I'm sorry, Comrade Cerny.'

'You've really done it this time.'

'But—'

'It doesn't make sense,' he continued. '*You* don't make sense to me. Killing a nonentity like this Jakob Bieniek. You know how much I hate psychological pedantry, but it seems to me you've got a very self-destructive impulse. This really isn't important to you, is it?'

'Comrade Cerny,' said Brano, 'you're absolutely correct, this makes no sense at all, which should make it plain that I am innocent.'

'Innocent?' Cerny sounded amused.

'I was framed. And I know who did it.'

'Who, then?'

Brano glanced back; Rasko was not in the room. 'Our informer, Pavel Jast.'

'That's ludicrous!'

'It's true. I believe he's turned against us. He wanted me in jail so he could help the Sorokas escape. I expect he's leaving with them.'

Cerny paused. 'What about Soroka? Whether or not he remains in the country is a minor concern. I want to know what he's up to. Any results?'

'I've spoken to him once, but as yet there are no results. I've only been here four days.'

'Spare me your excuses, Brano.'

'Yes, Comrade Cerny.'

'Take care of your job and stay out of jail. I don't want to have to repeat myself. We understand one another?'

'We do.'

'Good. Now let me talk to the captain.'

He called for Rasko, gave him the phone, and returned to his cell. Through the doorway he heard the captain's weak voice murmuring, *Yes, Comrade Colonel, yes, I understand, immediately.*

Cerny, like any man of importance, had many faces. He

knew when to sympathize and when to attack. And when his temper flared, Brano would remind himself of a cold night in 1960, a month after Cerny's wife, Irina, shot herself with her husband's Walther PPK. Brano had gone over to the colonel's apartment to draw him out of his depression, but the depths he'd reached were a surprise. Cerny took out his insulin syringe and placed it on the coffee table, beside his vodka. *I don't need a gun,* he said. *It's simple, ending everything. All it takes is a little air.* He lifted the syringe, pulled the plunger, then slowly squeezed it shut again. When Brano told him he couldn't do that, the colonel, drunk, smiled strangely. *Because it's a sin, One-Shot?*

Because there's nothing on the other side.

Sounds peaceful.

And besides, said Brano, *I need you.*

The colonel smiled then, dropped the needle on the floor, and began to weep.

Brano refused the ride the captain offered and left as the sun was setting. He wandered back up to the empty bus stop at the main road and settled on its bench. The church grounds, too, were empty. He took Jast's white, unmarked matchbook from his pocket, ripped out the insides, and tossed the leftover cardboard under the bench. It was beginning to snow.

Mother was at the window again, her hands now by her side, but she did not come out to meet him. She waited inside and kissed his cheeks hesitantly. 'Is it all right?'

'Yes. But I'll need to go out again. There's someone I need to talk to.'

'A moment,' she said, raising a finger, then went to the kitchen. She returned with a small sealed envelope. 'Pavel Jast dropped this off for you.'

'Pavel Jast?'

'I told him where to find you, but he was in a hurry. He had to leave town on some business.'

'What kind of business?'

'He didn't say.'

'Did he say anything else?'

'He was in a hurry.'

As he headed off to his room, she asked when he was going out; she would heat some soup. 'I've changed my mind,' he said, then shut the door and tore open the envelope.

He found a small slip of brown paper, ripped from something, with a single line of handwriting: *They're leaving very soon.*

12 February 1967, Sunday

Brano woke with the sense that the previous day had been a dream. Indeed, when he sat in the kitchen over a cup of scalded coffee and watched his mother amble through the cabinets, trying not to ask the questions she knew he didn't want to answer, it seemed that the previous day simply hadn't existed. He'd woken as a murderer, sat in a cell, then been released – all without any drama or outburst.

Yet everything was different now. Jast had framed him for a murder and fled town, but not before leaving word of the Sorokas' plans. These two facts simply did not match, unless Jast had lost his nerve at the last moment.

More urgently, though, back in the Capital, Colonel Cerny was impatient for results he still did not have.

And here was his mother. Those few lines in Jakob Bieniek's notes nagged at him, and when she filled his cup and sat across from him he involuntarily pictured her weekly visits to Juliusz's house, to fulfil her carnal desires. He rubbed the bridge of his nose.

'I imagine you don't want to go into it, Brani, but, you know, people will talk.' Her eyes were on his shirt.

'What will they talk about?'

She stood again and poured herself a cup. 'Yesterday, Brani. The whole town knows.'

He wished she would stay quiet so he could think.

'They pester me. You know that, don't you? Lots of questions.'

'What do you say?'

'I tell them to ask you.'

'And that's what you're doing now.'

'I take my own advice, Brani.'

So he lied to her. He said that there had been a mistake. Captain Rasko, an admirable investigator in many respects, had gone with the word of a drunkard.

'Pavel Jast?'

'Yes, Mother.'

Pavel Jast had told Rasko that he had seen Brano fighting with Jakob Bieniek on Thursday morning, around ten.

'Ten?'

'Yes.'

'But weren't you with me then? At the shop?'

'We were having coffee.'

'Well, I'll tell that Tadeusz Rasko myself. You know, he's not very experienced. He's only been Militia chief a year.'

'Don't worry about it, Mother. He found a shirt in my car –'

'I know, I saw it.'

'But it wasn't Jakob's. He understands now.'

'If he's going to start arresting people indiscriminately—'

'He won't, Mother. I'll help him out.'

'I bet you will, Brani,' she said, then turned to the clock

on the counter. It was eight-forty. 'I need to . . . well, I'd like to . . .'

'When does it start?'

'Nine.'

'Then let's go.'

Brano walked with her through deep, fresh snow, and by the time they reached the gate, his feet were wet and very cold. There was a large crowd filing into the pale yellow church, and he scanned their backs until he spotted the trio Jast had assured him would be there: Jan Soroka, his wife, Lia, and their skinny, blond seven-year-old, Petre, holding his mother's hand.

'Will I see you afterwards?' Mother asked.

'I'll be around.'

The Sorokas entered the church.

A large hand settled on his shoulder. Lucjan was smiling foolishly, Klara coming up behind him. 'A bit of a surprise, eh?'

'What kind of surprise, Lucjan?'

'You're coming in?'

'Not a chance.'

'Okay,' he said, raising his open hands. 'No surprises today.'

Brano began to kiss Klara's cheeks, but she pulled back and looked closely at him. 'Well?'

'Well, what?'

'I see you're out. That's something. But is this just some kind of delay?'

'Mother will explain.'

She lowered her voice to a whisper. 'Brano. I don't know what's going on, but tell me . . . did you do it?'

He didn't answer at first, only gazed at her large, round eyes. Then he shook loose of the surprise. 'Of course not.'

*   *   *

The snow-whitened village was empty now, everyone packed into that little church. Brano Sev chose not to broach the subject of religion with his mother or sister, at least not here, because he'd always felt in his gut that the further he ranged from the epicentre of Yalta Boulevard 36, the more his authority waned. It made no sense (and if nothing else, Brano felt it must make sense), because anywhere within the borders of the country his legal abilities remained the same. But somehow, here on the northern edge, where the villagers walked boldly into their church every Sunday, he felt less of a man, his long-held convictions relegated to the opinions of an outsider.

So when he broke into Jakob Bieniek's house, he felt weaker than usual. He had to struggle a little with the boxes – the second seemed heavier than the first – as he dragged them into the living room. He sat on the floor, looking at the many hundreds of wrinkled and bent pages that reminded him of the overstuffed drawers in his old Militia-station desk. The world was full of danger, full of cheats and liars and murderers and informers, and he wondered how he could ever hope to sort through the contradictions and evasions to discover, finally, the truth.

But the truth was what he had always uncovered.

He took a breath and began.

JAST, PAVEL

26 January 1967: The gambler has been showing off his new toy, a debauched pen given to him by a friend he calls Roman. I saw it over Zygmunt's shoulder at the bar – a woman with clothes that slide off when you turn the pen over. A fool's pen for a fool . . .

31 January 1967: He must have won a lot last night. He bought 2 extra bottles of milk and, grinning like an idiot, offered me a tip. Who does he think he is? The rumour is that he cheats, but it doesn't stop the rest of the cows in this town from lining up at his trough . . .

5 February 1967: I'm amazed anyone talks to him. What he's done to Lucjan and Karel and Zygmunt through the cards, in any other town, would get him lynched. But he struts through the streets as if he's the most loved man in Christendom.

It surprised Brano, marginally, that Lucjan took part in these card games, but the surprise faded when he noticed the next, and last, entry, on the day of Bieniek's death:

9 February 1967: This morning, the gambler was in front of Iwona Sev's house, crouched behind the son's Trabant. He seemed to be waiting for something, but after a while he simply checked to see if the passenger door was unlocked – it was – and then crept away.

'You missed a great service,' said Klara, elbowing him. She was in a good mood now, her bright face alive with the peaceful ecstasy of the believer.

'I'm sure I did.'

Lucjan shrugged. 'Well, it was good enough. Not that I buy into all of it.'

Mother was behind him, glancing around at the other villagers. 'You'll be home for dinner tonight?'

'Sure.'

'Good, good,' she said, smiling at Krystyna Knippelberg's pregnant belly. 'Klara and Lucjan will come, too.'

Klara and Lucjan nodded obediently.

Brano spotted the face he'd been waiting for. He brushed past Lucjan and caught up to Jan Soroka, smiled, and nodded at Lia. Worry drew the edges of her puffy lips lower. Petre, whose face was marred by a brown blemish across the left cheek – a birthmark – looked up at him and squinted.

'Do you have a minute?'

Jan didn't slow his pace. 'Right now?'

'Just a few questions. About Pavel Jast.'

'I don't know him very well.'

'But you've talked with him.'

'A couple times, yes. Everyone has to talk to him at one time or another.'

'But about me,' said Brano. 'Did you talk with him about me?'

Jan stopped, while Lia continued on with Petre. 'Why do you think we talked about you?'

'Because he tried to frame me for murder.'

'And I would be involved?'

'We both know you're involved in the end.'

Jan looked at the ground, but there was no nervousness in him. He said, 'Jast was spending a lot of time around my house. He's an obvious guy. So I approached him myself.'

'He never told me this.'

'Of course he didn't. It was embarrassing for him. I told him that if he wanted to talk with me, we would go have a beer and do it like men.'

'What did he want to know?'

'The same things you want to know, Comrade Sev.'

'And what did you say about me?'

'I asked what he knew about you. This was a few days before you arrived, but I thought perhaps you would show up. You're Bóbrka's most famous son.'

'I'm hardly that.'

'Now you're being modest. It's a funny thing to see.'

Brano looked at him with an obscure face. 'And what did he say about me?'

'He acted like he didn't know anything about you. At first. But then he admitted he might be able to contact you when you came.'

'And this is what you wanted? To contact me?'

'I considered it. But you took care of it for me. You found me out in the fields. How did you do that?'

'Why did you want to contact me?'

'Because I don't believe in avoiding problems, Comrade Sev. I believe in facing them.'

'Is that why you ran off to Vienna?'

Jan's lip twitched as he glanced at his wife and son waiting beyond the bus stop. 'Funny, Pavel Jast didn't believe me, either. I went to Szuha. But yes, you're right. I was avoiding problems – running away from my marriage.'

'How much longer do you plan to stay here?'

'In Bóbrka? Not much longer. I'll need to return to the Capital and get back to work soon.'

'Okay,' said Brano. 'We'll talk later.'

'I've no doubt.' Jan raised a hand, then jogged to catch up with his family.

At Bieniek's, he collected the papers on anyone he knew. His mother, Pavel Jast, the Sorokas, Klara and Lucjan, Zygmunt the bread man, Eugen, and Captain Tadeusz Rasko. Then he spread the papers across the floor and sat on the couch. He felt strongly that the answer was here, because, despite Bieniek's inept conclusions, his eye for detail was unerring. He was a camera-eye to the anomalies of Bóbrka.

He picked up the one closest to him – MYMKO, EUGEN – and learned that his mother's assistant had masturbated in the cemetery on the cold night of 15 November. Bieniek was not impressed. On 31 December, during the New Year's gathering in front of the church, he had been particularly forward with the young daughter of Piotr Stepniak; his attempts, though, had been rebuffed.

Brano reached for WITASZEWSKI, LUCJAN.

His brother-in-law had begun attending Pavel Jast's games of luck in December. Bieniek speculated that life with Klara was not what it could have been, because why else would he leave her for Jast's smoke-filled shack three nights a week? Bieniek was a romantic, but he was also practical. He noted that during most of any given day, Lucjan could be found drinking with his workers on the grounds of the still-under-construction Ignacy Lukasiewicz Petroleum Industry Museum instead of working.

Captain Tadeusz Rasko was hardly controversial, as evidenced by only two brief entries. In September, he had taken his mother to Dukla in order to help her file divorce paperwork – again, Bieniek's morality erupted: *Does no one know the purity of commitment any more?* Apparently not, because in December Rasko split with his longtime girlfriend, Anita Gargas.

He went through more, but these papers told him nothing of importance. The answer, perhaps, was not here after all, and he was wasting a precious day burrowing through the inconsequential ramblings of a dead man. The window was dark – it was already evening. And he was expected for dinner. In his jacket pocket he found Bieniek's passport – the wide face, the mole. He closed it again, then sat on the floor.

There were two pages on Zygmunt Nubsch, most of it mundane. Each morning he drove to the factory in Dukla, picked up his order, and delivered bread to state shops in the region. He and his wife, Ewa, attended church regularly and sometimes joined the Knippelbergs and all their children for picnics in the countryside. And, like so many men, he made the pilgrimage to Pavel Jast's smoke-filled shack.

1 February 1967: There is a story going around that, at last night's game, Zygmunt lost more than his shirt. He was drunk, and when he ran out of money, asked for credit. Jast refused, said he was tired of Zygmunt not being dependable. He wanted something more than money. Zygmunt knew what he meant. The same as with Tomasz Sakiewicz's daughter. So he shrugged and bet his wife's life on the hand. The story is that he lost . . .

3 February 1967: Saw him on his bread rounds today. He looks sick and pale. It seems the story is true . . .

6 February 1967: He's smiling again. This evening he was in the centre with Ewa. She's alive, but now she's the one who looks ill. Maybe he told her that her time is limited – or maybe he made another deal with Jast, and it's only the knowledge of how close she came to death that's ruining her.

There were voices in the cloud-deepened darkness. A woman's shout from behind a closed door, the whisper of two children hidden in the shrubs, and a man's cigarette-congested cough somewhere ahead, to the left. But he ignored them all, even the snow that leaked into his shoes, the images in his head as clear as a memory of that night with Dijana Franković: Pavel Jast's smoky, cold shack, men around the dirty table, drunk, sweating over their game of Cucumber. Zygmunt, an old man with less sense than he should have, looks at what he thinks is a winning hand. But he's cleaned out; there's nothing left to bet. *No more credit, you deadbeat,* says Jast. *Give me something more than money.*

With the logic of a drunk and the narrow-mindedness of a villager, Zygmunt remembers Tomasz Sakiewicz. But all he remembers through the vodka haze is that Tomasz won his hand. He made the ultimate bet, and won.

So Zygmunt can, too. He says, *Ewa's life.*

They all pause, because even though this happens, it's rare, and never taken lightly. Jast even leans forwards, cigarette smouldering between his fat lips, and squints. *You're sure about this, Zygi? A bet is a bet.*

Yes, says Zygmunt. *A bet is a bet.*

'Hey!'

It was the man with the smoker's cough, wandering up from the bus stop. The illumination from the church lit the dirty snow around the man but kept him in shadow. 'Yes?'

He was tall, with a very long nose. 'You're Iwona's son, right?' He slurred the words.

'Yes, I am.'

Gravel crunched behind Brano; three more vague forms approached. All men.

'Why'd they let you out, Comrade Security?'

'Because—'

'Because you can't jail your own!' shouted a voice behind him, and laughter followed.

They were all very drunk.

Brano stepped back, but each direction brought him closer to one or another of the drunkards. So he waited. The first man was at his face now, looking down on him, those large nostrils flaring. 'You're a nasty son of a bitch, aren't you?'

A second one – fat, his old soldier's coat too small for his belly – had reached Brano's left side. Both stank of home-distilled rotgut.

'You come here and slice up a respected member of our little village.'

The third, hovering on his right, nervously rubbed one palm with the fingers of his other hand.

'In fact,' said Brano, 'that wasn't—'

The fourth, whom he never quite saw, threw a hard fist into Brano's kidney. The fat one grabbed his left arm, twisted, and pulled it down. Brano swung with his free hand, catching a chin, then tumbled into the snow.

What followed was a battery of sharp pains and stunned blows to the head and futile attempts to use what skills he had long ago been taught and had often practised. But those times he'd fought one man, maybe two, and there was a universal rule of fighting that, once a certain threshold is reached, talent and training are of no importance – the greater numbers always win.

He didn't know how long the blows were delivered and the alcohol-heavy spittle rained on him, but when they finally tired and wandered away after a last kick in the ribs, he could not move. He no longer felt the gravel digging into his back or the snow that had soaked through his clothes. His arms were as heavy as trees. He blinked teary eyes at the black sky, unable to make out the crescent moon breaking through the clouds.

He hurt, but he'd been hurt enough times to know how to deal with pain. Pain was mental; it could be coerced and tamed. He compressed the aches into a dense ball that he moved to his heavy hand. He breathed steadily, the cold night burning his lungs. Now all he had to do was move, pick himself up and figure out how to walk. It was simple, the kind of thing an infant learns to do. But, like Zygmunt Nubsch after he looked at Jast's winning hand, it took him a long time to learn to walk again.

* * *

His shoulder felt as if it had been ripped out and shoved back in, but he was able to let himself inside through the kitchen door. He heard their voices drift from the living room. A little laughter, and Mother's sudden, 'Is that you, Brani?'

He leaned against the counter and tried to take breaths. 'Yes,' he said, then said it again, louder.

'Late,' came Klara's unsurprised voice.

He found a glass and filled it from the tap, his shaking hands barely able to bring it to his lips. He sucked it dry, then looked at the muddy footprints he'd tracked across the floor. His head was pounding.

'I don't know about you, but I'm starving,' Lucjan said to someone.

Feet approached the kitchen as Brano refilled the glass. Then he turned and saw his mother stop, her face crumbling. '*Brani!*'

She was on him then, a white rag magically in her hand as she mopped the blood and grit that had smeared across his cheeks and forehead. 'Brani, Brani,' she whispered.

Klara was standing, stunned, in the doorway. Her mouth worked, but nothing came out.

Lucjan's voice: '*What?*'

He hadn't realized how much blood was on him until he took off his wet, spotted clothes in the living room. Before accepting a robe, he was for a moment naked in front of them, Mother kneeling, wiping his legs dry. He wasn't sure what he felt, shame or more, but the pain he'd been holding in his hand seeped from his grip and spread through him again. He thought his head might explode.

Then he was in the robe and stretched out on the couch. There were sores on his face and bruises developing across his chest. Both his knees bled. He told them what had happened, ignoring their dubious silence. He shrugged, sending a sharp ripple through his back, and said that he supposed his attackers thought they were making some justice.

'Savages,' said Mother.

Klara lit a cigarette and stared at him. Lucjan patted Brano's foot, which was the only thing that didn't hurt. 'Tomorrow we'll teach them a lesson.'

He sneezed, shooting agony through his temples. 'Don't – don't worry about it. I'll survive.'

'Maybe you will,' said Klara.

'I always do.'

He was able to get up again and, with Lucjan's help, make it to the dinner table. They served him his food, and whenever he began to reach out a hand they asked what he wanted and got it for him. As she passed him a plate with butter, Klara muttered, 'You'll survive until you don't.'

Brano smiled while Lucjan, sitting next to him, used a knife to carve him some butter. 'You've become a pessimist. I doubt your god would be too pleased with that.'

Klara considered that, then said, 'Brano, you and your kind will survive until drunk men in the street have had enough. And they will.'

'My kind?'

'Apparatchiks.'

Brano looked at his mother, but she was focused on pushing food around her plate; Lucjan, finished with the butter, had begun sucking on a glass of vodka. Brano said, 'This time you speak of. You think it's near?'

'Nearer than you think.'

'I suppose you learned this from your Good Book. Revelations. Fire in the sky and all that.' He said, 'Don't choose faith over facts, Klara. It'll always get you into trouble.'

'You pompous bastard.' She pointed her fork at him. 'What about Father Wieslowski? Huh? Was it a mistake of faith that got him thrown into prison and then murdered by his guards? And where are they keeping Father Wołek?'

Wieslowski was an old story, an easy one to dredge out whenever some Christian had run out of arguments. Wołek was one of his associates, arrested last June. 'Socialism is a demanding mistress,' he told her. 'And fragile. These so-called fathers were nothing more than hooligans undermining the foundations of our culture.'

'Did you just say, *our* culture?' She let out a rough laugh. 'Read your history books, Brano. Christianity is the foundation of European civilization.'

'I have read them,' he said calmly. 'European civilization survived despite – not because of – Christianity. There's a reason why the height of Catholic power is called the Dark Ages. Because facts were given less credit than faith.'

Klara fell quiet a moment. Lucjan shovelled food into his mouth. Mother stared intently at her glass. Brano kept his eyes on his sister. They had never been particularly close as children; fourteen years' difference and the sudden disappearance of their father had pushed her further away. Adulthood had done nothing to lessen this distance. Each sibling, in each town, had followed a different track, had built up his own values and hatreds, had formed his own language. Brano didn't understand her – he knew this – but there was no sense backing down from her stupidity.

Quietly, she said, 'You've got more faith than anyone at this table, you know that?'

'I don't know what you mean.'

'You're the most religious person I know. Your faith in your beloved *Ministry*.'

'You saw my work as a religion?'

'At least in ours we have salvation.'

'Of a kind.'

'And we're never alone. I don't think you can say that about yours, Brano. The religion of the apparatchik only gives you paperwork and a bad conscience.'

'You could turn it around,' he said after a moment. 'Maybe I'm not religious at all, and neither are you. Maybe you're all apparatchiks for God.'

Klara looked at him, but before she could answer, Lucjan slapped a big hand on Brano's back. 'Apparatchiks for God?' He was laughing a laugh that sounded like desperation. 'That's good! I like it!'

Through the fresh flood of pain in his back, he understood: No matter how upset he made Klara, Brano wouldn't have to deal with it at the end of the night; Lucjan would.

He said, 'Doesn't matter. I'm not in the Ministry any more, and we're just sharing our opinions. Right?'

Mother picked up her glass. 'That's the smartest thing anyone's said this evening.'

Klara, red-faced, shoved her fork into her potatoes. 'Just as long as no one arrests me for my opinions.'

13 February 1967, Monday

His back ached when he finally rose at noon; his ribs were tender, and his head still throbbed. A dark bruise had grown around his left eye. Mother was not in a good state, either. Her pale eyelids had swollen so that she peered at him through slits when he asked where Zygmunt Nubsch, the bread man, lived. 'Why on earth do you want to know that?'

'I need to talk to him about something.'

'About this?' she asked, and touched a finger to his injured eye.

He walked to Zygmunt's home, which was just across the

street from the graveyard. Passersby flicked their gazes over his beaten face, but no one spoke to him. He paused at Zygmunt's front gate and glanced back at the lines of stones, a jumble of styles, some clumsy and eroded, others fresh slabs with fine edges. A group of them were low and simple in the long grass, with Cyrillic names etched below five-pointed stars: Russian soldiers fallen during the liberation of their country from the fascists. He stomped through snow to the front door and knocked.

After a minute, a squat woman looked up at him, pulling a length of grey behind her ear.

'Ewa Nubsch?'

Though she peered at his bruises, she didn't recognize his face, but his accent – measured and purposeful, from the Capital – gave her pause. She placed a shrivelled hand on her breast. 'Yes?'

'I've come to speak with Zygmunt. Is he in?'

She shook her head. 'He's working. You can speak to him this evening.'

'Perhaps I could ask you a couple of questions, Comrade Nubsch.'

'I'm very busy now, Comrade Sev.'

'This is rather important.'

'But—' she said, then lowered her hand. 'Come in.'

The Nubsch house was tidy and proper. A small television in the corner overlooked a sparse living room covered with lace doilies and table runners. Ten paperbacks were on display behind a glass-doored cabinet, and an electric coil-and-fan by the kitchen door kept the place very warm.

'Something to drink?'

'If you're drinking.'

She hesitated again. 'Coffee?'

'Perfect.'

99

She limped off to the kitchen and ran water for a while, and he heard the pop and hiss of the gas stove being lit. Then she was in the doorway again, wiping her hands on a white towel. 'Something to eat?'

'No, thank you,' he said, and settled in a chair. She ranged further into the room but didn't sit down. He said, 'Do you mind if I ask a personal question?'

She shook her head with two tight jerks.

'Where did you get that limp?'

Ewa Nubsch looked down at her right leg, as if she had never noticed it before. She took a breath. 'Well, you know, I'm not a young woman any more.'

'Neither of us is young.'

She rocked her head from side to side. 'I twisted the ankle in one of those badger holes in the fields. I should have been watching better.'

Brano looked at his palms, then placed them on his knees. 'You know, Comrade Nubsch, there's a rumour going around that I wanted to verify. About the thirty-first of January, a Tuesday night, Zygmunt lost a hand of cards.'

Ewa blinked at him.

'People lose at cards all the time; it's seldom notable. But the story is that Zygmunt made a very rash wager. The same kind of wager Tomasz Sakiewicz made last year. But Tomasz was lucky enough to win his bet.'

She glanced into the kitchen, and by the time she turned back, she had found something to say. 'There are a lot of rumours in Bóbrka, Comrade Sev. I wouldn't believe them all if I were you.' She gave him a half-smile and limped off.

He followed her into the kitchen. It was small, but the space had been used economically. She poured the steaming water into a filter that dripped black coffee into a glass pot.

'Comrade Nubsch, we both know the story is true. I don't really care about gambling, but I do wonder why you're still standing here, living and breathing, making me a cup of coffee.'

Her eyes took on a forced vacancy, staring at the now-full coffeepot. 'I really don't know what you mean, Comrade Sev.'

'Card games in the provinces are a very particular phenomenon.'

'Are they?'

'Their rules are firm. And the gamblers, for lack of a better word, are like members of a cult. The rules give their lives extra meaning. So when Zygmunt bet your life and lost, he couldn't just change his mind. He had to follow through.'

She poured the coffee into cups, staining the counter with black puddles. 'This is sounding ridiculous,' she said without looking at him.

'The only way Zygmunt could get out of taking your life was to make a deal with Pavel Jast. You would remain alive, but another life would have to be taken.' He approached her; she flinched. But he only took a cup. 'The choice wasn't up to Zygmunt, or you. It was Jast's choice. Wasn't it?'

She didn't answer.

'Comrade Nubsch, I have no doubt that Jast cheated at that game – not because he wanted you dead, but because he wanted Zygmunt to commit a murder. He had someone particular in mind. Jakob Bieniek.'

She reached for the second cup but faltered, knowing she wouldn't be able to bring it to her lips. She tugged at her ear; she swallowed. 'Pavel Jast is a fiend. I've told my husband this for years, but the game – it's hard to explain.'

'It's an addiction.'

'More than that, Comrade Sev.' She focused on his

ear, considering her words. 'Do you know what Zygi used to be?'

'No.'

She paused, and when she spoke again the sentences were clear and without hesitation, as if part of a speech she had practised for years. 'He was the head manager of the Bóbrka Petroleum Works. He was an important man. But one day the Gas Committee sent some men from the Capital; they had no idea what they were looking at. A bunch of bureaucrats who made policies without understanding a thing.' She opened one hand and used the other to tap the wet countertop. 'Zygi was foolish enough to point out this fact, and two weeks later he received a notice in the post. He'd been given a new job. He was to deliver bread for Bóbrka and the surrounding villages. Do you know what that does to a man? A man with Zygmunt's talent and experience?' She shook her head. 'No, Comrade Sev. I don't think you have any idea.'

'Then explain it to me, Comrade Nubsch.'

This, at least, was understood. His pains receded, the barking dog behind the white wooden fence no longer distracted him, and he even found himself smiling as he walked past the church and the bus stop that still, beneath its bench, sheltered the empty book of matches Pavel Jast would never pick up.

Ewa Nubsch was the kind of person who, in the end, doesn't care about punishment; the guilt is so strong that all she desires is to be understood. And with the story came tears. She explained between sobs that they'd used razor blades because they couldn't be traced. *We thought we were being clever. We didn't use the shotgun. We thought we could find a vein. But we couldn't, and it only made everything more horrible.*

That was because they'd been drunk; it was the only way they knew to prepare themselves for murder. Then they'd got Jakob drunk and brought him out there. She was still surprised he'd come. He had seemed, almost, excitedly curious. But once they gagged him he fought back, and that was when she had hurt her leg.

And what about the matches?

The matches?

The matches you stuffed in his mouth.

That was Pavel, she said. *He wanted them to be on Jakob's body when it was found. And the shirt. Yes, the shirt. He wanted us to give him the shirt. And yes, yes – he even told us where to do it, behind the Emilia 4. He told us everything.*

And she told him everything, except the answer to the one question that mattered most – *Why?* Why would Pavel Jast frame him for the murder of a reclusive peasant? Pavel Jast had not run off with the Sorokas; he had simply disappeared.

'You look like hell,' the captain said as Brano approached his white Škoda at the Militia station.

'It's nothing. But listen.' Brano drew close as Rasko fooled with the lock on the front door. 'The Bieniek case is solved. It was Zygmunt and Ewa Nubsch.'

Rasko let go of the lock. 'Are you kidding me?'

'Pavel Jast arranged the whole thing. He made Zygmunt bet his wife's life in a Cucumber game, then he offered Zygmunt a trade – Jakob's life for Ewa's.'

Rasko got the door open. 'And they'll admit all this to me?'

'Ewa told me everything.'

'How did you get it out of her?'

'I asked.'

Rasko tossed his keys on the desk and dropped into his chair. He ran a hand through his black fringe. 'Let's see how it all turns out. First you might want to get in touch with the Ministry. They called for you this morning. Maybe they want you to go back home.'

Regina Haliniak, at the Yalta front desk, softened when she heard his voice. 'Hello, Brano. Are you enjoying the provinces?'

'Not particularly, Regina. Are you and Zoran well?'

'Well enough. Did you want to talk to the colonel?'

'Yes, Regina. Thank you.'

He listened to clicks and static.

'It's about time you called, Sev.'

'I just got the message.'

'What's the progress?'

'I'm afraid Pavel Jast's crime has been proven. He forced an old couple here to kill Jakob Bieniek.'

'Jakob who?'

'Bieniek. Jast used them to frame me for the murder. The wife admitted everything.'

'When I asked about progress, I wasn't talking about this murder. You know what I was talking about.'

Brano cleared his throat. 'I've had more contact with Soroka, and Jast told me he'd be leaving soon. But I no longer trust Pavel Jast's information.'

'Well, trust him, Comrade Sev. We have the same information. Jan Soroka is leaving in the next couple days, probably for Austria, and you'd better clear this up before that happens. If you can't manage to stop him, then you follow him and report back when you can. Do you understand me?'

'Yes, Comrade Colonel. But—'

'But what?'

Brano paused. 'I'm known there, Comrade Colonel. In Austria. If I enter the country without diplomatic papers . . . I don't think I'd be safe.'

Cerny gave one of his unimpressed exhales. 'You're exhausting, Sev. You've been given an opportunity few men receive. And who do you think insisted you could be trusted to come back on this case? It's my neck we're talking about.'

'I know, Comrade Colonel.'

'You know me, Brano. You know disappointment doesn't sit well with me – makes my bladder go awry. And it doesn't sit well with the Comrade Lieutenant General, either.'

'He knows?'

'The man knows everything, Sev. It's my job to keep him informed.'

His legs ached by the time he made it to the house, trying without success to evoke that memory of Cerny's suicidal weeping to settle his nerves. But the man was right – he'd been given an exceptional opportunity to redeem himself. He climbed into his Trabant and drove west.

Again, he didn't have to wait long. To the south, beyond the silent cows, a small figure materialized near the base of the mountain. He parked by the road, and his feet crunched through snow as he walked through the cold, hissing wind to meet Jan Soroka.

He suddenly remembered what Klara had said, the pink anger filling her cheeks: *The religion of the apparatchik only gives you paperwork and a bad conscience.*

This wasn't far from the truth.

Jan was crouched, looking at something on the ground. 'Hello!' called Brano, and Jan glanced back over his shoulder. He didn't stop what he was doing: using a stick to slowly pick apart a high, encrusted anthill. Brano squatted beside him. 'Going to destroy that thing?'

'I've always hated ants,' said Jan. 'When I was a child, a whole army attacked me. I'm a lover of nature in general, but not these things. Whenever I get the chance, I kill them.'

He brushed the stick through the base of the hill, quickly, and the tower collapsed, releasing a flood of confused black spots that spilled onto a patch of snow.

Brano said, 'Ants in winter. That's strange.'

'Yeah,' said Jan.

Then the two men began walking along the edge of the mountain in silence, until Jan said, 'How's that case of yours coming?'

'Which one?'

'That dead man. Bieniek?'

'Yes, Jakob Bieniek.'

'Any leads?'

'The Nubsches killed him.'

Jan, for once, looked surprised. 'So it wasn't you after all. But I'm not sure the village will believe a nice old couple like Zygmunt and Ewa sliced him up.'

'It doesn't matter what Bóbrka believes.'

'It might. From the look of your face, you could probably use some allies around here.'

Brano touched his sore eye. 'You're right about that.'

'But why did they do it?'

'The Nubsches? A bet.'

'Cucumber?'

'Pavel Jast got them to do it.'

'And why did *he* do it?'

'I have no idea.'

They stopped beside a boulder, where Jan took out a cigarette. Brano cupped his hands around the match to keep it alight. Jan took a drag and handed it to Brano. 'My father knew you didn't kill Jakob – he had Pavel fingered from the beginning.'

'Why?'

'My father's got intuition.'

'Well, he's a lucky man. I just stumble through the facts as I see them.'

'What about your father?' asked Jan as he took the cigarette back.

'My father?'

'Is he dead?'

'He was a farmer,' said Brano, 'and when the Germans came, the Wehrmacht forced him into service. He built anti-tank obstacles. All through the war he did this in a factory up in Rzeszow. By the end of the war, he was managing the factory, and by late 'forty-five, he was back to farming.'

'But he left the country, didn't he?'

'He had to. His name was put down as a collaborator. If he'd stayed he would have been arrested.'

'Arrested?'

'Yes.'

Jan handed the cigarette over. 'By whom?'

'By me.'

They didn't talk for a while, and despite the lingering memory of that trip to Bóbrka back in '45 to arrest the man he instead handed forged papers to and ordered to emigrate westward, Brano found it a peculiarly peaceful moment. He never learned what had become of Andrezej Fedor Sev; the few times he'd tried to look into it he'd come up with nothing. Perhaps he never made it out of the country, or he died in one of the many displaced persons camps of post-war Germany. He simply didn't know, and when he reflected on it, he found he didn't care. That man was part of another life.

Jan took out another cigarette and offered him one. They smoked and watched the cows standing in patches of snow. Brano said, 'Either you had an affair with Dijana Franković in Szuha, or you went to Vienna and left your family behind

107

– it really doesn't matter. But why would you leave at all? Lia's a beautiful woman, she seems like a good mother.'

Jan tapped his ash and thought a second before answering. 'Did you know that when I was sixteen years old I met Mihai?'

'Nineteen-fifty,' said Brano. 'You were a Red Pioneer.'

'You guys really do know everything, don't you?' He took a drag. 'Well, I was excited. I'd never been much for the Pioneers, but every now and then we'd do something interesting. This time we met the most powerful man in the country. And I, like any other kid, idolized Mihai.'

'A lot of people still do.'

'So I'm told – no one seems to idolize Tomiak Pankov. Anyway, we went to Victory Square, to the Central Committee building and his office on the third floor. You been there?'

Brano nodded.

'It was impressive. All that red satin, the paintings, that enormous desk. I remember a silver ink bottle – it had the hawk etched in it. It was a beautiful thing. And then I saw Mihai himself. You met him a lot, I guess.'

'A few times.'

'Well, the photos and newsreels never really showed how short he was, did they? He was a head shorter than me. This was a shock, I can tell you.'

'That he was short?'

'Not just that he was short. He had a cold at the time, and whenever he breathed you could hear how hard it was for him. I was a kid, you know, and I couldn't imagine how such a great man could be like this – short, snot-nosed, no better than the guy who sells vegetables in the market. And this was the head of our country?'

'Well, you were young.'

'I was. But I don't think that reaction ever really left me.

I got older, I married Lia – to me she was the most gorgeous woman in the Capital – but I was still a stupid teenager up here,' he said, tapping his skull. 'I didn't realize she'd catch colds, that she'd be lazy in the mornings and not make coffee. She'd be short-tempered and shout at me about things that weren't my fault; she'd be completely unreasonable sometimes. And no amount of expectation can prepare you for a child. Everything shifts and becomes a little dirtier. Your wife's body begins to fall apart.'

'You're brutal, Jan.'

'To be fair, I'm sure she had similar complaints about me. I was unreasonable *all* the time; I got fatter, lazier; I stopped talking to her.'

'And so you left.'

'At first I just had affairs. An afternoon, sometimes a whole night. And I saw some of what I was missing. I suppose I wanted to get out on my own and learn what life with another woman was like.'

'Until you became disillusioned with the new woman.'

Jan shrugged.

The cigarette was strong, and Brano's head buzzed as he wondered if it would have been this way had he stayed with his Dijana. 'Did you ever actually know her?'

'Who?'

'The real Dijana Franković. In Vienna.'

Jan smiled. 'I only knew the one in Szuha.'

Brano was smiling as well. He tossed his cigarette into the grass and felt, for the moment, that time had slowed. For the moment, there was no one in the Capital waiting for results, no press of minutes.

Then Jan said, 'I'm not sure I understand. You seem to believe a lot of bad things about me. Why aren't I in jail?'

Brano considered this. When he first arrived in Bóbrka, he believed that sticking to his cover story, that he was

109

simply a factory worker on holiday, would be simple enough. But no one in this town really trusted that, least of all Jan – he'd clearly been waiting for Brano's arrival. There was nothing left to hide. So he said, 'Arresting you isn't my job. I was supposed to find out why you came back.'

'And what's your conclusion?'

'My conclusion is that I really don't care.'

'Is that true?'

Yes, Brano realized – it was true. 'I came here to do a simple job. But immediately my one contact double-crossed me – he framed me for murder. And now that I've proven my innocence, the Ministry doesn't care. I went into this with all good intentions, and now,' he said, looking for the right words, 'now I have the suspicion I'm being used, but I don't know why.'

'Maybe it's all about Pavel Jast,' said Jan. 'Maybe he framed you in order to improve his position with Yalta. He probably wants to get out of Bóbrka and go to the big city.'

'Did you tell him much about yourself? I mean, the things you don't tell me.'

'I've told you much more than I told Pavel Jast.'

'Then that isn't the answer. He could only improve his position if he arrived in the Capital with all the information on you that I couldn't get.'

'But he could also improve his position if he stopped me from doing what I plan to do.'

'Which is to return to Vienna.'

'Or maybe I want to go to Moscow.'

They both laughed out loud, and Brano admired this clever man who could subdue his own fears and laugh with a man who might, at any moment, kill him.

Jan nodded past Brano's shoulder, towards the road, his smile fading. 'Isn't that Captain Rasko?'

110

Brano turned, peering through the winter dusk he hadn't noticed descending. The white Škoda was parked behind his Trabant, and Rasko took awkward, high steps through the snow towards them. They helped close the distance, and when they met, Rasko's face was pinked by the wind. 'Hello, Jan,' he said.

'Tadeusz.'

Rasko nodded at Brano. 'Can I have a word with you?'

'I'll talk to you later,' said Jan as he retreated towards the cows.

'What is it, Captain?'

Rasko was wearing a heavy coat – blue, Militia regular issue. He buttoned the top button. 'I went over to the Nubsches'.'

'And?'

'And nothing, Comrade Sev. They've left. Taken a lot of clothes and gone away. I called the Dukla factory, and it seems Zygmunt abandoned his bread truck on the side of the road this morning. They don't know where he is.'

'They fled.'

'They're your alibi, Comrade Sev.'

Brano looked into the captain's dark, steady eyes, then wiped his hands on his trousers. 'They're still my alibi. They left because they were guilty. It's obvious.'

'Not to Yalta.'

'What?'

Rasko arched a brow. 'They've been in touch the whole time you've been in Bóbrka. Seems they don't trust you completely. And when I told that colonel about the Nubsches' disappearance, I was given leave to arrest you again.'

Brano's hands jumped involuntarily from his hips. 'Colonel Cerny?' He settled them down again. 'This doesn't make any sense.'

'We live by our orders, Comrade Sev.'

That was a well-rehearsed line from the Militia Academy, the kind of motto only repeated at official functions. Now Brano Sev was hearing it in a field littered with blank-eyed cows.

He cleared his throat. 'Give me a little more time.'

'It's difficult.'

'No, it's not. Tomorrow. I'll have something for you by tomorrow.'

Captain Rasko squinted into the wind a few seconds, waiting for something more – a bribe, perhaps, or some sign of desperation – but Brano waited him out. The captain nodded. 'All right. Tomorrow.'

As Rasko made his way back to his car, Brano turned back to Jan, who – magically, it seemed – had disappeared.

The captain was right. The Nubsches' home, which he entered by reaching through the hole Rasko had broken in the window, was cleared out. Clothes had been thrown around the bedroom in a frantic act of packing, and remnants of a quickly thrown-together meal littered the kitchen: bread crumbs, cheese, salami. He went through each room, his calm slipping away, trying to find anything – a coat, perhaps – that connected them to Jakob Bieniek. But after tearing apart cabinets and wardrobes and searching under all the furniture, he realized it was useless. When he slammed the door behind himself, broken glass fell and shattered on the concrete steps.

As he drove through the darkness, he laboured with the mass of facts that were filling him with an acute sense of *zbrka*. What he'd said so casually to Soroka – that he was being used – now felt real. Cerny was pressuring him, either to get results or to flee – he didn't know which. There was no ready answer to the *why* of Jast's frame-up nor the *why* of Cerny's phone calls. Was it possible the colonel believed Brano had killed some nondescript milkman? Or was he only following the Lieutenant General's orders?

Again, the question: Why?

His mother was settled in the dim kitchen with Lucjan's vodka when he returned. Her head rolled back as she tried to get him into focus. 'He returns!'

Brano sank into a chair without removing his overcoat. 'Are you drunk?'

'What do you thing?' she said, slurring 'think'.

'That can't be good for you.'

Her eyes were shiny. 'Don't start telling me what's good for me. You're on your way to jail.'

'You know?'

'The whole town knows. My criminal son.'

'Criminal son,' he repeated, and reached for the vodka bottle. There was a dirty water glass on the table that he filled to the rim. 'But I didn't do it.'

'What do I know about that? You don't tell your mother anything.'

'I'm telling you now.'

'Just like you told me about your Tati.'

'I did what I could.'

She looked at him for a little while, then spoke slowly. 'You know, Brani, I'm an old woman now. I know a few things. I know, for instance, that life is sometimes too long. There are a lot of years. What do you think would have happened if you hadn't made your father leave?'

'You know what would have happened. He would have been sent to prison. I had no choice.'

'Yes,' she said, and brought her glass to her cheek, pressing it into the soft flesh. 'He would have gone to jail, but for how long? A couple years, maybe five. Then, my dear

113

son, my husband would have been returned to me. We would have been a family again.'

He did not answer.

She said, 'You think your life is going to be one way, then it isn't. Your son leaves for the Capital, then your husband leaves the country. Your daughter marries an idiot who can't give you grandchildren.' She took another drink and set her glass down. 'Tell me, Brani. Do you think this is the family I always hoped for?'

He lifted his glass to his lips.

She passed out in her chair, and Brano carried her to bed. He undressed her, then pulled the duvet to her chin before kissing her forehead. He felt very much like a father at that moment – at least, how he imagined fathers felt – looking down on this old woman who, in her more honest moments, hated him. She'd had to eke out a living without her husband and had never remarried – she instead lived on the fantasy that Andrezej Sev would return from the West. But unlike Jan Soroka, most people did not return when they escaped the Empire. If they survived, they made their way as best they could, despite loneliness and poverty, and became citizens of another world.

And she was only partly right about what he'd done. There was no telling what would have happened to his father in one of those labour camps. Many never returned.

He drank more in the kitchen, enough to maintain dizziness, and took his passport out of his coat pocket. He had a dull face, he knew, not the kind of face a young Vojvodina Serb living in Vienna would fall in love with. In his other pocket he found Jakob Bieniek's passport and flipped through its pages. Both men had features that suggested plainness, perhaps even stupidity.

He hung his coat by the door, then undressed in the

bedroom. There was nothing to do but wait. Tomorrow – yes, tomorrow – Captain Rasko would visit, with full Ministry authorization, and take him to that puny cell. The climax of a half-year of failures. Then Brano would be faced with the end of everything. He would be transferred to a holding cell in Rzeszow, given a trial, and moved to a work camp. Perhaps Vátrina, in the Magyar provinces, where he had once visited an old colleague who had been put to work digging a canal that had never been completed, and probably never would be.

A factory job would seem like a blessing.

He was, inexplicably, free from worry. Some of it was the vodka, but as Brano climbed into bed and closed his eyes, the darkness swirling around him, he felt that it had to do with Jan Soroka, the man who chose to wander with idiot cows while the apparatus of state security haunted him. Jan was a disciple of acceptance.

So it surprised him when he opened his eyes to that familiar voice in the darkness. He reached out to touch the shoulder of a coat and heard the voice again, as if from a dream: *Don't move, Brano. I've got a gun.*

Is this it? he asked the darkness.

The voice said yes, this was it, though it didn't mean what Brano had meant. *Right now. Come if you want, but now – grab your bag. No hesitation. But if you try to stop us, I'll kill you.*

Jan Soroka turned on the bedside lamp.

14 February 1967, Tuesday

Jan held the gun as Brano dressed and filled his suitcase with the clean clothes his mother had folded at the foot of the bed. Neither spoke. After a stunned moment, staring into Jan's bright face, Brano had understood that communication, more than possibly waking his mother, would introduce questions and explanations that undermined Jan's command for no hesitation.

He grabbed his coat at the front door, but Jan took it from him and patted the pockets. He handed it back and nodded towards the kitchen, where they left through the now-unlocked side door, into the cold. They marched through the deep snow in the backyard and climbed over the fence, landing behind the Grzybowskas' house, then cut around the side to the road, where a silent green Volga GAZ-21 with Uzhorod plates waited. Inside, dark forms shifted. Jan threw Brano's suitcase into the boot and opened the back door for him. Petre, sleepy eyes suddenly widening, was in the middle, and on the boy's other side Lia sat straight-faced, not acknowledging him. The fat man in the driver's seat was from Pavel Jast's house, the Cucumber game, the man who had put out his cigarette in a glass of vodka. He turned, reached a hand over the back of the seat, and narrowed his eyes. 'You been in a fight?' he whispered.

Brano touched the bruise on his face. He nodded.

The man gave a huge smile and shook his hand. 'Call me Roman.'

Jan sat in the passenger seat and closed the door quietly. 'Well, let's get going.'

Brano had expected none of this. The wake-up call had been as if from a dream, and his snap decision had been based on nothing. But his training had come back instantly – the requirement of all good agents that they learn to act, even without all the proper facts.

And this was the only move left to him. After clearly envisioning the end of everything, it was an amazing turn of fortune that he'd been awoken by another option.

Luck, though, was a suspicious animal.

Roman was a careful driver. He maintained a steady speed through Bóbrka, shifting gears smoothly, then exited from the west, passing the field with its dozing cows – then further, through Kobylany, and beyond. Petre, with the blemish covering his left cheek, stared at Brano, but after a while bowed his head into his mother's armpit and began to doze. Sometimes Jan glanced back at his wife, but Lia had closed her eyes as well.

He didn't understand the risk Jan was taking. Though Brano had surprised himself by opening up to Soroka in that field, he had no reason to believe Jan felt the same. Had they really made a connection?

And Roman. He was the connection between Jan and Pavel Jast; he was Jan's contact at the train station (watched by Jakob Bieniek) and Pavel's Cucumber-playing friend who brought him pornographic pens from West Germany.

Pavel Jast was no mere small-town informer.

Although in the darkness he sometimes became confused, he was able to track their progress by villages. Nienaszów, Toki, Nowy-Żmigród, Kąty. The names were familiar, and the hills around them were filled with partisan memories; but now, knowing that he was leaving, yet not knowing why, they began to sound exotic to him, precious.

They made gradual progress along side roads, only rarely spotting another car driving in the opposite direction. Once, a lorry appeared behind them, hovering close, and Lia craned her head around, the truck's headlights illuminating the fear in her face. Roman slowed and waved his hand out the window, and the lorry passed, soon disappearing.

Just after Krempna, they came upon a white Škoda blocking the road. Brano noticed the Militia hawk on its door. Jan reached for his gun, but Roman said, 'Nothing to worry about,' as he braked. He climbed out and conferred with an older, uniformed militiaman beside the Škoda's front bonnet; they shook hands and patted each other's shoulders, and once Roman tapped the militiaman's cheek with his fingers.

117

Then the money appeared and was quickly handed over, and they shook again. As the Militia car pulled back into the shrubs, Roman got back behind the wheel. 'This world is getting more expensive by the minute.'

Petre, as if in answer, whispered, 'I have to pee.'

By Brano's watch they had been travelling five hours; it was after seven, and an omen of sunrise lightened the sky. They had spent the last hour and a half winding slowly through the mountains north of Sárospatak and were now on the west bank of the Bodrog River, driving south through a birch forest. Roman pulled off onto the side of the road and cut the engine. Then he flashed his headlights – once, twice – and settled back.

'What is it?' asked Jan.

Roman grunted. 'We wait.'

Lia reached for her husband's shoulder, and he put his hand over hers, squeezing. Petre whispered, 'Can I pee *now?*'

They didn't have to wait long. A pair of headlights appeared, very bright, and it was soon clear that they belonged to a large lorry. Along the side, CARPATIA S.A. was painted in three-foot-high white letters. A thin, nervous-looking man climbed out. He had a moustache as thick as Stalin's and long fingers that tapped the roof of the Volga as he talked with Roman through the window. 'So many? You said three – come on, what're you trying to pull?'

'Don't worry,' said Roman. 'Everything's the same.'

The thin man looked at each face, pausing on Brano's. 'You know what this means, eh?'

'Of course.' Roman handed over a wad of bills. 'It's all there.'

The thin man counted the koronas with spastic fingers, his mouth forming numbers. 'Yeah, okay. Looks right,' he said, pocketing the cash. 'Let's get moving.'

118

Lia took Petre into the woods to urinate while Brano and Roman carried the suitcases to the lorry. It was filled with boxes of tinned plums that the thin man, with Roman's help, shifted aside. They made a narrow corridor to the boxed-in space in the back. Jan seemed to have disappeared. They deposited the luggage in the corner as Lia and Petre returned, the boy now very awake, scrambling inside while they helped Lia up. Jan appeared again, a burned-down cigarette in his lips, and they all retreated to the secret room behind the boxes. Before the driver and Roman walled them in, Jan asked how long they'd be driving. 'Four, five hours,' said the driver, but his voice wasn't very authoritative.

From the other side of the boxes, Brano and the Sorokas heard the men murmur to each other; then Roman's voice, louder, wished them luck. The men jumped down into the gravel, and the doors ground shut – first one, then the other – and the darkness was complete. Petre yelped, but Lia calmed him. A rusty squeal as the latch was pulled into place, then the snap of the lock being secured.

Brano sat against the luggage as the Sorokas huddled in the opposite corner, their whispers indecipherable above the knocking groan of the engine and bone-crunching thumps when they hit potholes. This man was not a careful driver; he sped and slammed the brakes indiscriminately, and occasionally they heard his voice through the wall, singing: *Infant holy, infant lowly, for his bed a cattle stall. Oxen lowing, little knowing, Christ the Babe is Lord of all.*

The song crept on, its melody circular and incessant.

> *Swift are winging,*
> *Angels singing,*
> *Nowells ringing,*
> *Tidings bringing,*

119

Christ the Babe is Lord of all,
Christ the Babe is Lord of all.

Despite himself, Brano found he was humming along.

Although he could neither see nor hear them, he knew the Sorokas were scared. He had watched them during Roman's drive, Lia most of all – her stern silence was a mask. She had never fled her country before, and here she was with her boy, at the mercy of strangers who handed the family off to one another like a shipment of . . . of tinned plums. Worse, they had brought along a state security agent neither of them had any reason to trust.

Brano closed his eyes – the darkness remained dark – and felt the lorry's erratic thumps and leaps dig into the old wounds from Bóbrka.

After three or four hours, the lorry stopped and idled. Lia whispered to her husband, and he whispered back. The lorry moved forwards a few feet, then stopped again. Petre asked when he'd be able to pee again, and Brano leaned in their direction. 'Stay quiet now. We're at the Hungarian border.'

They answered with silence. The lorry lurched, crept forwards, and stalled. Was restarted and crept again, then turned off. They heard the thin man climb out of the cab and talk with the border guards, make a joke and laugh. Then footsteps around the back of the lorry. The snap of the lock being opened, the doors unlatched. Brano heard the boy's quick inhale, and when the doors opened grey late-morning light bled through the boxes. Lia's hand was tight over Petre's mouth. Above her hand, his eyes were perfectly round, focused on Brano. Jan held Lia from behind, biting his lips.

The driver talked with the border guard about plums and how late he was running. The guard told him he was always running late. 'You shouldn't drink so much, Jaroslaw, it messes up your nerves. Know what my wife gets me to drink? Slivovitz, the kosher stuff. Wake up fresh every morning. Those Jews know what they're doing.'

'I'll remember.'

Then they closed the doors again and, after a few minutes and a couple more jokes, the lorry moved on. Once they were on their way, Jan said to the darkness, 'Welcome to the Hungarian People's Republic.'

The second roadblock only checked the driver's papers. It seemed that Jaroslaw knew all the people he ran into; he even spoke to them in Hungarian. This was his regular delivery route.

After a while, they stopped again, and Jaroslaw opened the doors. 'Let's move, everyone. I've got to get this stuff to Budapest.' He climbed into the lorry and started shifting boxes as Brano moved the ones on their side.

They were at the end of a long forest trail, beside a small dacha. Impatient, Petre ran to a tree and dropped his pants. Jaroslaw unlocked the dacha and beckoned them inside, nervous hands fumbling with the keys as he spoke.

'I'll be back this evening, and I'll be able to tell you what's happening next.'

'You don't know already?' asked Lia.

He raised the corner of his lip. 'I know what I'm doing, okay? I need to contact someone, and then I can get rid of you. But in the meantime, stay here and don't go out. If anyone knocks on the door, you're not here. Okay?'

Jan squeezed his wife's arm. 'We understand.'

There was stale bread and jam in the kitchen, so Lia made sandwiches while Jan and Brano sat in the main room, smoking Jan's cigarettes. Jan seemed nervous, but when Brano asked, he said, 'No, it's all right. This is the way they said it would be. It's still unnerving, though.'

'You didn't follow this route before?'

'Before when?'

'When you went to Vienna.'

Jan smiled, finally admitting the truth. 'No, that time I took a different route. Through Yugoslavia.'

Brano didn't ask anything more.

They spent that day floating through the dacha's two cold rooms. Lia and Petre took a nap together in the bedroom while the men talked. They discussed the discomfort of that lorry, both hoping they wouldn't have to board it again, and Jan told him that for the whole ride Lia had been sure they were heading to prison. 'She just can't believe what she's doing. I've done it before, but I can't, either.'

'Neither can I,' said Brano.

'But this time it's for real.' Jan lit a cigarette, forgetting to offer Brano one. 'This time I'm not going back.'

'And this is why you returned? To get your family?'

Jan shrugged. 'What better reason is there?'

'What about me? I don't understand why you brought me along.'

Jan looked at his cigarette, then, remembering, offered one. He lit it for Brano. 'Because I could tell you needed it. You were in a bind. Like everybody else in Bóbrka, I knew you were going to be arrested.' He paused. 'And I like you. It's as simple as that.'

'I'd like to believe you,' said Brano. 'But we both know it was decided long ago, in Vienna.'

Jan's cigarette stopped halfway to his mouth.

'Dijana Franković,' Brano explained. 'The Americans gave you that name to assure that I'd be the one sent in. And I suppose they paid Pavel Jast to give me a reason to leave.'

Jan Soroka stared at his hands in his lap. He took a breath. 'Well, Brano. Let's say this was true, that I was part of some conspiracy to get you out of the country. Do you think the

Americans would tell me everything?'

'I suppose they wouldn't.'

'So what will you do?'

Brano took a drag of his cigarette. 'What?'

'East,' said Jan, 'or West?'

Brano surprised even himself by dredging up another smile. 'I don't suppose I have a choice any more.'

While Jan slept, he watched Lia shepherd Petre around the dacha and intervene with a nervous smile when he began to talk too much to Brano. Perhaps she was afraid he'd repeat things he'd overheard. Brano hadn't had much experience with children, but he felt that, despite the blemish on his cheek, Petre was like most boys – he saw this trip as an adventure. He peed a lot and asked for more bread and jam and exclaimed unexpectedly about details that caught his eye – 'Mama, there's a spider!' He pointed, trembling, at a dirty corner, where there proved to be no spider at all – but a cockroach. Brano began to suspect the boy was a little dumb, then decided that he was only overenthusiastic, with a penchant for quick, unreflective judgements. Lia would crouch over him and point out his mistake, and the boy would nod, register the correction, and move on to the next mistake. It was like watching a puppy and its master.

After the tense silence had stretched long enough, he asked Lia about her work in the Galicia Textile Works back in the Capital, how long she'd known Jan, and how Petre was at school. At first, she answered his questions easily, folding her relaxed hands in her lap. Her cheekbones were very strong; when she paused, she pressed her thick lips together until they wrinkled. He asked, and she told him that her fear was lessening now that the trip was under way.

'It feels like there are no more decisions to make, you know? It doesn't matter if the original decision was wrong or not, because it's irreversible. I'm no longer responsible.' A cigarette in her right hand sent ribbons of smoke into her face. 'But what about you, Major Brano Sev? You've got a family back home.'

He adjusted himself in his chair. 'My situation is different from Jan's. My family survives well enough without me. In a way, it'll be a relief to them that I've gone.'

She nodded doubtfully, then looked up at the bedroom door. Jan stood in it, wiping his eyes with the back of his hand, smiling at her. 'Christ, it's good to see you here.'

When Jaroslaw returned that night, they were in the kitchen, drinking tea without sugar, because there was none in the dacha. Jaroslaw went directly to a kitchen cabinet, where he retrieved a small bottle of palinka that no one had noticed before. When he brought the bottle from his lips the ends of his moustache glistened. 'There's been a little delay – nothing to worry about.' But his nervous fingers flicked against the bottle. 'I'll get you to the outskirts of Budapest tonight. You'll stay with a friend of mine, then it'll be taken care of.'

'For how long?' asked Jan.

'Don't worry. We know what we're doing.'

Jaroslaw had picked up another shipment in Budapest; this time it was tinned apricots. They again camped behind the boxes, teeth rattling as Jaroslaw sped along and stopped twice for road checks. But he was a regular along this road, too, and the soldiers chatted with him and scolded him for his excessive lifestyle (he told them he was rushing back to see his Budapest mistress) and happily accepted the bottles of palinka he gave them.

They reached the maize farm east of Budapest a little after midnight. Jaroslaw ushered them out of the lorry, tossed the suitcases down, and knocked on the door of a farmhouse with a steep, clay-tiled roof. A short man with a heavy limp greeted them and introduced himself as Adam

Madai, the manager of the region's farming collective. As soon as they were inside, Jaroslaw shook the farmer's hand, wished them all luck, and left.

Madai was an energetic man, chain-smoking Moskwa-Volga cigarettes throughout the night. He kept getting up from the table to refill glasses and winked continuously at Petre – who, after blushing a few times, finally warmed to their host – the whole time chattering away. He knew their language well and said with visible pride that he was also adept at Romanian, German, and English and was now learning French from Juliette Gréco records. He learned these languages, he told them, at the school of necessity. 'No one, but no one, speaks Hungarian in this world.'

He said he'd gotten his limp in '56, during the Revolution. He'd been in the streets with his brothers – that was the word he used for them – shooting at Russian tanks from behind barricades. Brano listened to his descriptions of walls exploding over his head, seeing his brothers dead in the street, the dread when he realized he'd used the last of his ammunition. By the time the Russians retook Budapest, he had slipped into the countryside, having been lucky enough not to make the lists of those destined for prisons and firing squads. Brano listened to everything, and by the end decided that Adam Madai was lying about all of it.

But that didn't matter. Madai was a generous host, choosing to sleep on the couch while they used the two bedrooms. In a bedroom drawer, Brano found an electric bill in Madai's name – at least he hadn't used an alias with them. And when Brano poked his head out at three in the morning to make sure their host had not slipped away to turn them in, Madai sat up and offered him a shot of Unicum, the syrupy national liquor that few outside the country had a taste for. Brano politely refused.

Their breakfast was a plentiful spread of coffee, salami, cheese, and pickled peppers that Madai jarred in his own basement. 'The water around here is too hard, much too hard for pickling. So I have to drive over to Érd once a week for bottles. Érd water . . .' He closed his eyes. 'Soft water – you can taste the difference.'

'Yes,' said Brano, wiping his eyes. 'I can.'

'Have some more coffee. You look tired.' Madai reached for his hat. 'I'm going to run into town to set things up. I should be back by the afternoon.'

'When are we leaving?' asked Jan.

'Hard to say. I'm not the one to do it, so it's not up to me. But I need all your luggage.'

Lia, on the couch, said, 'You need *what*?'

'Your luggage,' he repeated. 'We'll ship it separately. It'll be waiting for you in Vienna.'

Lia raised her hands. 'My whole life is in that bag, and you expect me to just hand it to you in the hope that it'll make it over the border? I'll keep my things with me, thank you.'

'Li,' said Jan.

'What? Am I the only one who understands this?'

'You're right,' said Brano. 'But we don't have much choice. I imagine our escape path won't work if we're all carrying suitcases.'

'Exactly,' said Madai. 'I don't have to do this, you know. I've given you food and drink. I've kept you safe. At great risk to myself. Aren't you comfortable here?'

'I'm scared out of my mind.'

'Come on, Li,' said Jan.

'Don't talk to me like I'm a child!' She crossed her arms over her breasts. 'I don't know how you can do this. Giving yourself over to strangers.'

'You don't trust him?' asked Brano.

'About as much as I trust you.'

Petre bounced out of the bedroom and ran through the living room, making buzzing sounds like a plane.

'Well, I can't bring you along,' said Madai as he pulled on his coat.

'Why not?' asked Lia.

'First of all, you don't speak Hungarian.'

'I do,' said Brano. '*A Balatonnál tanultam mez magyarul.* I learned Hungarian at Lake Balaton.'

'And *second* of all, none of you have travel papers.'

Brano reached into his jacket and took out his documents. Inside his external passport was a slip of paper folded into quarters. Madai read it briefly and handed it back.

'Well, one of you has travel papers.'

'Then he can go with you,' said Jan.

Lia tightened her grip on herself.

'I don't know,' said Brano, rubbing his sore eye. 'If I'm caught . . .'

'But you won't be caught,' said Jan. He looked at Lia. 'Okay, then? Is that good enough?'

She glared at Brano. 'I suppose it'll have to be.'

'Well, then?' said Madai. 'Will you get your goddamned bags now?'

They took Madai's stumpy flatbed truck, a Russian UAZ, into Pest, the sooty Habsburg buildings growing more frequent as they neared the centre.

'I can't take you to him,' Madai said as he drove. 'You know this, don't you?'

'Of course,' said Brano. 'But we'll see how it goes.'

'What does that mean?'

Brano stopped gazing at the buildings for a moment to focus on him. 'Have you been told what I do for a living?'

127

Madai's tongue moved around his mouth. 'I was told what you *did*.'

'Yes, well, I think you know what I mean, then.'

Madai remained quiet until they parked along Kerepesi út, across from the rail tracks that led to Keleti Station. He opened the door and reached behind the seat for the luggage. 'Are you really going to follow me?'

'You point the way,' said Brano.

As they waited for the number 7 tram, each with two suitcases, Madai grew visibly nervous. He kept wiping his hands on his trousers, glancing at the crowd of young men and women waiting with them. Brano, though, ignored the others and kept his eyes on Madai, which only increased the man's panic. Then the yellow tram approached; above its front window perched a decorative red hammer-and-sickle.

They rode the bumping car westward to Blaha Lujza Square, then walked south along the busy shopping boulevard that looped around the city, split by sporadic electric trams. Brano's gaze wandered in a Balkan manner, taking in the exceptional faces of the Magyar women bound in their long coats and hats – pale cheeks, bold eyes. When they reached Rákóczi Square Park, Madai stopped beside a tree. 'I can't take you any further than this.'

There were two militiamen loitering on the opposite corner of the park, smoking in the cold. 'How can I trust someone I haven't met?' asked Brano.

'It's impossible. You know that. You just have to believe me.'

The two militiamen noticed them and began to walk in their direction. 'But what am I going to tell the Sorokas?'

'I don't care what you tell them. I'm doing all of you a great favour, and I don't have time for this.'

Brano set down his bags. 'Don't look, but two militia are coming over here.'

Madai paled. 'Do you understand now? Go. Meet me back at Kerepesi in two hours and we'll return together. Can you manage that?'

Brano smiled and held up his hand in farewell, as if they were old friends. *'Szia.'*

'Szia,' Madai replied, adding the other two bags to his load. They turned and walked in opposite directions. The militiamen, still far away, stopped again and rested against the fence of a small playground empty of children.

Despite a decade's passage, there was still lingering evidence of the '56 uprising in the bullet holes scratched in the Habsburg masonry he passed on his way down Rákóczi út towards the Danube. Workers in blue coveralls passed on the street, preceded by clouds of breath; women tapped by on well-worn heels; children stumbled along, packed tight in winter wear – as best he could tell, he was alone. He stepped inside the gloomy splendour of the Parisian Arcade at number 5 Ferenciek Square.

The dark, domed ceiling was stained glass, and the walls carved, blackened wood. A few shops hid in here, but he was only interested in the one at the arcade's elbow, where it turned to exit at Kigyó utca: the Párisi Udvar Könyvesbolt.

There were stacks of books in the window, where Brano paused, scanning titles, then shortened his focus to the glass-reflection of the archway where he'd entered – empty. He went inside.

The only customers were two women standing together before a display of picture books about the city. From their mutterings and their quality clothes, it was obvious they were Yugoslav tourists. He went to the counter, where an old man with glasses read the day's *Magyar Hírlap*.

'Jó napot.'

The man looked up. *'Jó napot kívánok. Tessék.'*

Brano placed his fingertips on the counter, leaned a little closer, and said that he was interested in a book on First World War automobile electronics.

The man opened his mouth, paused, and said, *'Talán Debrecenben, a Déry Múzeumban megtalálja.'* Perhaps you should try the Déri Museum in Debrecen.

'I don't have time. Maybe you have something on the Russian Enlightenment?'

The old man stood up, nodding. 'In the back . . . I think we have some titles for you.'

Brano followed him into a small room filled with boxes. The man pushed his glasses closer to his eyes and examined him. 'This is a surprise. I haven't heard from anyone in a while.'

'I need to talk to *az Orvos*.' The Doctor.

The man stroked his grey cheek. 'Yes, that shouldn't be a problem. I'll tell you what. In a half hour, be at the Grand Hotel Margitsziget. The bar. You know how to get there? Need some tram tickets?'

Brano nodded. 'I don't have a lot of time.'

'Don't worry. He'll be there.'

Váci utca was just around the corner, and he walked the pedestrian avenue with tourists from other corners of the Empire who gazed into shop windows. There were more tourists here than back in the Capital, and perhaps that added to Brano's sense of dislocation – everything was still so strange. All this place did was remind him of the understocked shopping streets that branched off Victory Square back home, and when he got to the Beograd Landing and looked across the broad Danube to the Royal Palace in Buda, it only reminded him of Mihai Boulevard, which ran alongside the Tisa and faced the less than grandiose Canal District.

He caught the number 2 tram, which carried him north along the Danube, looping around the Parliament, then to the end of the line where Balassi Balint ran into the Margit Bridge. He walked quickly across, coat tight against the Danube winds, and entered Margit Island at the bridge's midpoint.

He was running late, so he did not loiter with the occasional chilled tourists who stood around the dry Habsburg fountain and wandered the parks. Hands deep in his pockets, he half-jogged through the thickening woods until he saw the empty outdoor tables behind the Grand Hotel.

Around the front, he paused again beneath the long awning. Behind him, through a wall of bare trees, the Danube flowed. He seemed to still be alone.

Inside, he walked past a long lobby filled with men reading newspapers in many languages. Diplomats, Western tourists and businessmen, and spies. Brano had known so many hotel lobbies in his lifetime and had often been one of those men pretending to care about the current events of the world.

He continued ahead, up a few steps to a wide, marble-lined lounge littered with faux-Habsburg furniture and a small bar along the right wall. The chairs were empty except one in the opposite corner, where a young English couple sat with a pile of suitcases, arguing tiredly.

Brano took a stool, nodding at the fat barman. *'Egy tejeskávét kérek.'*

The barman started up his coffee machine, and over the gurgle asked, 'Cigarette?'

Brano shook his head. 'I've quit five times.'

'Six is the magic number.'

The barman grinned, took out a pack, and offered one to Brano. 'Who comes up with these passwords? I think they must be feeding him opiates.'

'I know someone convinced it's a computer under Yalta.'

'A computer wouldn't be creative enough. Would it?'

'I have no idea, *Orvos*.'

The Doctor placed a caffe latte in front of Brano, then a dish of crackers, taking one for himself.

'Better watch those,' said Brano. 'You're getting fat.'

'I'm getting settled, that's what I'm getting. Married two years ago, and all she does is cook. I think she's trying to ruin me for other women.'

'She's a smart girl.'

The Doctor forced a laugh and wiped the counter. 'So what the hell are you doing in Budapest, Brano?'

'I thought maybe you'd know.'

'I know a few things, but I didn't expect to see you.'

'I'm trying to close down an operation. Didn't think it would bring me this far. Do you have a pencil?'

The Doctor took one out of his breast pocket, and Brano wrote on a napkin.

'Roman' – Volga GAZ-21, UZ-546: path: Nienaszów, Toki, Nw.-Żmigród, Kąty, Krempna

'Jaroslaw' – deliveryman, safe house over Hungarian border

'Adam Madai' (not alias) – maize farm east of Pest

Madai's contact in 8th District, near Rákóczi Park

The Doctor glanced at the list, then slipped it into his pocket. 'I'll hand this over.'

'We'll be leaving for Austria soon. I don't know the route, but it doesn't matter. Send some men to Adam Madai's this evening, and we can learn the rest from him.'

'No problem.'

'This is important,' said Brano. 'I'm in a bind with Yalta, and to tell the truth I'm scared. I certainly don't want to end up in Austria.'

The Doctor winked at him. 'Nothing to worry about. We'll wrap this up for you and send you back a hero. You won't dirty yourself with Austrian soil.' He took Brano's empty cup. 'Better go now. The manager will be checking on me soon. But take this.' He reached behind the counter and took out a copy of *The Spark*. 'Keep it. You might be interested in page two.'

When Brano reached Kerepesi út, having taken a tram south from the bridge through the Fifth, Sixth, and Seventh districts, Madai was rounding the corner behind him. They met beside the lorry without shaking hands. 'I've been around this block four times,' said Madai. 'Standing still makes me feel conspicuous.'

They left town again along the same road, neither speaking until they were out of the city. Brano cleared his throat. 'So you made contact?'

'Yes, yes.'

'And?'

'And it's all settled, Comrade Sev.'

'You don't want to tell me?'

'There's nothing to tell. We'll be met by someone else, who will take over.'

'The man you contacted?'

'Probably.'

Brano looked at Madai's hand tapping the wheel, and the blank eyes watching the road. He imagined Madai complaining to his contact about the ex-state security officer who came with him into town, and the contact, alarmed, reminding Madai of the techniques of vagueness. *Don't give him silence – let him trust you. But avoid details at all cost.*

Madai kept the plans vague with the Sorokas at dinner. Jan nodded; he knew the routine. But Lia shook her head over her soup. She asked Brano if it all made sense to him as well.

133

Brano said it did, but he was still distracted by the news-paper he'd dumped in a litter bin on the edge of Margit Island. He had opened *The Spark* during that long walk back through the woods, and before scanning the headlines on page two, he had seen that it was yesterday's paper. That only made his surprise more acute when he found the photograph of himself halfway down the second page, an old one from his file, under the headline:

MAJOR BRANO SEV, ARCH-MURDERER, FLEES THE COUNTRY!

The words had nearly doubled him over; he had to fight to avoid vomiting in the litter bin. And it wasn't until that drive back to the farm that he understood what it meant. News of his escape had reached *The Spark* on the same day he had left. Pavel Jast had learned of it from his friend Roman, then passed the news on to his superiors, who had expediently printed it in *The Spark*. Pavel Jast had been working for Yalta all along.

Lia was saying something.

'Yes?'

'What did you do in town, Comrade Sev?'

'Since I couldn't meet our host's friend, I walked by the Danube.'

'Pretty, was it?'

'I prefer our stretch of the Tisa. Not as grand, maybe, but it has its charm.'

'I like to swim,' said Petre. His head was just high enough to rest his chin on the edge of the table. 'I'm a great swimmer.'

'I'm sure you are,' said Brano.

Jan rubbed his hair. 'Eat, Petre. We'll take you swimming in a few days.'

Again, Brano slept poorly. He lay in bed listening for feet in the grass outside, whispers, and a boot kicking in the front door, followed by shouts, screams, and perhaps even gunshots.

But *az Orvos*'s men did not arrive that night, nor the next morning, as the Sorokas used Madai's cards to play a game that lasted hours. Madai spent the morning in the fields around the house in a heavy coat, examining the stunted, long-harvested cornstalks, while Brano browsed a Hungarian book on maize cultivation. He learned in the introduction that evidence had been found in Central American caves that maize domestication had been going on for eight thousand years. That page had been marked by a fold in the corner, and he wondered if Madai, when he questioned what he did with his life, cited this fact to prove he was part of an ancient tradition that gave his pesticides and harvesting machines symbolic power.

The silence that day was unique. It was a day of waiting, and in such a situation conversation becomes banal. Over cards, Jan sometimes sat back and chewed the inside of his cheeks, opened his mouth and, after reflection, closed it again. Lia was less indecisive; her jaw remained clamped shut all morning. Brano looked up from his book at Petre, who crawled around with a wooden model car Madai had given him, but even he did not make engine sounds.

Madai returned from the fields with wind-flushed cheeks and made lunch, recruiting Petre to help plate the sandwiches. When the boy dropped one on the floor and grew visibly upset, Madai assured him that he'd happily make twelve more if necessary. Over the meal, he told everyone that it would happen today, but not even he knew more than that. Brano doubted this but let it go. Despite the man's petty lies,

Brano found himself pitying this farmer-turned-counter-revolutionary. Because when the Doctor's men arrived to take the Sorokas back home, Adam Madai, after interrogation, would end up somewhere in his fields with a bullet in the back of his head. The men were probably already here, crouched along the edge of the fields, watching.

Dwelling on the newspaper article gave him few answers. Yalta had commissioned Pavel Jast to kill Bieniek and frame Brano for the murder. Why? To give Brano a reason to escape with the Sorokas and track their route – and, he assumed, to close it down. Jast, using the murder as an excuse, spoke to Soroka, through Roman, to convince him to bring along Brano.

But killing an innocent man and framing Brano for it, then sending the story to *The Spark* – why this large machinery of conspiracy for such a simple case? The Sorokas weren't important, at least not important enough to warrant this.

It reminded him of a phrase the Lieutenant General liked to use to describe the mind of counter-intelligence, and particularly the mind of Colonel Cerny: 'a byzantine imagination'. And he knew from experience that this kind of thinking could seldom be unravelled by a single agent. It was even possible that Jakob Bieniek had been connected to another operation for which he needed to be terminated, which then proved useful for Brano's situation as well.

There was no telling, because Cerny had kept him in the dark. Perhaps Brano had not been brought back inside after all.

But there was another side at work. The West had given their amateur agent, Jan Soroka, Dijana Franković's name as a cover. The Americans wanted something from him. Information, or simply him. They had not got anything out of him in Bóbrka, and it was unlikely they'd try anything in Hungary. They wanted him in Austria, the one place he wanted to avoid. His safety lay on this side of the Curtain, with the Doctor's men, and on the other side his future was a black, inarticulate mist.

So when, a little after lunch, they heard a car engine outside, then footsteps, Brano twitched. He took a breath, waiting for the boots to kick the front door, shattering hinges, but exhaled when he only heard the soft rap of knuckles on wood.

Madai opened the door and kissed the cheeks of a small blonde woman whose thin jawbone shifted as she smiled. Under her arm was a brown paper package.

Madai turned to them. 'Time to go.'

The package contained three white outfits that the adults were instructed to put on. The clothes were loose fitting, like pyjamas, and when they stepped outside in their coats they saw a small white box-van with a beefy, white-uniformed man standing beside its back doors.

'Don't be afraid,' the woman said in Hungarian as they approached the van. 'The others are too full of drugs to be a bother.'

'What did she say?' asked Lia.

Brano said, 'The van is headed for a mental home. There are real patients in the back, but they're too drugged to cause trouble.'

'A *mental* home?'

'But what about the kid?' he asked in Hungarian.

The woman shrugged. 'He'll be up front with us. We'll say he's one of the patients' children, that I'm going to take care of him myself.'

'And his language?'

'He's a mute. Psychologically scarred.'

While the big man put their clothes in the space behind the front seats, Brano explained the plan to the Sorokas. Lia didn't want to be separated from Petre. 'This is unacceptable. I'm not going to do it.'

137

'Li,' said Jan.

'Don't try to calm me! I don't know these people – neither do you!'

Brano paused at the back doors. 'They don't send seven-year-olds to mental homes. If he sits with us, your whole family will end up in prison.'

Lia's crossed arms came apart. She crouched and hugged her boy, then whispered instructions to him.

There were three patients in the back, two men and a woman. The men hadn't been shaved in a few days, and all three shared a vacant, large-pupiled stare focused on nothing in particular. Straps from the wall kept them from falling over. Brano and the Sorokas climbed past the patients, deeper into the van. Madai stood at the doors, smoking and watching. 'Remember,' he said, 'you're all patients filled to the forehead with drugs. You don't understand what anyone says to you; you're not even aware of anyone. If the van stops, you put on those straps. Don't make eye contact and, most of all, never speak. Is that clear?'

They all nodded.

The large man closed the doors.

Then the van fired to life, and they began to move.

Brano could see little through the back windows covered in steel grating, but he mentally charted what seemed the most likely route. They crossed the Danube at the tip of Szentendrei Island, north of Budapest, then wrapped around the western side of the city to reach the northwest road to Győr. The van sped along and the Sorokas whispered. Lia sometimes held Jan's hand. Other times, the anger flushed her cheeks and she whispered something and crossed her arms. Jan held her elbow, trying to reason with her, then settled back. He gave Brano a nervous smile that Brano could not return, preoccupied by the hope that the Doctor's men were not far behind them.

All along, the three patients sat beside them, swinging in their straps to the rhythm of the road, because no one existed outside the drugged dreams in their heads.

They were stopped once before Győr, and as they slowed Brano strapped himself to the wall, nodding at the others to follow suit. They heard the woman telling a soldier the brief, sad tale of the mute boy and his insane mother, who was in the back, and how she was going to take care of the boy herself rather than give him over to the state orphanages. The soldier admired her maternal instincts, but when they opened the back doors, it was clear that he admired her body even more. He hardly looked at the patients at all.

The soldier who opened the door just after Győr was less taken by her shape, perhaps because the sunset had cast her in shadow. 'Where's this sanatorium?'

'Sopron,' she said.

He climbed into the van to get a better look at the drugged woman. He put his hands on his knees and stared into her eyes. 'Crazy,' he said. 'You, my dear, are insane.' He shook his head as he climbed back down and told the blonde about his grandfather, who stumbled around a sanatorium near Debrecen and never remembered his grandson's name. 'I don't know why we waste our time with them,' he said. 'Might as well just shoot them.'

'They're not animals,' said the woman.

'Are you sure?'

She closed the doors. 'Of course. They're human.'

The soldier laughed. 'If all there is to being human is standing on two legs and having a face that isn't a monkey's, then maybe there's nothing special about being human.'

*   *   *

It had been dark for a while when they stopped again and the large man opened the back doors. *'Gyertek ki,'* he said, and the Sorokas followed Brano around the patients' knees, out into the cold. Petre bounced from foot to foot, then threw himself into Lia's arms.

They were on a paved road surrounded by flat farmland. They took their coats and clothes, and the woman asked them to change.

'Out here?' asked Lia.

But even she submitted, undressing and redressing on the other side of the van. The driver took the hospital clothes and gave the woman a brief kiss on the lips before driving away. They watched the van disappear in the direction of a town. She turned on the torch to illuminate her wristwatch, then extinguished it. 'Come on,' she said. 'We'll hide in the ditch until it's time.'

'Time for what?' asked Brano once they were settled. The Sorokas mumbled behind him.

'Time to be picked up,' she said.

'We're near the Fertő Lake, aren't we?'

In the darkness he could just make out her head turning to him. 'Yes.'

'A boat?'

'A boat would be cut to bits by machine guns.'

'So we're crossing by land.'

'It's not your concern.'

Brano grinned, though she couldn't see his lips. 'I think it's all of our concern. I know a little bit about these kinds of operations, and I don't want to think I'm in the hands of amateurs. I suppose you have contacts within the border guards?'

She raised herself to look down the length of the empty road. 'Wait – there he is.'

A pair of lights grew from the direction of the town, then

stopped about thirty yards away. Brano was able to see, once the lights went off, that it was a small military lorry, its rear covered in canvas. From the driver's side, a torch beam flickered three times. The woman stood up then, and the lorry rolled closer. She jogged up to the window and began to speak with a man inside.

'What is it?' asked Jan.

'*Shh,*' said Brano, listening.

'. . . Zsolt knows, I'm sure he does,' said the man. 'The whole Fésűs Corner is covered with troops.'

'Not so loud,' she told him. 'What are the options?'

Brano couldn't hear what the man answered, but he could hear the woman's exasperated sigh.

'What are they talking about?' whispered Lia.

'Nothing,' said Brano. 'Just personal things. Everything's fine.'

The woman walked back to them. 'Everyone, let's go.'

Brano sat in the shadows by the canvas flaps, watching the road fade behind them, while the Sorokas, deeper inside the lorry, whispered among themselves. They didn't need to speak the language to feel that something was wrong. Brano knew of the Fésűs Corner, a small point of Hungarian territory wedged into Austria on the eastern side of the Fertő Lake – Fertő to the Hungarians, Neusiedl to the Austrians. The driver was no doubt a border guard under the supervision of the Hungarian Interior Ministry, and the woman had bought him, either with money or something less tangible.

Brano leaned back as they passed through a town that, once they exited, he saw by a sign was Fertőd. Then the road narrowed, and they passed through Sarród and, after a while, the tiny village of Lászlómajor. Then, off to the left, he saw the low, flat spread of the eastern edge of the lake.

And there was no sign that the Doctor's men were nearer to him than he was to the Austrian border. He briefly considered throwing himself out the back and running off. But he recalled Cerny's last order: *If you can't stop him, then you follow and report back when you can.*

He had reported to the Doctor, but no one seemed to care.

When the lorry turned and trembled across a rutted gravel road between the lake and a concrete canal, the obvious finally became clear. The Doctor would not come, because Yalta Boulevard wanted him in Austria. He covered his mouth with a hand, fighting a quick rush of *zbrka* and fear.

When they stopped it was in a darkness punctuated by the occasional flash of a spotlight sliding over the water from a guard tower north of them.

Both front doors opened and shut, and they waited. The woman appeared first, looking at them through the flaps without expression. Then she nodded to the right, towards a watery darkness thick with reeds. 'It's not far – about eight hundred yards that way. Once you're across, turn right and then wait at the dirt road. You'll be picked up.'

After Brano whispered his translation, Lia stuck her head out. 'We'll catch pneumonia.'

'That's the least thing you have to worry about,' she answered. 'Jan.'

Jan looked up from Petre, who was in his arms.

Brano translated her next words. 'You're responsible for watching the spotlight over there.' She pointed. 'When it approaches, all of you go under. Understand?'

'We won't make it,' Brano said in Hungarian. 'Will we?'

'We're more organized than you think. They're focused on the Fésűs Corner tonight, not here.' She looked back at the empty road. 'Hurry. They'll be here soon.'

'And what will you be doing when they arrive?'

She smiled at Brano as the driver, who he could now see was a fat soldier with a rough face, put his arm around her. She said, 'I'll be fucking my friend in the back of this lorry.'

As they crawled down from the gravel road into the cold water that rose to their knees, then their waists (Petre's neck), he let go of the last tenuous hopes that he would be saved from this. But this had always been part of his work – no matter how vast the security apparatus behind you, the fact was that, in the end, you were alone.

His wet shirt puffed around his neck, and he pushed it down, working hard to reach that stage that followed uncertainty, the one Jan Soroka had always seemed to inhabit – acceptance. He barely heard it when that same man whispered, 'Now.'

Brano looked around, saw the light sliding over the water towards him, and realized he was alone, ripples spreading through the reeds where his companions had been. Then he dropped into the icy water.

Images flashed. Bóbrka. Childhood. A quiet, shy boy, who never raised his hand in class. Unexceptional in school, where they used beet juice in lieu of ink, he was neither poor nor impressive, and it seemed likely that he would farm the earth in the same way his father and grandfather had. And this is what he did, from the age of twelve, tilling potatoes alongside his father in the arid fields.

His one lasting friendship, with Marek Piotrowski, was temperamental, based on this loud oaf's momentary whims. When dissatisfied, Marek could sometimes be found on a Bóbrka side street, kicking Brano Sev into the dust.

Then, in 1939, the Germans took over his country. He was twenty-two when the frantic soldiers marched into his house and handed his father a piece of paper, which told him he would no longer grow vegetables; he would spend his days in a factory, welding large strips of steel into anti-tank obstacles. Two nights later, with his friend's encouragement, Brano and Marek disappeared, soon finding what they sought: the partisan camp.

He came up, stifling a cough with his fist. His cold head was pounding. The others looked at him, Petre's wet face grinning. Black makeup dribbled from Lia's eyes.

A breeze iced his wet hair as he glanced back to where, on the road some distance away, a jeep was parking behind the lorry they'd left. A gathering headache pulsed behind his right eye.

They continued forwards, stumbling sometimes over the stiff reeds. Petre fell; Lia righted him. They could still not see the far bank, but Jan walked with stiff confidence, glancing occasionally back at the activity on the gravel road. He turned again and paused, noticing a flicker. *'Now.'*

The partisan camp was not what they expected. It was makeshift, ready to be transported at any moment, and when they asked to be shown how to use a rifle, the commander, a shopkeeper from Dukla, Laszlo 'Lion' Cerny (though he wore no stripes, he called himself a major), instead handed them a weathered book by Karl Marx. *Read this,* he told them. *Then we'll teach you how to kill Germans.*

Will this teach us to kill the proper way? asked Marek.

Shh, said Brano.

While the partisans snuffed the fire and raided German convoys, Brano read. *History is economics in action . . . The philosophers have only interpreted the world . . . the point, however, is to change it.* Marek stood over him with a pine branch held like a rifle. He made shooting sounds with his mouth. *What the bourgeoisie . . . produces above all is its own gravediggers . . . The workers have nothing to lose but their chains.*

In the end, reading didn't matter, because a failed raid on an officer's tent turned out to be an ambush and cut the partisan camp in half. *Want to learn how to shoot?* asked Cerny.

The two of them nodded.

Let's practise on Nazis.

And that was the day Marek was killed by a bullet from a machine gun mounted on a personnel carrier. Brano lay beside him in the grass, trying to deal with his jammed rifle (he had fired only two shots), and when he heard the quiet sigh to his left, through the grass, he knew before looking that his friend was dead. But he looked anyway. He stared at the hole in Marek's neck, which throbbed, producing an astounding amount of blood that glued the blades of grass together.

A hand pulled him, gasping, out of the water. Jan's face was close to his. 'Don't drown, stupid,' he whispered.

Brano blinked at him, the pain in his head sharp now.

As they continued, the reeds thickened and the water lowered to their waists again. They could no longer make out the lorry. Jan looked around, then said, *'Now.'*

The frigid water swallowed Brano.

Over the next years their raids became more frequent, and his rifle usually did not jam. He became familiar with the recoil against his shoulder and the uniformed Germans who crumpled quietly on the road. Sometimes they shouted and squealed, though usually they dropped in silence. Cerny said, *You've got an eye, Sev. You're a one-shot killer.* He became known as that – 'One-Shot' – by everyone in their mobile camp. He was respected for his efficiency and for his modesty.

Perhaps that was why, in the summer of 1944, Cerny took Brano out into the woods and sat him down.

It's winding down now, you know.

What?

The war. The Americans are coming in from the west, but the

Russians will be here first. You know what that means, don't
you?

Brano didn't want to disappoint. *It means the dictatorship
of the proletariat is upon us.*

*Don't give me dogma, Brano. What this means is that we are
going to run things now. Orders have come in from Moscow. We're
to organize.*

Organize?

Don't pretend you don't understand. Cerny ruffled Brano's
hair, and for the moment, Brano forgot that he was a twenty-
seven-year-old man being treated like a twelve-year-old boy.
The most important thing in an emerging socialist state is what?

Brano shrugged.

You know the answer.

He did. *Security against insurrectionists.*

Cerny smiled. *Now, comrade, you'll never be alone.*

And if Brano was angry about anything, it was for that
one lie.

Through his blurred, aching eyes he could see barren land
ahead, past the reeds, and when the light swung across the
water again, Jan said nothing. Because now they were
beyond the reach of the spotlights; they were in Austria.

At the bank, the upturned hull of a shattered blue rowing
boat stuck out of the water. Petre pointed at it as he struggled through the reeds, and whispered something to his
mother. Lia told him to be quiet.

'Don't worry,' said Jan. 'We've arrived.'

'My God,' said Lia, but she whispered it.

They were exhausted and cold when they staggered onto
the muddy grass that sucked at their feet. They collapsed. They
lay in silence, breathing heavily, shivering. Brano rubbed his
temples to get rid of the pain, while Jan smiled blankly at the
night sky.

Brano forced a soft, slow laugh. The Sorokas looked at him.

'What?' said Lia.

He raised himself on his elbows and laughed again – it came from deep inside himself, a strong, convincing laugh, but nonetheless an act. 'Now I'm the one who has to pee.'

Maybe it was the stress finally rolling off their shoulders, but the Sorokas, after a second, laughed as well. Petre, delighted, said, 'I can't pee at all!'

Brano wandered back to the broken rowing boat and urinated into the water, watching the out-of-reach spotlight turn in the distance. The pain in his head was becoming manageable. He zipped himself up and reached into his soaking coat pocket. He took out Jakob Bieniek's passport and wrapped it tightly in a handkerchief, then squatted. He glanced back, but the Sorokas were unaware, huddled together for warmth. Then he hid the package in a dry pocket under the hull of the boat.

Brano returned, watching the faint western horizon. 'They should've found us by now,' he said to Jan. 'Where are the Austrian border guards?'

'I don't do the planning, but it doesn't matter. We're safe now.'

'She said we go to the right?'

'To a road,' he said, a grin playing on the corners of his lips. 'From here it's simple.'

So they followed Jan across the grassy field. Brano caught up with him, hopping over occasional rocks. 'You might as well tell me now.'

'What should I tell you?'

'What you sold the Americans. You opened a Viennese account with their money.'

'Why should I tell you that now?'

'Because in a few minutes I'm not going to be a problem

147

any more. Your friends will take me away, because I'm the reason they helped you get your family back. So you might as well tell me what information you sold them.'

Jan looked at him, for a moment stunned, then he snorted a half-laugh. 'Information? Honestly, Brano, I've got no idea what you're talking about.' He squinted ahead to where a raised dirt road was just visible. A little to the left, Brano saw the silhouettes of two cars waiting in the darkness. He could make out the lights of the cigarettes held by men who leaned against the bonnets. Five in all.

One stepped on his cigarette and jogged out to greet them, holding towels under his arm. He was tall, with a grey Viennese suit and a big smile. *'Grüß Gott,'* he said, shaking Jan's hand furiously, then gave them each a towel. He shook Brano's hand, then kissed Lia's with excited intensity. He crouched beside Petre and produced a bar of Toblerone chocolate wrapped in foil. 'Been saving this for you, young man,' he said, and stood up. *'Herzlich willkommen in Österreich!* I'm Ludwig.'

'Pleased to meet you,' said Lia, but with a flat, emotionless tone.

Jan, one hand rubbing a towel over his hair, placed the other on the Austrian's shoulder. 'I don't know how to thank you.'

'My absolute pleasure, Jan. It's time for a new life!' He took Lia's limp hand and kissed it again. 'I'm sorry about the sudden change in plan – you never really know how these things will turn out. But now it's time to get you into the warmth.'

As they approached the cars, the other four stepped on their cigarettes. They were all large men, their hats low, with significant bulges under their jackets.

When they reached the cars and one man put a hand on his shoulder, Brano did not resist. This was no surprise. He didn't even protest as another patted him down to be sure he was unarmed.

He looked at Jan to see what expression he might have, but Jan was helping Lia into the back of a car. He went out of his way not to look at Brano as he followed her inside.

PART TWO

The Jowls

17 February 1967, Friday

It had all been so predictable. The whole ride he didn't ask a thing, because there was no point. He could imagine the scene in the American embassy those months ago. Jan Soroka, no longer able to live without his wife and son, asked for their help. *Of course,* the Americans told him. *We are for freedom and the values of the family. Just one little thing you can do for us.*

Brano Sev wasn't vain; he didn't imagine they had desired him a long time. No, they simply looked at Jan Soroka's file, and some smart office boy lined up Soroka's family home with a list of known intelligence agents. It was simple; it was a given. No one helps without asking a price.

But these men were not Americans; they were Austrian. Members of military counterintelligence, the *Abwehramt,* like the man he had knocked out in the Vienna Airport's bathroom six months ago.

After ten minutes of driving, they passed a sign that said they were entering Apetlon, and Ludwig turned in his seat. He asked Brano, in German, to please excuse them. Then everything went black because of the burlap bag placed over his sore head.

So obvious. So predictable.

They didn't talk in the car, and when, after perhaps two hours, they stopped, the only thing said was a polite, 'Right this way,' as a hand led him by the arm into the cold night.

There was gravel beneath his feet and dirt. They were not in a city. The air through the burlap was fresh.

'Watch your step, now.'

He tripped over something, but they righted him – strong hands gripping his elbows. Someone cursed – *Scheisse!* – trying to work a set of keys into a lock, then they walked into a warm, dry place. Light bled through the burlap, and he could smell old cigarettes.

'Sit down, why don't you?' someone said, then eased him back into a thick-padded chair. Soft, comfortable.

The bag was taken off.

It was a living room. Comfortable, bourgeois. His chair matched the grey Bauhaus sofa on the other side of a low coffee table stocked with periodicals – *Der Standard, Stern*, and the dissident Filip Lutz's sounding board, *Kurier*. In the corner, between a large television and a cabinet of coffee cups and cocktail glasses, Ludwig whispered to one of the men, then checked his watch. He noticed Brano staring, and smiled.

'It's a relief to get that thing off, isn't it? Can breathe a little better.'

Brano glanced up at the fat man beside him with the bag in his hand. He was smiling as well. The third man walked out the front door and locked it behind himself.

'Something to drink?' asked Ludwig as he opened the cabinet door to reveal rows of bottles. 'Brandy to warm you up? It's a fully stocked bar.'

'Nothing, thank you.'

'How about some water?' As he spoke, he took out a plastic jug and began to pour a glass.

'I'm not thirsty.'

'It's not drugged, Brano. Here – ' Ludwig drank half the glass, his Adam's apple bobbing, then placed it on the coffee table and settled into the sofa. 'See? I feel fine. That's mountain spring water, pure and simple.'

'I'm not thirsty.'

'Well, then. Want to change out of that?'

Brano looked down at his soaked clothes. 'My clothes are supposed to be in transit.'

'No worries.' Ludwig nodded at the fat man. 'Get that robe, will you?'

He brought a thick yellow robe from the bathroom and handed it to Brano, who stood, then hesitated. 'Here?'

Ludwig grinned. 'We're not queer, Brano.'

So he undressed and put on the robe, watched carefully by both men.

'I suppose we should get to it, shouldn't we?'

Brano sat down again. 'If you'd like.'

Ludwig examined his nails, which were clean, like his long face and close-cropped hair. 'Let's establish some facts first. You have entered Austrian territory of your own free will. You don't have a visa, and there is no record of your entry. Bureaucratically, my friend, you do not exist.'

Brano's hands were on his knees, squeezing through the robe.

'We're going to talk. How long our conversation lasts is up to you. You can cooperate or not. That's your prerogative. But it will have a bearing on how long we keep you here.'

'I understand,' said Brano.

'Good. Good. Tell me, then, why you have entered Austria.'

* * *

155

Decades ago, when Brano Sev began his tenure at Yalta, then-Major Cerny put him through a mock interrogation that would prepare him for this kind of situation. As he left his apartment one evening, two men jumped out of a bread van, placed a burlap sack over his head, and took him to an old farmhouse. They told him to squat and hold out his arms, as if he were preparing to launch into flight. He was ordered not to move. After a while, his arms became heavy and sank, and they smacked his elbows with truncheons. When exhaustion overcame him and he started to doze, they lifted him by his armpits and dragged him outside – his numb legs could no longer move – and threw him in a lake, then dragged him back again. After a day of this, he was placed in a chair, a bright light shining in his face, and asked questions.

What is your mission?

I cannot answer that.

Who are your superiors?

I cannot answer that.

What is your name?

Brano Oleksy Sev.

And your mother's name?

I cannot answer that.

How about your girlfriend, Brano Sev? You've got a girlfriend, don't you?

I cannot answer that.

You're not queer, are you?

I cannot answer that.

Come on, Brano. This is just between us. You can at least deny it, can't you?

I cannot answer that.

Look, I'm just trying to help you. If I tell those boys outside that you're a shirt-lifter, you know what they're going to do, don't you? They're going to beat the shit out of you. So are you queer or not?

'I cannot answer that,' he told the Austrian.

Ludwig winked at the fat man with the bag. 'Looks like we're going to be here for a while.'

Brano had met Ludwig's kind often over the years. Well fed, confident, with a sense of something they thought was style. They played nice men because they believed themselves to be nice men who were in the unfortunate position of having to commit certain acts that, in themselves, were not nice.

The effect was accentuated by the fact that this man was Austrian – a race not known for its casual demeanour.

But for now, there were no prison cells, no truncheons, no electrical wires – this was unexpected. Just a living room, smiles, and questions. And that made it all the more difficult. Brano wanted to understand what was going on, and with understanding would come the acceptance he needed. He tried to hide his consternation as Ludwig leaned forwards and smiled.

'Let's start with what we know about you, Brano. You're half a century old, and in that time you've had your successes. After the war you even had some fame – your picture appeared in *The Spark* now and then when you uncovered another "fascist"' – he marked the quotes with the long fingers of his left hand – 'hiding in the hills. You have a good record. But the question I wondered about for a while was, Why is a man as accomplished as this working in a factory now?'

Brano blinked at him.

'Well, I wouldn't ask a question like that unless I thought I had the answer, would I?' He touched his chin. 'You're not a young man, Brano, but you think like one. You're an idealist. Perhaps you even believe that tripe your General Secretary Tomiak Pankov likes to mutter about international peace. When you did your job, you did it well, and you stayed clean. You were even approached – twice that we

157

know of – to turn to the side of right; each time you refused unequivocally, even when the price was good. You *are* clean, Brano, in your own way. And because of that, someone finally gave you the shaft. But even before that, you were never allowed to progress.'

Brano opened his mouth, paused, then said, 'That's not exactly true. I moved up in rank.'

Ludwig grinned. 'That's just uniform decoration, Brano! Look at the facts. You were sent on short trips to a lot of places. Tel Aviv, Athens, Belgrade, Moscow. But other than one instance, you weren't trusted to do any long-term work. And we both know that one exception: Free Berlin.'

'You mean West Berlin?'

'As you like, Brano. West Berlin. But even there, you weren't a *rezident*; you weren't controlling anyone. You were controlled. Because, in the end, you're not corrupt enough to be trusted by your Ministry. And so, after one year, they brought you back. And that was that, until . . .' He crossed his legs and gripped a knee. 'Until six, seven months ago, in July, when you visited Vienna. A month-and-a-half stay. That's it. Though your tenure was supposed to be a lot longer.'

'I was here as a temporary cultural attaché,' he said. 'I didn't need to stay long.'

'Cultural attaché – these labels they come up with for *rezident*s are wonderful!' Ludwig slapped his thigh, then shook his head. 'The day you left, a certain Bertrand Richter, another known spy, was found dead in the Volksgarten. You know anything about this?'

Brano blinked again.

'Perhaps you do, perhaps you don't. But spies don't end up dead in Vienna for no reason. And he was one of your men. Certainly you're concerned about what happened to Bertrand.'

'I don't know anything about that.'

'And you don't care?'

'It's not my problem.'

'Well, it obviously was at the time, because you were stripped of your uniform and packed off to assemble tractor gauges.' Ludwig checked his watch again and rubbed his thighs. 'We'll get back to this, okay? Right now, I have some things to attend to, but in the meantime I have something for you to consider. A deal, if you will. See, I don't expect something for nothing. Others have different opinions, but today you're dealing with me, and I'm a realist. I can give you something if you give me something.'

Brano looked at his hands and waited.

'It's no secret you made a blunder back in your hometown. You're a murderer, Brano, and as soon as you set foot back in your country, you're going to be arrested.'

Brano didn't answer, because there had been no question.

'So you can talk to us, and we'll not only give you asylum, we'll set you up with a nice apartment in downtown Vienna. But if you don't talk to us, we'll put you on a plane back home. I'm sure your friends would be happy to meet you.'

Brano settled deeper into his chair.

Ludwig grinned. 'Why don't you think about it a while? We're in no hurry. While I'm gone, my men will be happy to listen if you feel like talking.' The fat man, beside Brano, nodded his agreement.

February to March 1967

Ludwig did not return that night, nor the next day. Brano took a bath and then slept in a bedroom with boards nailed over the windows. The lock on the door worked only from the outside, and each morning the guard who unlocked it was different from the one who had locked it the previous night.

159

His guards seemed never to tire. They stood with their hands crossed over their groins and watched him. This was how it worked. Time was a formidable tool, and it could be used in many ways. In the morning, the fat guard opened a cardboard box filled with pastries and coffee, and Brano ate with him. The tall one arrived much later with dinner. On the third day, the fat guard opened a second box as well: Brano's clothes, cleaned and pressed. No one spoke. Time and silence.

At first Ludwig's offer had shocked him – not the fact that a deal had been offered (he'd suspected something in exchange for his cooperation), but the nature of the deal itself. In all his worries and predictions of the last week, it had never occurred to him that he would want to stay in the West, particularly in Vienna. It was a cold city, all charm removed by the flagrant displays of capital: the bankers, international corporations, the trite exploitation of their musical history. It was a city without a soul, and it was the scene of his greatest failure.

And why would he leave his country? He knew why others left: they were impatient. Socialism, like any egalitarian system, is not born whole. It moves slowly from the inequities of capitalism to the long restructuring of the dictatorship of the proletariat, before finally reaching the full glory of pure communism. Lenin made no secret of progress's sluggishness. Those who left were individualists, or opportunists, who felt that the realization of true human equality was not worth a few years of discomfort. Brano felt differently. He did not mind the occasional breadlines, the glitches in production that filled the shoe stores with only one style of footwear, nor the periodic interruptions in hot water and electricity that individualists decried. Perhaps Ludwig was right; he was an idealist.

The opaque byzantine machinations of Yalta were also

becoming clearer. If Cerny knew he would be picked up in Austria – and he had to suspect this – then printing his murder conviction in *The Spark* made sense, as did the Doctor's failed promise. Cerny knew the Austrians would never believe Brano had left his home for ideological reasons. So he had given Brano a personal reason.

Brano, in the eyes of the Austrians, would be another Bogdan Stashinski, the KGB assassin who had defected in 1961, in Paris, after just two jobs. Simply because he couldn't take it any longer.

But again, why? Soroka was far from his reach, and once again Brano was alone with the enemy. Ludwig's threat to send him back home was merely that – a threat. So, here he would stay.

On the third night, Ludwig settled on the sofa and crossed an ankle over his knee. 'Tell me, then. Why have you come to Austria?'

'I've been framed for a murder, and the only way out of it was to leave the country.'

'Of course. An ex-member of the Ministry for State Security is framed by a drunk peasant, and he can't get himself out of the mess? You must think we're idiots, Brano.'

'I can only tell you what I know.'

'Which is all we ask.'

Brano waited.

'All right. Your people run a lot of operations out of Vienna. Who doesn't, these days? Neutral countries breed this kind of intrigue. Tell us about them.'

'I cannot.'

'Because you choose not to?'

'I simply cannot.'

'Okay,' said Ludwig. He got up again. 'We'll talk later.'

*　　*　　*

Ludwig was patient. He came and went many times, and in the periods between, Brano ate pastries with the fat guard, and sometimes they watched television – insipid programmes with names like *Batman* and *Gespensterparty*.

The struggle, it seemed, was not against fear but boredom.

His guards were polite but well trained; they knew their duty. Their silence was meant to give Brano a sense of relief each time Ludwig returned and spoke. That relief would help Brano to eventually open up.

At least, that was how he understood the technique until the seventh time Ludwig returned to the house, three weeks into his stay.

He smiled like every other time, but now he had a small briefcase. He placed it on the coffee table. 'You're feeling well, Brano?'

'I feel all right.'

'Good, good.' Ludwig's eyes wandered, lost for a second, then he sat down. 'You'll never guess what happened today, in India.'

'I probably won't.'

Ludwig smiled. 'Svetlana Alliluyeva walked into the United States embassy in Delhi and asked for asylum.'

'Stalin's daughter?'

'The very one. Seems she was delivering her lover's ashes to the Ganges, and after thinking it over decided there was no longer any reason to remain in that hellhole they call the Union of Soviet Socialist Republics.'

'I don't believe you.'

'Well, believe it, Brano. It'll make the news by tonight. Want to know what's in here?' he said, tapping the suitcase.

Brano shrugged.

Ludwig opened the latches, then raised the lid. He turned it around so Brano could see.

Inside was a corroded battery a little smaller than one

used in an automobile – red letters told him it was made by the Italian Fiamm company. Attached to the terminals was a red switch with two long leads ending in alligator clips.

'What's that for?' he asked stupidly.

'Karl,' said Ludwig.

The fat one stepped behind the chair and grabbed Brano's arms, twisting them back and quickly tying his wrists together with a braided rope.

'I don't understand,' said Brano.

Ludwig tied his ankles together, and then Karl placed the burlap bag over his head again.

Through the darkness, Ludwig spoke to him. 'You've been through these sorts of things. We know this. And it was my hope that, knowing what was possible, you would choose to work with us. But you've been stubborn. So, then. Austrian hospitality, it seems, can only get one so far, and now we must rely on the methods of our fathers.'

Brano felt hands on his chest. They grasped his shirt and ripped it open. He heard the click of a button hitting the floor. A sharp, cold pain in his left nipple – the first alligator clip – then the other.

'Karl?' he heard. 'Can you show me how to work this damn thing?'

This, then, was what he was trained for. No longer boredom, but fear – not of pain, but of the knowledge that your life is no longer in your hands. How long he lasted he wasn't sure, but the cold, jaw-grinding shocks went through him many times – short pulses that became, over time, longer. Sometimes he could hold the pain in his hand, but often it slipped through his fingers and filled his rigid body. His organs hardened with each shock, and his fingers clenched behind his back. And, like everyone in the end, he talked.

He gave them a list of names. That was where he started, with the list of Yalta Boulevard's local informers, because the first impulse of anyone who has been broken is to give away others. Retribution isn't a worry – all you want is your life back.

Then he gave them two names they already knew: Austrian agents who also worked for Yalta. One had been bought, the other blackmailed with photographs of him in bed with a young Polish boy. Brano told what little he knew of the information they had handed over.

But these admissions were decisions; even through the pain he could still think. The two double agents had served their purpose months ago and were no longer of use. The informers he handed over were a mix of the uncooperative and unproductive. And in a city like Vienna there were so many of these that the names could go on for a long time, giving the illusion of completeness yet in reality telling nothing.

Then Ludwig reached further back, to 1964. He was in West Berlin, no? Brano quickly verified this. And who was the West Berlin *rezident*? Again, this was a man who had since been brought back home, so he answered. And what did Brano do there? He followed orders.

Ludwig closed the circuit.

'More specific, Brano.'

He told them of various operations he'd taken part in over that year, none of which concerned Austria. He'd helped manage three informers, had once run a disinformation campaign against British intelligence, had arranged the practical details of two incoming operatives, and had killed one man.

'Name?'

He admitted that as well, because by now he could no longer distinguish what was important from what was not. All questions had answers.

'What about Bertrand Richter?'

'He was giving you information.'

'What made you think that?'

'I gave him false information, and he delivered it to you. He told you a West German lorry would carry guns into Hungary. He had to be eliminated.'

'By whom?'

'By Erich Tobler,' he lied.

The sound of paper shuffling. 'That's the informer who lives on Hauptstraße.'

'Yes,' said Brano. 'He's the one.'

'We assumed it was you. You did leave Austria the same evening the body was discovered.'

'It wouldn't make sense for me to do it myself – I was the *rezident*. There are people trained for that.'

'Okay,' said Ludwig. Papers again. 'Tell me why you're in Austria.'

'I've told you a hundred times.'

'You've lied to me a hundred times.'

'It's the truth.'

'Try again, Brano.'

'What do you want from me?'

Movement. Then a hand removed the burlap bag. He blinked, the light stinging his eyes, and looked down at the metal teeth digging into his nipples, the bruises around them, and the blood. He could no longer feel his chest.

Ludwig was on the sofa, and between them the coffee table was covered with scribbled pages ripped out of a notebook. He leaned forwards, elbows on his knees. 'I don't know why you're being so unreasonable. We all know you're not here because of a drunk peasant. You're here for another reason. And this reason has a name: Dijana Franković.'

Brano stared at him, unable to answer. After all the secrets spilled and networks made useless, Ludwig was asking about a matter of personal desire. Perhaps they thought she was part of his network, he didn't know. But bringing her up provoked that one thing Brano had been able to sidestep for three weeks. It was one of Cerny's dictums: *Never hate your enemy. Hatred means you underestimate; your hatred makes you blind.*

'Dijana Franković is connected to nothing. I can't explain it.' He inhaled, trying not to weep, his stomach knotting. 'Dijana Franković is an innocent. She just stumbled into the wrong man. She fell in love.'

Ludwig smiled doubtfully, the same smile Colonel Cerny gave him when he told Brano she was obviously a spy. 'Tell me, Brano. You were sent to follow Jan Soroka, to track his path. Why, then, once you knew you'd be picked up by us, didn't you arrest the Sorokas, or simply turn back?'

Brano was asking himself the same question. He took a deep breath, and the tight flesh on his rising chest began to ache. He'd had orders, but he could have interpreted them however he liked. 'Perhaps you're right,' he said.

'About what?'

'It wasn't just her in love with me.'

'I knew it!' Ludwig slapped his knee and turned to Karl. 'Didn't I tell you? All idealists are, beneath the surface, just romantics. Didn't I say that?'

Karl nodded.

Brano exhaled and closed his eyes. Then he opened them, blinking, but couldn't quite get the living room into focus. He felt very old.

19 March 1967, Sunday
He'd spent the last week sore and sleepless, fearing each night that when Ludwig came the next day, it would

166

be with Dijana Franković in tow, and he'd give way to the hatred that tugged at him. But when Ludwig arrived each morning, it was with a notebook and pen, and the questions continued. Until Sunday, when he brought a cardboard box. Brano shifted uncomfortably on the sofa. Ludwig set the box on the coffee table. 'Go ahead, Brano. Something for you.' Brano reached forwards and opened it.

Inside was a suit, slate grey jacket and trousers, and beneath, a pressed white shirt.

'Try it on. I guessed your measurements yesterday. Let's see how well I did.'

Ludwig had guessed perfectly. Despite the soreness in his nipples when he buttoned the shirt, each piece of clothing fit as if it had been measured for him, and the material was strong and very fine. Ludwig put his hand on his chin.

'Like new, Brano. Very good.'

'What now?'

'Now, we take you to your new home.'

They used the burlap bag again, and when it was removed they were making their way through farmland towards Vienna. It was the same car that had brought him in from the Fertő Lake, the grey Renault. Karl sat in the back seat with him while the tall guard drove. Ludwig, in the passenger seat, gazed ahead as the road widened and rose, the familiar cityscape coming into view.

'Where's my new home?'

Ludwig twisted back and winked. 'A surprise.'

They entered Vienna from the southeast, through the Simmering and Landstraße districts, then along the Ringstraße that circled the inner city, past the Stadtpark and the immense buildings of the Museum Quarter. Along Mariahilfer Straße, shopfronts loomed, the pavements packed. A left just before the Westbahnhof, a few more streets, then they parked.

'Not a bad area,' said Ludwig. 'You can do your shopping just up the road.'

'So I'm allowed to leave?'

'Leave?'

'My new home. You're not taking me to prison.'

Though he'd often smiled, this was the first time Ludwig laughed in Brano's presence, a choked sound from a red face. 'Christ, Brano. You've got an imagination.'

His new home was a quaint apartment building at number 25 Web-Gasse. White Secessionist women's faces looked down from a high floor.

'How long?'

'What?'

'How long are you going to let me stay here?'

'As long as you want, Brano. Just check in with us weekly – each meeting we'll renew your visa – and sometimes we can talk. Why should we treat you the way you treat people?'

'How do I treat people?'

'Just read the newspaper, Brano. Everyone knows what you guys do.'

Brano almost replied, but the week-old soreness beneath his shirt convinced him otherwise. His impulse was to give a list of agents who had been lost in Vienna over the last three years. Ignac Janke had turned up in a landfill outside town with burn marks covering his chest and two fingers missing. Alfonz Schmidt drowned, but from engine oil poured down his throat. Kristina Urban, the old Vienna *rezident*, at least experienced a moment of flight when she was thrown from that high window of the Hotel Inter-Continental. And last September, after returning to the Capital, Cerny told him that one of his three agents suspected of being GAVRILO, Theodore Kraus, had turned up at an Austrian farmhouse. He had somehow escaped his captors, though by that point he was blind and mute, the result of haphazard operations with a kitchen knife.

'There's a war on,' he said. 'None of us knows what to expect.'

The Austrian shrugged. 'You're right about that, Brano. Just consider yourself blessed.'

They took a rickety elevator to the fifth floor; then Karl placed Brano's suitcase just inside the barred door of number 3.

The apartment was large enough for a family – two bedrooms and a vast kitchen, a dining room filled with a huge polished table. Everything was stocked: food, furniture, linens; his clothes had even been hung in the wardrobe. It was unimaginably large compared to his twelfth-floor two-room in a concrete tower back in the Capital. 'Hope you don't mind the style,' said Ludwig.

'Doesn't matter.'

'Tell that to my wife.'

Karl seemed to think that was funny.

'No one lives on this floor, though some old folks are below you. They shouldn't be any trouble.'

'I'm sure they won't be.'

In the living room, by the twenty-inch television, Ludwig sat on the blue sofa. 'It's an easy deal, you can't deny it. Once a week you and I meet. Let's say Sunday, at one. Sound good?'

'Okay,' said Brano. 'Where?'

'Café Mozart on Albertinaplatz. You know it?'

'Of course I do.'

'Good. Café Mozart at one every Sunday.' He placed Brano's maroon passport on the coffee table. 'This has a one-week visa stamp. Each Sunday I'll give you a new one.

For that, you and I talk, and I don't do all the talking. You understand?'

'I understand.'

'If you're contacted by anyone – and I'm sure you will be at some time – you let me know. Okay?'

'Okay.'

'And you don't leave Vienna.'

'I expected that.'

'You should, Brano. Because we're giving you everything. Here,' he said, handing over a small stiff card with a long number on it. 'That's your account number at the Raiffeisenbank. Don't go crazy, now. We're just civil servants, after all.'

'Of course.'

'On the other side I've written my work number. For emergencies.'

'Okay.'

Karl took a ring of three keys out of his pocket and placed it on the coffee table. 'Any questions?' asked Ludwig.

Brano looked at Karl standing behind Ludwig, smiling, his hands clasped in front of himself. Then he focused on Ludwig. 'Why?'

Ludwig flared his nostrils and breathed loudly. 'Because, Brano, we're no fools. You'll only be of use to us when you're on the street. In a prison cell you're no use to anyone.'

'But why do you trust me?'

'Who ever said I did?' He forced a chuckle. 'Brano, I don't trust you at all. But consider this a job. Right? We've got enough unemployed in Vienna.'

He patted his thighs and stood up. He stuck out his hand.

Brano shook it.

Then Ludwig and Karl walked out the door.

For a while Brano stood in the empty living room, staring

at the door. He thought nothing, except that silence – the physical silence of an empty room – was a strange thing. Then he snatched the keys from the coffee table and locked the door.

He crept back past the sofa to the French windows. They were open, covered by translucent white curtains that stirred in the breeze. He tried to see the street but couldn't without leaning his head out to where it could be seen from below. So he parted the curtains and quickly peered down.

The space where they had parked was empty.

He looked again to be sure, then gazed down the length of the street – from Mariahilfer down to Gumpendorfer Straße – and saw only a few car roofs and some pedestrians, small from this height, going to and from their homes. His hands on the window frame shook, but not from elation. He knew that what he did not see still existed. To prove it to himself he walked over to the beige telephone that hung on the wall in the foyer, beside the bare coat-rack, and lifted the receiver to his ear. He hung up and repeated the procedure three times, each time recognizing that additional *click* of the phone tap he would have installed had he been them. Then he turned back to the living room, and in the fan-shaped overhead lamp, in the dials of the large television, in the electric clock hanging on the wall – in all these things he knew he had an enemy.

24 March 1967, Friday
Day 5. The Subject, it seems to this agent, is a man in love with ritual, with repetition. He rises at 6.30 each morning and makes one cup of coffee in his apartment, then showers and dresses. Around nine, with a book in hand, he strolls up Liniengasse to where it meets Gumpendorfer Straße, purchases a copy of Kurier *from a kiosk, then continues to Eszterházy Park. On a bench in the shadow*

of the flak tower, he skims the newspaper, then reads his book. (Purchased 21 March, but title not yet ascertained.) The morning's coffee runs through him, and he walks to a tree – the same one each day, three back from his bench – and urinates. (This agent hesitates to mention it, but this strikes him as evidence of the Subject's degraded social conscience – a result of the socialist mentality.) At noon, the Subject walks into the inner city, buying a sausage from a Würstelstand *and eating in the street – a different street each day – window-shopping and sometimes settling on a bench to watch passersby. Each evening, he finds a bar – again, a different one each day – and settles with his book or newspaper and a beer in the back corner, often ordering a schnitzel and fried potatoes for dinner. After two beers, he pays and returns to his apartment (never after 21.00), watches television, and goes to sleep.*

The only significant diversion from this routine occurred on Monday, 20 March (Day 1), when, at 11.00, the Subject entered the Raiffeisenbank at Michaelerplatz and withdrew a significant amount of money. He hides the schillings in an ice-cream box he keeps in the freezer.

'*Grüß Gott,*' said the waitress, a pretty blonde in a foolish-looking folk costume.

Brano placed his book on the table, facedown. '*Grüß Gott,*' he said. 'May I have a mélange?'

'Anything else?'

'Some water. Sparkling.'

He watched her weave around full tables to the pastry counter and give the order to a big man beside an espresso machine, who looked as if he ran the Espresso Arabia. Around him Brano heard German, French, Italian, and English. Children sat sullenly with their parents, who flipped through guidebooks. Through the window, Kohlmarkt was full of businessmen and tourists; leaning in a doorway, his shadow, a heavy man with a sunburn, wiped his nose.

Brano had lived under observation before. In West Berlin, he lived for months with the knowledge that he was being watched. The KGB, whether or not they were doing work in the interests of socialism, kept an eye on agents from both sides of the Curtain. It helped a man to stay on the correct path. Cerny had once joked that the Russians couldn't get anything done in Berlin because they used all their manpower to watch one another, and this was perhaps true.

But he had never quite got used to surveillance. It made even a man as self-conscious as Brano Sev more self-conscious, so that when he paused on a street corner, it felt like a pose, and when the second beer in a Viennese bar caused his head to tingle, he made a special effort to walk straight when he left, so that his shadows would have nothing of interest to report.

Over that first week he established a dull routine for his watchers' reports, wondering all the time if Ludwig really expected him to walk to the embassy on Ebendorferstraße, drag Josef Lochert outside, and announce that he was the local *rezident*. Maybe he did. Instead, Brano gave him tedium. That, within the confines of his comfortable imprisonment, was rebellion enough.

On the second day, Brano had purchased a book – *Stratégie Ouvrière et Néocapitalisme*, by André Gorz – visited his local park, and wandered the streets of Vienna. To avoid anything of interest, he hid his distaste for the monoliths of the old Habsburg regime, the equestrian statues and palaces from a time when even his own country was ruled from this capital. Although he sometimes paused to consider baskets of painted eggs sold by old women from the countryside, he spoke to no one save the occasional waitress.

The sunburned man followed him most days, and by

Wednesday he seemed to have caught a cold – he wiped his nose with the side of his hand all the way through the Volksgarten. Brano considered offering him his handkerchief, but instead stopped a moment by the Temple of Theseus, with its naked young man whose genitals were covered by a leaf. The concrete base read DER KRAFT UND SCHONHEIT UNSERER JUGEND. *The strength and beauty of our youth.*

It made as little sense to him then as it had seven months ago, waking up with a headache and no identity.

'Mélange,' said the waitress as she placed an Austrian caffe latte on the table. 'And water.'

'Thank you very much.'

The waitress began to turn, then paused, looking at the book on the table. 'Is that André Gorz?'

Brano tilted his head. 'It is.'

'I find his analyses a little weak, but he has some good ideas, don't you think?'

'I haven't read much yet.'

She squatted so her head was just above the table and lowered her voice. 'Maybe I don't know what I'm talking about, but I think in the end he's becoming too much of an apologist for capitalism. And of course they eat this up. Anyone who suggests that violent revolution isn't necessary is just not seeing things straight.'

'That's a good point,' said Brano. 'I'm not from here—'

'I know. Your accent.'

'Do you think Austria's ripe for revolution?'

'Oh, I wish!' She laughed expressively. 'But no. There's too much American money coming in. If Austria were left on its own, then recession would come, and there would be a move towards revolution. But everyone here thinks the Americans can do no wrong. As if they're saving us from some horrible fate.' She tapped the table with a long, red-painted fingernail. 'I was in Zagreb last year. No one can tell me those Yugoslavs are hating their lives. They own their own apartments. Half of them have bought a summer home on credit. I can't even afford my rent!'

'More people should travel.'

'You're not kidding.' The waitress glanced back, then stood up. 'I suppose I should get back, so I can pay my rent. Geez. What a scam.'

Brano smiled.

It was good to break the silence, good for his head. Days spent inside himself led to unreal perspectives. This was why the intelligence services of the world used silence to tame their subjects. Emotions became too acute, and paranoid suspicions became facts. This was what silence had done to Jakob Bieniek.

Brano found the waitress, paid for his coffee, and added a handsome tip.

'For the Revolution,' he said, and she winked at him conspiratorially.

His sunburned shadow followed him from the Espresso Arabia, down Kohlmarkt, and to a bus that brought them back to Mariahilfer, a few streets before his. Then he backtracked, turning down Theoboldgasse, thinking of betrayal.

He could not be sure, but a week of silence had begun to take its toll, undermining his conviction that he was less a victim than a pawn in a grandiose plan dreamed up by Yalta. All he could see was a series of betrayals. The Doctor had not done what he had promised outside Budapest, and Pavel Jast's betrayals were blatant. Captain Rasko, it turned out, was only interested in closing his little murder investigation as easily as possible, and, yes, he had even begun to trust Soroka – there were moments during that long ride through Hungary when he almost accepted that Jan simply had pity on his situation. Brano hated his own naïveté.

Most important, Colonel Laszlo Cerny had ignored the evidence Brano had collected on the Bieniek murder and had obviously been behind the Doctor's failure to appear at the Madai farm. He'd allowed Brano to be questioned with a car battery in an Austrian safe house for a month. Now, five days into his comfortable imprisonment, no messages had been left for him at the Eszterházy Park dead drop. He was beginning to suspect that Cerny, and therefore the Ministry, had abandoned him.

But he would continue, because there was nothing else left for him to do.

Brano paused at the corner of Eszterházy Park. His shadow stood at the other end of the block, wiping his nose again. Brano crossed the park and sat on his bench near the base of the enormous flak tower – a remnant of Hitler's last-ditch efforts to defend his Reich – then opened his book.

Capitalist planning exists for the express purpose of maintaining the existing social relationships and orientations, of consolidating capitalism by rationalizing it, and, by co-ordinating private and public decisions, of reducing the inherent risks . . .

But he was barely reading, distracted by the stiffness in his left pocket: the bent nail he'd extracted from the frame of his sofa that morning. Around it he had wrapped and taped a piece of paper on which was written a series of numbers that, when decoded, read WEB-GASSE 25, V/3 – B. SEV.

He stared blankly at the book for almost an hour, the *zbrka* of his thoughts keeping him warm, before he finally closed the book, stood up, and walked three trees behind his bench. He transferred the nail to his right pocket, the one he'd ripped a hole in, and unzipped his trousers. There were some Japanese tourists taking photographs of the flak tower, but they didn't notice him. As he urinated, he dropped the nail through his trouser leg and stamped it into the wet ground.

26 March 1967, Sunday

The Café Mozart was around the corner from the Hotel Sacher, at Albertinaplatz's crosscurrent of traffic, across from the Kapuzinerkirche's equestrian statue. Brano had walked the whole way into town, crossing empty streets and closed shopfronts. Even for a Sunday, Vienna seemed to have shut down. The vacant buildings of the Museum Quarter were stone sentries over an evacuated city. Only once did he spot a crowd, hovering outside a church, but he was running late and didn't want to investigate.

Brano paused in front of a pastry counter laden with Austrian sweets. The café was full, perhaps the only open place in town. Ludwig waved from the corner, where he sat with a small black briefcase beside his crossed legs. Brano passed four old women in mink stoles smoking at a round table as the Austrian rose to shake his hand. 'A very happy Easter to you, Brano.'

'Oh, so that's what it is.'

'What?' asked Ludwig as he waved to a waiter.

'Nothing.'

'Mélange good for you?'

'Of course.'

'One mélange,' he told the young black-and-white-suited waiter. 'And a small whisky.'

'It's early, Ludwig.'

'And it's a holiday. Tell me,' he said once the waiter had

left, 'how are you settling in? You look tired. There are bags under your eyes.'

Brano looked at himself in the bevelled mirror behind Ludwig's head; the Austrian was right. 'I'm not sleeping well.'

'Well, that's bad news. Loneliness can be a difficult thing.'

'I'm used to it.'

'Maybe we can set you up with some introductions.'

'I'll be fine.'

'What's that book you've got? None of my boys can figure out what it is.'

Brano showed him the cover of *Stratégie Ouvrière et Néocapitalisme*.

'Trying to start world revolution in France, Brano?'

'We have to start somewhere.'

'Did you bring your passport?'

Brano took it out of his jacket and handed it over.

From his briefcase, Ludwig took out a slip of paper, a stamp, an inkpad, and a stick of glue. He found a clean page in the passport, rubbed glue on it, and pressed the slip into the page with the side of his fist. Then he used the inkpad and stamp to place the blue seal of an eagle with ruptured shackles on the page. He waved the open passport like a fan. 'Any friends show up?'

'Friends?'

'Old friends. They're bound to find you soon.'

'No, no old friends.' Brano took back the passport. 'Have you received inquiries about me?'

'Your people seem to have counted you among their many losses. They're silent.'

'What about my other old friends?'

'Which ones?'

'The Sorokas.'

Ludwig peered out the window. 'I suppose it's no secret.

Their kid got a nasty cold after swimming that marsh. It's to be expected. He's in a London hospital now, while they wait for American visas.'

'Feel insulted?'

'That they didn't stay in Austria? No, we don't have the mystique of the New World.' He looked up as the waiter set down a whisky and a mélange, then raised his glass. 'To the people who do, surprisingly, prefer it here.' He knocked back the shot. 'You might hear from one of them.'

'Yes?'

'Fräulein Franković.'

To avoid betraying his feelings, Brano took a quick swallow that burned his tongue. 'She knows I'm in town?'

'We choose our secrets very carefully. Your presence in Vienna is not one. Anything you want to know?'

'About what?'

'About her.'

Brano shook his head and settled back into his chair. He wanted to know everything, but not from this man; instead he gazed out at the street, where his chubby, sunburned shadow was blowing his nose. 'He's not up to your regular standards, is he?'

'You get who you can these days.'

'How is Karl?'

When Ludwig slapped the table, his empty glass rattled. 'I knew you liked that guy! Karl worried you hated him because of that battery trick, but I told him – I said, *Karl, you're just too damn likable!'*

'Sure,' said Brano. 'He's a fine man.'

'Know why we're here, in the Café Mozart?'

'Because this is where you've installed the microphones.'

Ludwig shook his head. 'We can install microphones anywhere we like, Brano. No, it was for you. A little fun. Ever see the film *The Third Man*?'

179

'I've never been much for moving pictures.'

'Oh, you should be. One of these days they'll get rid of books, mark my words. But this particular film is a little about what we do.'

'It's about imprisoning people in apartments?'

'Not that literal, Brano. Come on. It's from just after the war, a kind of spy movie. Takes place in Vienna. And while Graham Greene was writing the script, he lived in the Hotel Sacher and came here each day to take notes. How do you like that?'

'Graham Greene,' said Brano. 'I believe he's a good friend of Kim Philby. Maybe I should see his film.'

Ludwig crossed his arms. 'Unfortunately, the place I'd rather take you has been closed since the war. The Café Central. I think you'd prefer it there. Your proletarian hero Comrade Trotsky used to play chess on those tables.'

Brano tapped the table with his fingertip. 'He's no hero of mine. Trotsky was a class traitor who deserved what he got in Mexico.'

Brano was pleased to see that the Austrian didn't know whether he should take the comment seriously. 'You know,' Ludwig said finally, 'something's bothering me.'

'What's that?'

'Our old dead body, Bertrand Richter.'

'I told you what I knew.'

'Of course you did. But we picked up the guy you said killed him. What was his name?'

'Erich Tobler on Hauptstraße.'

'Right, right. Well, the thing is, he's never heard of Bertrand Richter.'

'And you believe him.'

'I don't know what to believe, Brano. I'm of half a mind that you're the one who killed poor Bertrand. But Erich and I have more talks scheduled. We'll get to the bottom of it.'

180

'I'm sure you will, Ludwig. You know what you're doing.'

The smile returned, broad and toothy. 'You're quite a charmer today, Brano. It's nice to see that side. Go on. Enjoy the day.'

'I'm curious about something.'

'What's that?'

'It's Easter Sunday, and you're here with me. Don't you have a family to spend the day with?'

Ludwig's smile faded. 'I don't think we're here to discuss my personal life.'

Brano nodded at his empty coffee cup. 'Will the Second Republic take care of this?'

'Business expenses.'

'I guess that's one advantage.'

Ludwig squinted as Brano stood and picked up his book. Then he nodded as he got the joke.

Brano walked back home slowly, watching churches along the way spill the faithful into the empty streets. The sunburned shadow remained a half block away, leisurely wandering, and at Web-Gasse 25 Brano noticed a second shadow sitting in a new Volkswagen across the street. An old man with a thick, white moustache and beard, to compensate for his decaying hair. The old man looked vaguely familiar – perhaps a face from West Berlin. He watched Brano unlock his door and go inside but made no move.

Ludwig's shadows were more conspicuous by the minute.

Through the holes in his mailbox door he spotted a letter. He retrieved the unstamped envelope as an old woman nodded a *Grüß Gott* at him on her way out, and in the lift opened it. Inside was a yellow English-language pamphlet published by the 'Committee for Liberty in the Captive Nations', titled *A Communist War?* Below the title was the image of a hammer striking a sickle.

He opened his door, then went inside and locked it. He took the pamphlet to the living room and tilted it in the sunlight, looking for invisible indentations that weren't there. He sat on the sofa, smiling as he read, for it was clear then that Ludwig, or his bearded associate, did have a sense of humour after all.

A COMMUNIST WAR?

Dear Friend,
There is much talk these days of an impending war between Red China and the Soviet Union. Optimism, to be sure. Such an argument encourages the feeling among Leftist professors that détente with the Soviet Union is the best course of action, to prepare for a war against the Red Chinese. Is this truly the best course of action?

THE HYPOCRISY
What these communist/détente sympathizers forget is that war between two communist powers is, by their own logic, impossible. Communists believe war is caused by the retention of profit by a small group of capitalists, leading to the roller-coaster ride of inflation and depression. The moneymaking machine of war, they say, is the one thing that can repair a capitalist depression.

Therefore Communism, not burdened by profit, cannot lead to war.

The academics had better reread their hero, Karl Marx!

THEN WHY TENSION?
There are many reasons for the present tension between these two godless nations, and I will mention just a few:

1) The truth is that these two communist powers are, in fact, 'capitalist'. That is, a small group of men hold the wealth, leaving the great masses with next to nothing.
2) Just this year Brezhnev, the Soviet Communist leader, spoke angrily against Red China for blocking arms shipments to the North Vietnamese Communist aggressors. It seems that while both Brezhnev and Chairman Mao wish to 'bury' Capitalism, they cannot agree on the proper method.
3) The Soviet Union, desperate to keep its hold on World Communism, has united the Communist Parties throughout the world in an attempt to end the other, Chinese, form.

RABID DOGS!
What the Leftist professors will not tell anyone is that these are the precise reasons why détente must NOT be followed. At this moment we have two communist giants glaring at one another like rabid dogs, and this is when it is most important to ACT. The Captive Nations of Eastern Europe, so long under the boot of the Soviet Menace, must be set free of their chains!

Be one with us, and appeal to President Johnson to push forwards efforts to roll back the Iron Curtain.

God bless America.

Dr Ned Rathbone
The Committee for Liberty in the Captive Nations
December 18, 1966

30 March 1967, Thursday
Day 11. The Subject began Thursday with the same routine as previous days. The Subject's regularity has been a source of surprise, only interrupted by occasional visits to bookshops (often

loitering in the political section). This agent has, however, noted an increased level of drinking. The Subject's one or two evening beers have turned into two beers at a bar, followed by a bottle of wine from his 24-hour local, brought back home to drink in front of the television.

Perhaps the drinking explains the acts of 30 March.

This agent stood beside the flak tower at the corner of Eszterházy Park as the Subject read on his usual bench and, at noon, urinated on his usual tree. Rather than returning to his seat, he walked down Windmühl to Fillegradergasse, then, just before the Hotel Terminus, jogged up the steps leading to Theobaldgasse, turning left on Mariahilfer (effectively doubling back on himself). This agent, fearing he would lose contact, jogged as well. The Subject turned right at Stiftgasse, then took another right on Siebensterngasse. This agent rounded the corner as well, but found the Subject staring at him through the rear windshield of a taxi that was pulling away.

This agent immediately telephoned his superiors.

'Innere Stadt, you said?'

'Yes. The centre.'

'But where in the centre?'

Brano looked back at the sunburned man dwindling to insignificance. 'Turn here. Right. Then go to the Westbahnhof.'

'Westbahnhof? That's not in the centre!'

'Please, just do it.'

Brano paid the driver and jogged into the modern, airy train station. There were three people in line at the ticket counter. The heavy woman in front of him wore a kerchief around her head and leaned on a cheap, heavy bag, much like the fat provincial women of Bóbrka, sweating beneath too many layers of skirt. Soon he was at the window.

'Salzburg,' he said. 'First class.'

The clerk looked at a list of cities and numbers on the wall. 'It's leaving right now.'

'I'll make it.'

'I doubt it.'

'Just let me worry about that.' Brano glanced behind himself, then handed over his money.

Ticket in hand, he ran up the stairs to the second level and paused, looking back again through the windows that covered the front of the Westbahnhof, his thumping heart reminding him he was old for this kind of action.

Then he spotted it: the grey Renault that parked along Europaplatz. Two men bolted out the back and across the concrete towards the station.

Instead of approaching the platforms, he exited left beneath a sign that said FELBERSTRAßE. He jogged through the station's car park, north along a back street, then, panting, caught a tram along Lerchenfelder Gürtel. The tram was tight with warm Viennese, and when he began to laugh involuntarily, many turned to look at him.

He got off at Gablenzgasse and returned on foot, taking the narrow backstreets overlooked by dirty buildings and shops, until he was back at the corner of Tannengasse and Felberstraße. Across the street an old woman moved slowly with her cane; on his side a drunk counted coins. *'Fünfundsechzig . . . siebzig.'* When the woman had finally made it to her door and the drunk had shuffled past and disappeared around the corner, Brano turned to face the wall.

He counted three bricks from the bottom, then five bricks from the edge. The brick left grey marks on his fingers, and he had to use a key from his pocket to loosen it, but after a minute he was able to pull it out of the wall.

The back of the brick had been chiselled away, so that a

small space remained between it and the next layer of brick. In that space lay a ring with two keys.

Number 20 Felberstraße was covered with a fine layer of soot from the train yard across the street. The tiles in the wall of the foyer had cracked a long time ago, and in those gaps spiders built webs. As he entered the second set of doors, an old man leaving the lift held it open for him. *'Grüß Gott,'* they said to one another.

It was a small wooden lift from before the First World War, with the name of a Budapest company on the plaque above the buttons. At the third floor he got out and closed the doors behind himself; the lift returned to the ground floor on its own.

The apartment was to the left, and in the dark corridor he leaned close and listened, then used the key.

During his time as *rezident*, safe houses had been minimalist affairs – a mattress and a telephone. Nothing else was required. But Josef Lochert, it seemed, had taken it upon himself to decorate. He stood in a comfortable living room not so different from the one where he'd been imprisoned in the suburbs. A sofa covered with a lace blanket sat across from a television, and a china cabinet held trinkets of a life that was still being lived.

Then he understood.

'Peter?'

He looked towards the closed bedroom door.

'Peter?' the woman's voice repeated. 'Peter, you didn't forget my chocolate, did you?'

Brano stepped back towards the front door and opened it.

'Peter, you better answer me now, you understand?'

On his way out to the street, he passed a fifteen-year-old with a large bar of chocolate in his hand. Brano smiled at the boy, who looked back curiously.

*   *   *

Further north, Brano found a post office with a row of public telephone booths. He approached the woman at the desk and asked if he could place an international call. She accepted his deposit of schillings and the telephone number, and told him to wait in booth number 5.

He went in and leaned against the glass door, looking out at Viennese talking into their phones, Viennese in line to buy stamps, and sullen Viennese women behind the counters who took envelopes and gave out change.

The telephone rang.

'Hello?'

There was a series of clicks, followed by a long hiss through which he could barely hear a telephone ringing. Then a faint woman's voice, in his language, said, 'Importation Register, First District.'

'Regina, it's Brano.'

'Hello?'

He raised his voice. 'Regina! It's Brano!'

'Oh, Brano! Where are you?'

He sighed, wanting only to listen to Regina Haliniak's comforting provincial accent. But he said, 'I don't have time to talk. Can I speak to the Comrade Colonel?'

'Colonel Cerny?'

'Yes.'

'One minute.'

The phone clicked four times, then began ringing again.

'Brano? You're on a clean line?'

'Public telephone, I think it's clean. The Felberstraße safe house is no longer safe. Lochert must have sold it for another.'

'Right,' said Cerny. 'Where are you?'

'Where do you think?'

'Don't be smart.'

'I'm not being smart, Comrade Colonel. You've kept me

in the dark. You wanted me in Austria from the beginning, didn't you?'

He heard Cerny's long sigh as static. 'Brano, everything has gone to plan. Now hang up and return to your flat on Web-Gasse and await further instructions.'

He almost didn't say the words, but they'd come to him so many times over the last week and a half that by now there was no holding them back. 'Have you abandoned me?'

Another pause. Brano glanced up at the man in the next booth, who was sinking down the wall, crying into his telephone. Cerny said, 'Comrade Sev, you will receive your orders when I want you to receive them. Is that understood?'

'Yes, Comrade Colonel. I just felt –'

'I don't care about your feelings, Brano. Not at this moment. I care about the security of socialism. You'll learn everything you need to learn, but only when you need to learn it. And stay away from our embassy – your presence is not their business. Are you reading the *Kurier*?'

'Every day, Comrade Colonel.'

'Good, Brano.' His voice lowered. 'Just tell me that everything's all right. You're not hurt?'

'No.'

'You're under observation?'

'Yes, but I've broken away.'

'Not for long, I hope.'

'No, Comrade Colonel.'

'Is there anything else you need?'

'Need?'

'Yes.'

'No,' said Brano. The man in the next booth had hung up the phone but was still in the booth, on the floor, weeping.

'Okay, Brano. My only order for you now is this—'

'What?'

'Be patient.' Then the line went dead.

The grey Renault pulled alongside him four hours later, as the sun was descending behind the Hofburg Palace. He heard the engine rumbling, then a squeaky window rolling down. Ludwig's voice: 'Come on now, Brano. Take a rest, why don't you?'

The car pulled a little in front of him and stopped. Karl stepped out of the back and touched the brim of his hat.

Ludwig's head popped out of the passenger window. 'Enough. Now get in.'

Brano climbed into the back seat, and Karl followed him inside.

They turned right onto the Ringstraße and rode without speaking for a while, the driver, Karl, and Ludwig preferring to gaze out the windows at their capital.

'You like Vienna, Brano?' Ludwig didn't look back when he asked it.

'It's a nice city.'

'It's a big city with a lot of history, and that's why we get all these damned tourists. Not that I mind so much – if it wasn't for tourist money we'd have more war ruins – but sometimes you don't want to see crowds of Japanese with their little cameras. Know what I mean?'

'Did you pick me up to talk about tourism, Ludwig?'

'It'll get me as far as any other subject.'

'Try me.'

Ludwig turned in his seat. 'How about hospitality, Brano? You're a guest in our lovely city. That's agreed, isn't it?'

'Sure.'

189

'And I don't think you could really call us bad hosts, could you? Apartment, money, the freedom to move around – that's not so bad, is it?'

'It's very fine,' said Brano. Despite everything, he found himself admiring Ludwig. His insistent good humour was a rare thing in their business, and sometimes Brano could even imagine liking the inept Austrian. In another life, perhaps. In another war.

'So you can imagine our frustration when it turns out our guest isn't being polite. When he in fact tries to send us to Salzburg to make fools of us. Can you imagine our frustration?'

Somewhere along the way, they had turned around and were driving in the opposite direction. 'I can imagine that,' said Brano.

Karl was looking out the window, smiling.

'Listen,' said Ludwig. 'I'm not going to try to be discreet about this. If you keep this up, we're going to take you out into the suburbs and fire up our battery again.'

Brano didn't answer.

'But, hey, none of us wants to do that. Right, Karl?'

Karl nodded at the window.

'So where were you?'

'Here and there.'

'You were gone almost five hours.'

Brano stared at his hands, which looked very small in this light. 'I was at the Espresso Arabia, on Kohlmarkt, for the first couple hours.'

'And what were you doing?'

'I read the newspaper a little, but in general I was enjoying myself. The coffee there is very good.'

Karl sniffed.

'And then?' said Ludwig.

'And then the Espresso Josefstüberl.'

'On Alser Straße.'

'That's the one.'

'Again, just reading?'

Brano nodded.

'Anything of interest in the news?'

'I was learning more about the recent coup in Sierra Leone. And it seems they're unable to sink the *Torrey Canyon* oil tanker. The Scottish coast is covered in oil.'

'Anything else?'

'Yes,' said Brano. 'There have been more protests in America against Johnson's imperialist war in Vietnam.'

Ludwig stared at him a moment. 'We'll check on those cafés, you understand? I don't want to find out you've been lying to me.'

'Anke, the waitress at the Arabia, should remember me. We had a nice discussion.'

'About what?'

'About the demise of capitalism.'

Ludwig looked ahead a moment. 'So now can you tell me why?'

'Why?'

'Why you're acting like a spoiled child.'

Karl was watching the enormous Natural History Museum slide by.

'I suppose I'm bored.'

'Bored?'

Karl turned to look at him.

'I've been here a while, and I've only talked to you. How else am I supposed to feel?'

Ludwig pursed his lips. 'Well, what do you think of that, Karl?'

Karl shrugged.

'I told you this before, Brano. You need to meet people. Who doesn't? Maybe some of your own kind?'

'My kind?'

'I don't mean spies, Brano. I mean your own countrymen.'

'Maybe.'

'I'll tell you what. You go over to Sterngasse. You know where that is?'

'I can find it on the map.'

'Good, good. There's a bar there. The Carp. Maybe you've heard of it?'

'I think I've heard of it.'

'Well, you go there, and I assure you you'll make friends.'

'Okay,' said Brano.

'You'll give it a try?'

'I will.'

'Good, good. You make some friends and try to be nice. Is it a deal?'

'Okay.'

Ludwig smiled finally. 'Because I know that Karl, for one, doesn't want to have to put those clips on your tits again. Do you, Karl?'

Karl shrugged and stared out the window.

31 March 1967, Friday

Of course he knew the Carp. It was a dingy place in the narrow maze of Vienna's old fishing district – on Sterngasse, off Desider Friedmannplatz. He knew what and where it was, though he'd avoided it personally. He'd instead sent his informants into its dark interior to listen to the exiles' stories of dissatisfaction. Ingrid Petritsch had been one of his better informants; she could manoeuvre herself among the barstools and flirt the information out of any man, because the exiles would say anything to impress a beautiful woman. They would always explain to her, as if to a child, that their own capital was superior to cold Vienna, though none of them had the courage to return home. Then Ingrid would touch their arms and ask for more.

But Ingrid, after Bertrand Richter's death, decided she'd had enough. Cerny had told him this over drinks. She married an English businessman and was now living in London. *A goddamned waste,* he'd said. *She won't even talk to our local man now.*

In the morning he woke later than usual and did not bother with Eszterházy Park. Instead, he picked up a *Kurier* and took it east, to the vast grounds of the Schönbrunn Palace, where, when he wasn't reading the newspaper's personals, he gazed at squares of black soil in the enormous gardens being tended by workers in preparation for spring. He mixed with a busload of Italians who shouted at their wives and children, then stopped beside a Grecian sculpture and stared at the crisp blue sky, where a single unformed cloud floated.

At sunset, he took the tram back into town, to Schwedenplatz by the Danube, then found Sterngasse. It was a short pedestrian street ending in stairs, dirty by Viennese standards but relatively clean to Brano's eyes. Arched above the door was a wooden carp, silver paint peeling off its ribs.

There were only a few customers this early, so Brano settled at the bar. The black-haired barmaid, a woman of about sixty, smoked beside a wall of palinkas and vodkas, reading a newspaper. She wore large hoop earrings. Behind the bottles, a large mirrored wall allowed him to see his own tired face. In the corner, a wide, glowing jukebox played jazz music.

'*Guten Abend,*' she said when she noticed him.

'Good evening.'

She smiled. 'One of our boys. What can I get you?'

He rapped the counter with a knuckle. 'A beer, I think.'

Her name was Monika, and she asked how long had he been here, where was he from, and was he going to stay?

He nodded morosely into his glass, as if he really were one of them.

'Don't worry, dear.' She placed a callused hand on his wrist. 'It gets better.'

He looked at her.

'You did the right thing,' she said. 'You came here. It's all going to change from this point on.'

'That's good news.'

For the next hour, he drank while Monika asked the occasional question – not probing, just to show she was interested. She seemed to respect his vague answers, because she had been around long enough to know that not all exiles wanted to regale the world with stories of their escapes. When she asked what he did for a living, he paused. He would have liked, at that moment, to speak of one of the elaborate pasts he'd toyed with in the Schönbrunn gardens, but one never knew who would walk through the door and prove him wrong. He didn't know how long he'd be here, and with each week the chances of being discovered would multiply. He said, 'I was a spy.'

She stopped wiping the glass in her hand. 'You're kidding.'

'I finally saw the error of my ways.'

'You're not pulling my leg?'

'I wish I was.'

'What did you do?'

Spies come in different flavours, and Brano chose the blandest. 'I worked in the Metropol, mostly. I spent time with Western businessmen and passed on what I learned.'

'To Yalta?'

Brano nodded.

She put down the glass. 'That's the last thing I'd expect someone to admit. So it must be true.'

A low-level operative – really, a mere informer – was an easy cover to maintain. No records were kept on such people, and while it was an embarrassing thing to admit, it was better than the complete truth. He smiled at Monika – a shy, embarrassed smile – and said, 'It's not the kind of thing I'd want to advertise, but I should come clean about it sooner rather than later.'

Then the noise began, in the form of a short blond man who stomped through the doors and shouted in German, 'Where the fuck is he, huh? Where the fuck is that useless bastard?'

Monika raised her voice. 'Don't shout in my bar, Ersek.'

Ersek's watery eyes blinked at her a few times. 'Just tell me where the fuck Sasha is.'

'I haven't seen him all day.'

'Don't give me that, Monika. You're protecting him.'

'You're a paranoid man. Have a beer and shut up.'

Ersek looked around the bar, then grunted and climbed onto a stool. He nodded at Brano and accepted a beer from Monika. She said, 'You better stay calm in my place or I'll kick you out.'

Ersek smiled, lips wet. 'No you won't.'

She winked at Brano. 'On top of being a pain in the ass, this guy's *Norwegian*. Don't know why I let him in here.'

'Because I publish half your clientele.' He turned to Brano, his high voice warbling. 'You'd think there would be some appreciation, wouldn't you? A guy from Oslo starts printing up all the half-intelligible mutterings of these barely evolved people, and what does he get for it? He gets a guy like Sasha who doesn't turn in anything because he's *meditating* on his compositions. Tell me, back in your country is "meditating" a euphemism for "drinking"?'

'Sometimes it is,' said Brano.

'Well, then, I won't start printing your stuff, either.'

'Meet Ersek Nanz,' said Monika.

Ersek stuck out a cold palm, and Brano took it. 'Brano Sev.'

'You're new?'

'A couple of weeks old.'

'You're not a writer, are you?'

'Not at all.'

'No,' Monika said under her breath. 'He isn't.'

'Good.' He took a swill of beer. 'People seem to think that being oppressed is the only qualification you need to be a writer.'

'Sometimes it's enough to give you a story to tell,' said Monika.

'But you have to know how to *write* it.'

'Then why do you bother?' asked Brano.

Ersek looked at him. 'Huh?'

'Why waste your time with bad writers?'

Ersek blinked a few times, and when he spoke he almost whispered. 'Because Monika's right. Someone's got to get their stories out.'

'Then stop complaining.'

'Your second one's on me,' said Monika.

Ersek tilted his head, paused, then moved his stool closer as Monika placed another beer on the counter. He'd been a publisher here, he told Brano, for the last five years. 'A guy told me it was an easy gold mine. I think he was trying to ruin me.' The idea had been that there was no reputable publisher printing first-person accounts of Eastern Europeans who had fled to the West; the only publishers were receiving funds from the CIA, 'making crappy propaganda'. Ersek shrugged. 'And it made sense to me. You've got a ready market in all these exiles, wanting to hear their own stories. But you know what I didn't take into account?'

'What?'

'Exiles are cheapskates. That's what they are, down to the last man. And in the end, they don't give a damn about their fellow exiles.'

'Is that really true?'

'Take it from me, friend. I've seen them all.'

And he had. He'd published many names Brano had heard before in the Ministry. There was Bálint Urban, who fled just after the war and wrote narrative poems about wartime misery. Stanislaus Zambra, 'like most of these guys', was obsessed with a single event that he re-created in each novel; for him, it was the murder of his sister in 1961 in the prison beneath Yalta Boulevard, committed while he was in the same cell, watching.

'I don't know why I bother with Sasha Lytvyn, though. Even when he's sober his writing isn't all that great.'

Brano leaned forwards. 'Sasha Lytvyn?'

'You know him?'

Brano shook his head, but he did know Sasha. He'd last seen him over a decade ago, in the early fifties, when Sasha Lytvyn parachuted with a partner into the forests north of Sárospatak with a pistol, a map, and a shortwave radio transceiver. He had been recruited by the benignly named Office of Policy Coordination, which, under the Truman administration, carried out a clandestine war, parachuting recent émigrés back into the East in order to foment revolution. That CIA office had built its army from the ranks of the displaced persons camps of postwar Europe, trained them in sabotage, and tossed them out of aeroplanes.

But almost nothing they did was secret, at least to the East. The Office of Policy Coordination was riddled with leaks, including the famous Kim Philby; and in the end its leader, Frank Wisner, had a mental breakdown, living out his final years with the English until paranoia and mania finally led him to end his own life two years ago.

That evening in 1952, Brano had been on the reception committee when Lytvyn and his partner descended through the birches into a ring of well-informed soldiers. He'd been an amiable prisoner, answering questions with the carefully constructed cover story Brano and his associates had already been briefed on. But, with time, Lytvyn did deliver his secrets, as they always do; his partner, however, didn't survive the interrogation. Once it was over, Lytvyn was put to work in the eastern mines. Then, like many, he was released in the ill-planned amnesties of 1956. After that, he must have found his way here.

'He's got a lot of stories,' said Ersek. 'But these stories have made him a dribbling wreck of a man.'

'I imagine,' said Brano. 'Who's the best?'

Ersek didn't hesitate. 'Filip, hands down. Filip Lutz. You heard of him?'

Brano, smiling slightly, shook his head.

'But even the great Filip Lutz,' said Ersek, 'even he suffers from the condition all these exiles share.'

'What's that?'

'Insufferable goddamned nostalgia.'

And as if on cue, someone put a coin into the jukebox and the bar was filled with a melody Brano knew, played on strings, the prewar national anthem that had been banned in 1947. A couple of drunks in the back stood up on wobbly legs, glassy-eyed, and placed their hats over their hearts.

2 April 1967, Sunday
'What do you think, Brano?' Ludwig spoke today without inflection.

'About what?'

198

'The Carp. You spent a long time there Friday night, talked to a lot of people.'

'It's good to talk with your own kind sometimes.'

'Any of them old friends?'

'I did recognize a couple of faces, but I don't think I ever knew them.'

'And no one approached you.'

'Just to introduce themselves. We're a polite people.'

Ludwig nodded into his whisky. 'But you did it the smart way.'

'Smart?'

'You told them the truth. Or a kind of truth. It surprised me at first – I thought you'd arrange some innocuous cover.'

'Too complicated,' said Brano. 'Thanks for the mail, by the way.'

'Mail?'

Brano reached into his pocket and brought out the pamphlet *A Communist War?* Ludwig raised his eyebrows as he accepted it.

'Your reading materials are improving, Brano.'

'You didn't put it in my mailbox?'

Ludwig shook his head, smiling as he read. 'The Committee for Liberty in the Captive Nations? When I give you political tracts, they won't be from American fundamentalists.' He shook his head. 'Maybe Friedrich did it. He's quite the churchgoer. But these people . . .'

'What about them?'

Ludwig handed back the pamphlet. 'Unimportant. They want a war to eradicate communism. Not a cold war, but a hot one.'

'Everyone has an opinion.'

Ludwig nodded.

'Tell me something,' said Brano. 'Why did you bring me here?'

'To the Mozart?'

'To Austria. I don't have much useful information for you, and we both know my people won't contact me while you're watching. You're spending a lot of resources on an operation with little payback. It doesn't make sense.'

Ludwig emptied the whisky into his mouth and signalled the waiter for another. 'What makes you think we were responsible for bringing you here?'

'I know the Americans arranged it – Jan Soroka went to their embassy – but I haven't seen an American since I arrived. Just you.'

Ludwig shrugged. 'All I had to do was clear our side of the border and share the information on Hungarian border movements – times and locations – so you and the Sorokas could walk through. Pretty easy. In return, I got you.'

'For how long?'

'That's for me to know, Brano. Let's change the subject, shall we?'

'As you like.'

'Remember Erich Tobler on Hauptstraße?'

'Of course.'

'Well, we've had a pretty extensive talk with him. At first he said he didn't know Bertrand Richter. He'd never heard of the guy.'

'I remember.'

'He stuck to his story a long time.'

'So he's stronger than you thought.'

'Well, not so strong.'

'No?'

'We became a little inventive with him, coming up with persuasions. And, finally, he did admit to the murder.'

'Then what's the problem?'

'The problem is, Brano, I don't believe him. He doesn't know any of the details of the killing. He can't verify a thing.'

Brano put his chin in his hand. Ludwig looked very tired, as if he'd spent the whole week working on poor Erich Tobler. 'You know,' he said, 'I once interrogated a man in East Berlin, at the Gedenkstätte Hohenschönhausen.'

'The Stasi's interrogation centre.'

'Yes. We suspected he had killed one of our men not far from the Brandenburg Gate. He told us he didn't even know the man. Then, after a while, he told us everything. He had killed the man, and he offered details of the killing. As with Erich, the facts didn't match, and we were sure he was just giving us what we wanted to hear so the interrogation would end. But we were wrong. He'd planned everything; he'd had his layers of cover carefully set up. After we let him go, he killed another of our operatives – this time there were witnesses – and . . .'

'The man you told me about. The one you killed.'

Brano shrugged.

Ludwig accepted a fresh whisky from the waiter and held it beneath his chin. 'Unfortunately, we can't follow the matter any further with Tobler.'

'He's dead?'

'Let's just say he's disappeared.'

The jukebox was playing very loud rock-and-roll music. Brano didn't recognize the tune, and he didn't think he wanted to know it. Ersek Nanz was at the bar with a fat man who needed a shave. Ersek swivelled on his stool, already drunk, though it was only eight. 'The mysterious Brano Sev. Where have you been?'

'Here and there.'

The fat man turned in his chair to look at Brano, using thumb and forefinger to adjust his wire-rimmed glasses, while his other hand clutched a newspaper.

'Meet my best and brightest,' said Ersek. 'Filip Lutz.'

Filip Lutz cocked his head and stuck out a big, wobbly hand as Ersek leaned close and whispered something into his ear. Lutz's eyes widened. 'The spy?'

'Ex-spy,' said Brano. He'd expected Monika would spread the word, but he hadn't expected it to come back to him so soon.

Lutz wouldn't release his hand. 'We, my man, must have a talk when I'm sober. I want to know your whole story.'

'It's not very interesting.'

'They're all interesting,' he said, letting go finally and waving to signify the entire bar. 'All of them. I'm collecting stories from everyone, for a new book, called *Escape from the Crocodile*.'

'Crocodile?'

'You know that nightclub in the Capital? The one all the Russians go to?'

'Ah,' said Brano. 'I see now.'

'Not bad, eh?'

'Not bad at all,' Brano lied.

'Tomorrow, you come to the Café-Restaurant Landtmann – you know it? By the Burgtheatre.'

'I know it.'

'That's my office. Can't stand to make my own coffee. You come by any time you like and tell me your story. It's a deal?'

'It's a deal.'

'Monika,' said Ersek, 'set our friend up with a palinka.'

'Did you see this?' asked Lutz. He handed over yesterday's *Kronen Zeitung* and pointed at a photo on the front page of four young men with outlandish scarves around their necks walking away from an aeroplane. The headline: ROLLING STONES EHER ZAHMER.

'They're a musical group, aren't they?' asked Brano.

Lutz glanced at Ersek, then laughed. 'You really haven't been out long, have you?'

Brano shrugged, which allowed Lutz the opportunity to launch into a monologue on the cultural relevance of the Rolling Stones' appearance in Vienna. 'It's the new generation making itself heard. And it doesn't matter how poorly these kids play their instruments. They're becoming the mouthpiece of the world.'

Ersek said, 'I give rock and roll five more years at most. At *most*.'

Brano's palinka arrived, and Lutz proposed a toast to the children of the world, but Ersek refused.

'They want to destroy European culture, and I can't toast that.'

'They are European culture,' said Lutz.

'My sister,' said Brano, 'thinks European culture is Christianity.'

'Isn't it?' asked Ersek.

'They call it the Dark Ages for a reason,' Brano said.

'You're right,' said Lutz. He looked at Ersek. 'He's right. Christianity just slowed culture down.'

'Exactly,' said Brano.

'It was capitalism that got Europe on its feet again.'

Brano looked at him.

'Burgeoning middle class and all that. Who do you think commissioned the best painters of the Renaissance, Nanzi?'

Ersek shook his head. 'Christ, I don't care. Let's just toast something. How about your new car?'

Lutz raised his glass. 'To my Fiat Dino. The most stylish creature to ever grace the motorways of Europe.'

Brano drank with them, lipping the bitter brandy. He cleared his throat. 'Is it really so lucrative?'

Lutz furrowed his brow.

'Collecting exiles' stories. A new sports car can't be cheap.'

'I'm a busy man. I write my column for *Kurier*. Maybe you've read it.'

'Once or twice, yes.'

'I've got other projects in the works, though, more *active* journalism.'

'*Shh*,' said Ersek. 'The secret works of a mad genius.' He raised his glass to Filip Lutz's mad genius.

Lutz winked at him. 'I'm going to shake up a few Politburo lackeys before I'm done.'

'Oh?' said Brano. 'How are you going to do that?'

Filip Lutz shrugged, the first and last sign of modesty that night. 'You, like Ersek, will know when the rest of the world knows.'

'The whole world?' asked Brano. 'You're an ambitious man, Filip Lutz.'

'The only man in this bar,' said Ersek, 'whose ambition matches his ability.'

'Come on, boys. I'm turning red now.'

So Ersek returned to his favourite subject, the incompetence of writers from their country, though Lutz shook his head. 'You've never been there, Nanzi. You don't understand where these people come from.'

'I don't understand? Are you telling *me* I don't understand?'

'Did you know,' said Lutz, 'that the Americans have invented an oven that doesn't use heat? It uses radiation – *micro*waves. That's a culture worth studying, Nanzi. I don't know why you bother with us.'

Ersek waved for another palinka. 'An atomic bomb to fry a chicken?'

'They're a bright people,' said Brano.

The jukebox was playing the old national anthem again. Lutz stared into his empty glass, then slid off the stool and stood rigidly, hands by his sides, and began murmuring the words.

> *Look! Look! The hawk is flying low.*
> *From the Carpat to the steppes, he marks his territory.*

Ersek winked at Brano. 'Are you busy this Friday?'
'I'm never busy these days.'

> *The borders are ringed with fire!*

'I'm having a party at my place, and you're most definitely invited. Time to get some new blood into this dull scene.'

Brano thanked him for the invitation. When he looked back, he saw tears spilling from Lutz's baggy eyelids as his lips worked out the words.

> *But we'd burn our great Tisa*
> *Before we'd forsake our Land!*

5 April 1967, Wednesday

Perhaps because of Ludwig's encouragement, on Wednesday Brano watched a film, an English film. It was dubbed into German and concerned an English spy who wore horn-rimmed glasses. From what he understood, the spy was in fact a thief who had been coerced into working for the queen under the threat of being returned to prison. He didn't know if this was the filmmaker's criticism of British intelligence services or simply narrative flavour.

Most of the action took place in Berlin, which was part of the title; some scenes were set along the Wall. He'd seen the Wall up close enough to know these scenes were filmed in a studio, but the effect was not bad. There was a Russian general who reminded him of the Comrade Lieutenant General he'd known before his last return from Vienna – all jokes, drinks, and backslapping, which cloaked his darker intentions. In fact, some of the more opaque scenes seemed, in retrospect, to have been comic, but Brano was unable to quite find the humour in them at the time.

Although he did not want to return to the Carp, he felt it was his duty. He was in a foreign city, and his only order – from both the Austrians and Cerny – was to wait. And there was always the possibility that useful information would pass by him, so he should be there to pick it up.

The world of the affluent political exile, it seemed to Brano, was cursed by two deficiencies: its miniscule size and its inflated sense of self-importance. While a great city surrounded them – be it West Berlin or Tel Aviv or Vienna – the exiles consistently walled themselves off from their new homes in well-heated bars and cafés and dinner parties, and occasional visits to the brothels; expatriate communities were always very masculine. In these small ponds, medium-sized fish seemed enormous, and the largest were those with the most fluid tongues. And because they lived outside their native language and country, these exiles no longer felt responsible for what they said. They lived entrenched in their narrow-minded theories and petty jealousies, never quite part of the real world. So they spoke endlessly, adapting to the quick-step of empty dialogue. And any words they uttered were assumed to be as valuable as a piece of china, pristine and vague.

Of course, for Brano Sev there was a level of insecurity beneath his harsh judgement. Linguistic cleverness had never been his strong trait, and he could remember many times in West Berlin falling silent as his fat acquaintances spoke over him, provoking laughter and table slaps. When

Brano chose to speak, there was seldom a reaction. Silence, maybe; sometimes a nod of agreement. But only rarely laughter, for Brano had never been, and never would be, an entertainer.

He considered this as he walked from the cinema to the Carp. Why would he never feel part of these expatriate cliques? Was it really that he had no humour about him, that he was always heavy, without the idle buoyancy that makes a born entertainer?

But this was not the right question for him to ask himself, and he soon realized this. The real question was, Why should he care?

He mounted the stairs at Sterngasse as the sun was beginning to set and understood why he cared. When he was with the exiles, he felt as if his documents and rank and even the medals he'd garnered over the years were just pieces of paper and iron. It was as if he, like them, had just been born when he entered the West and now had to start all over again. It was as if the scars and sweat of his long past were no longer of any consequence.

Monika served him beer, then settled her elbows on the bar. 'How are you making out?'

'It's a difficult transition.'

'Of course it is.' She lit a cigarette. 'The thing I've noticed over the past twenty years is that those who do well are those who recognize the situation.'

'How do you mean?'

She took a drag and considered her words. 'Well, we're all in a foreign country. We didn't choose to come here because we're in love with Austria. We came because it was convenient. Maybe we want to be back home, maybe we don't. It doesn't matter. The thing is, we're all here for the same reason.'

'What's that?'

'We're all running away from something. That's the only reason anyone leaves his home.'

Brano sipped his beer and looked into the mirror. Behind him, two old men played backgammon by the wall. 'I know someone who left Yugoslavia. She wasn't running from anything. She simply decided she didn't want to be in that country any more. She told me that it had become a country of losers, and she didn't want to become a loser herself.'

Monika shrugged. 'And what's that? She was running away from boredom or emptiness or whatever. And if she's been here long enough, she's probably come to terms with the fact that she can't escape any of those things. Certainly not here. You know what's interesting?'

'What?'

'Ask anyone around here for their story. Ask what happened to them. If they just arrived, you'll find that their story goes on for a long time, with details on top of details, and you can watch them get upset – I mean, visibly – as they tell it to you. Ask someone who's been here a few years, and they'll have it condensed down to a sentence, maybe two, and that's it.'

'Interesting.'

'It's inevitable,' she said, then put out her cigarette. 'Over here, your past is just a story. It gets smaller with time, until it's just a haiku. Until it's got no more emotion in it.'

'Until it's cold.'

'Until your past can't touch you any more,' said Monika. 'Watch out you don't turn cold, too.'

Rather than wait for the cold exiles to fill the bar, Brano returned home. He was unsurprised by another piece of propaganda in his mailbox. The Committee for Liberty in the Captive Nations explained that, because of its godless nature, the believer in Communism could not feel emotions beyond fear and pride. 'Little more than animals,' Dr Ned Rathbone argued. He had studied the Communist Menace since 1938, and the one thing he knew above everything was that the Christian faith and the Communist faith could never exist in harmony on the same planet. And the martyrs of the side of Right demanded that the war be brought to the steps of the Kremlin itself.

Brano unfolded the pamphlet in his living room, flattening it with the side of his hand. He folded it down the long midpoint, then folded it a few more times until he had it right. Then he opened the French windows and tossed out his paper airplane. A breeze held it aloft for a moment; then it began to spin and plummet to the street, where Ludwig's old white-bearded shadow leaned on his Volkswagen and watched it crash into the pavement.

7 April 1967, Friday

Ersek Nanz's party was in Kahlenberg, in a house perched beyond the woods on the last dying bumps of the Alps. The taxi driver made noises under his breath as they approached the iron gate in front of a wide, modern bi-level. Brano looked over from the passenger seat. 'What was that?'

'Nothing. Just wishing I had the money to live up here.'

'One day, comrade, maybe you won't need money to live up here.'

The driver squinted as Brano grabbed his bottle of red wine and climbed out.

A man in a tuxedo opened the gate. Brano began to reach for his documents but stopped when the man simply smiled and nodded him on, up the paved drive, to the house. Another tuxedoed man opened the front door and took the wine and Brano's coat.

Beyond a stark white foyer, the living room opened up, rising two dimly lit floors to a glass wall that looked down on Vienna. About fifty people milled around, clutching champagne glasses and murmuring steadily. A few glanced at him. He was underdressed.

'Jesus Christ, Brano. You're late. I thought you were different than your brethren!'

'I'm just the same, Ersek. You live well.'

The Norwegian smirked. 'I wish this was mine. On loan from the Italian ambassador.' He raised a finger. 'One benefit of always gravitating towards power.'

'I'll keep that in mind.'

'Let's get you a drink.' Ersek walked him over to a white table covered with a hundred full glasses of champagne. 'Don't worry, there's more in the kitchen. Unless this guy already sniffed it out,' he said, nodding at Filip Lutz, who reached for another glass.

'It's our spy!'

'That's one thing you're right about,' said Brano.

Lutz patted the lapel of his tuxedo. 'I tell you, Nanzi, she wants it.'

Ersek looked around. 'Who?'

'Who do you think? The interpreter.'

'I'd give it to her in a second.'

Their longing looks were directed through the terrace doors, to where a tall, thin-boned blonde stood; her broad, sculpted jawline suggested she had come from the Slovak provinces of their country. She held a long cigarette beside her head as she laughed at a short, bearded man's joke.

As Brano took a second champagne and wandered past the Bösendorfer grand piano to a dark corner, he heard Ersek mutter, 'Little Rolf thinks he's going to give it to her.'

'I'd just like to see that,' said Lutz.

Some faces he recognized, though they did not know him. In late July, he'd gone through the files in order to uncover the identity of GAVRILO, and before settling on his short list of suspects, he'd come across half these faces. They were in the files because they were of use, because they could be of use in the future, or because they posed a threat. A tall man in the corner, a chain-smoker, looked familiar – yes: He'd been marked as a possible resource, because Yalta held a roll of 16 mm film of the man in a local brothel with a nine-year-old girl.

He wanted another champagne, but over by the drinks table he spotted a small, beaten-looking man hoarding glass after glass. It was Sasha Lytvyn.

He did finally talk to people, though without enthusiasm, always sidestepping the drunk man from his past who didn't seem to recognize him. A journalist from *Die Stern* explained to him the intricacies of recent Egyptian-Israeli tensions, as if Brano had never heard of the state of Israel. 'When Israel shot down those Syrian MiGs, it was a provocation. Now, I'm no anti-Semite, but . . .' Another man, young and pale, quoted Svetlana Alliluyeva from a manuscript supposedly awaiting American publication – *God grants an easy death only to the just* – then smiled rapturously. A gaunt woman with large glasses, originally from Sighet, described herself as an actionist painter, which to Brano meant nothing. When he asked, her explanation only confused him further.

'People like to say that painting has moved across the Atlantic to New York, but seriously, Europe is the centre of art civilization as it has been for centuries. I doubt a bunch of monkeys with paintbrushes would be able to take that from us. Do you?'

'I really don't know,' said Brano, edging away.

Lutz elbowed him in the ribs. 'My friend, I've had a brainstorm.'

'Tell me, Filip.'

'I suggest you find yourself a Viennese girlfriend. Best way to ease into the transition. Yes, what you need is a nice fräulein.'

'You sound like my mother.'

'Well, you've got a very progressive mother. Does she also do this?' Lutz reached into his jacket and pulled out a small wooden pipe. He squinted into the bowl.

'What's that?' Brano asked stupidly.

Lutz stuck the pipe in his mouth and flicked a lighter over the bowl. As he inhaled, the flame bowed, crackling the hashish inside. He held the smoke in his lungs a few seconds, then exhaled.

'Here.' Lutz handed him the pipe.

In another situation, Brano would have declined, but nothing so far had helped him relax. Even the champagne seemed of a light variety. And when Lutz exhaled, that pungent aroma reminded Brano of the few times he'd smoked it, back in Tel Aviv. It had been available everywhere, sticky clumps in a wooden box in everyone's home. When he'd smoked it there, his heartbeat had settled as he warmed into an easy languor, in which everything – even the complexities and brutalities of his job – seemed manageable.

'Are you coming Monday?' asked Lutz after they had finished.

'Where?'

'To my lecture. "The Lies Behind the Communist Dove of Peace." Didn't Nanzi tell you?'

'Where is it?'

'The Committee for Liberty in the Captive Nations, over on Schulerstraße.'

Brano snorted, then covered his mouth. Half laughter, half surprise.

Lutz leaned closer. '*What?*'

'The Committee for Liberty?'

'Yes.'

'The Christians?'

Lutz frowned, and Brano covered his mouth again as the stoned, monotone laughter rolled out of him.

'You don't understand,' said Lutz. 'They sound a little crazy sometimes, but they're not. No, not at all.' Lutz made an expression that looked similar to pain. 'Like many opposition groups, they have their use. They have money, influence. If you have their ear you have . . .'

Brano nodded, but he wasn't listening any more. The tingle at the base of his neck had spread over his scalp, and his blank smile no longer meant a thing.

Frustrated, Lutz sneaked off after the interpreter, and Brano took another champagne to the glass wall, staring at the dancing lights of the city down below. From this height he found himself thinking mystically, like Dijana Franković, as if the lights were stars to be read. In them he read the truth of Vienna's underbelly: conspiracies. There were so many conspiracies going on in that city – simultaneously, often bumping into one another. In neutral Vienna the intelligence services of the entire world converged to talk and trade and do battle, and up above it he was stoned, drinking expensive champagne.

By the time the pianist started, he was deep in a padded chair, trying to see if there was anything left in his glass. There wasn't. It was a Bach piece, a – if an overheard voice could be believed – *Fantasia*, the one in C minor, and it played in his muscles and bones, the high notes tickling his shoulder blades. He peered past the thin, tuxedoed man swaying at the keyboard, past smoking groups, into the darkness under the staircase leading to the second floor. He thought he saw the reflection of water there, maybe plants, but wasn't sure. And why plants in a dark spot? So he closed his eyes. He hadn't realized how exhausted he was – this was the first time he'd really relaxed since he had left Bóbrka, a world away. A family that hated —

The piano played and he tapped his foot, unsure if he was keeping time but not caring. Through the notes, a voice said, *Brani?* but he didn't look to see who it was. The music was warm and excellent, and he didn't want inane conversations destroying something that perfect. He sank deeper into the chair and tried to ignore the hand shaking his shoulder.

'Brani, you is sleeping?'

For the second it took his drug-stunned eyes to adjust, he tried to imagine what she would look like. All that came to him was a moment during their one night together, when he opened his eyes to find her head at the foot of the bed. He'd first noticed her feet by his face, then the long calves that disappeared beneath folds of white sheet. Then he'd sat up and looked at her sleepy face beside his feet, puffy cheeks covered by a splay of dark hair, the light from the scarf-muted lamp lighting the soft down on her cheeks. He'd paused then, staring, before realizing he should leave.

But the dim light here was entirely different, and when she came into focus she looked like another woman. The down was gone from her cheeks, and her hair was different; it was short, cut like a boy's. Her mascara was thick. And unlike in sleep, she was smiling a smile he knew was not authentic.

She blinked three times. 'I am in the shock!'

Then all relaxation left him, as if through a hole in his foot. He stood. But the hashish was still with him, fiercely, and he wobbled as he kissed her cheeks and awkwardly hugged her, taking in the aroma of some Viennese bottled scent.

214

'Oh, Brani,' she said, and looked down at her champagne glass. 'I have so much for to tell you.'

He was flushed; the blood beat in his head, and everything was too warm. The piano player didn't notice the change in temperature; he tapped on. Then, for an instant, he could see through her eyes and mouth to the dark staircase behind her that hid an entire forest. That was when he decided she was not there. She was an illusion.

But she did not dissolve into mist.

So he told her she looked good. She stared at him as if she didn't understand. 'Really, you do.'

'Why you are here?'

'I've left.'

'Left?'

'I've moved to Vienna.'

'You – ' She squinted at him over the rim of her glass. Then she lowered the glass. '*Here* now?'

'*Pa da,*' he said.

She exhaled. 'We go to the terrace, no?'

When she turned and he followed, he saw that it was true; she did look good. Where on that August night she had been clumsy and drunk, now she seemed to have gained many years. Maybe it was the sobriety, or the haircut, that had smoothed the movement of her hand when she stopped by the table and lifted a fresh glass, that made her new smile seem easy and unaffected. Maybe it was simply that over the last months she had grown accustomed to a life with no word from him.

Or maybe it was the easy idealization that comes from a vivid, drug-induced hallucination.

There was a drunk man with his own champagne bottle sleeping against the steel railing; he didn't wake as they closed the glass doors and Brano lit a cigarette. She watched him inhale, rubbed her arms against the cold, and shook her head.

'You looking very good, Brano.'

'No I'm not. I look old.'

'Like strong old man. Is very attractive.'

The dancing lights from the city blurred in his periphery. He wondered why she had cut her hair like that. Before, it had reached her shoulders, a loose bundle she would tug behind her ear. Now she looked like a little boy. He wondered if he should ask, then wondered how he could wonder such stupid things at his age. Cerny had spelled it out for him. No matter the haircut, she remained what she had always been, from the beginning. A spy. Who met with Russian agents in her apartment. 'Don't lie to me any more, okay? I've had enough of that.'

She furrowed her brow, then relaxed. Then, with effort, she furrowed again. 'I not know what you saying.'

It was strange, how easily she lied, how her inept grammar gave the illusion of innocence. 'I almost came back here,' he said. 'I did. Almost. I almost had the ticket.' He stopped; he was rambling.

'What you mean?'

'I'm not a fool, Dijana. I don't like being used.'

'What?' Her teeth were gritted behind her lips. 'What you say?'

He didn't answer. He waited. If this was a hallucination, he had a better imagination than he thought.

'Why you are here?'

'Because.'

'Because?'

'Because.'

Her glass was already empty, so she set it on the railing, then smiled thinly – yes, another false smile. 'Maybe we have coffee when you not so drunk.'

'I'm not drunk,' he said, but when he turned to the cityscape he almost tumbled.

'I think it not a bad idea I go.'

He looked back at her and, seeing her green-edged eyes again, felt the air leave him. Quietly, he said, 'Am I really that stupid?'

'Now – yes.' She squeezed his arm. 'But tomorrow, what knows?'

She smiled and leaned forwards, her lips brushing his cheek. He could not hear the kiss, but he felt it.

The drunk man was waking up. He slid a little to the left, hanging on the railing. And she was walking away.

Brano wasn't sure what had happened. He felt an urge to grab her arm, or to shout some stupid lie like *I love you* – any cheap trick to keep this remarkable illusion a little longer.

Through the terrace doors, Brano watched her glide across the floor, find her coat on a rack, and leave.

'Everyone's stupid,' said the drunk man. He slid a little more to the left, trying to rise, and knocked Dijana's glass off the railing. After a second they heard the crash against the concrete patio below.

Brano fought an urge to throw Sasha Lytvyn over the railing as well.

Day 20. The Subject left the party at one in the morning, meeting a taxi by the front gates. This agent followed the car into the centre, but it did not take the Subject to his apartment. Instead, he was delivered to the Volksgarten, the Dr K. Renner Ring entrance. As the park was closed, the Subject was forced to climb over the gate – a difficult manoeuvre, as the Subject appeared to be very drunk. This agent followed him to the Temple of Theseus, where he circled the structure a few times, then stood in front of the statue and spoke to it. He spoke primarily in his own language, though occasionally he

217

switched to German. Phrases included: 'Find a nice girl for me, will you?' and 'Paperwork, yes, and a bad conscience.' This agent is unable to make sense of the words.

By three, the Subject had passed out, and this agent carried him to the Hofburg gate, then radioed for assistance. This agent then took the Subject home. He said little on the ride, but did thank this agent for his assistance, asking at his door if he was really alone. 'No,' this agent told him. 'You're not alone.'

The Subject seemed very pleased with that answer.

9 April 1967, Sunday

'You look well, Brano. Not so lonely any more?'

'I get out some.'

'Sure,' said Ludwig. 'It's good to see. We were a little dismayed by that depressive crap you pulled at first. But we know as well as you that Vienna can be a very alienating place. It's funny how, the bigger a city is, the more people it has, the more alienating it becomes.'

'Yes. That's a funny thing.'

'And you know what, Brano? You're a damn lucky man.'

'I never thought of myself that way.'

'Open your eyes. I once knew a girl in Heidelberg. A beautiful girl. We were going to school together. She was from Amsterdam, over for a few weeks. On her last night we – well, you can imagine. It was dark, the stars were out, I was charming . . . it was wonderful. Really. I think back, and even after all these years, that girl was the best I ever had. Can you believe it? A nineteen-year-old girl.'

'I can believe it.'

'But then she left. The next day. I was completely and utterly in love, and you know what?'

'What?'

'Her parents had moved while she was gone, so the address and phone number I had were no good. I learned this from the new tenants, but they didn't know where the family was. I was truly and completely screwed.'

'Is this leading somewhere, Ludwig?'

'I think you know what it's leading to. Your girl is back. It was obvious to even to our denser associates on Friday that you are still hooked.'

'Then it must be true.'

'Don't kid me, Brano. You're a romantic, just like the rest of us. You've found her again. Don't tempt fate by screwing this up.'

'You know what, Ludwig?'

'What's that?'

'I just might do what you suggest.'

The Austrian raised his whisky. 'I give a lot of useless advice, I know this. But with love I know what I'm talking about.'

'You seem to.'

Ludwig grinned. 'Okay, Brano. Enough of that. Tell me what you and the great Filip Lutz have been talking about.'

'A lot of things. Primarily him. He's got a huge ego.'

'That's true. But he's good at what he does.'

'If what he does is being a slanderer.'

'You're kidding me, right?'

'He talked about his interviews with exiles. I suspect he embellishes their stories before they make it into print.'

'Why would he do that?'

'Because otherwise you won't pad his bank account.'

Ludwig's grin spread over his face and his lips parted to let out one short laugh – *Heh.* 'You really believe that?'

'He's got a new car, a Fiat.'

Ludwig shrugged. 'He's just a smart capitalist. You know how much longer Lutz thinks your anachronistic system has left?'

'Three years.'

'What do you think of that?'

'I think Filip Lutz is an optimistic man.'

Ludwig crossed his arms over his chest. 'You want to take a little walk? It's a beautiful day.'

Ludwig paid, took the receipt, and gave Brano his hat. They made themselves small to squeeze around the packed tables, and once they were outside, the Austrian asked Brano if he had a cigarette. Brano lit two. As they passed the flags of many nations fluttering in front of the Hotel Sacher, Brano said, 'What's on your mind?'

Ludwig took a drag. 'I just wanted to give you some advice.'

'I thought you'd already done that.'

'Not about love, Brano. I want to warn you not to escape any more.'

'We've been through this, haven't we?'

Ludwig didn't say anything until they had turned onto Kärtner Straße. 'It's different now. You have to realize that when I picked you up and then gave you that flat, I did it of my own accord. My associates have never made a secret of their disagreement.'

'What do they want you to do?'

'They don't care what deals I've made. They want you in prison, Brano. And they don't want you to ever come out.'

'I see.'

'I'm not sure you do.' Ludwig tossed away his half-smoked cigarette. 'I've had a few poor years in the service. Some mistakes have been mine, others were my responsibility. And when you eluded us a couple weeks ago, my associates reminded me of each mistake. I've had to fight hard to maintain our deal, to keep you out of prison. But if you leave again, it will be out of my hands.'

'And what about you?'

'What?'

'What happens to you?'

Ludwig frowned. 'There's an open desk in Accounting – I've been told this more times than I'd like to remember.'

'Oh.'

The Austrian patted Brano's shoulder. 'Just go see your girl and get out of my hair, okay?'

Brano caught the number 38 tram north to Döblinger Hauptstraße, got out, and paused, looking up. Hers was the concrete tower near the corner, up from the train overpass. It was noticeably plain in a city of Habsburg baroque. He waited with a small crowd for the light to cross the street. Once he reached her building, he glanced back as the sunburned man sneezed into a handkerchief. Brano entered the building.

On a panel were three strips of buzzers above a speaker grille, FRANKOVIĆ halfway down the last row. He pressed it and waited.

Through the glass doors behind him, the sunburned man took a small 35 mm camera from his trench coat and brought it to his eye.

'*Ja?*' said the speaker. '*Wer ist da?*'

He opened his mouth.

'*Hallo?*'

'Dijana?'

A pause. Then his language. 'Is you?'

'*Pa da,*' he said.

The door buzzed, and he pushed through.

He couldn't remember if she was on the third floor or the fourth, so he took the stairs instead of the lift, recalling the last time he'd taken these stairs, in August, following as she walked in her tight, flesh-coloured trousers, one hand reaching back, holding his. But unlike then, his knees

221

tingled, and he couldn't tell if he was moving fast or slow until his quick, shallow breaths began to make him dizzy. His palms were dripping.

On the third floor, he heard her voice from above. 'Brani? You is there?'

He galloped the next flight to find her in her doorway, pink-cheeked, wearing jeans and a black turtleneck. Self-consciously, she pushed dark hair behind an ear, but, trimmed short, it wouldn't stay.

Somehow, he had forgotten that she was taller than he. Her hesitant smile, which brought out a dimple, was glued to her face as she kissed his cheeks. He wanted to squeeze her entire body but was afraid that would scare her.

'So you really are here,' he said.

'We talked, no? You was too drunk to remember?' Even her high voice seemed different.

'I thought maybe you were a hallucination.'

'Well, I'm not,' she said, then cocked her head. 'You stop writing. I don't know how is your life.'

'Things didn't go well for me back home. I thought it was a good idea to leave.'

'To come here.'

'To leave,' he said. 'And what about you? How are the cards?'

For an instant, she didn't understand. Her eyebrows came together, and her lower lip rolled out. Then she smiled. 'Oh, *tarot*? No, no, Brani. I'm not do that any more.'

'Why not?'

She laughed. 'You want we go in?'

He laughed, too, easily, relieved.

Her apartment was airy, with wood floors and old, heavily padded furniture. Essentially the same as August, except for a new beige chair, where, with one knee propped up to support an acoustic guitar, sat a young man with a moustache and blond curly hair long enough to cover his ears. He nodded at Brano.

Brano nodded back.

'Wolfgang,' said Dijana as she walked on to the bathroom. 'Introduce yourself to my boyfriend.' She said this in German.

Wolfgang's face shifted, as if the bones beneath his skin had moved. He leaned the guitar against the arm of the chair, stood up, and stuck out a hand. *'Grüß Gott.'*

'Grüß Gott,' said Brano.

Wolfgang settled back down, opening a hand towards the sofa. Brano sat. They said nothing, half-smiling and listening to Dijana run water in the bathroom, humming. When she reappeared, she smiled at Brano. 'You like my boyfriend?' she asked Wolfgang.

The young man stood up. 'So I guess today's lesson is cut short, Dee?'

Dijana nodded sternly. *'Pa da.'*

The men shook hands again, and Dijana walked Wolfgang to the door, closed it after him, and turned to look at Brano on the sofa.

He didn't say anything at first, because her long body seemed unapproachable. There were so many things that Brano, the *zbrka* rising again, did not understand. He didn't understand how he could be here in her flat – how he ever could have been given access; he didn't understand why she had sent away her handsome friend for him. He didn't understand how she could be looking at him in that way. He supposed Cerny had always been right, and she was a spy. What else could explain her desire for an old man with a cold heart? But right now – right now, he didn't care.

She squatted beside him. 'Wolfgang, he manage the bar where I work. Jazzklub Abel, on other side of canal, at Große Mohrengasse. Maybe you hear of it?'

Brano shook his head.

'Easy work, I wait the table.' She shrugged. 'A real job, no? But I like people what is there. Musicians. Folk music. You like?'

'I don't really know it.'

'Wolfgang, he teach me guitar. Just little. And I'm thinking maybe it's not bad idea I learn to sing. What you think?'

She smiled hugely, waiting for his approval. He couldn't say anything for a moment, because she was here, finally, with him. She smiled a lot – he'd forgotten that – and her teeth were large and clean and straight. He felt like he'd been drinking, but he hadn't been.

'I think it's a great idea, Dijana.'

'*Dobro,*' she said. Good.

'And you're finished with the tarot cards?'

She nodded seriously.

'Why?'

'Because it's silly,' she said, standing again. 'That's something what you know. Okay, I thought maybe there is something in it. You know. Something like truth. But I change a lot since August. *Da.* First you come. Then Bertrand die. And tarot, it seem . . . I don't know. Stupid. Wolfgang, he say to me about tarot, *You know, Dijana, that is old world.* Is true. This is new world.'

'You're brand new.'

'And my hair?' Hesitantly, she touched it. 'You like my hair?'

'I love it,' said Brano.

They talked, and Brano slowly readjusted to the peculiar rhythms of her speech, the forgotten flow of her thoughts. She laughed regularly, and while in his career he often associated laughter with nervousness, this was not the case with

Dijana. She simply found more things in this world funny than he did.

As she told him more about her life, the job, the music, the friends, and even her developing interest in Buddhism, Brano realized that they were just as unlike as before, perhaps more so. Her evenings were spent in smoky music clubs discussing political hymns and peace marches and mysticism. His evenings were spent planning his survival. And she *was* young – even Cerny had pointed this out. A woman in her midtwenties was still jumping around the spectrum, trying to find something that would settle her nerves and guide her through the *zbrka* of modern life. She had left her own country behind, which only added to her need. The tarot cards hadn't done it, so now she was throwing herself into the world of popular music and Eastern religion. That, no doubt, would not satisfy her either, and she would be faced with more years of dissatisfaction.

He watched her face as she explained to him the idea behind reincarnation, and to avoid making an expression that betrayed his real opinion, he stopped listening and noticed how her cheeks puffed up when she spoke, her fingertips tapped the table, and her neck, just visible above her turtleneck, was very pale.

'You know what?' she said.

'What?'

'You listening to anything I saying.'

He remembered that that night in August she had often confused 'anything' with 'nothing'. He laughed, then she laughed. 'You're right,' he said.

She stood up. 'Is okay. But you must to go now.'

'Go?'

'*Pa da.* I have things I must to do.'

He patted his thighs and stood up, warmth rushing to his

face. He started to look for his coat but realized he'd never taken it off. She walked him to the door. 'Really, you are here?'

'Really, I am.'

Then she reached her arms around him, squeezed, and kissed him on the lips. She tasted of chewing gum, but he hadn't seen her using any. Her lips parted, and he felt her large, strong teeth against his tongue, then her tongue entered his mouth. He held her tight until she let him go.

'I not drunk this time, *dragi*. Yes, but not now, okay?'

'Sure,' he said, nodding dumbly. 'But when?'

'I just – ' she began. 'Only not so fast. Okay?' When she smiled again her shoulders settled.

Then she closed the door.

When he left the building, Brano spotted the sunburned man putting away his camera. Brano caught his eye by waving and, inexplicably, blew the man a kiss.

10 April 1967, Monday

Brano knew a little about the Committee for Liberty in the Captive Nations. Their primary work was using tourists to smuggle pamphlets and Beatles records into the East, where they tended to litter the corridors of the Hotel Metropol. Among the groups devoted to ending the communist experiment, they were low on the list of priorities. They were, like most émigré groups, more style than substance, only platforms to be heard from, because their new countries never listened. And so they spoke to their own kind, received applause, and returned to their empty apartments rejuvenated. The Committee was different in that it was formed not by exiles but by American Christian fundamentalists who plucked their workers from the exile communities.

The Committee's Vienna branch lay in the Innere Stadt, part of a Habsburg complex on Schulerstraße, behind St Stephen's Cathedral. He had expected something further out, in the cheaper districts, but at number 9 he found the small bronze plaque with a symbol of a sun rising over

CLCN

INTERNATIONAL

He pressed the buzzer.

'Hallo?'

Brano leaned close to the speaker. 'I'm here for the Filip Lutz lecture.'

The door hummed.

The office was on the second floor, and as he climbed the stairs Brano tried without success to push Dijana from his mind. It irritated him that he had been too confused to leave his phone number, but he assured himself that she was resourceful enough to track him down when she was ready, when she had done those unknown things that were required of her first.

There was another plaque on the open door that spelled out the name of the organization, above a Latin motto: IGITUR QUI DESIDERAT PACEM, PRAEPARET BELLUM. Whoever wishes for peace, let him prepare for war.

In the foyer, beside a rack overflowing with coats, stood a small woman with thick eyebrows. She pumped his hand energetically. 'So glad to *meet* you,' she said in childlike English. 'So *glad* you could make it! I am Loretta Reich, the Committee's press agent, and you—oh!' She put a hand to her mouth. 'I mean, is English okay?'

He nodded. 'I'm Brano Sev. Filip invited me.'

'A friend of *Filip's*!' She placed a finger on Brano's forearm.

'Well, we're just tickled *pink* he agreed to do this for us. You know, without Filip we'd hardly get a thing done around here. He's *invaluable*. Oh!' She looked around. 'Let's get you out of that coat and get you something to drink.' Then she laughed, showing all her teeth.

Loretta brought him into the large main room, where twenty people milled around rows of metal folding chairs, drinking. Lutz was beside a tall window that overlooked Schulerstraße, entertaining a semicircle of admirers, both men and women. Others looked American – tall young men with tans and tailored suits they wore with ease. One stood in a corner quietly talking to an old man with a white moustache and beard – the shadow with the Volkswagen who liked to sit outside his apartment. The old man noticed him looking, then gave a smile and a half nod.

'I hope you don't mind zinfandel – the cabernet's all gone!' Loretta laughed as she handed Brano a glass. 'These people know how to drink!'

'How long have you been here in Vienna?'

Loretta tilted her head. 'Well, *I've* only been here since November, but the office . . . we started it three years ago, in 1964.' Then she took a breath. 'We do a lot of good work.'

'Like what?'

'Anti-communist seminars, mostly. Oh, we've had some success in the Austrian universities, particularly the Christian schools. And we've lobbied members of the Austrian and West German governments to include anticommunist education within their national curriculums.'

'You're not recruiting again, Loretta?' Lutz tapped her shoulder with a cylinder of papers, which seemed to be her cue – she moved on. In his other hand was a glass. 'Brano, glad you could make it.'

'You ready to speak?'

'Trying desperately to get drunk first.' He looked back over the crowd and took a sip. 'See anyone you know?'

'A few familiar faces. Who's that guy with the beard?'

Lutz squinted at the corner, where the white-haired man was still talking with his American friend. 'Oh, that's Andrew. Andrew Stamer. Left our country a while ago. Now I suppose you can call him an American. One of the founding members of the Committee.'

'He's not Austrian?'

Lutz shook his head as Brano gazed at the old man, reviewing the two times he'd seen him outside the Web-Gasse apartment. Not one of Ludwig's men, then, but a lone crusader who had somehow learned who and where Brano was, and was trying to reeducate him with cheap pamphlets.

Lutz noticed him staring. 'You probably don't want to meet him unless you're planning to convert. He can be very persuasive. Most of these Christians are.'

'So you're saying this isn't a front for the CIA?'

Surprise slid into Lutz's face. 'I keep forgetting what you used to do.'

Brano cocked his head, as if agreeing.

'Which reminds me, you still need to tell me your story. *Escape from the Crocodile* needs some tales of adventure.'

As the crowd swelled, Brano recognized more faces from his Vienna files and heard accented English everywhere – Hungarian, Polish, Yugoslav, Czech, even Russian. They met and hugged and kissed cheeks, as if part of a secret society. But there was nothing secret about any of them. They all wore their faith on their sleeve; they were apparatchiks for their most precious word: *liberty*.

Ersek Nanz arrived a few minutes later to harangue Brano for not spending more time at the Carp. Brano shrugged and went for another glass of zinfandel. Beside the bottles were stacks of the Committee's pamphlets with such titles as *What Is Communism?* and *Watch Out! There's a Marxist Behind You!* and *Christ's Words on Profit*. On the wall was a line of bronze plaques mounted on wood; on each was a name and a year.

Loretta came up. 'You like our wall of martyrs?'

Brano squinted at the names. There was the man his sister praised, Father Jacek Wieslowski, as well as Yuli Daniel, a Russian writer who had been given five years' imprisonment last year for publishing anti-Soviet works in the West. At the end was the old head of the Office of Policy Coordination who had killed himself, Frank Wisner.

'Frank Wisner?' he asked.

Loretta nodded earnestly. 'Yes, yes. A great man, sadly gone. Andrew knew him well.'

'They were old friends?'

'I think so, yes. During Wisner's last year, in London. Very close, those two. Frank Wisner's determination is an inspiration to us all.' She touched the corner of Wisner's plaque wistfully, then wandered away.

Brano looked around for Andrew Stamer, but he was no longer in the room. He felt a tap on his shoulder and turned to find the pockmarked, scarred face of Sasha Lytvyn. 'Brano Sev.'

'Hello, Sasha.'

The man smelled of something stronger than zinfandel, but he held no glass. Instead, his hands twitched at his sides. 'I thought I saw you at the party.'

Brano held his wine glass between them. 'I saw you as well.'

'You've been in Vienna a long time?'

'Not very long. You?'

'A decade. But I never forgot you, Brano.'

'How is your arm?'

'My—' Sasha looked down at his left arm, then unbuttoned the cuff. He slid back the sleeve to expose a forearm covered in mottled, burned flesh.

'About the same,' said Brano. Lutz was taking his place at the head of the room, behind a small podium. 'Take care, Sasha.'

Brano walked to an empty seat in the rear, and when he glanced back saw Sasha Lytvyn in the foyer, reaching for his coat.

A small American with round glasses stood beside Lutz. He looked nervous, but once the room quieted he took a piece of paper from his jacket pocket and began to read, introducing Lutz as a 'distinguished scholar of the communist world' who was 'famous for his insightful articles in *Kurier*'.

The applause was loud, vibrating the walls. Some men whistled.

Lutz smiled and pressed the air for silence. Finally the crowd settled, and Lutz licked his teeth. 'I didn't know we had so many fans of yellow journalism in Vienna!'

Laughter.

'But, really, it is an honour to be invited here to speak to all of you. Thank you, Jeremy,' he said, nodding at the small man, now sitting in the front row. A smattering of applause. Lutz took a sip of wine from the glass sitting on the podium, then said, 'We like to make jokes, but what I've come here to talk to you about tonight is a deadly serious subject. Over the last years we've heard a lot of talk coming from Moscow and Bucharest and Warsaw and my own home about the idea of international peace. The communist world, the message goes, is focused on the aim that all good men have in their hearts: peace in our time. And I think that all good men, upon hearing this for the first time, think, *Well, why not? That's an admirable thing for them to say.*'

There were a few chuckles from the audience.

'No, don't laugh. This is an honest response to the press releases issued by the International Communist Party. But the problem is that honest responses assume that the original statement is honest. And that is what I've come here to examine today.'

Lutz went on, but Brano focused instead on the heads lined up in front of him. Men and women alike seemed transfixed by Lutz's vibrant voice, and sometimes they nodded ecstatic agreement. Lutz was casual. He could have been standing in a bar, giving a lecture on seduction. He knew all these people and was speaking to friends about something they all already agreed on. And when he said, 'You know the old Hungarian joke: We're a three-class society – those who have been in prison, those who are there, and those who are heading there,' everyone nodded because they already knew this as well. There was no one – except, perhaps, himself – to convert. The lecture, it seemed, had no point.

Then he felt a soft hand on his shoulder.

Dijana took the seat beside him. Her skirt was short, and she looked, he thought briefly, very bourgeois. In an exceptional way. She kissed his cheek and whispered, 'I hear you will to be. Here.'

Brano felt an easy warmth fill him, as if he'd known all along that she would arrive and both of them were merely fulfiling their roles. 'I'm glad you came.'

She placed a finger over her lips and looked up as Lutz enumerated the various corners of the world to which the Soviet Union had sent its troops and advisors in order to create wars, rather than end them. 'Vietnam, Korea, Africa . . . the list goes on.'

She leaned close to his head. 'You are liking this?'

'No.'

'Well, maybe it's not bad idea we go.'

Lutz spread his arms to show just how much evil the communists of the world had committed.

'*Pa da,*' said Brano.

The Oskar Bar lay on the ground floor of a large, modern office building facing the Concordiaplatz car park. It was dark and empty, and when they settled at the bar Dijana grinned. 'We don't see no one what we know here. Is good?'

'It's great,' he said, then placed a hand on her knee. 'Have we waited long enough yet?'

She nodded seriously. 'I sorry. But was something what I had to do first.'

'What?'

'You want to know?'

'Of course.'

'Okay.' She pursed her lips, then opened them and sighed. '*Well,* I had to say bye for someone.'

'Bye?'

'*Da.* Goodbye. A man what was my lover.'

'Wolfgang?'

'*Wolf*gang?' She thought that was funny. 'No, I like the old men. Was Abel, a friend for Wolfgang. He also own the club what I work at, is his name. The Jazzklub Abel.'

'You were sleeping with your boss?'

Dijana started laughing. '*Da da da!* Is funny, no?' Then she tilted her head.

'What?'

'I think it's not bad idea we go home now.'

The number 38 tram took them north along Nußdorfer, and though Dijana held on to his arm, they did not speak. That pressure on his arm, the fingers she sometimes tapped against the inside of his wrist, and the blank smile she gave the passing street – they all helped to make the silence an ideal thing. It was different from the silence of the Bóbrka countryside, different from the silence of an empty flat. He remembered their walk last August, which had been loud, because she had been loud. Now she wasn't drunk, and she showed no signs of nervousness. And he, surprisingly, felt none.

For a few moments, he even forgot about Vienna – he forgot about Ludwig and the sunburned shadow; he forgot about the Committee and Andrew Stamer, even Yalta Boulevard and poor Sasha Lytvyn; he forgot that he was an exile here, just like everyone else.

11 April 1967, Tuesday
Brano Sev was not a young man. He'd had half a century to acquaint himself with the other sex, and when he was younger he put much effort towards that. Those years just after the war, when he was building his career, he'd had brief affairs with women he met in bars. They were often a little older than him, war widows who knew what they were looking for when they sat alone at a bar. He'd go home with them and perhaps stay until the next morning. A few of these affairs stretched the length of a week, until the cold sexual calculation began to wear on both participants, and they would quietly call it quits.

He'd never lived with a woman, and this was something he regretted. He'd had one year-long relationship, when he was forty-two, with Regina Haliniak, who still worked the Yalta front desk. That relationship, like this one, was prompted by the woman's forthrightness. Three months into it, he suggested they move in together, and Regina laughed at him. *Do you think I'm going to fall for that?* He never quite understood what she meant, and by the end of the year it didn't matter. In the canteen of Yalta 36, she informed him that she'd begun sleeping with a lieutenant named Zoran, and she thought she might be in love. That word had never crossed her lips in the last year. Brano had looked at the gravy-smothered bread on his plate and shrugged.

Since then he'd stopped trying, settling for the brief, cool greeting of prostitutes living in the Canal District. Brano was self-aware enough to realize that he was no woman's ideal. He was neither particularly attractive nor virile. He spoke too quietly, and when he was entertaining, it was by accident. He wasn't even particularly loving – he knew this. He had learned the techniques of coldness because without them he wouldn't have survived for this many years, but they had also assured that his many years would be spent alone.

Which is why he never quite trusted Dijana Franković. A young woman, even one with a fixation for older men, would be a fool to choose him. There were far more accomplished men in this city, more entertaining men, rich men. So even when he followed her up her stairs that second time, eyes on her skirt, he was still far from believing. He half expected to find that young man with his long hair sitting in her chair, or her boss, Abel – for these had to be her real lovers, and Brano was a game, something to pass the time. Or perhaps it was more sinister, and Wolfgang would attempt to strong-arm Brano out of his meagre Raiffeisenbank account.

But the apartment was empty, and once they were inside her youth came out as she tore off his clothes and tried to take him there, on the floor. Later, in bed, she cried once, and apologized. 'I don't want you to thinking I am strange. Impulsive, I know this. I am. But, *da*, just what I know. This is the right thing.'

And when they lay there afterwards, her head fitting so

well against his chest, he asked her, because he still wasn't sure. He knew what kind of man he was, he said, and maybe she didn't, but he wanted to tell her, because someday she would realize this and leave him. He told her he was an old man who had spent years dulling his emotions until they were almost nonexistent.

'But they exist?'

'Yes, somewhat.'

'For me they exist?'

'*Da.*'

She nodded into his chest and said that she understood his doubt and knew the kind of figure she cut. 'People, you know, they not always trusting for my . . . honestly?'

'Your sincerity?'

'*Da.* My sincerity. But this is because I am too much sincerity too much of the time.'

He said he could see that.

'I am not blind,' she said. 'I can to see your faults. And the future . . . what knows? Maybe we can to be together only one week, maybe five years. Maybe we cannot to live together. I don't know. All what I know is this, Brano Sev. When I am with you, it feels like correct. And when you is not here, I want you to be with me. You understand?'

He took a breath. 'Yes. Yes, I understand.'

'Was not like that with Bertrand. And for certainly not with Abel. Good men, but . . .' She shrugged. 'Maybe it just pheromones.'

'Pheromones?'

'*Da,*' she said. 'Smell. Maybe only you have smell what for me is very good.'

He liked that theory, because it was biological and felt unchangeable. But when he slept, the doubt returned, making him restless, and when he woke, he kept his eyes shut, listening. He heard her steady, quiet breaths. Then he turned his head towards the sound and opened his eyes. The morning light lit the dribble of saliva that had drained from her lips into the pillow.

He made his way quietly across the creaking floor to the bathroom. He urinated and brushed his teeth with her toothbrush but avoided looking into the mirror. He didn't want to compound his overwhelming doubt. What he wanted was to leave, so he crept back into the bedroom, where she still slept, a calf sticking out of the sheets, her toes curled tight. He put on his underwear and brought the socks into the living room, where he gathered the rest of his clothes. He put on his shirt, buttoned it, and pulled on his trousers. Then, as he was tying his shoes, he heard her. *'Dragi?'*

He looked down at the shoelace knots he'd been mishandling. 'Yes?'

'Dragi, where *are* you?'

He went to the bedroom doorway. She was wiping her eyes with the back of her hand.

'Why you have on your clothes?'

'I always get up early.'

'Come here.' He walked over to the bed and sat beside her. She looked up at his face. 'You are going?'

'Just getting breakfast for us,' he lied.

She stretched her arms high over her head and yawned. 'That is not bad idea. But wait,' she said, and unzipped his trousers. She stuck her fingers inside, tugging on him. 'I want we make more sex now.'

He was naked again, and back in bed. His flight instinct had dwindled to nonexistence during their sex, so that now he couldn't imagine leaving. They smoked using an ashtray balanced on Brano's stomach. 'You know, I knowed this. I knowed at Ersek Nanz's party. I can see we will be together.'

'You mean you could smell it?'

'*Da,*' she said, letting out a little laugh. 'I could smell it.'

'Do you want breakfast now?'

'Coffee, *da*, and cigarettes.' She lifted her pack from the bedside table and showed it to him; it was empty.

'I'll get some more.'

'Then I will make for you coffee. You like?'

'*Da.*'

He dressed, then trotted down the stairs and out to the street, unable to control his grin. He didn't see Ludwig's men around, though he knew they were there. This, finally, was something worth reporting. Where the road split just past the tram station was a tobacco shop, and he bought cigarettes and the day's *Kurier*. When he returned, he found Dijana in the kitchen, naked, preparing coffee. He settled on the couch and opened the newspaper but watched her. She was not shy with her body, and sometimes she glanced over her shoulder to smile at him, or to slap her own behind then laugh. He watched her arch over the counter to reach for the sugar, and at that moment he felt sure that she had been right all along. Because, *da*, it was the right thing.

'I can read the paper?'

'Of course,' he said, and brought it over to her. She lit a cigarette and began reading on the counter while he reopened the personals. As he did every day, he scanned them quickly, but this time one caught his eye.

Franz F, »Gedicht-1«

Franz F, 'Poem-1':

Lieb + Ebenbild sterben in Kampfgas.
Warte ich auf Lawinen? Schlau . . . hab dich!
Acht Jahre! 00 Leute, 0 Reich!

Love + *image die in War-gas.*
Do I wait for avalanches? Sly . . . gotcha!
Eight years! 00 people, 0 empire.

He didn't understand the poem, and that made sense. This was written not for a surface meaning but for a hidden one, the small grammatical blunder of the first line – *in* instead of *im* – helping draw his attention. And the code was simple. Brano looked at the date on the newspaper – 11 April 1967. 11-4-1967. Poem, minus one. 11-4-1966, or 1-1-4-1-9-6-6.

'You are finding a lover?'

Brano could feel himself reddening. 'No,' he said. 'Just reading poetry.'

She smiled, rocking her head as she returned to the world's headlines. 'So my Brani like *poetry* . . .'

Brano got up after a while and, on her bedside table, found a worn pencil. He took it, with the newspaper, to the toilet, closed the door, and began underlining letters based on the code 1-1-4-1-9-6-6.

L̲ieb + E̲benbild st̲erben i̲n Kampfga̲s.
Wart̲e ich auf Law̲inen? S̲chlau . . . ha̲b d̲ich!
A̲cht Jahre! 0̲0 Leute, 0̲ Reich!

L-I-E-B-E-N-G-A-S-T-E-W-C-A-B-D-A-C-0-0

The first part made sense: a meeting place – Liebengaste WC; the bathroom of the Liebengaste, a restaurant north of Mariahilfer, on Neubaugasse. But the rest – ABDAC00 – did not. Which meant they were numbers. He transformed the letters into numbers, based simply on their alphabetic order, and found 1241300. A date and time – 12 April, 13.00.

'You will live in there?'

239

He looked up at the door, and when he spoke he found he had little air to work with. 'No, Dijana. I'm coming.' He tore out the poem, dropped it between his legs, and flushed the toilet.

12 April 1967, Wednesday
He returned to Web-Gasse the next morning, with the excuse that he needed to bring over clean clothes. Dijana frowned when he said he'd rather go alone. 'But why?'

'You want me to get tired of you?'

She punched him in the stomach. 'You better not.'

He loaded some clothes into a small bag he found at the back of his wardrobe, then followed the old routine, sitting in Eszterházy Park, trying to read the last pages of his French Marxist tract. A different man watched him read – a little fat, with a blond crew cut – until, at a quarter to one, he followed Brano up to and across Mariahilfer Straße.

The fresh spring weather was apparent in the Viennese women's freshly pressed short skirts, showing off their tapered legs and high heels as they strode to lunch meetings and offices. He wondered what Dijana was wearing right then; he wondered if she was wearing anything at all.

Neubaugasse was choked with little eateries, clothing and junk shops, and parked cars. He paused outside the Liebengaste, a small traditional restaurant on the sunny side of the street, then found a table inside, where he placed his bag beside his chair. There was only one other guest, a large man with a thick grey moustache buried in a newspaper. Brano didn't recognize him. It was five to one. He asked the waitress for a beer and schnitzel, and the location of the toilet. She smiled and pointed to the back of the restaurant. As he got up, he noticed the man with the crew cut through the front window, hands in his pockets, as fast-moving Viennese passed him.

The bathroom door was unlocked. He opened it and switched on the harsh light. Beside the sink, on which sat a brown hat, Josef Lochert stood, smiling. The tall man had lost weight since that day he'd driven Brano to the Vienna airport. He was rubbing a thin beard he'd added to his juvenile moustache.

Brano closed the door and locked it.

'It's about time I heard from you.'

Lochert chewed the inside of his lip. 'There's a sale at the tricot store.'

'What?'

Lochert raised an eyebrow. 'I said, *There's a sale at the tricot store.*'

Brano looked blankly at him, then closed his eyes and spoke the old, coded reply as it came to him. 'But I've always been suspicious of cotton.'

'Okay, Sev.' Lochert stuck out his hand.

Brano gripped it but didn't let go. 'Why?'

'Why what?'

'You were the one who hit me in the Volksgarten, and then—'

But Brano didn't finish the sentence. Instead, he punched Lochert in the eye, then let go of his hand.

Lochert stumbled back against the wall, holding his face. 'Okay,' he said. 'Okay, Brano. I deserved that. But you were endangering our mission with that woman. I thought I was doing the right thing at the time.'

'No, Josef.' Brano took another step towards him. 'You deserve a lot more than that. You tried to set me up for Bertrand Richter's murder. And when that didn't get me arrested by the Austrians, you took advantage of my condition and packed me off for home. I imagine you also called

241

the Austrians who almost got me in the airport. Then you sent in a report that ended my career. You wanted Vienna to yourself.'

Lochert rubbed his eye; the other one squinted at him. 'I don't know what to say, Brano.'

'Well, you got what you wanted, didn't you?'

'Yeah,' he said. 'I suppose I did.'

Silence followed, and Brano didn't feel the need to fill it. Lochert finally lowered his hand from his wet, bloodshot eye. 'Are you being followed?'

'Of course; he's outside. I think I might want to do that again.'

'Enough, okay?' Lochert raised his hands. 'Let's consider ourselves at peace for the moment. Can we do that?'

Brano shrugged.

'Your instructions are simple,' said Lochert. 'Yalta wants you to take care of Filip Lutz. I see you've already made contact with him.'

'Take care?'

'Kill him, Comrade Sev.'

At first Brano couldn't think of anything to say.

Was this the answer he'd been waiting so long for? This? He shook his head. 'I'm not the man for this. There are others.'

'Not this time.'

'Why me?'

'Orders.' Lochert took his hat from the sink.

'Wait a minute.'

'I'm not waiting for anything, Sev. I'm going.' He stepped towards the door, but Brano gripped his arm. Lochert looked at Brano's hand.

'You're not walking away,' said Brano. 'I've been stuck in this country a month and a half now, and I don't have any idea what's going on. I'm not an amateur. I should have been told from the beginning.'

'So you could spill it to the Austrians?'

'You're the usual hired gun, Lochert. And even if you're the temporary *rezident*, there are plenty more of your kind around.'

'Think about it, Brano.' This close, below Lochert's dripping eye, he noticed scars from old acne.

'Because Yalta can deny it if I'm caught.'

'You haven't lost it all yet.'

'I don't even work for the Ministry any more. I'm just a murderer who fled the country.'

'Very good. Can I go now?'

'Wait.' Brano frowned. 'A frame-up in a village, all the operatives I had to turn in here, letting Soroka out of the country – all this was to get rid of one troublesome journalist? I don't believe it.'

'Do you want me to tell Cerny you're refusing?'

'No.' He squeezed Lochert's arm tighter. 'What I want is for you to tell me why we want Lutz dead.'

Lochert sighed and, when Brano let go of his arm, settled on the toilet. 'I was only supposed to tell you if I felt it was necessary.'

'It is necessary, Josef.'

'Well, then.' Lochert's hands hung loosely between his knees. 'You were at Lutz's speech to that Christian organization, weren't you?'

'Yes.'

'They're Lutz's connection to the CIA.'

'I suspected as much.'

'But what you don't know is why the CIA is giving him money. It's not for those silly articles he writes.'

'Then what's it for?'

Lochert paused. 'You remember after the war, Truman's plans to roll back the Iron Curtain?'

'Of course. I've seen Sasha Lytvyn around.'

243

'Well, they're doing it again, with Filip Lutz at the head. It's better organized than the one Frank Wisner led. It's completely airtight, too. We don't have anyone working on the inside. We've tried, of course, but come up with nothing. All we know is that something is being planned – probably an armed insurrection.'

'Something to shake up the Politburo,' said Brano. 'That's what he told me.'

'Lutz talks a lot, but only when he's being vague.'

'Then we should interrogate him.'

'No.' Lochert shook his head. 'That's out of the question. He's being watched too well, and we don't want the Austrians to learn of this. At this point, they don't know a thing – the Americans haven't involved them. We want to keep it that way.'

Brano nodded, the *zbrka* of the last weeks dissipating. Explanations, however distasteful, and even from someone as distasteful as Lochert, were what he needed. 'Is Jan Soroka connected to this?'

'Not that we know.'

Brano pressed a finger to his lips. 'But it's not Lutz heading this. There's an old man named Andrew Stamer. He knew Frank Wisner. They were friends.'

'Yes, we know about Andrew – he was just a go-between. He passed Wisner's knowledge on to Lutz. At most, he's an occasional advisor, a nobody.'

Brano stepped back and leaned against the wall. He didn't like that all-knowing look in Lochert's good eye. 'Tell me, then, why would the Americans be involved in a scheme they know will fail?'

'We're here to be sure they fail, but don't think it's pre-determined.'

'It'll be the same as Budapest in 'fifty-six,' said Brano. 'They can start a revolution, but Russian tanks will end it.

The Americans won't send their army to back it up, and even if they wanted to they'd have to go through Hungary or Czechoslovakia or Yugoslavia first. No. It's impossible.'

'Maybe they know something we don't,' said Lochert. 'Or maybe they just want to disrupt things. We can't take chances. The CIA have placed themselves far enough away to deny they had any part in it. To Yalta, that suggests something quite serious.'

Brano nodded.

'And you had better watch your back with that woman.'

'What?'

'Your Fräulein Franković. She's working with the Russians.'

Brano smiled. 'That's the story you gave Cerny, but don't think I'll believe it.'

Lochert reached into his jacket pocket and took out an envelope. He held it out.

Inside, Brano found four black-and-white photographs. In the first, two men in suits entered Dijana's tower block. The next three were taken with a telephoto from another building through her window. Dijana with a tray of drinks, smiling at the men, then talking very seriously.

'You know the tall one, don't you?'

Brano had trouble bringing Lochert into focus. 'Major Alexis Gogol, head of KGB counterintelligence in Austria.'

'I don't have to tell you why we don't want the Russians getting wind of this. The Ministry has enough problems maintaining any sense of autonomy. This would ruin us.'

Brano went through the photos again.

'Keep them if you want,' said Lochert. 'I just want to be sure you understand your orders. Do you, comrade?'

Brano said that he did.

Lochert stepped over to the door and touched the handle.

He looked back. 'I don't imagine killing Lutz will be easy, but trust me – it's a vital operation.'

Brano nodded.

Then Lochert walked out the door.

That evening in her apartment, Dijana cooked a layered Balkan pastry with a mixture of ground beef and pork and cream. *Gibanica*, a dish he'd had in Belgrade years before, and though it was a favourite of his, he couldn't taste a thing. They ate at the cramped kitchen table and drank red wine from coffee mugs – she didn't own any wineglasses.

He had watched her carefully since returning from his meeting. He was trying to read signs of betrayal in the way she kissed him when he arrived and helped with his coat. What before had seemed the lucky virtues in a woman who loved him had become the techniques of seduction. There were schools in the Soviet Union that taught pretty Russian girls how to become, in the vernacular, 'swallows'. They learned how to extract information from travelling Western businessmen and diplomats, or simply to bed them for the hidden cameras. Before eating, as he washed his hands in her bathroom, he even cupped his hands around his eyes and leaned close to the mirror, as if there really would be two-way glass and a remote 35 mm.

'You like?'

Brano nodded, stuffing more *gibanica* into his mouth. 'You're a good cook, Dijana.'

'I must to be. You don't cook?'

Brano shook his head.

'What I thought. You are not comfortable at the kitchen.'

'How long have you lived in this apartment?'

She rolled her eyes, thinking. 'One year? *Da*, one year.'

'Is it expensive to rent?'

'*Da*. But I not rent. It's mine.'

'You own it?'

She nodded.

'I didn't think you earned that much.'

She waved her fork at him. '*Pa da*. Is true, but – you want I should tell you?'

'Of course.'

She frowned at her plate. 'Was Bertrand. He buy it for me. I say no, really. I like Bertrand, but know I won't be with him so long. I tell him this, too, but he was – I don't know. He say it's okay, he just want to buy it for me.' She smiled. 'He was good man, no?'

After dinner, they settled on the couch and listened to one of Dijana's records, an American folk singer named Joan Baez. 'I not understand so much,' she told him as she settled into his arm. 'But I think maybe I can to learn English with this music, no?'

'I knew a man who was learning French from Juliette Gréco records.'

'Really?'

They fell quiet as the young American sang in her soft voice, but Brano was not interested in the music. He wanted to ask her directly about Lochert's accusations. She had met with Russian agents in this very apartment, in this room – through the window he could see the building across the street where the camera must have been placed. But if he brought it up, she'd demand to know how he knew. So he said, 'You liked Bertrand, didn't you?'

'Of course,' she said into his chest. 'I don't go to the bed with a man what I don't like.'

'Of course.'

'But you know something?'

'What?'

'Bertrand, he scared of you.'

'Me? He mentioned me?'

'Once, *da*. He was drunk, and he say, *That Brano Sev – he is a dangerous one.*'

Brano's arm around Dijana became cool. 'Why did he say that?'

'He say you are a spy.' She shifted a little. 'That is true?'

'I was a spy, yes.'

'You kill people?'

He looked down at the crown of her head, encircled by his tingling arm. 'No,' he lied. 'I wasn't that kind of spy.'

'I thought not.' Then she sat up and looked at him. 'But you can? You know how.'

He nodded.

She looked at the record player. It had reached the end, and they could hear the quiet *shht shht* of the needle's revolution. She smiled. 'So you can to protect me?'

'Of course.'

She turned the record over, filling the room with music again, then sat down and stared at him a moment before speaking. 'Why you are cold tonight?'

'Am I cold?'

'Yes,' she said. 'You not kissing me.'

'Sorry.' He leaned over and kissed her, but she didn't return the kiss.

'Why you are not a spy no more?'

'Because I didn't want to be.'

She nodded. 'How long will you staying in Vienna?'

'I don't know.'

'Long time?'

'Maybe forever, Dijana.'

That answer seemed to satisfy her, and she settled again beneath his arm. Brano watched her face as she gradually fell asleep.

13 April 1967, Thursday

The Café-Restaurant Landtmann sat across from the Burg-theatre, part of the ring of enormous Habsburg buildings around the Innere Stadt. In its dark wooden walls, mirrors and intarsias of bouquets – blond walnut inlaid in the dark walls – looked down on a cramped scene of marble-topped tables stuffed with politicians involved in serious discussions over late breakfast. A woman offered to take his coat; when he declined, she frowned and told him it was the tradition, that all coats were taken, so he handed it to her. She gave him a slip of paper with a number on it. Again, Brano felt underdressed.

He found Lutz in the back, beneath a tall, narrow mirror in which he could see himself approach, a short man in this crowd. Lutz's tiny table was overflowing with empty cups and saucers, dirty spoons, and a full ashtray. He was reading from a stack of typed pages that he put away when he noticed Brano. He smiled and stuck out his hand but didn't have room enough to get up.

'Delightful to see you, Brano. Delightful. What'll you have, a coffee? Something stronger?'

'Just coffee.'

Lutz took care of the ordering and stretched beneath the table.

'You've been working hard,' said Brano.

'As always, my man. As always.'

'Writing?'

'*Reading.* Government reports, that sort of thing. It's dull enough to make you want to shoot yourself.'

'Why are you reading government reports?'

'Sometimes it's the only way to learn things.'

'Is this that Politburo-shaking project?'

Lutz considered him. 'You, my friend, are going to have to wait, just like the rest of the world.'

Brano prodded carefully. He'd been given a clear, un-ambiguous order, but nothing quite added up. His imagin-ation could not manage a buffoon like Lutz at the helm of an international conspiracy. The answer would only be found in whatever Lutz was now working on behind a pile of extinguished cigarette butts. But this was the one subject Lutz refused to expand on. Brano's casual questions met with the defiant answer that his work was not yet ready for public consumption and, once, the reminder that Lutz, because of his writings, was a dangerous man. 'Come on, Brano. You're my friend. Why would I want to put you in danger?'

Brano found he had no good answer for that.

'So?'

Brano furrowed his brow as the coffee arrived in a cup so delicate he feared he might break it.

'So are you here to tell me your tale of intrigue? For *Escape from the Crocodile*?'

'That's just what I was here to do.'

Lutz took notes in a worn spiral notebook as Brano spun his story. Like always, he stuck close to the truth. He talked about a childhood in Bóbrka and his move, after the war, to the Capital. They'd both been there at the same time, so they shared stories of deprivation and the Russian soldiers' atrocities. Brano said that this had always been difficult for him, that he could see the moral problems inherent in his career. A large part of his job had been to cover up Russian crimes, while arresting those who had, it seemed, done nothing.

'I thought you were just an informer.'

Brano had considered sticking to the bland version he'd told Monika – a trench coat in a hotel – but Lutz, given Lochert's assessment, would be able to see through the lie. 'That's the story for the Carp.'

Lutz took a breath. 'Then why did you stay with it?'

'Because it was all I had. I couldn't be a farmer any more – my family no longer owned land. What else was I to do? And you remember, it was no small thing in those days to be in a position to get a little extra bread and salt.'

'You kept your family in salt.'

'In a manner of speaking, yes.'

Filip Lutz looked at the notes he'd written, then back at Brano. 'What, exactly, did you do?'

'I tracked down dissidents.'

That earned a raised eyebrow, then a nod when he explained that he even measured the loyalties of people within his own Ministry for State Security. He kept a desk in the homicide department of the People's Militia, measuring the loyalties of the militiamen as well.

'Did you arrest many of them?'

'Not many. A few.'

'Did you only work inside the country?'

'No.'

'Exotic places?'

'Some.'

'Where?'

Brano cleared his throat and apologized. 'I'm not really comfortable with too many details. Not yet.'

Lutz said he understood. 'When did you become disillusioned?'

Brano paused, then lied smoothly. 'I'd always been disillusioned, in my own way. But it was always an abstract disillusionment.' He said he was a believer in Marx, in the promise of communism, and he knew sacrifices had to be made. But how many sacrifices have to be made before you stop and say, *This is enough?*

'How many does it take?'

'It takes hundreds. Thousands. Either that or simply

one sacrifice that affects you personally.' Brano told him that while he was at home he had been framed for a murder.

'Framed?' Lutz pulled back a little, elbows rising from the table. 'For murder?'

'My superiors, they framed me for murder in order to get rid of me. I'd already been kicked out of the service, but that wasn't enough. They wanted my career to end in a prison cell.'

Lutz stared at him. Then he wrote a few more lines and asked about Brano's family – his mother, his sister, his father. Brano told the truth. They lived in their village far from the Capital. His father had fled west after the war.

'Was that it, maybe?'

'Was that what?'

'Was that,' said Lutz, warming again, 'perhaps the seed of your discontent? That your own father refused to live under communist rule?'

'My father had no conviction. He was just a coward. And in the West he probably died a coward.'

'He's dead?'

'I assume so. There was never any word from him.'

Lutz, after a moment, wondered about any ex-wives or scattered children and was visibly irritated by Brano's negative answer. 'Something,' he said. 'I need something more. A story doesn't make a reader cry just because the main character gets into trouble. Something in the character must hook the reader, make him care. Make him think this guy's not just another state security officer who got uncomfortable. What's your hook?'

Brano stared at him, opened his mouth, and closed it. 'Why do you want to make your readers cry?'

* * *

Instead of taking the number 38 tram north, he returned to Web-Gasse and telephoned Dijana to say he would see her tomorrow. 'I just need a night alone.'

'You don't like it here?'

'I didn't say that, Dijana. You know I like it there.'

'Okay,' she said, then paused. 'I think I can to see what you mean. You will be alone?'

'Of course, Dijana.'

'*Poljubac,*' she said. Kiss.

'*Poljubac.*'

He turned on the television. He did not want to be alone, and he didn't want to be without her. More than that, though, he didn't want to treat her coldly, and he knew he would. He wanted to ignore the photographs he'd hidden behind his refrigerator but couldn't. Dijana was, at the very least, an informer for the Russians, who never trusted their satellites to do anything independently.

No, he would not see Dijana today, and perhaps not tomorrow, either. He had a man to kill.

But Filip Lutz, though he might have a certain misdirected talent for writing, was no organizer. He was the kind of man one used as a mouthpiece for an operation, or as a front. You put him in public so that attention would be drawn away from what was really going on. The Committee for Liberty in the Captive Nations was probably being used similarly. In public, they could be seen as the fools of reaction, while their quieter members, perhaps the old man Andrew, worked steadily in the background, with utmost seriousness.

Filip Lutz was simply unable to head a conspiracy that aimed at bringing down any government. He spoke too much; he lived too much on his pride.

Still, Yalta – and therefore Cerny – believed this so strongly that it had arranged a byzantine conspiracy to place Brano at Lutz's side, in order for him to kill Lutz.

He'd killed enough men in his time not to be dissuaded by the act itself. Murder is just a governmental tool, be it assassination or war. More than once, Brano had been called on to execute old comrades, a few he was even fond of; but in each instance he had understood the inevitability of that final option. *Mokrii rabota* – wet work – was never done without justification.

Perhaps the only justification he needed was that he had been given a clear, unambiguous order from Yalta Boulevard. There was a time when that had been enough.

14 April 1967, Friday
Day 26. The Subject has altered his schedule over the last two weeks. Beginning with visits to the Carp (suggested by our own people – see report of 30 March), then a party at the residence of the Italian ambassador – hosted by Ersek Nanz, Norwegian publisher – and a surprise: his visit to the Committee for Liberty in the Captive Nations for a lecture by Filip Lutz.

This agent's perception of the Subject's relationship with Lutz began as suspicion. Considering Lutz's role as a thorn – albeit a small thorn – in the side of the socialist world, any new figure in his life is examined carefully, and the Subject is a security risk of the highest order. But after a series of meetings between Lutz and the Subject, this agent has become less suspicious. First, at Ersek Nanz's party, the Subject was seen by sources sharing a hashish pipe with Lutz (which, we now understand, was one catalyst for the Subject's erratic actions in the Volksgarten that same night – see Day 20). Later, as mentioned above, the Subject attended one of Lutz's strongly anticommunist lectures. (He did, however, leave early, but only at the insistence of Fräulein Dijana Franković, Yugoslav, who invited him back to her apartment.) Yesterday, he visited Lutz at his local café, the Landtmann. The subject of their conversation was not verified, but from this agent's vantage point at the window, it seemed extremely personal. And

*today, the Subject returned to the Landtmann for another
conversation with Lutz.*

*This agent's assessment is that the Subject is genuinely inter-
ested in Lutz – in his stories and his persona, which we all know
can be very intoxicating. Considering the Subject's admitted depression after his arrival, it seems he has found in Lutz a possible, if
ironic, friend. The additional entrance of Dijana Franković into
his life can also be taken as a positive move, for the Subject will
not consider himself, as he put it the night of Ersek Nanz's party,
'alone'.*

Lutz had been talking for an hour, fat hands spread across
the table as he recounted his previous night with the interpreter from Ersek's party, who had come to the Carp at
his invitation. He'd manhandled her to another bar, where
they wouldn't be interrupted, then kissed her in a dark
corner. She wouldn't come home with him, but, he admitted, perhaps that was best, for on their walk to his car,
she placed her hands on her knees and vomited on the
pavement.

'And you? How's she treating you? Dijana – that's her
name?'

'Very well, Filip.'

'And?'

'And what?'

'You're not allowed to be discreet with me, my man.'

Brano ran his tongue over his teeth. 'Tell me about your
big project and I'll learn to be indiscreet as well.'

Lutz cradled his water glass below his chin. 'Something's
got into you, Brano, and I'm going to figure it out if it kills
me.'

'Only curiosity. Does it have something to do with those
American fundamentalists?'

'The Committee?'

255

'Yes, the fundamentalists.'

Lutz pursed his lips, half-considering. 'You know the difference between fundamentalists and your run-of-the-mill Christians? They don't half-believe. If something is true, it's goddamned true all the time. You've got to respect their lack of moral ambiguity.'

'I know some Marxists like that. How long have you been involved with them?'

'A few years now. They do great work in the schools.'

'Loretta told me. Is Sasha Lytvyn working with them, too?'

'Yeah, Sasha mentioned he knew you. Then he stopped coming to the Carp.' He shook his head. 'No – he's too scattered to join any organization.'

'Did he tell you how he knew me?'

'Just that it was a long time ago.'

Brano looked at him a moment. He said, 'Sasha parachuted into the country in 'fifty-two. He was part of an American operation to commit sabotage behind the Curtain. I caught him, then I interrogated him.' Brano waited a second, then added, 'You could say I tortured him.'

Lutz wiped his mouth. 'No, he didn't tell me that.'

'What about the old man I saw at your lecture? He had a white beard.'

'Andrew?' Lutz began tapping the table unconsciously.

'Yes,' said Brano. 'Andrew Stamer. American?'

Lutz nodded, tapping away. 'He's American now. He escaped back in the forties. Smart guy!'

'What does he do for a living?'

Lutz rocked his head as he spoke. 'He had some kind of business back in New York or New Jersey. Launderettes, I think. He made his money and retired early. That was smart, too. Then he helped Dr Rathbone start the Committee. He told me he wanted to give something back.'

'He's one of the quieter ones, isn't he?'

'How do you mean?'

'I mean he doesn't give lectures like you do.'

'I think his official title is international coordinator.'

'A grand title,' said Brano. He drank the last of his coffee and set the cup down. 'But listen, I actually could be of help to your project. We both know I have a few talents.'

Lutz stopped tapping and stretched his feet beneath the table. He cleared his throat. 'Take a rest, okay? You've got every reason to relax a while and just be satisfied. You're in the West. You've got a girl who's half your age. Hell, you're friends with me! But learn some patience, Brano. Trust me. Next month the world will look like an entirely different place.'

'And I'll have you to thank for it?'

'If you want to see it that way. But what about you? You're more relaxed than when you arrived – that's something. She's good in bed, is she?'

Brano blinked at him.

'My God, man, you're blushing! *Kellner!*' he called, snapping the air. 'A bottle of Veuve Cliquot!'

A waiter halfway down the room looked up from a table and nodded.

'So tell me everything, you dirty bastard.'

'I'll only say I'm very fond of this girl.'

'You should be,' said Lutz. 'Men our age don't get this every day. Watch out you don't get a heart attack in the middle of it.'

Brano and his sunburned shadow left the Landtmann an hour later, taking the tram back to Web-Gasse. Half a block away from number 25, the shadow paused, and when Brano looked he saw why. She was standing outside his door. She strode up to him in a short coat, then wrapped her arms around his neck. '*Dragi*, I am missing you. You are hungry?'

'I can be.'

'*Dobro.* I take you to dinner.'

Although he didn't want to go there, the only local place he knew was the Liebengaste, and so, with their sunburned companion just outside the window, they settled at a table. The waitress who brought the menus nodded at him, remembering his last visit. He ordered schnitzels for them both, then, after the waitress had left, leaned towards Dijana. 'I'm sorry, did you want schnitzel?'

'I don't care, Brani. I just want to seeing you.'

He lit her cigarette and tried to avoid looking out the window.

'Last night,' she said as she took a drag, 'I was at Jazzklub Abel. Not for the work, but a drink. Poor Abel – you should see him. He is very sad. But he asking me about you. He say, *What this Brano Sev do?*'

'Did you tell him?'

'I can't to say you was a spy, of course. I say I don't know. Something with business. And then I start to thinking – what I know about you?' She shook her head. 'Nothing. I know you was a spy, but that is not information. I know you was friend with Bertrand, maybe you is dangerous. I know you go back to your home and you start to writing me, then you stop. I not know why. I not know even if you have wife – do you have wife?'

'No,' said Brano. 'I don't have a wife.'

'Then what?' Her voice rose and her cheeks turned pink. 'I know I am a good girl, I not asking you questions because I have respect for the privacy. I waiting for you to tell me what you want to tell me. But you tell me nothing, Brani. I start to thinking maybe I'm stupid. You come again to Vienna and say nothing why you stop to writing.'

She placed her elbows on the table. 'Are you understand me?'

He moved his fork to sit beside his knife, then stared at it. He said, 'I stopped writing to you because I was told you were a spy.'

When he looked at her, the flush had gone from her cheeks. '*What* you said?'

'There are photographs,' he explained. 'Photographs of you with men from the KGB. In your apartment.'

'*Boli me kurac,*' she said, which was one of the few Serb phrases he knew – essentially, 'my dick hurts', meaning that this was simply not to be listened to. She said, 'You people, you are terrible.'

Then she dropped back in her chair and crossed her arms. Brano was overcome by an unexpected desire to apologize. He hadn't taken those pictures, but the pictures had come from his world. He was the kind of man who did this, who set up cameras with long lenses to see into a young woman's private world. It was his world that made such things acceptable. While he was thinking this, the waitress brought their food. She seemed to notice the awkward silence, in which Dijana, her face reddening again, stared at her schnitzel with something like terror.

Once the waitress was gone, Dijana straightened again and leaned towards him, over her plate. She whispered, 'Listen, Brano Sev. I don't must justify what I am doing to you, not to no one. This is why I not live in Yugoslavia. They ask me always questions. *Dijana, why you stop with your school? Why you not talk with your friends no more? Why, Dijana, your father is so sick – maybe you think he should not been in jail?* They ask me, *Dijana, why you want live someplace what is not your home? You are not patriot?*' Her eyes were very big. '*This* is why I go. Because I will not to have interrogations no more. And not from the man what is my lover.'

259

Brano nodded into the fist holding up his chin. 'If I were the manager of a club – if I were Abel – then you would be right, I'd have no need to ask this. But I'm not a restaurateur. I spent all my life doing intelligence work, and if you were a spy, it would matter to me. I don't want to think you're using me.'

'Using?'

He nodded.

'Too long,' she said. 'For too long you doing this, you don't see what is good no more.' She waited, but he didn't answer. So she shrugged and said, 'You want to know?'

'Yes.'

She touched the edge of her plate. 'Why you think Bertrand buy me apartment? Because he love me too much? I was thinking this at one time, but no. He use me for place to meet with his friends. Those Russians. Of course I did not know they was KGB – he telled me nothing. But it's not surprise me. He meet with them and I make coffee for them, and then he ask me not to stay there. He send me out to the store so he can to talk.'

Brano folded his hand over his forehead. 'Why didn't you tell me this before?'

'Why I should tell you?' She shook her head. 'It's not your business. And anyway, I sweared to him I will tell nobody. He make me swear. He was afraid Lutz will find out.'

'Lutz?'

'*Pa da*. Filip Lutz. They was friends, together all the time. Me, too, we all had good time together. In that time we was at the Carp. But Bertrand, he was scared from Lutz – he say if Lutz find out he is with Russians, then he is dead man.' She frowned then, momentarily confused. 'You think maybe Lutz, he find out? He kill Bertrand?'

'I don't think so,' said Brano. 'What was Bertrand doing with the Russians?'

'I don't know. Just talk. He meet them three times what I know of. In my apartment. But I don't know what they was doing – I am no spy.'

'Wait.' Brano tried to think through the fresh accumulation of *zbrka*. 'You and Bertrand and Filip were friends at that time.'

'*Da*. And that terrible Ersek Nanz, too, you know. But after Bertrand die I stop going to the Carp. It depressing. Anyway, I wanted to be with you, not in Vienna. You remember?' Finally, a brief smile.

'I remember.'

'And you was thinking I am spy!'

Brano rubbed his scalp. 'I wasn't sure, but I suspected.'

'You still suspecting?'

'No,' said Brano. Then he called to the waitress for a bottle of wine.

15 April 1967, Saturday

She didn't have to be at the Jazzklub Abel until one, so they spent the morning in her apartment lazily, eating and making love, until a headache crept up on him. She gave him aspirin and boiled tea.

Brano could think of a hundred different ways to punch holes in the story she'd told him. For any good operative there were many layers of cover, each more convincing than the next. The thing that worried him most was her acceptance. She knew that he had worked for state security all his life, yet she had decided to simply believe that his life's work was now over. Her father had been sent to a prison because of men like him, and she had left her country because of those same men. She had found refuge in the West and then, inexplicably, had chosen a lover from that world.

Brano found himself thinking over his tea that even if

she were telling him the truth, he would never be able to accept it completely. He was, as she had pointed out, terrible.

'You are cold again.'

'What?'

She pulled her robe over her shoulder. 'I can see when you, your head, it is far away.'

'Sorry,' he said. 'It's the way I am.'

She grunted and reached for her tea. '*Pa da*. Is what I am learning.'

In the afternoon he walked her to the Marienbrucke, which crossed the Danube Canal into the Second District, where the Jazzklub Abel lay.

'Why you not come with me?' she asked. 'You can to meet Abel.'

'I don't think Abel wants to meet me.'

'Why not? He's not boy.'

'Maybe I don't want to meet him.'

'*Dragi*,' she said, and kissed his cheeks. 'You is not so cold after all.'

He smiled.

'And your head? How is it?'

'It hurts.'

She straightened the lapels of his jacket and kissed his forehead, then whispered, 'I don't want to making your head more bad, but there is a man behind you what is watching us.'

'Does he have a sunburn?'

'You mean his face?'

'*Da*,' he said.

'Yes, is very bad.'

'He's just watching me, don't worry.'

'Who he is?'

'He's Austrian.'

'Ah,' she said, nodding and looking over his shoulder. 'He is always with you?'

'Always. To be sure I'm not getting into trouble.'

'You know what?'

'What?'

'I make stupid choice for a man, no?'

'Yes, Dijana. You made a terrible choice.'

She snorted a laugh, kissed him again, then headed off. He watched her cross the steel bridge, waiting until she was just out of sight, before turning back.

As usual, Filip Lutz was at his back table, surrounded by soiled cups and saucers, and a full ashtray. Ersek Nanz was there, too, leisurely stretched out in his chair, listening to his friend's lecture. Through the windows, Brano's shadow wrote something in a notepad.

'Our senior intelligence officer has arrived!' said Lutz. 'Come, come.'

Ersek turned in his chair with some effort, sticking out a hand. Brano patted his back and sat down. 'I'm not feeling particularly intelligent today.'

'Just today?' asked Ersek. He was brushing dry his upper lip, where the beginning of a moustache was forming. 'You're doing better than the rest of us. Turns out one of the principal shareholders in Nanz Editions just died of a heart attack. Now his executors want to sell his piece to pay off his debts. You want to invest in publishing?'

'With what? Ask Filip.'

Lutz opened his hands. 'I already own thirty percent.'

Brano scratched his sore forehead to mimic serious thought. 'I suppose I could get someone to sell my Trabant back home.'

That received a few seconds of obligatory laughter.

'How's your girl?' asked Lutz.

Nanz straightened. 'Yeah, you don't bring her out, do you?'

'Why didn't you tell me you knew her?'

Both men fell silent, until Lutz said, 'We don't know her that well.'

'Not from what she says.'

Ersek leaned forward. 'How does she say it?'

'She says you two and Bertrand Richter were all very close.'

'That's how it is among expats,' said Lutz. 'We form close friendships for a while, then we stop.'

'You stopped when Bertrand was killed.'

Ersek found a cigarette and popped it into his mouth. 'You have to admit, Brano, that puts a strange tone on a friendship, when your friend's dead.'

'Even more so when he's killed,' said Lutz.

'Do the police know who killed him?'

'The Austrian police couldn't find a hooker in the Canal District with a handful of koronas. But he was a good guy.'

'A bore, though,' said Ersek. 'You have to admit.'

'Sure,' said Lutz.

'I don't know about Lutzi,' Ersek continued, 'but to tell the truth, I was nice to him because he had a pretty girlfriend. I think a lot of people were the same way. And now – now I've got a reason to be nice to you!'

Lutz rapped the table. 'Let's change the subject, okay? It's no good for my indigestion.'

The change of subject seemed an excuse for Lutz to regale them with the details of his latest date with the interpreter, with whom, this time, he had finally achieved success.

'You're a bastard,' said Ersek. 'A lucky bastard.'

Lutz squeezed out from behind the table. 'That I am.' He patted Nanz's shoulder, excused himself, and lumbered off to the bathroom.

'What do you think of Dijana?' asked Brano. 'Honestly.'

Ersek considered him. 'I liked her. A little baffling, but you probably know that. All those Balkan chicks are. And she gets around, if you know what I mean.'

'No. I don't know what you mean.'

'You asked, right? But she's perceptive as hell, that one, and great to look at.'

'And Richter? Was their relationship good?'

'Who ever knows these things? He was crazy about her, that's for sure. He was paranoid someone would take her away. He accused each of us at one point or another. Me, Lutz, even that cold fish from the embassy, Josef Lochert – you know him?'

Brano hesitated. 'No. No, I don't.'

'Well, Lutzi brought him to the Carp one night for a good time.'

The air seemed to dry up. 'This Josef Lochert is a friend of Filip's?'

'Sure,' said Ersek. 'They've known each other years. Longer than I've known Filip. But if you meet Lochert, you'll understand why Bertrand got upset. He has a way of staring that's entirely impolite, and he gave it to Dijana. Bertrand went off the handle completely and tried to take him outside for a fight.'

'They fought?'

Ersek shook his head. 'Nah. I wanted to see Bertrand get kicked, but Lutz stepped in and made peace. What did he say? Yes. *If we fight one another, then there'll be no fight left when we need it.* Or something like that. Very poetic.'

When Brano realized he was tapping the table like a nervous old man, he placed his hands in his lap.

After a couple of drinks, Brano feigned fatigue, which the

men immediately associated with his sex life. They laughed as he reddened and gave him masculine slaps on the back, whistling as he walked away. His sunburned shadow followed him south, in the tram, all the way to Web-Gasse.

In his bathroom, he prepared the note that demanded an 11.30 appointment the next day, just before his scheduled meeting with Ludwig, and wrapped it around the nail. He stuck it in his pocket, grabbed his book, and left again. The light was failing, but he didn't care. He walked up Liniengasse to Gumpendorfer, then found his bench at Eszterházy Park. He stared at the open book.

Brano remembered a time, which seemed very long ago, when he could move slowly in the street and etch out a painstaking portrait of a dull, daily life, all for the benefit of the socially infirm men who followed him. But as he closed the book far too soon, the urgency came in the form of his mother's voice. *Brani, do you think this is the family I always hoped for?*

He pressed his hands to the bench to help himself up, wandered to the third tree, and unzipped his trousers. He had to concentrate to get anything out of himself, and when he transferred the nail to his right pocket, dropped it through his trouser leg and stomped, it was into earth that was dry and unyielding.

The sunburned man standing at the base of the flak tower watched him curiously.

Dijana stayed at Web-Gasse that night, and they cooked together, stopping once to make love on the kitchen counter. *'Dragi!'* she said, as if anything could surprise her. Then they half-watched late-night television and split a bottle of wine that they soon brought to his bed. She told him she wouldn't stand for masculine untidiness and would clean his apartment the next day. He smiled and rolled her over, into the pillow, so she could not see the *zbrka* all over his face.

Brano waited until the door to the Liebengaste bathroom was shut before reaching to turn on the light. White walls glimmered around him, and Lochert looked upset. He was sweating.

'What's going on?' asked Brano.

'I was going to ask you the same thing. You have your orders. There's no reason for us to meet.'

'We're going to talk.'

'What on earth do you need? You've met the guy I don't know how many times, you know what to do.'

'You've been lying to me,' said Brano. 'You never mentioned you were an old friend of Lutz's.'

'It's a small city.'

'Not that small. And you never told me that Bertrand Richter was holding meetings with the Russians. He was using Dijana's apartment for his sessions.'

'Did she tell you that?' Lochert raised an eyebrow. 'You're a sucker, Brano Sev.'

Brano ignored that. 'Richter believed that Lutz would kill him if he found out he was meeting the Russians. Lutz! He couldn't kill a man if he tried.'

'And?'

'And then we find the major players all together, in the Carp. Richter, Lutz, and you.'

'Don't forget your girlfriend,' said Lochert.

'How could I?' Brano stepped closer. 'Bertrand Richter tried to start a fight with you over her. What made him so nervous?'

'I like to look at pretty girls. What's wrong with that?'

'Bertrand was sitting with Lutz, whom he feared,' said

Brano, 'and Lutz had brought along a man with experience in killing. You. Richter feared that he had been uncovered.'

'What on earth are you talking about?'

'Richter never was GAVRILO.' Brano paused, the words making last night's insomniac suspicions real. 'He was leaking information, that's true. But to the Russians, not the Austrians. And he wasn't giving away our networks. He was exposing next month's insurrection.'

Locher's mouth worked the air.

'When we – or when you – killed Richter, we weren't working for Yalta. We were working for Lutz.'

Lochert rubbed his face, but when he brought his hand away, he was smiling. 'Come on, Brano. You've got paranoid in your old age. We had the evidence that Richter was selling information to the Austrians, and if he was also selling to the Russians, that's no surprise.'

'I never saw those lorries being checked on the Austrian border,' said Brano. 'You're the one who reported it back to me. No.' He pointed. 'You were probably the informer. You, or Lutz, were GAVRILO.'

Lochert, against the wall, waited a moment before answering. 'So you're thinking that I killed Richter in order to protect myself?'

'I'm not sure.' Brano stepped back. 'But you and Lutz were working together, and both of you wanted Richter dead. Now, though, you want me to kill Lutz. Why?'

Lochert found some confidence. 'I don't have to tell you anything, Brano. I'm your *rezident.*'

'Fine, then I'll walk over to the embassy and tell them everything I know. And I have some idea what the Lieutenant General will do to you.'

Lochert, to Brano's surprise, laughed quietly. 'You know, this is what happens when you give people half-information.'

He sighed. 'Maybe it's my fault. I'm secretive. It's my nature.' He looked away for a moment, into the mirror over the sink, then rested his hands on his hips. 'I'll be in trouble if this gets out, you know. We've had our problems in the past, but I don't want to think you'd reveal what I'm going to tell you.'

'Tell me,' said Brano.

'Okay.' Lochert placed his hands behind himself, on the small of his back. 'I've told you about Lutz's operation to start a revolution back home. That's the absolute truth. And it's true we don't have many details. Sometime in May, that's about it.'

'It's the fourteenth of May,' said Brano. 'That's what Richter said to me on the phone, back in August. You were with me when he let that slip.'

Lochert raised his eyebrows. 'Very good, Brano. Quite a memory. But Richter – he was selling out Lutz's plan to the Russians, yes. That's how we first learned of it. The Russians told us, and we told them we'd take care of it ourselves. We didn't want the KGB doing our work for us. But he was also central to the conspiracy itself. That's why I framed him in August.'

'But why didn't we capture Richter?' asked Brano. 'It would have been simple. He could have told us what we needed to know. That was stupid.'

'No it wasn't,' said Lochert. He paused, considering something, then brought his hands out from behind his back. In his right fist he held a pistol. Hungarian made, a Femaru Walam 1948, 9 mm.

Brano looked into Lochert's eyes. 'It wasn't stupid, because you're working with Lutz, and both of you needed to get rid of your leak.'

Lochert shrugged. 'It takes you a while, but in the end you do get to the truth, don't you?'

'And why do you want Lutz killed?'

'I think we'll have to end this conversation now.'

'You're going to shoot me?'

'We live by our orders.'

Brano's knees were weak, but when he dropped it was of his own volition. He crumpled to the tiles and kicked, catching Lochert's legs. Lochert tumbled, and an explosion filled the bathroom. Despite the buzzing in his ears, Brano caught Lochert's hand and twisted the pistol until it turned back and went off again, quieter this time, because it was buried in the soft flesh of Lochert's stomach.

Lochert's face tightened, reddening, his exposed teeth clenched. Then he coughed. Brano's knees ached as he stood up and stared at the dying man. Lochert coughed again, red spittle appearing on the white tiles. He seemed to want to speak but was unable.

Day 28. The Subject was seen entering the Liebengaste restaurant on Neubaugasse at 11.25. As it was a bright morning, the view into the restaurant was less than perfect visibility, but it appeared that the Subject sat at a table alone. He spoke with the waitress (who later said he simply ordered a coffee), then rose and went into the back of the restaurant, presumably to the toilet.

At 11.41, a gunshot was heard. Approximately thirty seconds later there was another, muted. This agent immediately entered the restaurant, weapon drawn, and proceeded to the rear. The door to the bathroom was open, and inside a man (later identified, via fingerprinting, as Josef Lochert, aka Karl Bertelsmann, known rezident *— see File 45-LOC) was found shot in the stomach. He was still conscious but did not speak.*

The restaurant staff claimed that, after the gunshots, an older man (presumably the Subject) ran out of the bathroom and into the kitchen, where he left by the rear door.

This agent followed his path into the alley behind the Liebengaste, but after fifteen minutes of searching was unable to find the Subject again.

Returning to the restaurant did not bring more facts to light, because Josef Lochert was dead.

PART THREE

The Inner Parts

18 April 1967, Tuesday
'Hallo?'

The sharp pain lay buried at the point where his skull met his spine. As if an ice pick had been shoved in, and occasionally someone tapped it, sparking white flashes in the darkness.

'Hallo?'

He was wet – through the pain he knew this. His lower half was freezing and rigid. And when he tried to open his eye – one, because only one would respond – he saw only blurred vertical lines.

'Ja, ja. Öffnen Sie die Augen.'

Beside the pain, and almost as intensely, he felt the déjà vu of a moment repeated. As if this day had been before, or this day was all of his days, and every day of his life he woke cold and wet, in excruciating pain, with a gravelly voice shouting inside his head.

Or outside his head. For he could now see, through the vertical lines, which were reeds, that the voice belonged to an old man with rubber boots squatting in the shallow water. The man leaned closer, licking his clean-shaven lips.

'*Sprechen Sie deutsch?*'

He tried to whisper, '*Ja,*' but his tongue wouldn't move. So he blinked.

'*Können Sie sich bewegen?*' Can you move?

He didn't know.

The old man reached out. 'Here. Give me your hand.'

He had to focus, but after a moment he could raise his right hand, and when the old man caught it the ice pick slid out a moment, then punched back inside to find a new spot in his brain. He gasped. The old man heaved and pulled him up like a sack of . . . something. His head spun, and he did his best not to scream.

'You all right? Not dying on me?'

The old man pulled his arm over his shoulder and helped him move forward, half-dragging him towards a rusting Volkswagen just beyond the water. Their progress was slow, but the old man's steadfastness kept them moving, and once they reached the car he used his free hand to pop open the passenger door. Then he slid his find into the seat.

The old man let out a rasping breath. 'You could've died.'

'Where am I?' he tried to say, but his voice came out of the side of his mouth, garbled. He repeated it, focusing on each word.

'You're by the Neusiedl Lake.'

He looked down at his body soaking the seat. His right arm and leg trembled, but he couldn't feel his left side. 'I am numb,' he enunciated carefully.

'Water's cold,' said the old man. 'Hypothermia, *ja*. That could kill you. Let's get going.'

He closed the door and walked around the driver's side. He sat behind the wheel and lit a cigarette, then, after a few tries, started the car and began driving down a dirt road.

Each bump, and there were many, was agony, and he

tried not to be sick. The road became paved, and a town appeared up ahead, but they turned off onto another dirt road that ended in a low, simple house with flower boxes in the windows.

The old man helped him to the front door and opened it without a key. He turned on a ceiling lamp and spread his hands to the mess around them. 'Wasn't expecting guests.'

'A bathroom?'

The old man pointed at a door. 'The aspirin's behind the mirror.'

He hobbled to the door, holding on to a chair and a table along the way.

'Say,' said the old man. 'You have a name, don't you?'

'Of course,' he said, then pushed into the bathroom, turned on the light, and pulled the latch.

After washing his hands and swallowing three aspirins, he stared at his wide, round face in the mirror, then touched the moles on his cheek. He had noticed the stiffness in his jacket pockets since the boat but hadn't touched them. Now he reached in his inner pocket, coming up with a passport – his face, his name – SEV, BRANO OLEKSY. The face in the mirror was different, though, the left half sagging weakly. There were Austrian schillings in his trouser pocket. He counted them with his good hand before, almost reluctantly, reaching into his left jacket pocket, the one he'd waited for with dread. He took out the pistol. He knew its make, its year, and that it was Hungarian, but he could not remember how he'd come across it. In his other pocket he found a stiff card with an account number from the Raiffeisenbank; on the opposite side was a handwritten telephone number.

The déjà vu held back the fear. His loss of memory was

not new – he knew this. Nor was the presence of a firearm. And the sense that he was a man in an immense amount of trouble – that was not new, either. He just didn't know what the trouble was.

It took some painful minutes of searching, but finally he found that the rusting lid to the drain in the middle of the floor was loose, held down by only one screw. He turned on the water to cover his movements and inserted a fingernail beneath the lid. He slid it to the side. There was just enough space to fit the pistol into the drain and close the lid.

He took off his wet clothes, which was difficult with only one hand, then washed his body in the tub with that same hand. The water jumped unpredictably between scalding and cold, and the soap seemed to be made out of sandpaper, but after a while he was, relatively, clean. He towelled himself off and found, beside a small electric washing machine, a robe.

When he left the bathroom, he smelled fried food – eggs, kielbasa – and coffee. 'Hello?' he called as he wobbled through the living room to the kitchen. Beside an icebox, the old man was on the telephone, smiling at him. He covered the mouthpiece. 'You look better, but your face is still funny. Have something to eat.'

'Who you are talking?'

'What?'

He focused. 'Who are you talking to?'

'I'm waiting to speak with Dr Simonyi. He can take a look at you later.'

'Hang up.'

The old man frowned. 'You sure?'

'Yes. Please. Hang up.'

The old man did as he was told, then cocked his head, but didn't ask the question. 'You must be hungry.'

They ate sitting on tall stools at the beige kitchen counter. He had a little trouble with the coffee – it trickled out of the corner of his mouth – but it was good, all of it, and it seemed to build energy beneath the pain.

'You know,' said the old man, 'I'm not a stranger to this. The lake's on the border, and we're used to finding waifs washed up. You're Hungarian, aren't you?'

He hesitated, then nodded.

'Usually, though, we find them washed up with a few bullet holes in them. Back in 'fifty-six, we got hundreds across this lake. Some even settled here. Dr Simonyi was one of those. First he tried his luck in Vienna, like they all do, but do you know how many Hungarian doctors showed up there? The competition was terrible. So he tried village life. He knows a thing or two about jumping the border. That's why I was calling him. I thought he could help you, besides the medical attention.'

'Thank you. Not yet. Now I need sleep.'

'Sure you do. You've been through a lot. Did you have that condition before? The face,' said the old man, touching the left side of his own face.

'Yes,' he said, though he didn't know.

They didn't speak as they finished their plates; and afterwards, when the old man offered him more, he just shook his head. He squeezed the bridge of his nose with his thumb and forefinger and asked if there was a bed he could use. The old man pointed at the door beside the bathroom.

He got up and limped across the living room, clutching anything for support, and when he got through the door, he dropped into the bed with his clothes still on.

Behind his closed lids the memories began as action – a train at night, sitting across from three old provincial women. Him, running through rolling vineyards with gnarled, barren branches. Then water and reeds, ducking his head into cold blackness.

22 April 1967, Saturday
He woke to a large face with a thick jawline. It was hand-some, with light blue eyes and flared nostrils. It smiled and blinked at him.

'About time you woke,' said the man, but not in German. Hungarian. 'Gerhard was worried you'd die in his bed. That would be bad luck. He'd have to throw the damn thing out!'

'Is it night yet?'

'Listen to you – *Is it night?* You've been in and out for four days. We got you up enough to put some food in you yesterday, but I imagine you're still pretty hungry.'

'You're the doctor?'

'Andras Simonyi. Gerhard said you're Hungarian. You speak it, but you're no Magyar. Where are you from?'

'What happened to me?'

The doctor paused. 'I don't know. It's possible you had a stroke. Give me your left hand.'

'A stroke?'

'A minor one, if one at all. Give me your left hand.'

It took some effort, but Brano was able to pull his hand from under the sheets and give it to the doctor.

'Make a fist.'

Though he could move his fingers a little, a fist was impossible.

'That's better than I expected. I can't say how much you'll recover, but you haven't done badly so far. How's your memory?'

Brano considered that. 'It was bad at first, but it's come back.'

'All of it?'

'Almost all.'

The doctor nodded, then took Brano's pulse and checked the dilation of his pupils. He seemed satisfied as he stood up. 'There's a robe over there with your clothes. Gerhard was good enough to clean them. Come out and join us. Let us know if you need some help.'

Brano said, *'Köszönöm.'* Thank you.

Once the doctor was gone, he slowly raised himself into a sitting position, feet just above the rug. He was naked, and he smelled sour, as if lake water had festered inside him. When he touched his face he felt a beard. His left side was still numb, but he was able to stand and make hesitant steps to the chair where his clean, folded clothes lay.

His memory, over the last four days of drifting in and out of sleep, had begun with a word from a dream – *zbrka*. Then other details followed, slowly filling him, telling him who he was, and why he was in Austria. He knew he had killed a man who had tried to kill him, and he remembered having the presence of mind, after shooting the man, not to run to the woman nor to the Westbahnhof, which was close to the restaurant. He'd instead walked quickly through the Liebengaste's kitchen, past confused cooks, into an alley, with the dead man's wallet and gun stuffed in a pocket. He'd taken a tram south to the Südbahnhof and boarded the first departing train, a slow regional with a rusting shell.

He remembered that he was sweating then, a spectacle for the prim suburban Viennese with their shopping bags and children. When the conductor arrived, he bought passage all the way down the line to Payerbach-Reichenau but instead got out at Neunkirchen. While waiting for the next train, he read a schedule he'd gotten from a sombre man behind the ticket window, then went through the dead man's wallet. He found the schillings and a driver's licence under the name of Karl Bertelsmann. He put the money in his pocket, then dumped the rest into a litter bin. That's when he noticed his shoe. He used his handkerchief to wipe the blood off of it.

He remembered taking the westward line to Mürzzuschlag, where the station bar was closed, and he paced the empty platform for hours as the sun set, wishing he had a heavier coat and trying not to wish for anything else. When he failed, it was her voice that came to him. *Dragi, where you are going?* The headache returned, pressing sharply behind his trembling right eye.

By the time his eastbound connection arrived, he was sneezing.

In the warmth of the full train, he became inexplicably dizzy. He worried that he would be recognized, but around him were old women who dozed, and when they woke they chose not to look at him at all. The only life in the car was a compartment of three drunk soldiers, howling into the night. One of the old women cracked her eyes at the sound, and he smiled and shrugged. She closed her eyes.

At Wallern im Burgenland, two stops short of Hungary, a soldier with a rifle smoked under fluorescent lights. He glanced up as Brano helped an old woman down, tensing his throat to suffocate a cough. Pain crackled through his skull.

He made the last bus to Apetlon as the station clock told him it was midnight. He and a smiling old man were the only ones on it.

From Apetlon he had walked, trying to retrace his path from months ago across the wet grass, but it was difficult; his memory was spotty. The headache surged again from the back of his head, and he found himself stumbling. But

282

there was only one desire in him by then, to leave this country and return to a place where he understood the rules.

He stopped once when the sound of barking dogs reached him. He waited, sinking into earth that had become mud. His headache had ebbed, but when it started again, his left leg became weak; his face tingled.

He fell sometimes, rising with mud-coloured hands. In spots he sank into brackish, cold water or stumbled over sharp reeds, and by the time he reached a marsh he thought might be the one he was looking for, he was soaked by cold water and sweat.

Then he stepped into the water.

His memory, perhaps out of revulsion, would not take him further.

Old Gerhard, boiling vegetables in a pot, was relieved there would be no deaths in his house. Dr Simonyi was curious. He complimented Brano on his admirable German and Hungarian. 'But what is your native tongue?'

Brano sipped hot tea. *'Mówię po polsku.'*

The doctor frowned, and Gerhard leaned forwards. 'What was that?'

'Polish. My language.'

'You know,' said the doctor, 'we're both familiar with your situation. I left Hungary in 'fifty-six, and Gerhard here has a soft spot for immigrants. Always has.'

'Beginning with this man,' said Gerhard.

'The point is, we're not going to hand you over to the police. You don't have to be shy.'

Brano nodded. 'I appreciate everything. But really, I can't remember much.'

The doctor sighed, either because he expected this or because he didn't believe it.

'What about your name?' asked Gerhard.

'I assume you know it already,' said Brano. 'My passport is in my jacket.'

The doctor smiled. 'And we also know your native language isn't Polish.'

'It's my family's language. So I wasn't lying.'

'You were just skirting around the truth.'

Brano shrugged.

'Listen,' said the doctor, lowering his voice. 'I imagine I have some idea what you're thinking right now. You're thinking you want to get out of here. But that's just paranoia, Brano. The best thing you can do for yourself now is to stay here. You understand?'

The doctor's eyes seemed to be saying something more. Or maybe they were just asking to be trusted. He tapped the table with a flat hand – a wedding ring clicked. 'Well, I suppose I should get back home. You can take care of our new friend?'

'Of course,' said Gerhard as he placed boiled carrots and potatoes on a plate. 'No more grease, like you said.'

'Thanks again,' said Brano.

'My pleasure.' The doctor and Brano shook hands, and Gerhard walked Simonyi out. Brano sipped his tea while they whispered by the front door. By the time the old man returned, he was finished eating, and he pushed himself into a standing position. 'I suppose I should take another bath.'

Gerhard sniffed. 'I was hoping you'd be the one to say that.'

The warming water ran into the tub, and Brano gazed at himself in the mirror above the sink. The weak half gave his face a suspicious look, like a wicked character in one of those films Ludwig loved. His left eyelid hung low, and his left cheek, beneath his spotty beard, had become flaccid. There was a razor behind the mirror, but he didn't use it. He did use Gerhard's toothbrush to scrape the detritus from inside his mouth. Then he sank into the water and, briefly, plunged his head under.

He had panicked – he knew this. After the one strand connecting him to his home had broken – or he had broken it, by killing Josef Lochert – Brano had panicked and fled. He hadn't even worried about the border guards along the lake, had only plunged in without forethought; this, in the end, worried him more than the possible stroke. He had, in the space of a few minutes in a Viennese bathroom, collapsed. He could have stayed in Vienna, could have even marched out to that shadow waiting on the street and explained that the Vienna *rezident* had tried to kill him. Ludwig would have been amused, but in the end he would have been satisfied that Yalta considered Brano a defector and was trying to silence him.

He came up and took a breath. He wiped his eyes with his right hand and blinked at the bathroom.

His mistakes were now irrelevant. Brano Sev was on the Austrian border, physically less than he had been, and he could either stay under the guardianship of these strangers, trying to find a way into Hungary, or he could return to Vienna.

That second possibility scared him most, so he set it aside for the moment.

Gerhard could perhaps be trusted, but the doctor was an unknown. He met with numerous people each day and had a wife, and one loose word to the wrong person could lead anywhere. The doctor was Hungarian, and as such he respected the legalities of paperwork; he would certainly feel the need to file something on the crippled, waterlogged stranger in need of his care.

So Brano would leave.

He could not walk through the border, because the Austrian post would be looking for him. He would have to wade through the marsh again, or find a point south of Sopron to make the farmland trek to the barbed wire. But in his state, that would be impossible.

And so, the option that he held at an arm's length came back to him.

Everything was in Vienna. In its intrigues lay the answers he'd been pursuing. In Vienna lay what was left of his career. And in Vienna, he thought as he stared at the murky water, lived Dijana Franković.

He unplugged the bath and reached for the towel. Insecurely, he stood and dried himself, then slipped into the robe. Before leaving, he squatted by the floor drain and popped it open. The pistol was wet, so he used the towel on it, then dropped it into the pocket of the robe.

Gerhard took out a bottle of Monopolowa potato vodka. He offered a toast to Brano's successful escape from the Empire, and Brano accepted the toast cordially. The alcohol warmed him, but after that he drank no more. He refilled his glass and affected sleepiness, but each time spilled his shot into the rug beneath the table, watching as Gerhard, always willing to accept one of Brano's inventive toasts – to Gerhard's health, to the spawning zander of the lake, to an end to the troubling situations history forces upon us – became more drunk and exhausted. Finally, around one, when Gerhard was having trouble remaining in his chair, Brano helped him to the bed. 'I'll stay on the couch tonight,' Brano told him. 'You deserve a decent night's rest.'

While the old man slept, Brano counted out two hundred schillings and left them on the kitchen table, then took one of Gerhard's overcoats from a rack beside the front door. Inside the pocket, he found the keys to his car.

There were no lights around the house, and for a moment it felt like Bóbrka, with its treacherous holes. He drove south, to where the roads again became erratic and the earth soft. This time he did remember, and repeatedly played the geography of his Austrian entrance in his head.

He parked near the marsh where Gerhard had found him, and only now understood that he had been at the wrong place. Had he not been incapacitated by that stroke, he would have struggled from one end of the marsh to the other and come out still in Austria. He had to go further.

His limp troubled him as he walked, but not as much as the low guard towers he knew were hiding not far away in the darkness. When an occasional flash of light came his way, he lay flat in the grass and waited, then, each time with more difficulty, climbed to his feet and moved on.

Then he spotted the upturned blue rowing boat on the bank of the marsh that he and the Sorokas had once waded across.

He looked up. The clear sky was choked with stars.

He squatted in the water alongside the cold hull. Then he plunged his hand into the water.

23 April 1967, Sunday
'So, I don't want to be rude, but what happened to you?'

Brano looked away from the road at the lorry driver, a big man with a moustache that curled up at the ends.

'You get into a fight or something?'

'Never know who you'll run into late at night.'

'That's for sure,' said the driver. 'I once picked up a guy north of Graz. Skinny kid, hair a little long, but nice enough looking. We started talking and he tells me he's trying to stop the war in Vietnam.' He grunted. 'A little kid. So I ask him how he expects to do that. *With this*, he tells me, and pulls out a gun as big as my forearm. Can you believe it?'

'Unbelievable,' said Brano, involuntarily touching the weight in his pocket.

'At the next petrol station you can *bet* I drove off before he was back from the toilet.'

Brano gave the man a half smile and returned to the road. The sun had just crested the hills behind them, casting long shadows, and ahead the outskirts of Vienna were coming into view. He'd parked Gerhard's Volkswagen on the northern shore of the lake and walked with a dead milkman's wet passport to the main road. He didn't have to wait long for a ride, and this talkative man, shipping lumber from eastern Hungary to Vienna, had kept him awake.

'I'm Heinrich. What's your name?'

'Jakob,' said Brano. 'Jakob Bieniek. You can let me off at Floridsdorf.'

'I can take you through the centre if you want. I've got to check in with my office.'

'Thank you.'

He got out at the Museum District and took a tram north along the Ringstraße. The morning was cool, breezy, and grey, the shaking tram filled with only a few early risers. They yawned into their hands, but Brano was too exhausted to do even that. More than anything, more than even Dijana Franković, he wanted a bed. He got out at Schottenring and crossed the street. The embassy was on Ebendorferstraße, between Universitätsstraße and Liebiggasse, so he took a parallel street to Liebiggasse, then approached the corner and waited.

There was the regular uniformed guard, standing outside

his pillbox with a machine gun hanging off his back. He was trying to light a cigarette with matches. Through the iron fence, a ground-floor light was on. At the very least, Brano would be something to brighten someone's otherwise dull Sunday morning.

The street was half full of parked cars. Those nearest him were empty, blocking the cars further up the road. He stepped out to get a better look, then slipped back behind the corner when the guard tossed down his empty book of matches, looked around, and crossed the road. He approached a car Brano could not see and bent over the window. The guard spoke a second, reached through the window, and brought a lighter to the cigarette in his mouth.

Brano backtracked and crossed Ebendorferstraße two blocks away, then approached again from the opposite side. From this corner, he could not see the embassy but could plainly see the grey Renault with the half-open window and the cigarette smoke misting out. Inside, Ludwig's crew-cut employee looked exhausted.

At ten, shops began to open, and he bought necessities – toothbrush and paste, a razor and shaving cream, and a cheap, wide-brimmed hat. He wore the hat as he left the haberdasher's, then took a bus to Concordiaplatz and walked the rest of the way.

He turned right at St Stephen's Cathedral and was soon on Weihburg-Gasse. Number 3's white façade looked as it had in August, but a different bellboy stood under the glass awning. The bellboy, however, said the same thing the other had.

'Grüß Gott.'

Brano nodded his reply and entered the Hotel Kaiserin Elisabeth.

The same woman sat behind the desk, now reading a different book. Her flaxen hair was styled differently. It was longer, more natural. He asked if they had a room free. They did, in fact. Then she smiled and asked for his documents.

'Sorry,' he said as he handed over the passport. 'It got wet.'

Although they were well trained and professional, both the bellboy and the receptionist had taken notice of his limp, of the way this man spoke through the side of his mouth, as if delivering secrets. Perhaps they also noticed that he did not remove his hat. He tried not to let this worry him. The one safe house he knew of was no longer safe, and he doubted that Ludwig and his associates would spend the manpower looking for him in the tourist centre.

She compared the photograph in Jakob Bieniek's passport to Brano's bearded face. She wrote down the passport number. She handed it back with a key and thanked him. 'Any luggage, Mr Bieniek?'

No, Mr Bieniek had no luggage.

But the bellboy, who had come inside during his registration, helped him with the lift nonetheless. Did he need assistance getting to the room? No, Mr Bieniek did not need help, but he still gave the boy a small compensation for his efforts.

In the room, he took apart the pistol, spread the pieces across the desk, and checked each for rust. There were five cartridges left in the clip, which he also laid out, to let everything air-dry.

24 April 1967, Monday
Brano didn't wake until seven the next morning. It had been a fitful sleep, but when he woke the fog had cleared from his head. He sat up and gazed at the disassembled pistol.

Before showering, he opened the Jakob Bieniek passport and propped it just below the bathroom mirror. Bieniek's expression was nondescript and bland, and Brano found it easy to imitate. The moles were placed differently, but no one would notice. His beard was a different shade, but that, too, was unimportant. The hair, though. Bieniek's scalp was wide, bald, and pale, while Brano's was not. He took out the razor and shaving cream, ran water over his head, and worked the foam into his hair.

He left the hotel at nine and spent the next hour on trams, changing often, until he had followed an arc around to Nußdorfer Straße. He got out one stop late and found a bookstore a half block north of her apartment.

'Grüß Gott,' said a spectacled woman behind a desk. He smiled at her, and she watched him limp to the wall of used paperback fiction beside the front window. The street was busy with traffic, cars parked tight against the kerb.

'Looking for something in particular?'

'Just browsing, *danke*,' said Brano. He gazed at the creased spines. Murder mysteries, cowboy fiction, sex-themed thrillers.

Across the street, a small Peugeot pulled out, giving Brano an unhindered view of the car behind it, where the driver was reading a newspaper. Brano picked a book at random – an English writer with a French surname – and flipped through it. The driver turned to the next page, and he caught a flash of sunburned face, more faded than before but still clearly damaged.

Brano closed the book, returned it to the shelf, and thanked the woman for her assistance.

He was running into dead ends. Ludwig had locked down the two obvious places Brano would be drawn to – one for safety, the other for sentimentality. He found himself respecting Ludwig's fortitude.

So Brano would ignore safety and sentimentality for the moment and focus on what was probably most important: information.

He walked east, towards the Danube Canal, and found a post office near the university. The woman at the desk told him to go to booth number 7, and he waited there, watching strangers until the telephone rang.

'Hello?'

Regina Haliniak, her voice muted by miles of telephone line, said, 'Importation Register, First District.'

'Regina, it's Brano.'

'Good to hear from you, Brano.'

'Can I speak to the Comrade Colonel?'

'He's not there with you?'

'In Vienna?'

'He left . . . four? Yes, four days ago. I thought he was going to meet with you.'

'Oh.'

'You all right? There was some fuss a few days ago about you, but no one tells me anything.'

'I'm fine, Regina.'

'Hold on, Brano. Let me put you through to the Lieutenant General. He wanted to speak to you if you called.'

'No, wait – ' Brano started to say, but she was already gone, replaced by a monotone ring. And though he considered it, he did not hang up.

'Brano,' said the congested voice that took him back, briefly, to a small, humid room in the basement of Yalta 36. 'Where are you?'

'Vienna.'

'What on earth is going on over there?'

Brano paused. There were no men standing over him with fists, but he felt the same anxiety he'd felt in August. 'I'd like to know what's going on myself, Comrade Lieutenant General.'

He heard static, then: 'Tell me, Brano. Why is Josef Lochert dead?'

'Self-defence.'

'And why, then, would you need to defend yourself against the Vienna *rezident?*'

'Because I learned he was a traitor.'

The Lieutenant General didn't answer at first. There was noise on his side, perhaps papers being shuffled. 'You damn well better be able to prove this. Or else a factory job will be just a dream.'

Brano gazed across the post office, where people were becoming blurry. 'I believe I can collect the evidence.'

'Go to the embassy, Brano. Major Romek will take your statement, and then we'll decide what to do.'

'I can't, comrade.'

'What?'

'The Austrians are watching it. I wouldn't be able to make it to the front gate.'

'Then come home. We can arrange a pickup in the Stadtpark.'

He rubbed his face. He had nearly died trying to get home. 'With respect, I suggest I wait for Colonel Cerny. I was told he's in Vienna.'

'I see,' said the Lieutenant General. 'That's the way you'd like to play it?'

'That's the way I'd like to play it. Please let him know that I'm staying at the Hotel Kaiserin Elisabeth, under the name Bieniek.'

'Bieniek?' The Lieutenant General let out a laugh that became a cough. 'Priceless, Brano.'

He waited until nightfall before visiting the Carp, spending the intervening hours at cafés further north. He limited his

293

outdoor time, and when he was on the street, he kept his hat low over his forehead, stroking his beard.

He approached Sterngasse from Fleischmarkt, waiting near the top of the steps, at Desider Friedmannplatz. From there he could see down the short pedestrian street to the next set of stairs leading down to Marc-Aurel-Straße. It was almost eight o'clock and had become cool. He buttoned his jacket and leaned against the railing, clearing his mind for the mental silence that made surveillance work bearable.

Through the window he saw a small crowd of familiars. Lutz's translator sat with the short man from Ersek's party, and Ersek was explaining something to Monika at the bar. Lutz was not around, but Brano did recognize the man with faint features who wobbled towards the front door and leaned against it, pushing through to the street.

He took two steps back, deeper into the darkness.

Jan Soroka came out, then paused by the Carp's window, breathing heavily, talking to himself. 'Yes, you know you can make it.'

Then Jan turned and wandered down the stairs leading to Marc-Aurel-Straße.

With his hands in his pockets, Brano stayed close to the opposite wall as he passed the Carp, then descended the steps. Jan was extremely drunk. He paused now and then, and once he put a hand against the wall, bowed his head, and rested before moving on.

They shared a tram southward, past the Stadtpark, Brano sitting in the back of the car while Jan slumped in the front. Occasionally he raised his head, shook it, and squinted out the dark window. He seemed to know where he was going.

They got off at Salesiandergasse, and during that last

stretch along the pavement, Soroka spoke to himself again. Brano couldn't make out all the words, but twice he heard 'Li', the second time louder than the first. Soroka stopped at number 6 Jaurésgasse and began searching for his keys.

Brano closed the distance between them as quickly as possible, his left foot dragging across the wet pavement as he pulled out Josef Lochert's pistol and pressed it against Soroka's back.

'Hello, Jan.'

Soroka fell to the steps. His hands fluttered a moment, then settled. He squinted. '*Brano?* Jesus, you know how to fucking scare a man.'

Brano switched the gun to his weak left hand and helped pull him up. 'The keys?'

Soroka looked at the gun. 'Sure. Here. It's the big one.'

Brano used the long key on the front door and walked with him to a ground-floor apartment. Just outside the door, Soroka looked at the gun again.

'Brano, should I be scared?'

He opened the door. 'No, Jan. I'm the one who's scared.'

While Soroka collapsed on the sofa, Brano went to make coffee. He stuck his head out of the kitchen now and then to be sure Jan hadn't left. By the time the coffee was poured, Brano had to shake him awake.

'Come on, Jan. Drink this. We need to talk.'

Soroka forced himself into an upright position and accepted the cup. 'It's a bad night for talking.'

'It's the only night we've got.'

Soroka sipped, then pursed his lips. 'This isn't bad.'

'I make a good cup of coffee. Can you focus?'

'Just barely.'

'Then drink more.'

Brano waited until he'd finished the first cup, then poured

295

him a second. Jan squinted at him. 'Something wrong with your face?'

'I'm bald.'

'Yeah, yeah. But your mouth. It looks kind of funny.'

'It's nothing.' Brano turned on a radio beside a few books on a shelf and found a station playing Austrian waltzes.

Jan smiled. 'You like this stuff?'

'No, but it's lively.'

He tilted his head, unsure if he agreed, and started on his second cup. He looked tired, but it was more than the fatigue of a drinking night.

'Why are you here, Jan?'

'In Vienna?'

Brano nodded.

'I thought you of all people would know. Everyone else does.'

'Lia?'

'Yeah. We got to Chicago, Illinois, and that's when she told me she wanted a divorce. She didn't want to be with me any more.'

'Did she give you a reason?'

'She said she couldn't trust me. I get her out of that hellhole, I bring her to the richest country on earth, and she can't trust me?'

'Well, Jan, you did leave her behind at first.'

'That's what *she* kept saying.' He looked into his cup, frowned, and put it on the coffee table. 'So I think to myself, where do I go now? Do I stay there? My English is terrible, and Chicago is . . . well, it's huge. Have you been?'

Brano shook his head.

'Don't bother. It's *cold*, too. My God, is it cold.'

'Then I won't bother.'

'This was the only place I could think of. But I've been

here a week, and now it's coming back to me. Why I didn't want to stay in the first place. I've got to get out of here.'

'Where?'

'I don't know. Sometimes I think I should just go back to Bóbrka. You ever think that?'

'Tell me. Tell me what you've heard since you've returned.'

'About you?' Jan grunted. 'Ludwig was all over the place last week. You've really pissed him off. He says you killed a man and ran away.'

'Does he think you know where I am?'

He shook his head. 'Not at all. He keeps asking about . . .'

'About what?'

'I don't suppose it matters now, does it?'

'What doesn't matter?'

Soroka settled his forearms across his knees. 'What you always asked me – what did I sell the Americans?'

Brano sat down finally. 'What did you sell them?'

'A story. Well, not the story, really, but my silence.'

'Explain.'

He took a breath. 'You know where I was before I went to Vienna?'

'At a conference.'

'That's right. On "the future of power in the socialist neighbourhood". Sounds good, doesn't it? It wasn't much of a conference, though, just a lot of empty speeches, but Gyula was quite nice for a spa town. Remember I told you about my visit to see Mihai?'

'Of course. When you were sixteen.'

'Turned out that another of the Pioneers in that group, Gregor Samec, grew up to be a scientist. Working in nuclear energy. He was one of the speakers at the conference. So I got in touch with him, and we went out to a bar. You've been there, to Gyula?'

'It's very nice.'

'It's excellent. You take the baths, then go get drunk. Gregor, though, wasn't enjoying it. He was nervous. It took a couple bottles, but I finally got it out of him: He thought he was being followed.'

Soroka blanked for a moment, as if he'd pass out, until Brano said, 'Why did Gregor think he was being followed?'

He blinked. 'Because he'd seen something he wasn't supposed to see. He was helping set up a test reactor in Vámosoroszi, near the Hungarian border. On the previous Saturday, he'd returned to pick up some papers he'd forgotten and found two men taking photos of the reactor and the field around it.'

'What men?'

'Wait.' He held up a finger. 'Well, he told them they were breaking the law. One of the men answered by showing him the cover of his identity card. It was from the Ministry for State Security. He told Gregor that if he mentioned this to anyone, he was a dead man.'

'Is this true?'

'He said it was. But I tried to calm him. After all, he hadn't seen the men since then, and I suggested he was just becoming paranoid, which was understandable.'

'And that's what you told the Americans?'

'I told the Americans that the next day I read in *The Spark* that Gregor Samec was found outside one of those wine bars. He'd been shot in the head.' He snorted. 'And so I was scared, too. Some Yugoslav gas researchers helped me leave with them, and from Zagreb it wasn't too difficult to get to Vienna. The Americans. They paid me not to tell anyone else the story.'

'Why?'

'How should I know?' he asked. 'And why should I care? I was broke, and they were willing to pay me. But I'm not as slow as I look. You see, Gregor, that night in Gyula, when he told me his story, he said that there were two men. A state security agent and someone else.'

'Yes?'

'That someone else, he told me, was an old man who didn't say a thing. He had a white moustache and beard. And as I was sitting in the American embassy, across from a white-bearded old man telling me not to breathe the story to anyone, I realized that *this* was the bearded man from Gregor's story. He's the one who paid for my silence, then later brokered the other deal – the Americans would get me inside only if I got you out. That was the deal.'

Brano pressed his palms together in front of his nose. 'Andrew.'

'Yeah. That's how he introduced himself to me,' said Soroka. 'You know him?'

'Why did he want me out?'

'I don't know.' Soroka shook his head. 'But he knew a lot about you. Names of your family, what to do to provoke you.'

Brano let this sink in. He'd always suspected the Committee was behind smuggling him here, but now it was clear. Not only the Committee but Andrew, the old man who left their literature in his mailbox.

'What about the other man? At the reactor. What did he look like?'

'Gregor didn't say; I didn't ask.'

'Have you seen Filip Lutz?'

'He's disappeared. Ersek said he heard about what you did to this Lochert character and is scared you'll be after him next.'

'Why does he think that?'

'Because you're a spy, Brano.'

'I was a spy.'

Jan looked at him. 'How should I know the difference?'

'Do you know anything about the fourteenth of May?'

'What day of the week is that?'

'Sunday. Do you know something?'

'Should I?'

Brano tried to cross his left leg over his right, but it was difficult, so he left both feet on the floor. He covered his face and rubbed his palms into his eyes.

'Have you talked to your Dijana Franković yet?'

Brano uncovered his eyes. 'Why?'

'She's worried to hell about you. She goes to the Carp every night and asks if anyone knows where you are. She's making a real nuisance of herself.' He smiled. 'My professional opinion is she's in love with you.'

Brano nodded.

'Are you in love with her?'

Brano looked up, but Jan wasn't smiling. 'I'm afraid so.'

Then Jan nodded as well, seriously. He allowed a small grin to creep across his face. 'I know I look like hell. But you – Brano, you look even worse. This is what love does to a man. No?'

25 April 1967, Tuesday

He waited until ten, when the tourist crowds began to swell. He had told Jan to stay quiet about his presence in Vienna but had no faith in the man's silence. So he mingled with the foreigners and their cameras, crossing to the edge of the old town, where the streets were emptier, then bought cigarettes in a tobacco shop and gazed out the window a few minutes, unwrapping the pack, before leaving again.

He walked the rest of the way, up Nußdorfer to the railway bridge, and bought hot tea in a paper cup from a kiosk. From where he stood beneath the bridge, he had a clear view of the front of her building.

300

He left his spot twice during the next three hours, once for another tea, once to urinate in an alley. Then, around two, he saw her cross the parking lot in front of her building, wearing jeans and a short brown leather jacket. Passing cars briefly obscured her, but when the traffic cleared he saw the sunburned man as well, just behind her, both waiting for the light to change. They crossed to the tram stop in the centre of the street. Brano walked to the opposite side, hat low, and continued to a doorway just past the stop.

When the number 38 pulled close, Dijana stepped forward, as did the sunburned man. Brano crossed the street behind the tram, hobbled up, then climbed into the third carriage as they boarded the second. Others piled on behind him, but he clutched a pole to hold his position by the window.

Dijana and her shadow got off at Haltestelle, where she entered a clothing shop, and her shadows, on either side of the street, looked at window mannequins. The sunburned man smoked three cigarettes during the half hour she shopped, glancing up and down the street while Brano walked to the corner, rounded it, and turned back, avoiding his gaze. When Dijana finally left the store, she hadn't bought a thing.

This was a young man's job, creeping around a metropolis, tracking people while remaining invisible. Decades ago, Brano had found the minutiae interesting, sometimes exciting, but he no longer remembered why. All the older Brano found himself desiring, as he followed Dijana and her shadow further down the street, was a life that looked a lot like retirement. Maybe Gerhard's small house on the Fertő Lake, and a woman not so different from Dijana Franković. A child as well? No. Brano Sev did not have the imagination to encompass all of that.

It was a little before four when, after more of Dijana's seemingly random stops, the three of them made it to Sterngasse. She did not hesitate as she entered the Carp. The sunburned man settled at the point where the Sterngasse stairs descended to Marc-Aurel; Brano, again, waited at the Friedmannplatz end of the street, leaning against the corner of a building. When he looked, he could just make out Dijana's form through the window as she fended off an old man with a white beard who had approached her. Andrew Stamer first put his arm around her shoulder, but she shrugged it off and threw some earnest words at him. The old man raised his hands, eager not to offend, and talked with her a while. She calmed and nodded; then the old man wrote something on a napkin and passed it over. He tapped her on the shoulder again before taking his shot glass with him to a back table.

She had a second beer, and as she talked with Monika, the barmaid shook her head sympathetically. Perhaps he was the subject of their talk. Whatever the subject was, it seemed to agitate Dijana. She kept using her palms to pull the sides of her short hair over her ears, to where it wouldn't reach.

Darkness had fallen by the time she left, and she trotted obliviously down the stairs past the sunburned man. From Marc-Aurel they walked east, towards the Danube Canal. They reached the Marienbrucke, and Brano, feeling weak from the exertion, realized this could go on forever.

He counted three other people on the bridge, men with ties and briefcases. But witnesses no longer mattered. Ludwig no doubt already knew he was back in town. Brano quickened his pace.

They were halfway across the bridge. The sunburned

man was five paces ahead of him; Dijana was ten more. The street was empty of traffic. Brano jogged those first five paces, his left leg cumbersome, pulled out the pistol with his right hand, and swung its butt into the shadow's neck.

He let out a shout but did not fall. Brano swung again as the man thrust back an elbow, catching his ribs. But the pain stayed solidly in Brano's fist, and he hit the neck again, then leapt on the man's back, an arm over his trachea. The sunburned man fought back, and they wrestled to the railing.

'*Brani!*'

He ignored her and twisted a pistol from the shadow's hand, tossing it into the canal. Grunting, Brano struck his neck again and felt the body relax. The man was weak but not unconscious. Brano hefted the man's top half over the railing, ignoring the moans – '*Nein, nein*' – and grabbed his kicking feet. He lifted, and the man tumbled over the edge.

'*Brani!*'

He waited for the break in the water, the shadow's head surfacing, arms splashing. German curses burst from the man's lips.

'Brano Oleksy Sev!' said Dijana.

When she hugged him, her leather jacket squeaking, he smelled the cigarettes in her hair.

She pulled her head off his shoulder to look at the railing. 'He is—'

'He's all right. I didn't want to kill him.'

Three men in ties fidgeted nearby, as if something were required of them but they didn't know what it was.

'I'm a policeman,' Brano told them.

The men looked at each other.

Very seriously, he said, 'Now, please excuse us.' He took Dijana's hand and began walking away.

'What you are doing?' Dijana whispered, barely suppressing a giggle.

'Just keep walking.'

Once they'd reached the other side of the bridge, Brano glanced back. The men were gone.

'Brani, what is happen?'

'Follow me.'

Still holding her hand, he led her to the end of Gredlerstraße, then left on Taborstraße, to the Church of the Brothers of Mercy. He pushed through the wooden doors into a plain entryway with notices for upcoming sermons.

'*Dragi* is Catholic now?'

They continued into the church, but an iron gate closed off access to the pews, so they moved back into a dark corner, beneath enormous portraits of saints.

'*Dragi*,' she said. 'What is wrong with you? You look bad. Your hair . . .' She removed his hat and touched his shaved scalp with cool fingers, her nose wrinkling.

'It's a kind of disguise,' he said.

She put her hands on his beard, a thumb touching the sloped left corner of his mouth. 'What is—'

'I'm all right, don't worry about me.'

She hugged him again. 'I was very worry.'

'I'm sorry,' he said. 'But I had to leave.'

'Who is this men?'

'What men?'

'They come,' she said, looking at his forehead. 'They ask where are you. This man, Luvi—'

'Ludwig?'

'*Da*, Ludwig. He say you kill a man. Brani, tell me. This is true?'

'Yes.' When he said this he was looking at the marble chessboard floor. 'He was trying to kill me.'

'Kill you? But *why,* Brani?'

'I can't explain.'

'*Dragi,* you make no sense.'

'I'm sorry,' he said. 'I just had to talk to you again.'

'And I to you, but what you must say?'

He had nothing to say. He'd followed her all day and had attacked a man to get to her. All that he'd known was that it was necessary. He rubbed his eyes.

He had become that thing that for men in his business was the beginning of the end. Dijana had turned him into a sentimental old man.

He stroked her hair as far behind her ears as it would go and whispered, 'I just want to say I miss you.'

Then he pinned her to the cold church wall and covered her mouth with his. After a minute, he pulled back, watching how she licked her lips. 'I like the way what you miss me. But I must to tell you something.'

He waited.

'I was on the Carp today. Of course, like every day, I looking for you. But this man, he come and talk.'

'His name is Andrew. I saw him.'

'You saw him?'

'I was following you.'

She arched an eyebrow and cocked her head. '*Da?*'

'*Da.*'

She kissed him again. 'Well, this man, I knowed him, too. From before. He was friend for Bertrand.'

'Not one of his Russian contacts?'

She shook her head. 'No. He friend for Lutz and for that Josef Lochert. And now he looking for you. He say he your father.'

Brano looked into her eyes, waiting for something to clear up the grammatical mistake that had obviously ruined the sense of what she wanted to say. 'Can you repeat that?'

305

'This man, he your father. Well, he want to meet with you. He say if I see you, I will to tell you.' She leaned closer. 'Brani?'

He had stepped back a few paces, his back now against the iron gate protecting the pews. Andrew, they had called him. The Americanization of Andrezej. How could he not have seen this? How could he not have recognized him? She put her hands on his shoulders. He leaned his head close to her ear and whispered, 'My father?'

'*Pa da*. You not know?'

He shook his head against her shoulder as she rubbed the back of his head.

'*Shh*,' she said. 'I am sorry.'

Brano could not remember the last time he had wept. Perhaps when Regina Haliniak left him for Zoran the lieutenant – but no, not even then. It was possible that the last time he'd wept was during the war, after his friend Marek Piotrowski was killed. But that time, at least, there had been a reason for weeping. Now, in a Viennese Catholic church, he was crying uncontrollably on this girl's shoulder, and he didn't know why. She cooed and kissed his bald head, and her voice finally brought him out of it.

'You will to meet him?'

He wiped his nose with a palm, then raised his head. 'I should. What else did he say?'

She thumbed some wetness from his cheek. 'He say he is reason what you are here. In Vienna. And he give me this.' She reached into a pocket and handed him a napkin from the Carp, with *Inter-Continental 516* written on it in pencil. 'He say you call him, and he will come right away.' She touched his face again. 'You will call? He seem very worry.'

'Yes. I will call.' He sniffed again and looked around.

The church's arid smell was getting to him. 'We should go now. They'll be looking for me.'

'You come home, I will take care for you.'

He kissed her, and she held on to his neck as he explained. 'If I stay with you, they'll find me. They're already watching you – the man I attacked was with you all day.'

'*Pa da*. I knowed that. He's very bad, no?'

'It's my fault. They're looking for me.'

'Then we go,' she said, smiling. 'We make a trip to Salzkammergut and swim in the lake.'

'We will, but I need a few more days to work things out. Right now, I'm confused.'

'*Zbrka?*'

'*Da*,' he said. '*Zbrka.*'

'What you must work out?'

He sighed, staring at her ear as he brushed down her hair. 'I never left my job.'

'You never – ' She shook her head. 'You say that again.'

He continued staring at her ear to avoid her eyes. 'I'm still working for the Ministry for State Security. That's why I'm in Vienna. And now I have to decide what to do.'

When he finally looked at her eyes, they were wet. She did not know whether to be angry or not.

'You're going to the jazz club now?'

'*Da*,' she muttered. 'I must to work.'

'Then work,' he said. 'I'll find you in a few days, and hopefully we can go to the lake. Really.' He raised her chin with a forefinger. 'It's the only thing I want now.'

She nodded.

'And, of course, you didn't see me.'

'Of *course*,' she said, and punched him in the ribs.

In the entryway she wiped some tears from her eyes, then kissed him. She straightened the lapels of his coat.

'You will to grow out your hair again?'

'You don't like it?'

She snorted when she laughed, and Brano hugged her. Over her shoulder, he saw the bulletin board of notices for future sermons, and one caught his eye. It was for the fourteenth of May, to celebrate when the Holy Spirit descended as tongues of fire and a rushing wind, and gave Jesus' disciples the power to speak so that all languages could understand them.

The fourteenth of May, a Sunday, was Pentecost.

She pushed him back and gave a teary smile. 'You will to talk with your father?'

'I will, Dijana. I will.'

'Good,' she said. 'I think it good we know our parents.'

26 April 1967, Wednesday

Brano chose the Café-Restaurant Europa because of the telephone booth across the street from its wide windows, which allowed an unhindered view of its long interior. He first bought tea in a paper cup from the pastry counter and told them he would need to reserve a table that afternoon for a business meeting. 'How many?' asked the woman behind the counter. Brano said he didn't know, but if he could have their phone number, he would call an hour before they arrived. She wrote it down for him.

He crossed to the telephone booth and dialled the Hotel Inter-Continental. A receptionist put him through to room 516. The voice that picked up was deeper than he remembered, but there was still that lisp to each *s*, caused, he had always assumed, by that chipped front tooth.

'Yes?'

'It's me.'

'Brani. I'm so glad you called.'

'The Café-Restaurant Europa, on the corner of Kärtner

and Donnergasse. You'll be here in fifteen minutes if you leave now.'

Brano hung up. He had also chosen the Europa for its distance from the Inter-Continental. His father could arrive quickly enough, but not so quickly that Ludwig, with his resources, would not arrive first.

But over the next fifteen minutes, as he stood in an apartment doorway and watched cars glide by, sometimes honk, and Viennese cross the street, read papers, and scold children, nothing struck him as suspicious.

Though there were plenty of holes in the story, he felt he understood the outlines. The Committee for Liberty in the Captive Nations was planning a coup d'état. He could doubt this if he were only going by Lochert's word, but Jan's friend Gregor had been killed after spotting Brano's father and a Yalta Boulevard officer at a nuclear reactor. Lutz had made no secret of a May event, and Bertrand Richter, on the night of his murder, had let the date slip: 14 May, which turned out to be the kind of Christian holiday the Committee for Liberty would naturally choose – tongues of fire and rushing wind.

But why? Why had Brano been drawn into a fundamentalist conspiracy? Only Dijana's revelation suggested an answer, and when he looked up he saw the answer approaching from the east, along Himmelpfort. Though Brano had seen him before, only now, with the knowledge of who he was, could he imagine away the beard and take off years. Andrezej Fedor Sev was a little shorter than he'd been in '45, and he'd grown thick around the torso beneath his badly pressed raincoat. The white beard gave his round, pale face a generous feel that Brano could not recall from childhood.

He reentered the phone booth and took a few breaths to get rid of that choked feeling in the back of his throat. His father stopped at the café door, peering through the window. Then he went inside. Perhaps for Brano's benefit, he chose a table by the window. A waitress took his order, and he rested his chin in his hand. He seemed neither agitated nor confused by his son's absence.

Brano took a couple of minutes to check the street again, then put a coin into the telephone.

'Europa,' said a woman.

'*Bitte*, may I speak with one of your customers? He's the older gentleman sitting next to the window, alone.'

He could see the woman behind the pastry counter look up from the phone. 'Moment.'

She came up to Andrezej Sev's table, bent over him, and spoke. He got up and went with her to the counter.

'Yes?' said Brano's father.

'I'm afraid I'm very careful these days.'

'Brani. We could have just talked on the phone in my hotel.'

'I wanted to find out if I could trust you.'

'And? Can you?'

'Dijana said you wanted to tell me something.'

'I'd rather see you face-to-face.'

'Let's take this in stages.'

His father nodded into the telephone, then looked around to be sure no one was listening. He was a careful man, more than when Brano was a child. 'I'm the reason you were brought over. A deal with Jan Soroka – I'd help him get his family if he would lure you out.'

'I know this. But you couldn't do it without Austrian help.'

'Yes, another deal. They called off their border guards and helped with the Hungarian side. In exchange, they were allowed to question you for a period of time.' Andrezej Sev paused. 'I heard about the car battery. I'm very sorry,

310

I didn't think it would come to that. I won't let it happen again.'

'Why did you want me here?'

'You're my son, Brano. You saved me once, and when I heard what happened to you back in August – that you made a blunder – well, I thought I could save you as well. Your only safety lies on this side of the Iron Curtain.'

It was just a voice, he kept telling himself, a voice on the phone. Nonetheless, that *zbrka* of childhood crept upon him. As if he were a confused child returning home to his father's stern voice, knowing he'd done something wrong but not knowing what it was. 'How did you learn about that?'

'I keep an eye on my children. How's Klara?'

'She lives in a house with bad paint.' He paused. 'And I believe she hates me.'

'Nonsense.'

'You couldn't have sent a letter?'

His father paused again. 'What do you want from me, Brano? Apologies? You're the one who sent me away.'

He placed a hand on the window of the booth to steady himself. 'You sound like Mother now.'

'Brano Oleksy Sev,' said that voice.

'Yes, Tati?'

'We'll get sentimental later. You can even hit me if you like. But now I'm trying to save your life. You killed Josef Lochert, and, no matter the reason, you know the only thing that awaits you back home is a firing squad.'

Brano nodded into the phone because he'd known this ever since the Comrade Lieutenant General mentioned a pickup in the Stadtpark. He sniffed, then cleared his throat. 'You and Filip Lutz are trying to overthrow my government.'

'You make it sound so easy.' Andrezej Sev snorted a

laugh. 'Is that what Lochert told you before you killed him?'

Brano closed his eyes. 'Lochert tried to make me believe that Filip Lutz was running the operation, but that was only to protect the real head. You. You were the one seen last June at the Vámosoroszi test reactor by a worker named Gregor Samec.'

'I don't remember being there.'

'But you were. Perhaps you were scouting landing areas, or perhaps you were figuring out how to create a meltdown. I don't know, and it doesn't matter now. But you were with someone else, a state security agent. I want to know who it was.'

'I don't remember that at all, Brani.'

He opened his eyes as Andrezej Sev broke away from the telephone to speak with a large man in a white chef's hat.

'They want their phone back. Can I answer your questions face-to-face?'

'One last thing,' said Brano. 'Are you going to wildly parachute soldiers into the country on Pentecost? While the Hungarians or the Czechs just close their eyes as you fly over their territory?'

'You've been doing so well up to now, Brani,' said Andrezej Sev. 'You've been making your father proud. But of course we're not parachuting anybody in on Pentecost.'

'Because,' said Brano, scratching the paint flaking off the telephone. 'Because they're already there. You've already sent in your men, probably through the same path Jan used to get in.'

'You can think what you like, Brano. I have a feeling Yalta Boulevard will find your stories hard to swallow, given the storyteller. *Ja, ja,*' he said to the chef. 'Brani, can we meet?'

'I'll call.'

'Well, I – ' Andrezej Sev began, but by then Brano had hung up.

His father had changed in the last twenty years. It was the same man – he had no doubt of that – but perhaps it was the American lifestyle that had made him into such a natural liar. He knew how to tease his son with half facts and outright fabrications. There was no reason to believe that he had brought Brano here for his safety; the fact was, it was his father's operation that had ended his career back in August. Andrezej Sev worked with the American fundamentalists, and the CIA was likely part of his background as well. There were too many loose threads; everything remained just beyond his reach. And this, as Dijana had explained, was the essence of *zbrka*.

He took a tram down to Soroka's neighbourhood and rang his bell but got no answer. Behind the building was a large courtyard with grass and picnic tables and groups of mothers chatting while their children ran in circles. He sat at an empty table and stared at the children without seeing them.

He understood the outline. His father, using the cover of the Committee for Liberty, had worked with Lochert, Lutz, and Richter over what must have been a number of years, recruiting émigrés, training them, and then sending them back into the country to wait. Loretta Reich, the Committee's secretary, had been kind enough to point out that his father had been close to Frank Wisner, who ran the earlier attempts to undermine the People's Democracies. Andrezej Sev had no doubt learned from Wisner's endless mistakes. Now their men had been placed – all they were waiting for was the prearranged date.

313

And in the middle of it all, his father was trying to convince him to defect.

Brano rubbed his head as children squealed, running past him.

There had been perhaps three moments during that phone call when he wanted to cross the street, walk up to Andrezej Sev, and hit him. Because he sounded like all fathers of the world who drop contact for years and then expect to be welcomed back. Like exiles, they live so long in their cloistered worlds, distracted by their petty obsessions, that it never occurs to them that their families no longer need them and, in fact, no longer want them.

But that wasn't it, he realized as a small blonde girl ran over to him to retrieve her ball. Narrow-mindedness and stupidity were no reasons to strike a man. It was commonness. It was that Brano's father turned out to be like all fathers in the world. He was a disappointment.

By evening he had returned to the Kaiserin Elisabeth. The woman at the desk set down her book when he approached. She stood up. 'Mr Bieniek?'

'Yes?'

She handed him an envelope. 'This is for you.'

'Thank you.'

There was a brief note inside, on Kaiserin Elisabeth stationery: *Johannesgasse 4, 11.20.*

'When did this come?'

'Around noon. A phone call.'

'Where is Johannesgasse?'

'Very near. Down Kärtner Straße, away from the cathedral, two blocks.'

'You don't know the name of the person who left this?'

She shook her head. 'I asked, but he said you'd know who he was.'

Johannesgasse 4 was a cinema, the Metro Lichtspiele, and its first show of the day, to begin at 11.20, was *Det Sjunde Inseglet – The Seventh Seal –* by a morose Swede named Bergman. That was an hour from now, so Brano wandered back down Kärtner and looked into the clothing shops and through windows at the faces of those who passed. He was back at the Lichtspiele by eleven, as the box office opened. He bought a ticket, went inside, and found a seat in the rear.

The cinema was empty for the next ten minutes, and he looked around at the ornate walls and the curtain covering the screen, waiting. The first visitor was an old man with a cane who took a centre seat. Then a young couple appeared and sat in the front.

Two serious-looking young men with glasses arrived. One returned his stare, but they continued ahead, sitting near the old man.

The crowd consisted of mostly older Viennese looking for a brief escape from the boredom of their retirements. One of the old men, behind a small crowd, turned and looked back. It was that familiar, moustached face he was beginning to fear he'd never see again. Cerny lit up when he spotted Brano, smiling as he twisted to fit between rows of seats. He took the one beside Brano.

They didn't shake hands, but Cerny patted his thigh. 'I can't tell you how relieved I was to get your message from Regina, One-Shot. I was afraid we'd lost you.'

'It was close. I got sick.'

'Sick?' Cerny squinted at him. 'Your face – it's different.'

'It seems I had a stroke, Comrade Colonel.'

'A—' Cerny didn't finish the sentence. 'Well, I guess that decides it. I'm sending you home.'

'What?'

Cerny's next words were drowned out by a blast of music. Then it silenced and the lights dimmed.

Brano leaned closer. 'I didn't hear that.'

'I said that you've done more than enough for the cause of socialism. I'm not going to lose one of my closest friends. Just tell me what you know and we'll put you on a plane.'

In a whisper, Brano outlined the plot as he understood it. A league of men trying to start a revolution on Pentecost. 'The Committee for Liberty in the Captive Nations. One of the conspirators, Bertrand Richter, tried to sell the plans to the Russians. Lochert learned of this. He had photographs of KGB agents in the apartment Bertrand Richter bought for Dijana Franković. Lochert used Yalta Boulevard to get rid of Richter and protect the conspiracy, as well as himself. He was GAVRILO all along. Dijana Franković was never a spy.'

Cerny nodded at the screen, where a bird hovered against dark clouds, then a Crusade soldier rested on a barren beach; subtitles told them what happened when the Lamb opened the seventh seal. 'Go on.'

'It's become clear that everything is in place for the fourteenth of May. My father's operatives are already in the country, waiting for the moment to attack.'

Cerny squinted at him. 'Your *father*? I thought he was dead.'

'I did, too. His new name is Andrew Stamer.'

'Andrew Stamer? *Christ*. Are you all right?'

Brano leaned closer. 'What?'

'It must have been a shock.'

'I've got over it,' he said, unsure if that was a lie. 'But the crucial point is that someone in the Ministry is working with him. Last June this person helped my father enter our country, and they visited the Vámosoroszi test reactor together.'

'June?'

Brano nodded. 'This is what separates his plan from Frank Wisner's operations. Wisner never had a highly placed insider. If we find this person, the whole thing might fall apart.'

Cerny squinted at him, taking this in.

'Now you,' said Brano. 'You have to tell me what's going on.'

'Sounds like you've figured it all out, One-Shot. We first learned of the plot from the Russians, who had got what they knew from Richter.' He grinned. 'If that bastard hadn't been so greedy, wasting time trying to raise the price for his information, it would have ended last August.'

'So you knew about it that long ago? And you didn't tell me?'

'All we knew was that something substantial was going on. The only name Richter had given the Russians was Filip Lutz. At the same time, our Vienna network was being decimated by the Austrians, and we felt that if you could reconstruct it by finding GAVRILO, then we'd be able to deal with this properly. But we all know how that tour of duty ended.'

Brano touched his shaved scalp. 'But if you knew Richter had information, then why did you give the order for him to be executed?'

'We didn't know,' said Cerny. 'I guess the Russians knew we had a mole, because they wouldn't tell us who their informant was.' He licked his lips. 'Anyway, it was the Comrade Lieutenant General's decision to kill Richter.'

'And what about Bieniek?'

'Who?'

'Jakob Bieniek, the man I was framed for killing.'

Cerny again looked at the screen. 'He was the key to getting us inside. We knew about this Andrew Stamer, that he wanted to get you west, through Jan Soroka, but we didn't know why. We certainly didn't know who he was.'

'How did you learn that he wanted to bring me west?'

'Josef Lochert. He said you would only be held a short time and then be given freedom within Vienna. That was Andrew – your father's – deal with the *Abwehramt*.' Cerny wrinkled his eyes. 'Your *father*?'

Brano nodded.

'Well, we decided to use their plan against them, but since you would be interrogated, we couldn't brief you. You'd come to Vienna, and then you'd be able to get rid of Lutz.'

'But I'm telling you,' said Brano, 'Lutz isn't controlling the operation. He's better to us alive.'

'That may be true, but at the time we thought otherwise. The Lieutenant General wanted Lutz dead. You were the one man I knew I could trust to do this.'

'But I failed.'

On the screen, Death told the Crusader that, yes, he was quite a skilful chess player.

'You were faced with unprecedented complications, Brano. It's not your fault. I know this. You can go home without shame.'

'And the inside man?'

Cerny cleared his throat. 'Let me make some calls from the embassy. I have friends at home who can make inquiries.'

'What can I do?'

'You can go home, Brano. I've got papers for you, and there's an eleven o'clock flight tonight. I'll drive you – I've got a diplomatic car.'

'And you?'

He sighed. 'I'm going to kill Filip Lutz.'

'But I told you –'

The colonel raised a hand. 'It doesn't matter if he's important or not. If we don't get rid of Lutz, suspicion in Yalta is going to fall on you – don't forget that. You don't have evidence, only speculation. Lutz's death will buy us time to collect evidence on the mole in the Ministry.'

Brano looked at his hands on his knees, then said, 'No.'

'What?'

'I killed Lochert. I dropped out of contact for a long time. I even gave information to the Austrians. When I spoke with the Lieutenant General, it was clear. If I go back now, it'll be to a firing squad,' he said, realizing he was echoing his father's words.

Cerny considered this, his face impassive. 'Perhaps you're right. Okay. Stay in Vienna until it's done, and I'll tell them you took care of Lutz. That should help your case.'

'I don't want you to lie for me.'

'I don't mind lying for you, One-Shot.'

'They'll interrogate you.'

Cerny gave him a pained expression. 'If you insist, I'll let you do it. Tomorrow morning. Can you get to the Schönbrunn Palace at nine-thirty? Lutz is meeting someone there at ten.'

'Who's he meeting?'

Cerny smiled. 'He thinks he's meeting Andrew, your father. But we'll be there instead. At the Roman Ruins. You know where that is?'

'Of course.'

'Are you staying at the hotel tonight?'

'Yes.'

'Fine,' said Cerny. He looked up to where the Crusader and his assistant were riding horses along the shore. 'You know, I always hated this movie.'

*   *   *

319

Brano returned to the Kaiserin Elisabeth, nodded at the bell-boy, and took his key from the woman at the front desk. In his room, he pulled the curtains shut and lay down for an afternoon nap. There was nothing to do but wait for the execution of Filip Lutz, then the flight back home. For the first time in months, he felt he knew what tomorrow had in store.

Yalta Boulevard, like any office in the world, was riddled with alliances and feuds. One vice of the dictatorship of the proletariat was that absolute power led inevitably to favouritism, cadres, and corruption. Those in the Ministry devoted to the original ideals had to be vigilant in order to keep the Ministry pure. This in turn led to schisms and power struggles. The ideals of the Ministry, like socialism itself, were under constant threat. For twenty years, Brano had remained in Cerny's camp, and together they had fought skirmishes to hold on to their positions. The only difference between their office and most others in the world was that when they lost a skirmish, they could end up dead.

Which was why, drifting into an uncomfortable sleep, he began to picture a life in the Salzkammergut, a house on a lake, the simple existence of chopping firewood and visiting the local market, of mixing with the kinds of farmers who had once populated his childhood. Dijana was there, with her tarot cards and acoustic guitar and her inventive syntax. It was a world where the cost of any skirmish was only hurt feelings.

That's when he considered it first in its entirety. An escape. Finding her was simple. A car could be acquired. And under the names Herr and Frau Bieniek they would check into a quaint pension surrounded by mountains.

A first step, until he'd wandered the local graveyards to find a stillborn child born the same year as him, 1917, whose identity he could borrow.

He sank into his dream uncritically, slipping through years, houses in southern France or the Italian coast, and wondered why he'd never thought through all of this before.

The Jazzklub Abel was on the other side of the Danube Canal, over the Marienbrucke, past the Church of the Brothers of Mercy, at Große Moihrengasse 26. The evening shadows hid the grime as he walked down from Johannes-von-Gott Platz, and through the front door he entered a courtyard fallen into disrepair. There was no sign of Ludwig's men; perhaps he'd given up. In the back, beside a gnarled fence, was a flat, abandoned apartment building with a small, hand-painted sign – JAZZKLUB ABEL – attached to its windowless door. It was almost seven o'clock, but he heard nothing from inside. The door was locked. He rapped with the knuckles of his right hand.

After a minute, he knocked again and heard heavy footsteps on the other side. Then the door opened, and he was faced with a large man in his sixties, bald, wearing tortoise-shell glasses like the British spy in the film Brano had seen a long time ago.

'Ja?'

Brano tried to smile. 'Is Dijana here? I'm a friend.'

'Dee?' Abel Cohen frowned as he made the connection. 'So you're the one.'

Brano shrugged.

'Well, come in.'

He opened the door for Brano, then trotted down concrete stairs without looking back. Brano followed him into a long basement with a low, arched ceiling blackened by decades of cigarettes. An empty wooden stage sat at the far end, and crowded throughout were round tables and chairs.

'No business?' asked Brano.

'We're just opening,' Abel said tonelessly, then walked behind a wooden bar through a door. 'Dee!' he called as he disappeared.

'*Da?*'

Whispers.

Then she was in the doorway, wiping her fingers quickly with a white towel. 'Oh, Brani.'

She flung herself at him, kissing his face as she held on to his neck. Each time he opened his mouth to speak, she covered it with hers, humming *mmm*. Finally, she pulled back.

'Where you have been?' she said with feigned anger.

'I've been working.'

'My *spy*,' she said. 'And you feel . . . how you feel?'

'Excuse me.'

They both looked up at Abel, who stood in the kitchen doorway.

'I need to open up. And a cigarette.'

'You need a cigarette?' Brano reached into his pocket.

'No,' said Abel. 'I'll have a cigarette outside.'

'*Danke*, Abelski,' said Dijana. 'We'll talk quickly.'

Abel, more sheepishly than his size would suggest, jogged up the stairs. They felt a cool wind as he opened the door and stepped outside.

'He is good, no?'

'He seems so.'

'Tell me, *dragi*. You stop to working and I take care of you. You are sick. We go to Salzkammergut?'

Her expression was hopeful in a way that only women can make convincing. Childish and naive. Brano had spent a life-time taking apart the imperfections in earnest expressions, but with Dijana it was impossible. Her earnest expressions were exactly what they seemed. He imagined that face in that house on that lake. Earnest, trusting.

322

During his walk from the hotel to here, he'd gone through that dream again, but critically, picking it apart, analysing it. There was only one flaw he could find, but it brought down everything: What would the lies, and a mind like his, corrupted from a young age, do over the years to a woman who could not be taken apart, who did not calculate and scheme? On the Marienbrucke the answer came to him: They would ruin her.

He said, 'There's something I have to tell you first.'

'*Da*,' she said. 'I know. You is a spy for your country. You tell me that.'

'There's more,' he said. 'You have to know this.'

'Okay.' She nodded, her face very serious. 'I am on the ready.'

What he wanted to do now, more than anything, was to come up with some innocuous fiction – that he had no money, or that he was married. Or even the simple truth that he was leaving. But despite the sometimes comical effect of her grammatical blunders, Dijana Franković was the most serious of women. She had spent the last years rebuilding her life from nothing and would not accept half measures. Her decisions – whether her decision to be with him or her decision to take on a low-paying waitress job because she'd uncovered the fraud of her previous career – were absolute. She had more integrity than anyone else in this cold city, and she deserved the truth. So he said, 'Bertrand. I was involved in his death.'

She let go of him. 'You kill Bertrand?'

'No,' he said, 'but I arranged it. I believed at the time that he was selling information. He worked for us – for me – and I thought he was selling our secrets to the West. It was a mistake. I was wrong. But I had reason to believe it. There was a reason, it seemed, at the time.'

He was babbling, so he stopped. Her expression was more

like surprise than anger, and perhaps that's why he clarified it for her.

'I ordered his execution.'

Footsteps clattered behind him. Two young men – Wolfgang and another long-haired friend – followed by Abel. They all nodded hello as they passed.

'I must to working,' said Dijana. She brought a hand to her mouth, the nail of her thumb caught between her teeth.

'I had to tell you.'

'*Da*,' she said, staring at some point in the air between them. 'Thank you for your honestly. But I must to working.'

She turned away; and he, feeling as if he were at that party again, stoned, wanting nothing more than to keep this remarkable illusion, reached out and grabbed her wrist.

With more speed than he would have expected, she spun around and struck his face with her open hand.

'Get away from me, Brano Sev.'

28 April 1967, Friday

Brano raised the mélange to his lips, sniffing the frothed milk sprinkled with cinnamon, but found no scent. It was fatigue, he knew, the result of a night in an uncomfortable bed, reviewing each moment leading up to that still-sore bump on his head. He drank the coffee quickly, feeling it scald his throat, then motioned to the waiter for another. He lit a cigarette.

It was shocking, the amount of abuse his poor body had survived.

He'd been in Austria over two months now, but it felt like two years. Last night he'd replayed all those people in an endless loop. Lutz and Nanz, Ludwig and Franz. Monika at her eternal bar, and even the pitiful Sasha Lytvyn. His father was no longer just a chipped front tooth, and Dijana – she was so much more than the memory of a single night that had kept him warm at the Pidkora People's Factory those final months of last year.

The waiter placed a fresh mélange on the table and took the empty cup. He smiled at Brano, then walked away.

Should he have told her? There were moments last night, tangled in his wet sheets, when he had been sure that with those few words he had killed any possibility of his own happiness. Now, bringing the cup to his lips, that conviction returned.

No lakeside house, no acoustic guitar. No charming sentence structures and no more desire.

He'd once believed that those who fled socialism were opportunists, and perhaps that was true of him as well. Dijana was an opportunity to have something that his own country had been unable to give him.

And what was left to him now? An assassination, and then the possibility of a firing squad.

A clock on the wall told him it was nine.

He paid and started down the busy street, following the stone wall of the Schönbrunn grounds. He touched the spot on the back of his head, then lit another cigarette.

Cerny had once said that young men were ideal for assassination. They didn't overthink. For them, the only worry is their own safety. Will they be able to get in, do the job, and make it out again? Unlike old men, they don't concern themselves with the whys and the repercussions, as Brano found himself doing as he approached the front gate.

The colonel's reasoning was valid enough. Lutz's death would hold the Ministry wolves at bay until they could uncover the mole. The Lieutenant General, in particular, was waiting for the opportunity to finish what he'd started in August. This time, as he'd said, a factory job would be just a dream.

Brano paused in front of the unbearably regal palace, then followed a crowd of tourists around the left side, to enter the gardens.

Filip Lutz was connected to a conspiracy to undermine socialism. He had no doubt about this. But Lutz was, like Brano, a pawn. His death would not frighten the surviving conspirators – Andrezej Sev and the unknown Ministry figure – into inaction. Lutz's only value was the information he carried in his head. Which meant that the only reasonable course of action was to make him talk. And then, if necessary, kill him.

He walked down the long stretch of garden leading behind the palace to the Neptune Fountain as he considered his phrasing, how he would explain this simple fact to Cerny. They could return to the Capital with enough information to salvage their position.

At the end of the Great Parterre he turned left, trees rising on both sides. The tourists thinned here, and up ahead he could see the imitation antiquity of the Roman Ruins.

By the time he reached the half-buried columns and worn arches and started walking around the pool filled with shattered fragments of lost splendour, he believed he had assembled the correct argument. That conviction only accentuated his surprise when he reached the hidden side of the pool and found Cerny with one knee in the dirt, a pistol equipped with a silencer in his hand, looking down on Filip Lutz. Lutz lay face down at the edge of the water with a hole in the back of his skull.

Cerny looked up, his face inert. He wiped his moustache. When he spoke his voice was almost a whisper. 'Brano,' he said, then looked back at Lutz's body. 'You're here.'

'You've already done it.'

'The first one didn't,' Cerny said. 'The first one didn't kill him. It was in the stomach. So I had to do it again.' The hand on his thigh shook. 'It's horrible, isn't it?'

'He came early.'

Cerny rose to his feet and wiped dirt from his knees. 'Yes.' He blinked a few times. He rubbed his eyes.

Something smelled strange here. Sweet. 'He would have been more use to us alive.'

Cerny gazed at the body. 'I don't know.' He looked past Brano, and Brano followed his gaze through the under-brush, but they were alone. Cerny's face was very red as he stepped back and leaned against a tree. 'I haven't been in the field for over a decade, do you realize that? I send you guys out here all the time, but I forget it's the hardest job in the world.'

Brano nodded.

'I did it for you, One-Shot. For both of us.' He took a long, loud breath through his nose and tapped his head against the bark. 'I forgot.'

'Forgot what?'

Brano looked at his red face, which was covered in sweat. 'Comrade Colonel?'

The colonel bit his lower lip and reached into a pocket. 'I forgot.' His hand came out holding a long syringe. 'Jesus, Brano. I don't think I can do it.' He slid, panting, down the tree as Brano ran over to him and took the syringe. In the same pocket he found a glass bottle of insulin and began. The colonel fell to the side, trying to pull out his shirt. Brano filled the syringe with insulin, then held it up to the light, squeezing, until all the air was out.

'*Christ,*' muttered Cerny.

Brano tugged the colonel's shirt out of his trousers and gripped the ample fat around his waist, which was cold and wet. Then he plunged the needle in, trying to ignore the dead body lying just behind him.

He waited for the colonel to recover, then helped him back through the gardens, out the front of the palace, to the car park where Cerny's diplomatic Mercedes waited. Some tourists watched, and a Frenchman offered assistance, which Brano declined. The colonel took the wheel but didn't start the ignition. His breaths were heavy.

'It's all right,' said Brano. 'You're not expected to do fieldwork. It has to be difficult.'

'I'll be okay.' Cerny patted Brano's knee with a weak hand. He took a deep breath. 'But I've learned a few things. Since we last talked.'

'What?'

'My contacts,' he said, then cleared his throat. 'My contacts have made some progress back in the Capital. During the months you've been in Vienna, one officer is on record as having made more than twenty calls to speak with our dear departed friend Josef Lochert.'

'Who?'

'Take a guess.'

The answer slipped from his mouth without reflection. 'The Comrade Lieutenant General. Who also ordered Lutz's execution.'

Cerny nodded. 'You know what's going to happen when we get to the embassy, don't you?'

'I have some idea.'

'I'm not sure you do,' he said. 'I know you killed Lochert in self-defence, but as far as Major Romek's concerned, you're a murderer. And probably a double agent.' He frowned, as if realizing something else. 'He's going to want to interrogate you, and it won't be easy. There's nothing I can do about that. I don't know who I can trust.'

Brano nodded.

'I'll tell the Ministry you took care of Lutz, but they won't believe that until the Austrians print his death in the newspaper. They know how loyal I am to you.'

Brano didn't answer, and the colonel started the car. He drove slowly.

'What about your father?'

'What about him?'

'He wants you to defect, doesn't he?'

'Yes.'

'Father and son, but so different.' He smiled. 'Irina used to say that children always act the same as their parents. Either they do it for the same beliefs, or they reverse those beliefs but commit themselves in exactly the same way.'

Brano nodded as Cerny leaned into a turn.

'Listen, One-Shot. I'm worried about you.'

They were driving east towards the Ringstraße. A light ahead of them turned red, and Cerny slowed. Brano said, 'I don't have any choice. I have to go to the embassy and tell them everything I know.'

'I can tell them everything,' the colonel said as he rolled to a stop. He turned to Brano. 'There's no need for you to return if you don't want to. You've done your service to the state. You've earned this right more than anyone. I can delay a search for a day or so, but you have to make the decision now. Before this light turns green.'

Brano gazed at the dashboard. 'Leave?'

'You killed Lutz before I arrived, then left. I never saw you. But *now*, Brano. It's your choice.'

Brano put his hand on the door handle. 'What about my family?'

'I can protect them, Brano. No problem.'

The colonel's pink face was very serious. Brano nodded

329

but took his hand off the handle. The yellow light came on below the red. Cerny sighed.

At Ebendorferstraße, Brano spotted Ludwig's grey Renault but couldn't see the man inside. They stopped at the iron gate, where a guard checked both their papers. When Brano rolled down the window and handed over his real passport, he glanced back at the Renault. The crew-cut Austrian stared at him a second before fumbling for his radio.

A short paved driveway led around the side of the building, and they got out together. Through the front door they arrived in a foyer with a bulletin board covered in notices for upcoming symposiums on international peace and, in front of them, a desk below the bronze crest of a hawk with its wings folded into its side.

'Good afternoon, Silvia.'

A petite woman with thick black hair smiled at Cerny. 'Hello, Comrade Colonel.'

'Do you have the plane schedules?'

While Cerny leaned over the desk and discussed flight arrangements, Brano wandered to the bulletin board and read a warning, drafted on Yalta Boulevard, about enemy intelligence officers.

WARNING SIGNS:
1. UNPROVOKED FRIENDLINESS
2. INTEREST IN YOUR PRIVATE LIFE
3. TENDENCY TO AGREE TOO QUICKLY WITH YOUR UNDER-
   STANDING OF THE IMPERIALIST THREAT

The notice ended with a final thought:

THE COUNTERREVOLUTIONARY INSTIGATOR OF IMPERIALIST

330

'Comrade Major Sev?'

Brano turned to face a thin man whose eyes bulged from a chronic glandular problem. He was the Ministry representative in the embassy, responsible for the staff's political education. 'Comrade Major Romek, it's good to see you again.'

Major Nikolai Romek spoke with a slight quiver. 'Comrade Major, would you come with me?'

'Why?'

'So we may discuss your adventures.'

Cerny hurried over from the desk. 'Comrade Romek, I've already debriefed Comrade Sev.'

'I understand,' he said, then shrugged. 'I'm afraid, though, that I've been asked to repeat the procedure. I'm sure you understand.'

'Who ordered this?' asked Cerny.

'The Comrade Lieutenant General.'

The colonel gave Brano a look. 'All right, but don't take too much time. We're flying out in the morning.'

Romek smiled. 'Of course, Comrade Colonel.'

29 April 1967, Saturday

Although there were no windows in his cell, he was sure that by now the plane home had left. Romek, with the assistance of a guard, had brought him downstairs to an empty office with a lock on the outside of the door, asked him to take a chair – there was one on each side of a table – then left and locked the door. Someone had turned off the lights after a few hours, and Brano climbed on the table to catch up on his sleep. He woke to a bright room.

The walls were white and clean. He couldn't remember if they had someone to clean up after each interview session, or if, as at Yalta Boulevard, they simply repainted such rooms once a week to cover the blood.

In other circumstances he would not have been afraid. Although he and Major Romek had had their differences, Romek was in all ways an officer of the state, a simple man who had devoted himself to that training-school creed of living by his orders. But now, his orders came from Yalta Boulevard, specifically from the Lieutenant General.

Major Romek arrived, followed by a squat, heavy man with a black beard who stood silently in the corner. Romek sat behind the table, and Brano took the seat opposite him.

'Brano, I can tell you I was surprised when I heard you'd walked in here. I thought we'd lost you.' The quiver had left his voice.

'As you can see, Comrade Major, I didn't run away.'

Romek smiled. 'Before we get started, though, let me tell you that I've always admired your work. Last year, if you remember, I was upset that you questioned my security in this building. You had my men sweep the offices and, upon finding microphones, gave me quite a reprimand. At the time, I took this personally. I did. But later I realized that you were right. So, before we begin, I want to tell you that I bear no ill will towards you.'

'I'm pleased to hear that.'

Romek scratched the corner of a bulging eye. 'But since then, the world has become a little more complicated, hasn't it? You attacked Josef Lochert in August – yes, he was open with us here at the embassy about what you'd done to him – and after returning home you murdered an innocent worker and have since finished what you began

332

with Lochert. You've spent a lot of time in this city with known counterrevolutionaries – the moderately famous Filip Lutz, as well as a whole cast of curiosities connected to the Committee for Liberty in the Captive Nations, which we believe to be a front for the CIA. Do you deny any of this?'

'I did not attack Josef Lochert last year, nor did I kill Jakob Bieniek. But the rest is true.'

'Better than I expected,' said Romek.

'I came here of my own free will.'

'Free will.' Romek grunted, as if this were funny. 'I suppose you did. But now, what I need from you is complete and utter honesty. Forget about the outside world. There are prisons and work camps out there, but they have nothing to do with what we are doing in here. What I want from you is the whole story.'

So Brano Sev began with August 1966, outlining what happened with Josef Lochert and Bertrand Richter. Romek used his notepad sometimes and did not interrupt. Brano told him about the appearance of Jan Soroka and about the murder of Jakob Bieniek, arranged by Pavel Jast. Then he explained why all of this had happened, that it was the Ministry's plan to get him into Austria for his mission.

'Wait,' said Romek, frowning at his notes. 'You're telling me that all this was simply to get you into Austria?'

'That's what I'm telling you. Colonel Cerny will verify this.'

'Okay. Go on.'

Brano described his time with Ludwig in that suburban house and told him what information he'd been forced to give.

'That's all you told them?'

'It's all I remember. I might have told them more, but I don't think I did.'

'Well, Brano. It's important we know everything you told them. So we know what's been compromised.'

'Of course. I'll work on it.'.

'You do that.'

Brano outlined his time in Vienna, his meetings with Filip Lutz and Ersek Nanz, the lecture at the Committee for Liberty. He told them the names of everyone he recognized there.

'Andrezej Sev?'

'Yes.'

'Your father, huh?'

'Yes.'

Romek wrote something down.

Brano gave a step-by-step review of his two meetings with Lochert, ending with his murder.

'But you're leaving something out, Brano.'

'What am I leaving out?'

'Your girlfriend.'

Brano closed his eyes and told everything he knew about Dijana Franković, including the information she'd given him about Bertrand Richter's meetings with the Russians.

'And she didn't ask him about it?'

'She believes in privacy.'

'Go on.'

The stroke was only a brief story, though he gave the names of the men who helped him on the border. 'They don't know anything about me.'

'You're sure of that?'

'I am.'

'What about when you came back? You were no longer being followed, so why didn't you report here immediately?'

'I tried, but I wouldn't have made it to the gate. There was an Austrian watching the street. He's still there now.'

'Oh, is he?'

'He has a crew cut, and he's sitting in a grey Renault.'

'Dragan,' Romek said to the big man in the corner, and Dragan stood up and left the room. Romek smiled at Brano. 'Go on.'

'I called Yalta Boulevard on Monday. I spoke with the Comrade Lieutenant General.'

'Yes,' said Romek. 'And he ordered you to go home. Who else have you spoken to since you returned?'

'My father, Jan Soroka, and Dijana Franković. Yesterday, Colonel Cerny contacted me.'

'And so?'

'And what?'

'Now, Brano, it's time for you to tell me exactly what's going on.'

Brano almost smiled. It wasn't the kind of tale a simple man like Romek would be able to absorb. It was too confused, too indirect. But more important, Romek would pass anything he heard in this room directly back to Yalta Boulevard. 'That's classified information. I'll have to talk to Cerny first.'

Romek shook his head slowly. 'And I thought you were being cooperative, Brano. Remember what I said, everything outside this room does not exist.'

'I can't take that leap of faith, Nikolai.'

Dragan didn't speak when he returned, only nodded at Romek's questioning gaze.

'Okay, at least one part of your incredible story has been verified. Shall I go and get the Comrade Colonel?'

'If you want to learn more, yes.'

Romek patted the table and stood up. Before leaving, he gave a quick nod past Brano's shoulder to Dragan, similar to the one Dragan had given him, and said, 'Not the head. We don't want another stroke.' Then he walked through the door and locked it.

For a moment there was nothing. Brano stared at the closed door, listening to Dragan's light breaths behind him, waiting. Then Dragan approached. He had the heavy, flat-footed step of his kind. The young, unreflective violence that served the Ministry so well. And when Dragan said, 'Stand up,' Brano was surprised that the voice was so high, and light. The voice of the kind of man who tended flowers in his free time.

He stood and turned to face the man. Dragan had bright, twinkling eyes, too, but no smile. He punched Brano in the stomach.

Brano did not fight back, because he knew his role here. To be cowed. A second fist struck his chest, knocking him across the table. *This is nothing,* he told himself, but without conviction. Dragan stepped around the table and lifted him again, then kneed his testicles.

Dijana was right. This world of men with endless questions that no answers would satisfy was a hateful place. He'd always known this, despite the meagre justifications he had clung to for years. There had been so many justifications, hundreds, but now he was having trouble remembering what they could have been.

Brano was in the chair again when the door opened. His limp hands hung between his knees, his head fallen to the side. He tried to make out Romek through the tears, and Romek leaned close to help. 'Brano,' he whispered. 'There's someone to see you.'

Then he straightened and stepped back as Cerny leaned down. The colonel sniffed, wiped his moustache, and said, 'Tell them, Brano. There's no reason to hide it now. He can't get you here.'

Brano raised his head. 'Who?'

'You know who. Just tell them everything. You can trust

336

Comrade Romek. I have his promise that he'll keep this quiet for as long as necessary.'

'Dragan,' said Romek. 'You're not needed now.'

Dragan walked out.

'And you, Comrade Colonel.'

Cerny looked at Brano. 'Remember what I told you. We'll get him, don't worry.' The colonel left.

Romek returned to his seat on the other side of the table. 'Now, if you please. I don't have all day.'

So Brano began to speak, and in speaking felt that the world had become less infused with *zbrka*. Despite the pain, the world was now simpler, a place where he could share the burden of his knowledge.

There was a conspiracy, he told Romek. A conspiracy to undermine socialism in their country. The conspiracy would take the form of an armed revolution, its soldiers made up of émigrés who had, over the past few years, been smuggled back into their country. Unlike similar operations conducted in the early fifties by the Office of Policy Coordination, under the stewardship of the CIA, this one was run by a religious group – the Committee for Liberty in the Captive Nations – with only a loose, probably financial, connection to the CIA. The central conspirators included Filip Lutz and Bertrand Richter, both now dead, as well as Brano's father. Lochert had been among their number, which was why he had attempted to kill Brano – because Brano was asking too many questions. There was also another person, placed inside the Ministry itself, who could retard their government's reaction to the uprising.

'Who is this person?'

'Comrade Cerny and I suspect it is the Lieutenant General.'

'Then why hasn't he been arrested?'

'Because we don't have enough evidence.'

Romek touched his pencil to his lips. 'The Comrade Colonel told me that you were responsible for Filip Lutz's death. Correct?'

Brano hesitated. 'Yes.'

'Why didn't you instead interrogate him? If the crux of the problem is a mole in Yalta, then why did you kill a man who could identify this person?'

'I was following orders.'

'Whose?'

'The Comrade Lieutenant General's.'

Romek smiled and pointed at Brano, as if he'd made a particularly good point. 'But Lutz wasn't the only one, was he? Josef Lochert could have given us the information.'

'I was acting in self-defence.'

'Of course you were. But you weren't acting in self-defence when you, or Lochert – it doesn't matter, but you did it together – killed Bertrand Richter, who was making a deal to sell this name to the KGB.'

Brano looked at him.

'It seems to me,' said Romek, touching a finger to the table-top, 'that you have got rid of anyone who could implicate you in the whole scheme. I imagine the final conspirator with this knowledge – your father – would be difficult to capture, wouldn't he?'

'I imagine so.'

'And what, then, would you suggest?'

Brano looked at his swollen left hand on the table. 'I'm the one person who can talk to him. He wants me to defect.'

'Defect? To America? Well, that would be something, wouldn't it?'

'If I wanted to defect, I would be gone already. I've had plenty of opportunities.'

'I suppose you have,' said Romek. He stood up, walked

around the table, and squatted beside Brano. 'Tell me,' he whispered. 'Tell me what you would do if our roles were reversed.'

Brano looked into Romek's strange eyes that seemed to want to flee his head. They both knew what Brano would do. He would place Romek on a plane home and pass on the order for Ministry interrogators to pick him up from the airport and place him in a cell. He would make sure Romek was worked on until he spilled the truth.

'Tell me.'

Brano cleared his throat. 'I would send me to the Hotel Inter-Continental to speak with my father. Andrezej Sev will only talk to his son.' He paused. 'If he believes I'm defecting, I might be able to get the name of the inside man.'

Romek looked at him a moment, immobile, then the laughter came. High and melodic, like a girl's. 'Oh, Brano!' He caught his breath. 'That's really very fantastic. Really. I'm supposed to give you the opportunity to, first of all, warn your father of everything we know. Second of all, to defect. And *third* of all, to live out your days in comfortable anonymity with your hot little Yugoslav!' He shook his head. 'No, Brano, I'm not quite the clever man you are, but I'm not stupid. Come on.' He stood again and reached out a hand. 'Why don't you get some sleep while I consider my options. Who knows? In the morning you just might be dead.'

Dragan walked him upstairs to one of the third-floor bedrooms. It was small and modest, as only socialist diplomatic suites are, with grey walls and bars over the windows, through which he could see stars hovering in the night. Dragan didn't say a thing, and when he left he locked the door from the outside.

Brano washed in the bathroom and shaved with the razor they had supplied – a convenience Brano would have denied Romek. His left hand moved well, though it sometimes tingled when he reached above his head to wash his prickly scalp. His forehead throbbed, so he covered it with a cold, wet towel and lay in bed.

He didn't know if he should have taken Cerny's offer to leave at that traffic light yesterday. He'd refused because of some kind of integrity he was having trouble finding in himself now.

If he had taken Cerny's offer, what would have followed? That dream returned – a car to the Lake Districts, a new name, a new life with her. But after his session with Major Romek, he knew that that new life would have been a troubled one, always waiting for that quiet, lurking death brought on by some young, soulless boy trained on Yalta Boulevard.

No. He wouldn't have done this, he now knew. Brano would have left that car, considered his options, then visited his father in the Inter-Continental. Because the only safety lay in his father's hands. In America. A new identity, and a new life an ocean away from this one.

There was a knock at his door.

'Come in.'

He sat up as Cerny entered. 'Look at you. Come over here, in the light. Let me see.'

Brano came over to the desk lamp, letting Cerny touch a bruise at the bottom of his neck. Brano grimaced.

'Goddamned savage,' said Cerny. 'I told him to go easy on you. I told you were to be trusted. But he'd got orders from someone higher than me, to do as he liked.'

'From the Lieutenant General.'

'Which is why we're keeping everything from him for now. Romek told me what you'd suggested. He thought it was funny. Ha ha. Well, I told him it was the only chance we had to end this thing.'

'Do you really believe that?'

'I can't see any other way.'

Brano sat on the bed and looked up at him, but the bright desk lamp behind the colonel's head obscured his expression. 'Tell me. Why did you do that in the car?'

'I – ' Cerny paused. He sat beside Brano, then cocked his head. 'The first reason I told you. You've been through too much on this operation. Far too much.' He put a heavy hand on Brano's shoulder. 'You mean a lot to me, One-Shot, even more since Irina's . . .' He snorted, then wiped his moustache. 'I wouldn't have survived without you. And in a way, you're the only family I have.' He looked into Brano's face. 'There's so much I would do if I thought it would make you, finally, a happy man. Something we both know you've never been.'

Looking into those familiar, damp eyes and at that unkempt moustache, Brano felt something like rest. They'd had so many years together, and in that time Cerny had never actually said such things to him. He'd shown it, sometimes, in their quiet moments, particularly during those months after Irina's death, as Brano helped raise him out of that suicidal depression.

Then he felt something he was not used to: shame. He was ashamed that he usually forgot those tender moments, remembering only the times Cerny reverted to the colonel whose job it was to punish Brano's mistakes.

Cerny patted Brano's back, stood, and cleared his throat. 'Don't worry, One-Shot. I'm not half done yet.'

30 April 1967, Sunday

He woke to Cerny's face hovering over his. 'Good news.'

Brano rubbed his eyes. 'Yes?'

'You're going to try it.'

Brano sat up, awake now. 'What about the Lieutenant General?'

'He doesn't know a thing. I stayed up late with Romek and worked on him until he agreed.'

'You convinced him?'

'Remember, I know a lot of things about a lot of people.' He shrugged. 'I blackmailed him.'

Brano dressed while the colonel sat at the desk, watching. Beside him, on the desktop, lay a pale cloth harness and a small box. 'Here,' he said, reaching for the harness. 'Romek wants you to wear this.' He helped Brano put it on – a strap went over his left shoulder and the harness wrapped around his chest. Cerny did the buttons in the back, making it tight. From the box he took a small wire recorder with three leads and slipped it into the pocket of the harness, just under Brano's left armpit. Two leads ended in a tiny square microphone he hooked to Brano's undershirt; the third, ending in a tiny switch, he let hang loose. 'Put on your shirt.'

Brano did so, and Cerny stepped back, nodding.

'Listen,' he said as he grabbed Brano's trousers from the bed. 'About the car. What I said yesterday.'

'Yes?'

Cerny used his thumbs to tear a small hole in the left trouser pocket. 'Well, I still feel the same way.'

Brano looked at him.

'Here,' he said, handing over the trousers. 'Put these on.' As Brano did so, he lowered his voice. 'I want you to get the information from your father, yes. But what you do afterwards . . . that's your business. This,' he said, tapping the bulge by Brano's left arm, 'can always go in the Eszterházy Park dead drop. And besides.' He bobbed his eyebrows. 'You could be of use to us in America.'

342

Brano slipped the on/off switch through the hole in his pocket, then put on his jacket. Cerny shook his head, smiling.

'It's small as hell – technology amazes me.'

Brano nodded.

The colonel's smile went away. 'Don't consider this anything other than what it is. My desire for your happiness.'

'I know,' said Brano.

They walked together into the corridor and down the stairs to the foyer, where Romek was waiting. 'You're looking rested, Brano. Are you ready for this?'

'Yes, comrade.'

'And you're wired.'

'It's taken care of.'

'Good,' said Romek. He scratched his cheek. 'I'm not going to threaten you, because I don't have to. You know what will happen if you try to get away.'

'Yes,' said Brano. 'I know.'

The Hotel Inter-Continental sat at the far end of Johannesgasse, a grey, glass-plated monolith dominating the Stadtpark. The embassy Mercedes dropped him off a couple of blocks short of it, then drove on. He walked past the wide front entrance, avoiding the lobby that would be packed with businessmen and tourists and informers of all nations. No doubt Ludwig's men were lounging there now. He instead walked around to Am Heumarkt, where, next to the Putzerei Wäscherei, he found an open door marked

PERSONALEINGANG

STAFF ENTRANCE

HOTEL INTER-CONTINENTAL

WIEN

*

343

He glanced back. On the opposite corner of the intersection, hands deep in his pockets, Romek leaned against a store window. Brano entered the building.

In the long tiled corridor, he passed trolleys overflowing with the day's dirty towels and uniforms, and when staff members passed him he avoided their eyes. Not obtrusively, but in a casual way that suggested he was a preoccupied man who belonged here. It was a difficult look that took years of experience to acquire, and was made no easier by the bruise creeping up his neck. But he did not hesitate, and that look brought him to the stairwell at the end of the corridor.

When he reached the fourth floor, he had to stop to catch his breath before continuing to the fifth. The corridor was empty, save a maid's cart with cleaning fluids and towels and sheets beside an open door.

Room 516 lay at the end, by a window that overlooked the skating rink behind the hotel. Children and adults slid around, sometimes falling, helping one another up, then continuing on their circular path. As he stared, he listened to the door beside him, waiting a full minute. He heard a television giving news in German. A toilet flushed; a door opened and closed. Bedsprings. Brano reached into his left pocket and pressed the switch. Although there was no noise, he could feel, beneath his arm, the vibration of the recording wire being pulled into the take-up reel. He turned to the door and knocked.

The television silenced and the eyehole darkened. Then the door was open, Andrezej Sev smiling at him.

His father's face, this close, was as it had always been in the photographs that filled that guest room in his mother's house. There was the addition of age, a beard, and when he smiled his front teeth were clearly visible – clean and white and strong. But this was truly his father.

Brano touched his own front tooth. 'What happened?'

Andrezej Sev looked confused a moment. 'Oh, this!' He still lisped his *s*. 'American dentist – he capped the tooth. I see yours are looking good as well.'

'I got braces some years ago.'

'So we both share the sin of vanity. But what happened to your neck?'

'I'm clumsy.'

Andrezej Sev kept a poor home. Dirty clothes lay in a loose pile in the corner, and the sheets had tumbled off the bed, as if after a night of hectic sex. This was nothing like the brutally tidy farmer he'd once known.

'Ludwig went crazy looking for you,' said his father, smiling. 'He called me every day demanding your whereabouts.'

'He's given up?'

'It seems he was transferred to a new desk.'

Brano opened his mouth, then paused. 'Accounting?'

'That's what I heard.'

Standing here beside his father, he found himself regretting Ludwig's demotion. Brano placed his hat on the small desk, where, beside a portable Remington typewriter, lay a short stack of typed pages.

'Your memoirs?'

Andrezej Sev flushed. 'Letters,' he said. 'To my family.'

'Your American family.'

'My wife's named Shirley. From Tennessee.'

'Tennessee.' Brano settled in the desk chair, picturing Loretta Reich from the Committee for Liberty and her expressions. 'Children?'

'Two girls.'

'And they have names?'

'Stacy and Jennifer.'

Brano, despite himself, cracked a smile.

'I didn't want to burden them with foreign names.'

'I imagine.'

Andrezej Sev, still standing, looked at his feet. 'Brani?'

'Yes?'

'How's your mother?'

'She's fine,' he said, wondering why the question, from this man, irritated him. 'I mean, no. She feels her life's a waste without you. And Klara, beyond the bad paint job, married an idiot. But she seems happy with her life.'

Andrezej Sev settled on the bed and patted his thighs, his voice deepening. 'No one's happy with their life. You don't fool yourself into believing that kind of rubbish, do you?'

'That would be asking a lot. But my life functions. I make do.'

'Make do.' His father smiled. 'I used to think that way, before I came west. It's hard to explain, but when you arrived in Bóbrka and told me to leave, I was almost . . . well, I was relieved.'

Brano adjusted himself in the chair, crossed one leg over the other, and looked at Andrezej Sev looking at his son's knee.

'You remember what the war was like for me,' he said. 'A German factory. I'd return home, and your mother was – she was . . . I don't want to talk ill of her, but she wasn't easy to live with. But back then I thought like you do. Happiness wasn't what this world had to offer. Survival, yes. Survival and making do. Then I got out of that world. First to a displaced persons camp in Hamburg. There were some American soldiers there, collecting information from émigrés. I made friends with them. And by 'forty-eight they asked me to join a new organization.'

'The Office of Policy Coordination.'

He nodded.

'We're all apparatchiks for someone.'

346

His father squinted, then went on. 'I moved to Virginia and helped train agents.'

'How long did you do this?'

Andrezej Sev shrugged. 'Until 'fifty-three? Yes, 'fifty-three.'

'Until the rollback operation was shut down.'

The elder Sev got up and took an ashtray and a pack of cigarettes from the dresser. He offered one, but Brano declined. So he lit one for himself and sat on the bed again. 'We're getting off track. The point is that my relationship to happiness changed. I still knew I'd never achieve happiness, but the Americans firmly believe you must try to find it. It keeps them in motion.'

This was a different man. The younger Andrezej Sev would have never gone into lengthy discussions of the intangibles of *happiness* or even *love*. Andrezej Sev had had the classic provincial mind – survival and subsistence. America had changed him into a creature with the leisure time to worry about such things; he'd become a creature of weekend television and football games and Main Street parades, while his new country's soldiers slaughtered villagers in the jungles of Asia. And he'd become proud – pride was all over him. They were strangers on opposite sides of an iron fence.

'It's my fault,' said Brano.

'What?'

'That you've become . . .' He tried to think of the right word. *'This.'* His father stared at him. 'Maybe Mother was right. Maybe I should have put you in prison.'

Andrezej Sev's face dropped. He licked his lips. 'You're blaming yourself for what I've become?'

'Maybe.'

'Well, don't.' He took a drag and spilled smoke into the room. 'If you want to know the moment that changed me, you have to look later. A Saturday afternoon in 1951. It was summer, and I went with my new wife down to Virginia Beach with the other thousand vacationers.' He grinned. 'Shirley had bought me an an inflatable mattress, because she knew I didn't like to swim. Well, the fact was I *couldn't* swim, but I didn't want to admit that to her. We blew it up together, and I took it out to where the water came to my waist and climbed on it. I lay on my back and closed my eyes. It was very peaceful, and I must have fallen asleep, because when I opened my eyes again I was far out, past the pier. I panicked. I don't know why, but I completely panicked. I began screaming like a child and fell off the mattress, into the water, and sank like a rock. I was sure, at that moment, that I was a dead man.'

'But you made it to shore,' said Brano.

'Not on my own, I didn't. I got to the surface, yes, and I clutched the mattress to stay up. I kicked and splashed and made it to the end of the pier and held on to the piling. It was covered with barnacles that scratched the hell out of my chest and pierced the mattress. It deflated. I tell you, I was crying then. Weeping uncontrollably. And the next thing I knew, this big strong man – he'd seen Shirley screaming from the beach – had swum out to me, and he was telling me very calmly to let go of the piling. He carried me back to shore.'

There was silence for a moment, as Brano looked into his father's eyes. 'Why are you telling me this story?'

'You're not going to like the reason.'

'Try me.'

'Well,' he said, leaning back, 'I got to the shore and Shirley dried me off. She was crying. She thought I'd drown out there. And when I saw her tears, I knew. I learned it in one moment.' He paused again. 'Brani, God truly exists.'

Brano felt the vibration of the wire recorder against his heart. 'Is that what you call a miracle?'

'It's what I call knowledge.'

Brano felt an urge to stand up, walk out of the room, and throw himself down the stairwell. This was more than he wanted to know. His mother had been right all along. But the vibration kept him in his seat. 'So I suppose this explains your Christian friends.'

'They're good people.'

'Maybe,' he said, rearranging the lines he'd put together on the way over here. 'But if I come to America, you won't force me to attend your church, will you?'

A large smile spread over his father's face. 'All I want is for you to be near me. I want to know my son again. Don't worry, I'm not as evangelical as my friends.'

'That's good to hear.'

Andrezej Sev leaned forwards and patted Brano's knee. 'You've made me a happy man, Brani. You really have.'

'How do I do it?'

'We can do it now, if you like. I make a phone call and wait for my friends to show up. Then it's just a trip to the embassy. You'll be completely safe.'

'And then what happens?'

Andrezej Sev's eyes grew as he lit another cigarette. 'Nothing much. A quick debriefing, no more than a day – and nothing like Ludwig's, you can be assured of that. Then we fly you to Virginia. A week or two more at Langley, and that's the end of it. A new passport with a new name. It's that simple.'

'And money?'

His father paused. 'Start-up finances, until you get a job. If you need more, I'll take care of it myself.'

Brano nodded, the lie becoming visual in his head: televisions, football games, parades – and possibly even her. 'But I can't leave yet. I have a few more things to do. We can meet tomorrow.'

'Where?'

'In the Volksgarten. You know the Temple of Theseus?'

'Of course.'

'Tomorrow at three, inside the Temple of Theseus.'

His father leaned back again and raised his hands towards his god, then clapped them together. His face reddened with pleasure. 'This calls for a drink!' He went to the bedside table, removed a metal flask from the drawer, and poured palinka into two glasses he fetched from the bathroom. 'To freedom,' said his father.

'To freedom,' said Brano, but inaudibly.

They drank their palinkas in a single swallow.

'I figured most of it out,' said Brano. 'This conspiracy you're hatching with Lutz.'

'And Lochert,' said Andrezej, refilling their glasses. 'Or we were until he decided to try and kill you. A terrible man. We never should have used him.'

'You smuggle in men – sleepers, told to wake up on Pentecost and start a revolution. There are a lot of them?'

'Enough.'

Brano took another sip. The palinka was rough on his throat. 'The CIA tried this before, when you were working for Frank Wisner. Nearly every operation failed. I couldn't understand why you'd try it again.'

'One thing we've had,' said his father, 'is security. The Wiz – he was a genius, but his operation was full of leaks. Kim Philby, for example.'

'You had a leak, too. But you and Lochert used me to get rid of Bertrand Richter.'

'Yes. And I have to admit Josef did knock you out under my orders. I hoped that you'd be picked up by the Austrians for killing Richter, and then I could bring you home with me. If we just kidnapped you off the street, Yalta would suspect something.' Andrezej Sev smiled. 'But you, Brano, you're better than that, aren't you? I was there in the park when you woke to that policeman. You talked your way out of that pretty well.'

Brano blinked, recalling the bearded man in the Volksgarten, watching him struggle with his memory and a haughty Austrian policeman.

His father pointed a finger. 'But you didn't remember a thing. Lochert called me from your hotel room, and I told him to take you to the airport. Then I called my Austrian friends. I thought they'd be able to catch you without much trouble. Hmm.' He shook his head. 'And the next thing I knew you were back in the Capital.'

'I returned to an interrogation, and then I lost my job.'

'I heard about it from Lochert. That report he filed was not sanctioned by me, rest assured.'

'Maybe your inside man sanctioned it.'

Andrezej Sev looked at him.

'It's not enough to get your soldiers into the country,' said Brano. 'You need someone to stall the reaction to their uprising. Otherwise it'll be crushed in an hour. Who was the state security officer you were with at Vámosoroszi?'

'I wish I knew what you were talking about.'

There was a knock on the door, and Brano stood.

His father patted the air for calm. *'Ja?'*

'Maid,' said a voice.

'Please come back later. I'm working.'

They heard the trolley squeak down the **corrid**or.

Brano settled down again and reached for the flask. 'In the end, there's one thing I don't understand. You might cause trouble for a few days, but the Russians will come in, the same way they did in Hungary. Executions will follow, and in the end it'll make no difference.'

'Brano,' said Andrezej Sev, taking on a tone that seemed very proud and fatherly, 'neither of us knows what will happen. But even if it does fail, do you really think it'll make no difference? Humans have the gift of memory. They learn from their mistakes, so that when they try again they will succeed.'

'And it doesn't matter that hundreds will die.'

'This is history, Brano. It's bigger than anyone. Even your dear Stalin understood this. *A million dead is a statistic.* What we're doing is not about today; it's about tomorrow.'

Brano looked into his glass, his cheeks warm. 'It's easy to talk about history in this hotel.'

'You understand, but you don't want to. We fight in the same way. Your Ministry sacrifices agents all the time – not to win battles, but in order to win the war. Don't underestimate the strength of collective memory. When the Russians marched into Budapest, the International Communist Party lost members in droves. It will happen again. And by the end they will have no support outside the countries they hold by force. The Empire will crumble, captive nation by captive nation.'

His father's eyes were rapturous, reminding him of Klara's when she left her church. There was no point debating with this man.

'So tell me, Brani. What made you decide to come over? Have you finally had enough?'

He shrugged.

'You've been a good soldier, Brano. I've seen your files. But every good soldier reaches a point where the lies and the double-dealing finally take their toll. They start to lose the sense of why they do what they do. They start to forget who they are.'

Brano forced a smile. 'You're not far from the truth.'

'And the loneliness?'

'I'm tired of that as well,' he said into his glass. 'But that doesn't really matter, does it? Like you said before, if I return home, it will be to a firing squad.'

'Don't hate me, Brano.'

'I never hate my enemy.'

Andrezej Sev frowned, then began to say something that was interrupted by another knock at the door. Two raps, a pause, then one more. He smiled, patted Brano's knee, and walked to the door as Brano stood, unsure. Then his father opened it.

Standing there, watching it open, Brano felt sure it would reveal Ludwig, or Karl, or maybe even the Lieutenant General. Nothing prepared him for Dijana, a hat in her hands, below a hopeful face.

Brano started to smile but didn't. 'What are you doing here.'

'I told her to come,' said Andrezej. 'A dirty trick, I know,' he added as she rushed past him and grabbed Brano.

He thought he would fall, but he didn't. He wrapped his arms around her waist and stared at his grinning father over her shoulder.

Her whispered voice in his ear was choked. 'I think it's not bad idea you come with me home, Brani.'

Brano kissed the hair over her ear. His father closed the door.

'Tomorrow,' he told her. He couldn't hear his own voice because of the ringing in his ears. 'We'll drive somewhere tomorrow. Is that all right?'

She pulled back, blinking. 'You mean it?'

'Pa da,' he said, then kissed her lips. He couldn't feel them, because only now had everything become clear, all the lies, and it numbed every part of him. He said, 'We'll go to the Salzkammergut.'

She nodded vehemently into his sore neck.

He kissed her again, then walked over to his father by the door. 'You're right, this wasn't fair, but I understand. Everything.'

'I'll do anything to keep you, Brani.'

He patted his father's cheek. 'Would you tell me the name of your inside man?'

Andrezej Sev smiled. 'I don't think you'll demand that of me.'

'You don't know me any more, Tati.'

'I know people.'

Brano reached for the door. 'This person, he's reached the rank of lieutenant general, hasn't he?'

The smile slid from his father's face; then he pouted his lips. It was almost obscene in its falsity. 'I'd heard you were one of the best, and it seems you really are. Ironic the ways your son can make you proud.'

'Are you going to let me leave this hotel?'

'I told you before. I'll do anything to keep my son.'

Brano nodded. 'Three o'clock.'

'At the Temple of Theseus.' His father leaned closer. 'You'll be happy,' he whispered. 'As happy as anyone can be. Shirley's looking forward to meeting you.'

Brano looked back at Dijana, who stood beside the desk, her hands fidgeting at her sides. He wasn't sure his tingling feet would carry him all the way out of the hotel, but they did.

1 May 1967, Monday

On the drive to the airport, they ran into a parade. The participants were dressed in everyday work clothes, and spread throughout were young men and women with long hair, who reminded Brano of Dijana's friend Wolfgang. A few held red flags with the hammer-and-sickle. One of them started a song, and that was when Brano remembered. *Arise ye workers from your slumbers*. Another red flag was raised. *Arise ye prisoners of want*. It was May Day, and even here the proletariat was showing its muscle. Cerny smiled, but Brano couldn't.

The Flughafen Wien was long and modern, the departures area shining marble and glass. In the line to the Tis-Air check-in counter, Cerny set down his bag and turned to Brano.

'How do you feel?'

'All right, Comrade Colonel.'

'You've done great work, you realize this?'

'Thank you, Comrade Colonel.'

'For God's sake, Brano, call me Laszlo.'

Brano smiled.

'You've earned this, you know.' He looked over Brano's shoulder at the taxi stand just outside the glass wall. 'By the time I get back and they realize you're not with me, you could be anywhere. Well, anywhere except the Salzkammergut – that's on the recording.'

Brano followed his gaze. 'So could you.'

'Me?' Cerny laughed. 'I've got a conspirator to nail against the wall!'

The line shortened, and Brano moved the colonel's bag for him.

'Well?'

Brano took a long breath and squinted at the sunlight pouring through the windows. 'I need to step away a minute.'

'Sure,' said Cerny. 'A minute.' He patted Brano's shoulder, then, hesitantly, gave him a hug, smothering him in the familiar scent of stale cigarettes.

Brano walked across the marble floor without looking back, then turned a corner to a line of pay phones by the bathrooms – where, many months ago, he had knocked out a man. He slipped a coin into the closest phone and took a stiff card out of his pocket. On one side was that Raiffeisenbank account number; on the other, a telephone number.

'Please state your extension.'

'Two-zero-eight is the old extension,' said Brano. 'But he should be in Accounting now. Ludwig.'

After some clicks, he heard two rings, then a man's voice. '*Ja?*'

'It's me.'

'It's . . .' A sigh. 'You fucking bastard.'

'Thank you for the hospitality, but I'm leaving now.'

'Do you know what you've done to my career, Brano?'

'Go to Schönbrunn, to the Roman Ruins. You'll find the body of Filip Lutz.'

'So he wasn't paranoid, was he? You did kill him.'

'Not me. It was Colonel Laszlo Cerny.'

'Of your ministry?'

'He's leaving as well, but I thought this might help get you out of Accounting.'

'What are you up to?'

'Just trying to return your hospitality.'

Ludwig grunted. 'You really are a queer one, Brano.'

When he returned, Cerny was at the head of the line, flirting with the girl behind the counter. Brano tapped his shoulder and watched the fog of surprise seep into his face. 'Brano?'

He shook his head. 'I can't do it.'

Cerny rapped the counter with his knuckles, regaining his composure. 'Well, I can't say I'm disappointed. It would be a terrible thing to lose you.'

They were squeezed into their cramped seats, thirty thousand feet above the Austrian border with Hungary, sipping from cans of Zipfer beer. Cerny stared out the window at clouds. 'It's funny.'

Brano saw nothing of interest out the window. 'What is?'

'Up here everything looks the same.'

'You're sounding as sentimental as my father.'

'It's true, though. And when we land we'll forget what it was like up here. We'll get back to work. We'll interrogate the Lieutenant General and search the poor bastard's belongings until we've come up with the evidence.'

'We don't need the evidence.'

'You want to just shoot him? Brano, there are some legal issues involved, you know.'

'We both know the Lieutenant General isn't the man we're after.'

Cerny looked at him.

'I'm sorry, Laszlo. It's you.'

The colonel brought his eyebrows together. He smiled. 'You need sleep, Brano.'

'You shouldn't have trusted my father. He's too sentimental. He wanted me to stay in Vienna so badly that he blew the entire operation.'

'I don't understand what you're talking about.'

Brano had known it ever since his father's hotel room, but only later, in bed, was he able to work backwards through each moment to convince himself of what he could hardly accept. 'My father knew I was coming to visit him. He prepared for it by inviting Dijana. How did he know?'

Cerny didn't answer.

'Only two people knew I was going to visit him. Romek and you. You called my father and told him to expect me.'

Cerny clapped a hand on the armrest. 'This is incredible, Brano! Of *course* your father knew – don't you see? We both know how loyal Romek is to the Lieutenant General. He lied to me and called him anyway. The Lieutenant General contacted your father.' He shrugged, as if this were simple mathematics. '*That* is how your father knew you were coming. And that's why we're going to have to be careful when we land.'

Brano sighed. 'Romek is a nuisance, but more than anything, he's honest. We all listened to the recording together – he believed that the Lieutenant General was guilty. If Romek had contacted him, he would have warned us before we left.'

'You don't know that.'

'I do. But more importantly, my father let me think that the Lieutenant General was the man. He was prepared to do it.'

'Like you said, he's sentimental. He'd admit anything to keep you.'

'And it doesn't matter how much history we have – I would never give you the opportunity to defect. Both of us could give away too much.'

The colonel's face loosened, and he turned to look through the window at the bed of clouds beneath them. 'Your father's a good man, but he's a fool.'

'I know,' said Brano.

Cerny pursed his lips.

'Maybe you can clear up some things for me, Laszlo.'

The colonel shrugged.

'Why did you want Lutz dead? He wasn't selling anything that I know of.'

He puffed up his cheeks and exhaled. 'No, Filip Lutz was always loyal. But it had to be done. Because of Bertrand Richter.'

He watched as the colonel's features relaxed; he was settling into a serene shock. 'The Russians knew Lutz's name,' said Brano. 'So he had to be sacrificed in order to keep you above suspicion. But Lochert could have done it.'

Cerny surprised Brano by smiling. 'If Lochert killed him, the Americans would think the operation was eating itself up. They'd take back our funding. The only way was to find someone else to do it. It was your father's idea to bring you over. He'd tried to make you stay in August, and he wanted to try it again. I told him it was too much of a stretch, but he can be very persuasive. He was afraid that if the operation failed, you'd be executed along with me. It made a kind of sense at the time – we get you into the West, and you take care of our problem. He already knew about Jan Soroka approaching the Americans for help. Sometimes circumstances come together in surprising ways.'

Brano touched the back of the seat in front of him, counting the levels of conspiracy. He dropped his hand. 'Why?'

'Why what?'

'Why *you*?'

The colonel considered that. 'Remember when Irina killed herself? Of course you remember. You were a great help to me then, and I've never forgotten it. But that was when it started.'

'When what started?'

'The doubt.' Cerny straightened in his chair and glanced over the seat at the heads of the other passengers. 'I can't say I didn't see it before, but in truth I didn't care. I saw the corruption. I was aware of how we throw around our power, stick our own people in prison, send them to camps, shoot them. Why?'

'You know why.'

'Remember back in the war, when we talked about the coming age of socialism?'

Brano nodded.

'Well, forget about it, One-Shot. Because it's never going to happen. The only thing going on east of the Curtain is a series of power struggles. The workers of the world don't even exist. We've become a three-class society – those who are in prison—'

'Yes, yes,' said Brano. 'I know the joke.'

Cerny shifted his knees against the next seat. 'I knew this before I ran into your father a couple years ago. He had already placed his first fifty or so in villages here and there, but he needed help from the inside. I made myself available.'

'And a year later,' said Brano, 'you were walking around with my father at that reactor in Vámosoroszi, doing reconnaissance. But you didn't expect someone would actually come to work on a Saturday.'

'You never expect that kind of work ethic in our country.' He shrugged. 'Jan's friend had a lot of questions.'

'So you killed him.'

Any hint of a smile disappeared. 'This operation is much larger than the lives of a few men – larger, even, than mine.'

'And the Americans paid Jan to keep it a secret.'

'The Americans know very little because they don't want to know. Despite what you think, they don't enjoy lying to their senators. Jan's payment was from your father, from the Committee. The embassy was just a meeting place.'

Brano looked past him through the window. Above the clouds, the sky was bright blue. 'You were the one who gave away our Viennese network. You were GAVRILO.'

Cerny rubbed his temples. 'They weren't supposed to use my information. That was the deal. Not directly, at least. But some idiot in Langley began trading it with your friend Ludwig. I have no idea why. And Ludwig, with about as much subtlety as an elephant, ripped apart the network. See, the danger of conspiracies is that the more people involved, the more chance there is for idiocy. Then Richter started talking to the Russians, and it felt like the whole thing was unravelling. So you were sent in to fix the situation.'

'You would be saved from suspicion, get rid of your leak, and keep the American money coming.'

'Something like that.'

Brano looked into his face. He had thought it would look different now, Machiavellian, but it looked as paternal as it always had. 'And do you believe like my father, that it doesn't matter that this whole thing will be crushed by Russian troops within days?'

'You don't understand,' said Cerny. 'You've been inside too long. We're not trying to *collect* power. We're trying to weaken an evil power, the one we've both served all our lives.' He shifted in the seat and grinned almost bashfully. 'Now, if you'll excuse me, all this talk is disrupting my bladder.'

Brano did not hate the colonel. Hatred and love were not things that mattered in the end. He simply wanted to understand, and he could not. He could follow the stories, the arguments, even the justifications. Yes, everyone knew the system was corrupt. But even if the system is corrupt, the fact is that it is your system; it is your world.

He got out of his seat to let Cerny pass. He watched the old man move slowly down the corridor and pause at the bathroom door, look back, and smile again before going inside.

Brano had wanted it this way, for him and the colonel to speak as equals, for him to learn all he could in a secure environment. He wanted to know as much as he could before handing the colonel over to the men who would be waiting for them at the airport. And the colonel, like Ewa Nubsch, felt the need to tell Brano everything. The colonel needed to make his first confession to a friend.

He didn't know how long he had slept; he only knew that he was waking. A voice, at first unintelligible, spoke to him through a speaker: . . . *making our descent. Please fasten your seat belts.* He opened his eyes and saw, first of all, that the seat beside him was empty.

He was on his feet. In the next seat back, a small boy stared at him, and at the front of the plane, an impatient-looking man stood beside the toilet door with his arms crossed over his chest.

That was when he knew.

He crossed the distance quickly but felt pain in his weak left leg, as if it were trying to hold him back. He reached for the locked door as the man said, 'Hey – I was here first.' He pounded on it and listened, but heard only the roar of the engines.

He told the man to get back.

'Look, I was—'

Brano grabbed the man's shirt and pushed him into a pair of empty seats, then banged again. He braced himself against the wall and shoved his right foot into the door.

It popped open a couple of inches, then slammed shut again.

Brano pushed and found resistance. As he pressed, something slid back and the door opened further, enough for him to stick his head in.

Cerny was on the toilet, his jacket and shirt off. His knees were tight between the door and the wall, and in his forearm was a syringe.

Brano squeezed through and got the door shut again. Cerny's blue head was tilted back against the wall, mouth open beneath that dishevelled moustache. When Brano removed the syringe, the plane trembled, the flaps tilting for descent, and he had to hold the sink to steady himself.

A woman's voice outside the door was telling him something.

Brano removed the plunger and brought it to his nose.

There was no smell. And when he touched the inside with a finger, it came up dry.

Then he leaned against the door and stared at the colonel. There are many ways to kill yourself. Sometimes all it takes is a little air.

Postlude

14 May 1967, Sunday
Brano Oleksy Sev paused at the top of the metro steps, a hand gripping the rail. Škodas and Trabants and Ladas shook over the cobblestones around the statue at the centre of Victory Square: a handsome couple sharing the burden of a flag held aloft. It was very warm, and as he made his way along the crosswalk to Victory Park, at the beginning of Yalta Boulevard, he unbuttoned his jacket. Behind him, the Central Committee building, wide and grey, looked over everything.

He walked through the gate to where more trees were covered in fresh yellow blooms and couples settled in the grass, eating bagged lunches. At the end of the trail lay a memorial to the war dead of all centuries, a bronze soldier sitting on a boulder, his rifle lying across his knees. In front of it, the wide back of the Comrade Lieutenant General faced him. Beneath his arm was a manila folder.

'Good afternoon,' he said as Brano approached. His red alcoholic's cheeks were puffy. 'How are you feeling?'

'I'm still easily tired, but otherwise I'm all right.'

'Excellent,' the Lieutenant General said. 'So you're happy.'

'I think that would be asking a lot.'

The big man frowned. 'Do you want to know?'

'Yes,' said Brano. 'I do.'

There had been four men at the airport when he landed, and they didn't wait for him to come out. They found him squatting beside Colonel Cerny's body in the back of the plane, mute, gripping the old man's hand.

Then, inevitably, they placed him in the back of a white Mercedes. Like Ludwig's men, they were adept at silence. They brought him into town, him staring through the window like a tourist at the dirty Habsburg buildings that were so much smaller than the ones in Vienna. They brought him to Yalta Boulevard, number 36.

He found himself dreaming of Austrian interrogation techniques when they tied him to a hard chair in the middle of a concrete cell, then turned off the light.

It didn't seem to matter how much he told them. He answered each question earnestly, hiding nothing, not even the existence of Dijana Franković, but still they treated him like a liar. And he found that, after a few days, he also began to wonder if he was lying. What was he leaving out? Who was he protecting? He wasn't protecting himself; he admitted his mistakes and lack of foresight. When they asked who was to blame for the death of Colonel Cerny, he told them he was to blame.

By the end of the week, he was unable to speak because his teeth, which had once been so perfect, were bleeding too much.

Then he woke in a hospital bed, the Lieutenant General gazing down on him. *Our celebrated Comrade Sev,* he said, but without a smile.

Now, though, the Lieutenant General was all smiles.

'You'll be happy to know the streets are peaceful, Brano. Generally so. We've had three incidents – two here in the

Capital, and one at the reactor in Vámosoroszi. Some joker tried to get inside, and we had to shoot him. The other two we picked up on the edge of town this morning. They had a truck full of old rifles. They were going to the Second District to distribute them to the others.'

'And the others?' asked Brano.

The Lieutenant General shook his head. 'No one showed up. It seems the scheme required a cue. The two arms dealers told us that. There would be a notice in *The Spark* announcing, of all things, a flower show. How do you like that? Flowers! Cerny's wonderful imagination yet again.' The Lieutenant General wiped his lips. 'But since he wasn't around to place the notice, well, no one came to get their guns. Pretty anticlimactic, don't you think?'

'Yes, comrade.'

'One of them told us their plan was to remove Adam Wołek from prison and place him at the head of our great country.'

'Father Wołek?'

The Lieutenant General nodded. 'Would've been a surprise when they learned he was dead. About a month ago he dropped while working on the Canal. Heart gave out.'

'I see.'

'Of course, we have quite a job ahead of us. There are enemies of the state to rout out. But we'll get it taken care of.'

'I'm sure we will.'

'Come on, Brano. Let's take a walk.'

They continued past the statue, off the path into clusters of birch trees, from which Brano could hear, but not see, birds.

'Your father, you may be interested to know, is back in America. With his family. Would you like to see the photographs?'

'No.'

The Lieutenant General laughed. 'You know who's most angry about this? Not you, not me, but your friend Ludwig. He complained directly to the embassy. He's demanding your extradition! But that was clever, what you did. Turning in Cerny before you left, so he'd be arrested if he returned.' He shook his head. 'That poor Ludwig has been in the dark about everything all along.'

'And you?'

'Me?'

'How long have you known about this?'

The Lieutenant General cocked his head, shifted the folder, and reached into his pocket for some cigarettes. As he explained his side of the story, his initial suspicion of Brano, Cerny's elaborate excuses for him and for his demolished Viennese network, and that final, exquisite plan to get Brano into Vienna – 'That man always had a byzantine sensibility for schemes, didn't he?' – it occurred to Brano that, although he had uncovered his own father's scheme, he was still under suspicion. The Lieutenant General paused now and then, working his way around occasional details, as if he were talking to a member of the opposition.

'Tell me,' said the Lieutenant General, 'why didn't you rest longer on the Fertő Lake?'

'I didn't want to be captured by the Austrians again.'

'So you didn't know.'

'What?'

'That the good Dr Simonyi was one of our men. He would have taken care of you.'

'No, I didn't know.'

'Here.' The Lieutenant General handed him the manila folder. 'You can dispose of these as you like.'

Inside was a stack of photographs. Half of them were of Brano, from a grainy distance. Brano in that Bóbrka bar with

Pavel Jast, Brano exiting the safe house on Felberstraße, Brano with Ludwig in the Café Mozart, Brano with Dijana outside the Web-Gasse apartment. Others were completely devoid of people. Brano looked at him.

'Seems our man fancied himself an *artist*,' said the Lieutenant General. He sniffed. 'Wasted a lot of film on empty streets and parks.'

'Who took these?'

'You lost my man a number of times, but he's persistent. I suppose that makes up for the artistic streak.' He winked. 'You never thought you were actually *alone*, did you? No, Brano. You'll never be alone.'

Brano gazed at the photos. Him in the Carp with Ersek Nanz, him in a nighttime street with Jan Soroka. Then, in the back, he found another one of Jan. He was with Lia and Petre in a street with English signs. Brano held it up.

The Lieutenant General took the picture and squinted at it. 'Just thought you'd like to know what happened to your friend. His wife had a change of heart.'

'I see.'

'And I suppose you heard about Fräulein Franković?'

'Yes, I did.'

'Like our photographer, she doesn't give up easily. She's been sending you letters, hasn't she?'

Brano nodded.

'I heard she visited the embassy again on Friday, with Ludwig. They both want to know what happened to you. Any message you'd like us to pass on? Want them to know you've been made a colonel?'

Brano shook his head. 'They won't care about uniform decoration.'

During the last week, as he recovered in his apartment from the bruises of the interrogation, he had received two visits from Regina Haliniak. She brought him the news she overheard from her desk – after his return, everyone seemed to know his story. She was sympathetic, arriving with food she had cooked in her and Zoran's kitchen. She made him sit while she shaved him, and sang folk songs while she ran his bath. She had seen photographs of Dijana Franković and told Brano that he was a fool. He could have given his information on Cerny to Romek and stayed in Vienna with Dijana. Everyone at Yalta had the same question: Why did he come back?

The Lieutenant General asked him the same thing. 'You could have even been of use to us there.' Brano shrugged, groping for an answer that he didn't have, and the Lieutenant General shook his head, perhaps disgusted, then left.

Brano descended the steps back into the metro, joining a crowd of young people with hair not quite as long as the Viennese youth's, and faced the cool wind that preceded the grey train. He got on, holding tightly to the leather straps as the floor shook beneath him and the train tilted into turns.

He got out in the Eighth District, where the grey towers spread out as far as the eye could see. He weaved between old cars in the cracked parking lot, on his way to Unit 57, Block 4.

The lift brought him to the twelfth floor. When he stepped out, he noticed that at the end of the hall a small child – the neighbours' girl – was staring at him. She held a ball in her hands. He gave her a smile, but it was too slight to be noticed, and she turned and disappeared through her door.

He hung his coat in the hall, then found a bottle of water in the kitchen that he brought to the living room. He looked at the coffee table, where Dijana's last, unopened letter lay. The writing on the envelope was erratic – some characters slanting to the left, others to the right – and perhaps that was why he hadn't opened it.

The telephone rang.

'Hello?'

'Brani?'

'Hello, Mother.'

'You're still coming tomorrow?'

'If you don't mind.'

'Why should I, dear?'

He nodded into the phone. 'You got my letter?'

She didn't answer for a moment, and he wondered if she was going to cry. He'd written her a story about her husband's flight west in 1948, about how he ended up in a displaced persons camp in Frankfurt and died the next year of tuberculosis. But she didn't cry. She only said, 'Afternoon tomorrow?'

'Yes.'

'I'll prepare something good.'

'You always do, Mother.'

He hung up, then sat a moment on the sofa, staring at his small television. He turned it on and flipped between the two channels, settling on a repeat of the May Day parade down Mihai Boulevard. He'd always avoided such celebrations, but next year, he promised himself, he would attend. Then he looked up at a sound.

Clicking, from the front of the apartment. Like a lock being turned. He stood and walked quietly to the foyer.

Beside the coat-rack, he waited, listening. More clicks, and then a quiet groan beneath the cacophony of trumpets from the television. But the sound was in the kitchen, and he knew then that it was only the water heater, trying desperately to raise the temperature. There was no one here at all.

The Istanbul Variations

Olen Steinhauer

A homicide detective boards a plane to Istanbul. Soon after, it is hijacked by contact. Then it explodes mid-air.

No negotiation, no explanation.

Why? Two men are sent to find out. One is Gavra Noukas, a homicide detective living a dangerous double-life. The other is Brano Sev, a loyal secret policeman well used to cover-ups. But this time, even he can't figure out what his superiors are hiding. As they start unravelling the elaborate mystery, a connection is made to a murder seven years previously – and Sev realizes the devastating consequences of a seemingly unremarkable killing.

'Steinhauer is a welcome addition to the wartime ground mapped out by Philip Kerr and Alan Furst.'   *Guardian*

ISBN: 0-00-723206-3